Reese Ryan writes sexy, emotional love stories served with a heaping side of family drama.

Reese is a native Ohioan with deep Tennessee roots. She endured many long, hot car trips to family reunions in Memphis via a tiny clown car loaded with cousins.

Connect with Reese via Facebook, Twitter, Instagram or reeseryan.com. Join her VIP Readers Lounge at bit.ly/VIPReadersLounge. Check out her YouTube show where she chats with fellow authors at bit.ly/ReeseRyanChannel

Fiona Brand lives in the sunny Bay of Islands, New Zealand. Aside from being a mother to two real-life heroes, her sons, Fiona likes to garden, cook and travel. After a life-changing encounter, she continues to walk with God as she studies toward a bachelor of theology, serves as a priest in the Anglican Church and as a chaplain for the Order of St. Luke, Christ's healing ministry.

Also by Reese Ryan

The Bourbon Brothers
Savannah's Secrets
The Billionaire's Legacy
Engaging the Enemy
A Reunion of Rivals

Dynasties: Secrets of the A-List
Seduced by Second Chances

Also by Fiona Brand

A Breathless Bride
A Tangled Affair
A Perfect Husband
The Fiancée Charade
Just One More Night
Needed: One Convenient Husband
Twin Scandals
Keeping Secrets

Discover more at millsandboon.co.uk

WAKING UP MARRIED

REESE RYAN

HOW TO LIVE WITH TEMPTATION

FIONA BRAND

MILLS & BOON

First Published in Great Britain 2021
by Mills & Boon, an imprint of HarperCollins*Publishers* Ltd,
1 London Bridge Street, London, SE1 9GF

www.harpercollins.co.uk

HarperCollins*Publishers*
1st Floor, Watermarque Building,
Ringsend Road, Dublin 4, Ireland

Waking Up Married © 2021 Roxanne Ravenel
How to Live with Temptation © 2021 Fiona Gillibrand

ISBN: 978-0-263-28284-9

0221

MIX
Paper from
responsible sources
FSC™ C007454

This book is produced from independently certified FSC™
paper to ensure responsible forest management.

For more information visit: www.harpercollins.co.uk/green

Printed and bound in Spain
by CPI, Barcelona

WAKING UP MARRIED

REESE RYAN

Thank you to all of my amazing readers and fellow authors who've read and helped promote my Bourbon Brothers series. Your enthusiasm for and willingness to recommend this series to fellow readers has meant so much to me.

To the phenomenal readers in my Reese Ryan VIP Readers Lounge on Facebook: y'all are the best! Thank you for your continued support, feedback and encouragement. I am forever grateful for it and for you.

One

Zora Abbott sat in the nursery at her brother and sister-in-law's home, holding her new niece, who was barely a week old.

Remington Renee Abbott—Blake and Savannah's baby girl—was the newest addition to their growing family. And Zora was already obsessed.

Zora smoothed down her niece's headful of soft, shiny black curls as she stared into the girl's wide, dark, expressive eyes. She gently tapped Remi's adorable button nose. Baby girl blinked in response, her mouth opening slightly.

Remi stared at Zora as if she was both slightly amused and mildly disinterested at the same time.

Zora glanced over to where Savannah had suddenly appeared in the doorway. "Remi's facial expressions crack me up. She definitely has her mama's no-nonsense fierceness."

"And her aunt ZoZo's ability to look right through you and make you question yourself," Savannah added, smiling.

"True." Zora grinned. "You and Blake are going to have your hands full with this one."

"I don't doubt that," Savannah agreed. "And I hate to break up the lovefest, but your brother asked me to remind you that you need to leave for the airport soon or you'll miss your flight to Vegas."

"I know." Zora brushed the backs of her fingers against the baby's rosy cheeks. Remi's skin was the same soft brown as her mother's. "I just hate to be away from her for three whole days."

"Remi will be right here waiting for her aunt ZoZo when you get back." Savannah stepped into the room with its

mauve-painted walls and straightened the dusty-rose bed-
ding draped across Remi's crib.

Zora kissed her young niece's forehead, then reluctantly
handed the baby to her mother. A hint of a smile ghosted
over Remi's little face as her eyes lit up with recognition.
Savannah cooed softly in the baby's ear, then nuzzled her
forehead.

Zora bit back the envy that knotted her gut the tiniest bit. More than anything, she wanted children of her
own. A startling realization she'd made nearly two and a
half years ago—the moment she'd first held Remi's older
brother, Davis. Zora had been sure it was a hormonal phase.
A passing mood she'd get over once she'd had her fill of
changing dirty diapers.

But the feeling hadn't passed.

Her desire to be a mother grew with each additional
child born into their family. Davis. Her cousin Benji's
twins, Beau and Bailey. Now Remi. Each wedding or baby
shower she'd attended made her painfully aware of her
deepening desire. Made her ache with a sense of loss over
something she'd never even had.

The night after Remi was born, Zora had lain in bed,
staring at the ceiling, preoccupied with her growing desire
to be a mom. She'd climbed out of bed in the middle of the
night, opened her laptop and researched the idea that'd been
brewing in her brain for months.

Who said she needed to wait for Prince Charming to
come along to become a mother?

Zora was the sales VP at their world-renowned family-
owned distillery, King's Finest. Her family was among the
wealthiest in the region. She certainly had the financial
means to raise a child alone. And her grandfather, parents,
brothers, and their significant others were all the village
she'd need to raise a child.

She was days away from her thirty-second birthday.

Why should she wait for some phantom husband who might never come along?

"Everything okay, Zo?" Savannah laid Remi down.

"Of course." Zora's cheeks burned, as if her sister-in-law had been privy to her thoughts. "Going over a few things in my head before the trip."

"Well, I'll go let your brother and nephew know you'll be ready to leave shortly." Savannah squeezed her arm. "That'll give you two a few more minutes."

Zora nodded at her sister-in-law gratefully, then returned her attention to her niece, whose heavy eyelids drooped as she drifted off to sleep.

She glided her fingertips over the signature burned into the wood of the crib. It was a gorgeous original piece, handcrafted by Zora's longtime best friend—premier furniture maker Dallas Hamilton. The reason for her Las Vegas trip.

Dallas was being honored with an award for innovation, thanks to a stunning line of furniture he'd designed the previous year. He'd spent months in Thailand working with native furniture artists, studying their designs and learning their craft.

He'd designed breathtaking pieces that were a marriage of Western and Eastern aesthetics, inspired by intricate Thai designs. And the award-winning collection included pieces designed by native artists.

Zora couldn't be happier for her best friend.

The award presentation in Vegas capped a whirlwind year in which Dallas had graced the cover of high-profile magazines, been asked to design furniture pieces for a growing number of celebrities and done a handful of television interviews.

Since they were both currently single, he'd invited Zora to Vegas as his plus-one for the award ceremony. Afterward, they would spend their final forty-eight hours in

Vegas partying—an early nod to her impending thirty-second birthday.

It was nothing unusual for them. Dallas had been her plus-one at countless weddings and business or family events. And whenever they were both single, which was far more often than she liked to admit, they vacationed together at least once a year.

Dal still owned the cabin his grandfather had left him years ago, complete with a workshop where he handcrafted pieces—like Remi's crib—or developed new designs. It was the workshop where his grandfather had taught him how to make furniture and cabinetry when he was just a little boy. Dallas still considered Magnolia Lake home, but he spent most of the year at various places around the world, opening new showrooms for his company, Hamilton Haus, teaching workshops and being inspired by the unique furniture designs of various cultures.

Zora tucked the soft blanket beneath her niece's chin and smoothed down her hair. "Goodbye, sweet pea. Auntie ZoZo will be back soon," she whispered to the sleeping newborn before slipping out of the room and quietly closing the door behind her.

Zora hated to leave her niece behind, but she was eager to see Dallas. She'd made an important decision, and she needed to ask a huge favor of him. Her stomach twisted in a knot when she imagined how he would react.

Two

Dallas Hamilton stepped out of the beautiful glass shower at the luxury hotel where he'd been staying all week. The suite, comped by the organization honoring him with an award later that evening, was far more elegant than anything he would've booked for himself.

His furniture design company had done quite well since its humble beginnings in his grandfather's barn ten years ago. Still, growing up, his family hadn't had much. So though he'd learned to enjoy the money, he hadn't been able to forget how quickly a person's circumstances could change.

He could still remember the day his mother had sat him and his older brother down to tell them that she and their father were getting a divorce. And that they would be moving into their grandfather's house.

That memory never left him. It reminded him that people and circumstances were temporary and to avoid getting too attached. Which was why his lifelong friendship with Zora Abbott was a minor miracle.

Dallas secured the towel around his waist and wiped the condensation from the ornate bathroom mirror. He scratched his stubbled jaw and surveyed his reflection.

His mother would say he needed a haircut and a shave, tasks he usually tackled himself. But this was one of those rare occasions that merited a splurge. So he'd booked an appointment for an obscenely overpriced facial and haircut in the hotel's posh spa.

"That's a pretty fancy towel and everything, but I think you can do better than that for tonight."

Dallas jerked his head in the direction of the voice as

familiar as his own. Even when they were at opposite ends of the world, Zora's voice was often the last one he heard before drifting off to sleep.

"Wasn't expecting you for a few hours, Zo. Or I would've closed the door." Startled by her surprise appearance, his heart was still racing. Dallas tightened the towel around his waist, lest he end up flashing his friend. His bare chest, on the other hand, Zora had seen countless times on the beach or at the pool.

"I know." Her dark eyes glimmered, and one edge of her mouth curved in a slow smile that honestly did *things* to him that it shouldn't.

Because they were best friends. Nothing more. Despite that inadvertent-ish kiss beneath the mistletoe a couple years ago that nearly derailed their friendship.

"I sent a text about switching my flight yesterday."

"Sorry, Zo. I didn't get your message."

He hated text messages and social media.

Anything worth saying should be said in person, or at least on the phone.

It was his grandfather's philosophy, which he'd happily adopted. Dallas used text messaging sparingly, out of deference to Zora, his older brother and the occasional girlfriend. But a good old-fashioned phone call was still his preferred method of communication.

"Sorry you had to make it here on your own. I'd scheduled a driver to pick you up at the airport."

"It's fine." A smile lit Zora's face, and her terra cotta–colored skin practically glowed beneath the bright bathroom lights. She stepped just inside the doorway and leaned her shoulder against the wall, her arms folded. The innocent gesture lifted her breasts and exposed more of her cleavage in the low-cut top.

Not that he was looking. He was observant, and he couldn't help noticing things.

Yep, that was why his eyes were drawn there, not because…

Dallas cleared his throat and scratched his chin, returning his attention to his own scraggly hair and face in the steamed mirror.

While most women he wasn't sleeping with would have probably taken the hint and retreated from the bathroom by now, his best friend wasn't shy. Nor was she big on privacy. Especially that of the men in her life, given that she'd grown up in a house with her father, Duke Abbott, and four older brothers.

She gripped her chin, her head cocked as she studied his face. As if they were sitting together fully clothed in the living room.

"I know, I know." Dallas ruffled his hair, which was a few inches longer than he usually wore it. "I need a haircut and a shave. My mother told me yesterday when we had a video call."

"Sounds like Tish," Zora laughed. She stepped closer and spiked her fingers through his wet hair, tugging it to its full length.

"The haircut I can't help you with," she said. "But I can definitely shave you. I've gotten good with a straight razor. Pops taught me how so I could shave him," she added when he cocked an eyebrow.

Pops was her grandfather, Joseph Abbott. Grandpa Joe was the Abbott family patriarch and the founder of the distillery that she, her siblings and her father now ran. He'd had a stroke several weeks ago. He was at her parents' house recovering and, according to Zora, driving all of them crazy while they looked after him.

"You're offering to shave me with a straight razor?" He guffawed. "Sounds like a setup to a really cheesy murder mystery, and I'm the guy who ends up on the floor with his throat slashed in the first five minutes of the film."

"Give me a little credit." Zora smirked, propping a fist on one generous hip. "If I planned to murder you, I'd be much more clever about it than *Oops, I s'pose the razor must've slipped clean out of my hand*." She pressed the back of her other hand to her forehead in a dramatic pose.

Dallas chuckled, rubbing his chin. "I have no doubt you're right about that. But I think I'll pass on the shave just the same." He winked at her. "I have an appointment for a haircut and a shave in the spa downstairs."

"Ooh. Look at you being all fancy. You're not turning into one of those high-maintenance men, are you? Because there is only enough room for one high-maintenance personality in this relationship, and I think we both know that's me." She pressed her open palm to her chest.

"Don't worry, your spot is safe, Princess." Dallas grinned, invoking the nickname that Zora's father still sometimes called her. A nickname he knew his friend hated. She was always competing with her brothers. She didn't want to be a princess. She wanted to be king of the hill, especially as they all jockeyed to be named the successor to Duke Abbott as CEO of King's Finest.

"*Don't* call me princess." Zora punched him in the gut playfully.

"Fine." Dallas chuckled. "But I have to get dressed or I'll be late for my spa appointment. So you've got exactly five seconds to get out of here or I'm ripping off this towel." He gripped the towel in what they both knew to be an idle threat.

"Hmm…" Zora rested her chin on a closed fist. "Is that supposed to make me want to leave?"

"Get out, Zo." He pointed toward the door, trying his best to maintain a serious expression.

"All right, all right." She turned and begrudgingly left the bathroom, then made her way across the large, well-appointed master bedroom. "But I'm starving. I'll go downstairs with you to grab something to eat."

"Perfect. See you in five." He shut the bedroom door behind her and changed into jeans and a T-shirt.

He'd invited Zora to stay the weekend with him in Vegas because he had this large suite all to himself and her birthday was coming up soon. It seemed like the perfect opportunity for them to have an early birthday celebration in Sin City, since he had plans to spend most of the next month traveling between his factories in Europe and Asia.

Normally, they would have separate rooms on a trip like this. But the suite was huge and had two master bedrooms on opposite sides of the living space. He figured the place was big enough for the two of them to share without any awkward incidences.

Clearly, he'd been wrong.

Then again, the situation just now had only been awkward for him. Zora, who was as comfortable in her gorgeous brown skin as any human being he'd ever known, hadn't thought twice about the encounter. In fact, she probably couldn't fathom why he would.

Maybe a few years ago, he wouldn't have. But since their kiss…

Dallas sank onto the bed and ran his fingers through his wet, too-long hair.

Things had been…*different* between them since Zora had kissed him beneath the mistletoe at a charity ball he'd attended with her in Nashville one Christmas.

The kiss had caught him off guard. He honestly would've been less surprised if Santa and an army of elves had raided the place. So he'd frozen like a deer caught in the headlights; incapable of reacting.

She'd taken his delayed reaction as a rejection. But before he'd been able to tell her that he'd wanted to kiss her, too, Zora had blamed it on the alcohol and the moment.

She'd apologized profusely and insisted that it would *never* happen again.

In the weeks following the kiss, Zora had avoided him. She wouldn't answer his calls and responded to his text messages with cryptic, one-word responses.

So he'd finally flown home from Thailand, gone to her office and insisted that they hash it out. And they had. They'd agreed to pretend the kiss had never happened and never to cross the line again. Because neither of them wanted to jeopardize their friendship.

Only, a part of him wondered if maybe they *weren't* better off being just friends.

There was a tap at the door. "Dal, I'm starving. Are you dressed yet?" Zora sounded like a petulant child on a long car trip asking, *Are we there yet?*

"Yes, I'm dressed." Dallas grabbed a pair of socks from his bag.

That was all the invitation his friend needed. She entered the room. "Ready?"

He slipped on his other sock. "Almost."

"Okay." Zora's voice suddenly seemed small, and her expression turned serious.

Not the reaction he was expecting.

Dallas reached for the burnished brown leather Tom Ford sneakers Zora had gifted him last year to mark the opening of a Hamilton Haus showroom in London. "Everything good, Zo?"

His friend glanced down at her clasped hands before finally meeting his gaze again. "I know you have an appointment to get to, but could you spare ten minutes? I *really* need to talk to you about something."

"Of course." Dallas slipped on his shoes, then patted the space beside him on the bed. "Sit."

Zora sank onto the mattress, her denim-clad knee brushing against his. Her soft scent—a mixture of floral and citrus notes—tickled his nostrils. The warmth from her brown skin seemed to embrace him. His heart beat a little faster, and he willed other parts of his body to behave.

She's your best friend. Mind out of the gutter, pal.

It wasn't as if he hadn't sat beside Zora on his bed before—both as kids and adults. But not since their unexpected kiss.

Dallas swallowed hard, hoping that his friend wasn't about to utter the words he constantly feared. That this would be their last adventure together because she'd fallen in love with some guy who couldn't deal with their friendship.

"What is it that you want to talk to me about?" It alarmed him that Zora Abbott—who had never in her life been at a loss for words—suddenly seemed reluctant to say what was on her mind. He covered her hand, flattened on the bed between them, with his much larger one and squeezed. "You know you can talk to me about anything, right? This—" he used his free hand to gesture between them "—is a judgment-free zone. Always has been, always will be. So whatever you need to say or ask—"

"I want to have a baby," Zora said abruptly. The words rushed from her mouth like a torrent of water, suddenly unleashed. She turned to him, her eyes searching his, as if gauging his reaction. "Not down the road when the right guy comes along," she added. "I want to have a baby *now, Dallas.*"

He was sure his heart had stopped momentarily. After all these years of friendship, Zora Abbott had a gift for surprising him. But never more than right now.

"You want to have a baby?" Dallas stammered, feeling a little light-headed. His throat was dry, and his heart was trying its best to beat right out of his chest.

She nodded, staring at him expectantly. For the first

time in a long time, the invincible Zora Abbott seemed vulnerable.

There were few things in the world Dallas would refuse this woman. But was Zora really asking him to father her child?

Three

Zora prided herself on being fearless. She had nerves of steel and wasn't easily intimidated. She'd stared down misogynistic liquor industry execs and vendors, never giving them a single inch of unearned ground.

But right now, Zora was filled with uncertainty and trepidation as she stared into her best friend's widened brown eyes. His warm beige skin had suddenly gone pale and his gaping mouth could catch flies. Dallas clutched her hand as tightly as he had whenever they went on some crazy roller coaster together, which he'd always ridden purely for her sake.

"You want…a baby?" Dallas repeated, his words stilted. "Now. With me?"

"Yes." She nodded—until his final words registered in her brain, as if on delay. "Wait…what? No, not *with* you, Dallas."

She tugged her hand from beneath his and stood, pacing the floor. What did he think this was? Some cheesy rom-com?

Dallas looked utterly confused and a little disappointed. He scratched the back of his head. "I thought you were asking—"

"For your support." She stood in front of him and folded her arms. "*Not* your DNA. After that kiss weirded you… I mean *us* out…the last thing I'd do is ask you to father my child."

God, it sounded so *real* when she said it aloud.

She was going to ask some random stranger to father her child. Well, not really random. Her baby's father would be screened and carefully selected for his mental acuity and promising gene pool. She'd make her selection rationally. Without mind-numbing emotions or messy attachments.

Zora expected Dallas to look relieved that she wasn't asking him for a sperm donation, but his frown deepened, and he looked more confused than ever. "You want to have a baby on your own?"

"If I could do this totally on my own, I'd be a mom already." She sank onto the mattress beside him again. "Obviously, I need a little help to make this happen."

"I'm aware of how babies are made, smart-ass." Dallas sounded only slightly irritated as he dragged a hand through his longish brown hair. "But if you're not asking me for…" Dallas's words trailed off and he cleared his throat. His forehead and cheeks flushed.

He was obviously uncomfortable with the idea of making a donation to the my-best-friend-wants-a-baby cause. She was glad she hadn't asked him for one.

The idea had certainly occurred to her. She'd known Dallas most of his life. She'd known and loved his grandfather and adored his mother. Dallas was a good, kind, decent guy. No, scratch that. He was an amazing man. Funny and smart. Creative and generous. And they had a great relationship that had spanned decades with only the slightest hiccup: their ill-advised kiss a couple of years ago.

She'd been more than a little buzzed. And Buzzed Zora lacked the filter that reminded her of things like the impropriety of staring at her best friend's rather impressive biceps and pecs. Or his generous ass, which she was pretty sure you could bounce a quarter on. Or the way he sometimes licked his lower lip in a move that would make LL Cool J proud.

Sober Zora realized it was a normal, hormonal reaction for her to notice those things. To maybe even have the *slightest* physical reaction to them. But Sober Zora realized she shouldn't dwell on such thoughts. And under no circumstances whatsoever should she ever act on them.

Buzzed Zora obviously hadn't agreed.

So she'd kissed her friend, sending him into minor shock that night. There were a few seconds when she'd wondered if the man was still breathing.

Thankfully, Dallas valued their friendship enough that he wouldn't allow her to slink off into the sunset, dying of embarrassment. She hated to admit it, but the fiery speech her usually even-keeled friend had given her after flying halfway across the world to set things right only made him more attractive.

Zora groaned quietly, just thinking of it. Her mind and body had been at war then, just as they were now. She found comfort in the quiet assurance conveyed by the grip of his strong hand. But it stirred feelings she'd rather not have about her best friend, just as the kiss and its aftermath had.

Yes, of course, she would love it if Dallas Hamilton was the father of her child. But she valued their friendship too much to risk it with such a monumental, relationship-changing request.

Gauging Dallas's reaction, she made the right call.

"Me wanting to be a mom probably comes as a shock to you." She studied his face and those expressive, whiskey-brown eyes.

"I've seen how in love you are with Blake and Benji's kids. And Davis and the twins certainly adore you. And then the way you gushed over Remi when she was born..." Dallas gripped her hand again. "No, Zo, I'm not surprised. And I know that you're going to be an incredible mother."

"Thanks, Dal. That means a lot." Zora was moved by her friend's words.

"But as your friend, I have to ask...are you sure about this? Yes, I know you're more than capable of caring for a child on your own, and that you'd have a ton of support from your family. But are you sure you don't want to wait until you find the right guy? Rather than having some stranger's kid?"

Zora yanked her hand back. She wasn't angry with her friend for being honest about his reservations. She respected Dallas's willingness to say the things she needed to hear, even when she didn't want to hear them. Still, the phrase *some stranger's kid* hurt.

"It wouldn't just be some stranger's kid," she said. "It would be my child. And the father would have no legal rights to him or her. I would make sure of that," she said firmly. "And as for this dubious Prince Charming...if he comes along, he would love me and my child...regardless of who his father was. And there's no reason we can't have a child of our own together. It's not like I only want one."

"Sure. That makes sense, I guess." Dallas cleared his throat and nodded, shoving his hands in his pockets. "You've given this a lot of thought, it seems. So what is it that you need from me?"

Zora stood, inching closer to him. "You're my best friend, Dal. I need you to tell me that I'm not crazy for wanting to do this. Especially now. While I'm competing with my brothers to be the next CEO of King's Finest. And I'd really appreciate it if you could be there when I tell my family."

"Zora, you're one of the fiercest, most determined people I've ever known." Dallas's eyes twinkled with admiration. "You've never been afraid to tell your family anything. And you've never allowed anyone else's opinion to sidetrack you once you're determined to do something. Why is this different?"

Zora wasn't afraid of bucking the Abbott family traditions or of ruffling a few feathers. She had a lifetime of practice doing both. But this was a monumental departure that would have long-lasting repercussions for her and her child.

"I don't know." Zora shrugged. "It just is."

"I think you do know," Dallas prodded, his arms folded.

He knew her too well. She did know; she just hadn't wanted to say it. But Dallas clearly wouldn't be satisfied until she did.

Maybe she needed to say the words aloud.

"Because a part of me really wants my family's blessing and yours. I love and admire all of you. So it does matter to me what you all think. Especially about something as deeply personal as my child."

Admitting the truth made her feel as if a weight had been lifted from her shoulders. But it also strengthened her resolve. Zora tipped her chin up and met her friend's gaze, folding her arms, too.

"But I *am* doing this. Regardless of anyone's objections, yours or theirs. Still, it would mean the world to me if you all did support me," she conceded quietly.

The sound of her heartbeat filled her ears as she studied her friend's handsome face and thoughtful expression. Dallas wasn't rash or impetuous. And as much as she knew he cared for her, she also knew he wouldn't placate her. If he thought it was a terrible idea, he'd tell her so.

Dallas heaved a quiet sigh and tapped his chest twice with his closed fist—his silent show of support. Something they often did.

A sense of relief flooded Zora, and her eyes stung with tears. She returned the gesture, then leaped into her friend's arms. "Thank you, Dal. I can't tell you how much this means to me."

"Well, you know how much *you* mean to me, Zo," he whispered in her hair as he hugged her. "So whatever you need on this, I've got you. Just tell me where and when, and I'm there."

"I will." She grinned, relieved. "I promise."

He released her. "Now, c'mon. If I'm late, they're gonna charge me a ridiculous missed-appointment fee and give someone else my spot. Besides, if you plan to grow an entire human being, we need to make sure you stay healthy and well fed."

Zora nodded and slipped her hand into his as they made their way out of the suite and down to the hotel's main floor, where they parted ways.

Dallas hurried off to his spa appointment, and she followed the heavenly scent of savory grilled meat emanating from the hotel's bistro. But a lovely turquoise-and-pearl statement necklace in the window of a jewelry boutique caught her eye.

The necklace and matching earrings were beautiful. They would look lovely with the evening gown she'd selected for the night's festivities. A sales associate stepped outside the store, a broad smile on her face.

"Stunning, isn't it?" the woman said admiringly. "I've been waiting for the woman who could pull off that engagement ring, and it would be absolutely gorgeous on you."

"Engagement ring? No, I wasn't looking at the ring, I was looking at the—" Zora's attention shifted to the ring in the display window near the necklace.

She was speechless.

Gorgeous was an understatement. The ring had a large, heart-shaped, pink sapphire solitaire flanked by two sizable diamonds, also heart-shaped. And it was absolutely breathtaking. Zora cleared her throat. "Sorry, but I'm not in the market for an engagement ring. I am interested in that lovely necklace and the matching earrings."

"Oh. Sure. Of course." The woman's eyes dimmed. She maintained her smile but was unable to hide her disappointment. The difference in the commission on the two items would be vast. "Right this way."

Zora followed the salesclerk inside and tried on the necklace. As she stared in the mirror, she couldn't help wondering what Dallas would think of the piece. Which was silly. They weren't a couple; they were friends. *Just* friends.

But for the first time since she'd decided to have a child on her own, she felt a true sense of relief.

Everything would be fine. Because her best friend would be there to hold her hand through the hard part: telling her family.

Four

Dallas stared in the mirror in his hotel bedroom as he re-tied his bow tie for the third time. He was much more of a T-shirt guy than a tux guy. Still, his mother had insisted that he learn to tie a bow tie rather than using a clip-on when he'd accompanied Zora to her first cotillion. In fact, nearly every time he'd worn a tuxedo, Zora Abbott had been on his arm for the occasion.

Either he'd served as her plus-one at some gala, charity ball or wedding, or she'd been his. Every time, he'd tied his own damn tie. So why did it seem that his brain and fingers had forgotten how to do it tonight?

Maybe it was because he was still in shock from Zora's news a few hours ago.

She wanted to have a baby.

Not some abstract child she'd have in the distant future with whomever she'd eventually fall in love with. She wanted to have this child now.

He'd spent most of the afternoon in a daze, going through the motions with Zora's words on his mind.

Mostly, he couldn't stop thinking of the few seconds when he'd mistakenly believed Zora was asking him to father her child. Despite the initial gut-wrenching shock he'd felt in that moment, the idea had been turning over in his head ever since.

Why couldn't he be the father of Zora's child? And rather than her going through some expensive laboratory proce-dure, why couldn't they just do things the old-fashioned way?

There was obviously an underlying attraction between them. And he and Zora knew each other better than anyone else. Wouldn't doing this with a friend be preferable to engaging the services of a stranger who might be lying about his Ivy League education?

Dallas huffed and undid the bow tie, which had turned into a disaster once again.

"Dal." There was the quiet rap of knuckles at the closed bedroom door. "I'm having a bit of a wardrobe issue. I could use your help."

Dallas opened the door. "What can I…"

The words died on his lips the moment he saw his best friend. Zora was always gorgeous. But today her beauty had ascended to a new level.

She was absolutely stunning.

Zora wore her dark brown hair, streaked with blond, in a partial updo. Part of her hair was swept into an elegant bun. The remainder of her natural curls were worn loose. Her dress was a vibrant pink perfectly suited to her skin tone.

The sleek column skirt of Zora's floor-length gown hugged her delicious curves. An overlay attached at the waist gave the magnificent dress an added flair of drama. The one-shoulder bodice of the dress revealed her shimmering brown skin with its red undertone, which seemed to deepen as his gaze drank her in.

"What?" Zora pressed a hand to her belly and glanced down at her dress. "You don't like it?"

"Are you kidding me? God, Zora." He was nearly breathless. "You look incredible."

"Thanks." She smiled, seemingly relieved. "You look pretty amazing yourself." She indicated his tuxedo. "Need help with that tie?"

"Please," he said. "For some reason I just can't seem to get the damn thing right tonight."

"It's just nerves." Her voice was soothing. "It's a big night for you and well-deserved."

Zora slipped the necklace in her hand onto her wrist before she began methodically tying the tie. A skill he knew she'd learned from her grandfather, well before he'd suffered his stroke.

"There." A bright smile lit her eyes. "Perfect."

"Thanks." Dallas tried to ignore the warmth of her body and her teasing scent. To focus his attention anywhere other than her pouty lips. And to drown out the voice in his head that mused about how sweet it would be to lean down and taste her mouth. "You needed something, right? What can I do for you?"

"Two things, actually. First—" She turned her back to him, revealing that her dress was only zipped halfway up. "If you wouldn't mind?"

"Of course not." Dallas zipped the dress, which fit Zora to a tee.

"And then if you'd help me with this clasp, I'd appreciate it." She handed the necklace to him, and he placed it around her neck and fastened it.

Zora thanked him and turned around, indicating the matching earrings. "Do I look good enough to be on the arm of tonight's guest of honor?"

"I have no doubt that you'll be the most beautiful woman in the room."

"Wow. You're swinging for the fence." Zora's eyes danced with amusement. "But it's sweet of you to say. I can always count on you for a boost of confidence." Zora patted his chest. "Ready?"

She turned to walk out of the room, but Dallas grasped her wrist stopping her. Zora turned back to him. "What is it, Dal?"

"I've been…that is, I was thinking that…" He was blabbering like a complete idiot.

She probably thought he'd already started drinking. Especially since he'd received several gift baskets that afternoon. Most overflowed with fruit, baked goods or coffee.

But at least two of the gift baskets included various types of liquor. Including one he'd received from his older brother, Sam, with explicit instructions not to open it until after the award ceremony.

"What is it, Dal?" Zora asked again. This time she looked slightly alarmed. "You're not getting a little case of stage fright, are you? Because everything will be fine. Just watch where you're walking so you don't fall off the stage. And even if you did, it's not the end of the world."

"Not helpful," he said. "But no, I don't have stage fright. At least, not about tonight."

Zora folded her arms. "Okay, now I'm curious. What do you mean?"

"I mean…" He took a deep breath, still not believing the words he was about to say. "I understand why you didn't ask me to be the father of your baby."

"Because it would be complicated and messy and just plain weird…for us and our families," she quickly pointed out. "Besides, that's a big ask of a friend. Not the kind of thing you put on your birthday wishlist."

"It is a big ask," he acknowledged. "But being a mother is obviously very important to you, Zo. So helping you achieve motherhood is important to me. Besides, regardless of the circumstances, making a baby with someone…that's a lifelong connection. Wouldn't you prefer to make that kind of commitment with someone you're already friends for life with, as opposed to a random stranger?"

"I know we're in Vegas, but I'm not going to the sperm slot machines, Dal. There's a careful screening and selection process. I'll know who this man is. That he's the kind of person I'd want half of my child's DNA to come from." Zora looked slightly flustered. "And I'm feeling a bit judged here, which is something I thought I could count on you *not* to do."

"I'm not judging you, Zo." He lifted her chin, forcing

her eyes to meet his. "I'm just saying I'm here, and I *want* to do this for you."

"And I love you for that, Dal." Her smile didn't quite reach her eyes. "But I won't jeopardize our friendship again. It means too much to me. So while I appreciate your offer, all I really need from you is your support. All right?"

He nodded, forcing a smile that probably didn't reach his eyes, either. "Fine. Whatever you need."

"Good." Her smile seemed more genuine now. "Now hurry up. I'm hungry again. Plus, there's an open bar. Let's get there before the good stuff is gone."

Zora had a gift for injecting humor into even the direst situations. She'd done that when his grandfather had died five years ago, alleviating a pain that felt simply unbearable.

"You're hungry again? Sure you're not already pregnant?" Dallas chuckled.

"Watch it, sucka." Zora pointed at him, doing her best imitation of Esther from *Sanford & Son*. "Don't make me strangle you with that bow tie."

He held up his hands in surrender, laughing as he turned off the bedroom light and followed her into the living space.

Zora grabbed her clutch off the bar, eyeing one of the gift baskets wrapped in purple cellophane.

"That one right there has my name on it." She pointed to the basket. "There's coffee liqueur in there, and those brownies look decadent."

"Probably the reason Sam doesn't want us to eat them until *after* the awards ceremony." Dallas patted his stomach, laughing. "Personally, I've got my eyes on that bottle of vodka." He indicated a different basket.

"It's a date, then. After the ceremony tonight, we come back here, change into our pajamas and plan how we're going to celebrate my birthday for the next two days." Zora grinned, then cocked one eyebrow and smirked. "Unless, of course, you hook up with some pretty brunette. If so, be sure to leave a sock on the door, so I'll know."

"Smart-ass." Dallas raked his fingers through his freshly cut hair before extending an elbow to his friend. "C'mon, let's get you something to eat."

Zora slipped her arm through his, and they headed for the door.

He should be relieved Zora hadn't taken him up on his offer to be her baby's daddy. She was right. It would be complicated and messy. They'd have lots of explaining to do to their families.

He was a happy bachelor, content to have his friendship with Zora as the only long-term relationship in his life. Fathering her child would change that.

Dallas was *not* his father. If there was a child in this world who was half his, there was no way he wouldn't be in his or her life.

But at this rate, maybe he'd never be anyone's father.

Given the shitty relationship record of the men in the Hamilton family, maybe being an eternal bachelor was for the best.

Five

"Okay, this one first." Zora brought the basket with the purple cellophane over for Dallas to open first. "Those fudge brownies and that coffee liqueur have been calling my name all night."

"Go ahead and open it. I'm working on my own basket here." Dallas ripped open the basket containing his favorite premium vodka and set the bottle on the bar.

The ceremony had been spectacular. The innovation award he received from such a prestigious organization was the highest honor of his career thus far. It meant a lot that his fellow designers had designated him for the award. He'd made some excellent industry connections and had a wonderful evening with the most stunning woman in the room on his arm. Plus, he'd managed to avoid tripping onto the stage for his acceptance speech.

Total win.

Zora's eyes lit up like a kid at Christmas. She carefully opened the basket, then unwrapped the brownies. She placed the bottle of coffee liqueur on the counter beside the vodka.

She took a bite of a brownie and moaned with pleasure. "*Oh. My. God.* Dallas, this brownie is a tiny slice of heaven. You *have* to try one."

"Seriously, Zo, no brownie is *that* good." Aside from a homemade pie, Dallas wasn't big on baked goods. But the sounds of indescribable pleasure his friend was making as she nibbled on the small square made him more than a little curious.

"I promise you, this one is. You have to try it." Zora broke off a piece and popped the morsel into his mouth.

He chewed slowly as he assessed the taste. It was rich and delicious. Filled with walnuts, and more like fudge than cake.

"Okay, you might be right about this thing," he acknowledged.

Zora finished hers, then picked up two of the other baskets she'd been eyeing. "Can we open these?"

"Absolutely." He grabbed two glasses from behind the little bar. "That's what they're here for."

Zora unwrapped the two baskets and removed the bottles of alcohol inside each one. She set a bottle of amaretto and a bottle of Irish cream liqueur on the counter beside the bottles of vodka and coffee liqueur.

She stood back and crossed her arms, her brows furrowed, as if she was in deep thought. Suddenly, her eyes lit up, and she snapped her fingers. Zora turned to him and grabbed his arms.

"I got it. You know what I could really go for tonight?" she asked, then excitedly answered her own question. "A screaming orgasm."

"You…wait…what now?" His throat went dry.

"A screaming orgasm," she repeated, one brow furrowed. "The cocktail."

He spiked a hand through his hair. "Never heard of it."

"It's something I had at a bridal shower once, and I loved it. It consists of vodka, Irish cream, coffee liqueur and amaretto." She pointed to each of the bottles in turn. "And I think I saw…" Zora rummaged through the already opened baskets, then triumphantly held up a small jar of maraschino cherries. "Aha! Now we just need to get room service to bring us up some milk and some whipped cream."

Honestly, he'd be happy with a beer or just a splash of his favorite vodka on the rocks. But they were celebrating his awards and her birthday.

So why not go all in?

"On it." Dallas called room service and ordered the missing ingredients. He could practically hear the person who took the order holding back a smirk. How often did the hotel get requests for a can of whipped cream?

Then again, maybe he'd rather not know.

Zora washed her hands in the small bar sink and rummaged through the cabinets. She found a half-ounce stainless steel jigger, a measuring glass and a mixing tumbler, then carefully poured measures of all four liquors into the cocktail shaker with the focus of a sci-fi villain working on a potion for world domination.

And though he tried mightily not to stare at the curve of her generous bottom in those cute little sleep shorts... well, he was her best friend, but he was also a man who had an extraordinary appreciation for a firm, well-rounded...

"You spent a lot of time chatting up the team from Iceland." Zora returned the last bottle to the counter and turned around.

Dallas's face flushed with heat. Had she caught him looking? If so, her expression gave no indication.

"Yes," he confirmed. "I mentioned a few months ago that they approached me about a possible collaboration. The owner of the company is very straitlaced and family-oriented. Believes in doing things the old-fashioned way. So he wanted to meet me in person before we move forward. They're a big, international player. So—"

"So this could be a *really* big deal for you. Not that you aren't already doing amazingly well," she quickly added, placing a hand on his forearm and smiling. "Because you've accomplished so much on your own already. You took a hobby your grandfather taught you as a kid and turned it into...*this*." Zora nodded toward the three awards lined up on the bar. "This past year, you've been *killing* it."

There was a knock at the door before he could answer. Dallas grabbed some bills off the nightstand in his bedroom for a tip. He retrieved the milk and whipped cream and brought them to his friend. Zora measured the milk and added it to the stainless steel cocktail shaker. She added a few ice cubes to each glass, then to the metal container before shaking it up.

Zora poured some of the creamy concoction in their glasses, topping each with some of the whipped cream and a cherry. She handed one of the glasses to him and then raised hers.

"Dallas Matthew Hamilton, I am so damn proud of you. Your grandfather would be, too. I only wish he was here to see it himself," Zora said with a sad smile, her voice trembling slightly.

"I think he would be proud." Dallas agreed, trying to ignore the twisting in his gut. "I wish Grandad was here, too. But I'm really grateful that you are. I know you have a lot on your plate with King's Finest right now. So I appreciate you dropping everything to come out here for this. It meant a lot to have you beside me when they called my name tonight."

"Wouldn't have missed it for the world." Zora clinked her glass with his, and they both took a drink. "Mmm…this is good. A little stronger than I remembered," she noted. "But good."

"Agreed." Dallas took another sip. He was a coffee fiend, so he'd always enjoyed coffee-based cocktails. He picked up the coffee liqueur bottle and examined the label. "Wow, Zo. This stuff is ninety proof. Maybe you should take it easy on this."

"I sell alcoholic beverages for a living, Dal." Zora's laugh came out as more of a snort. "I can hold my liquor. Don't worry, I promise not to take advantage of you if it's a little too much for you." She winked and took another sip.

"Smart-ass." He grabbed another brownie from the box and bit into it. "*This* is a damn good brownie." Dallas waved it for emphasis before taking another bite. "You weren't exaggerating."

Zora picked up another square and nibbled.

"I told you," she muttered through a mouthful. "Remind me to thank Sam next time I see him."

Zora ran a hand through her hair, which she'd taken down the moment they returned to their hotel room. The dark curls with hints of blond dusted her bare shoulders, exposed by the tank top she wore with her adorable little sleep shorts.

Dallas gripped his glass and tried to ignore the fleeting image of him running his fingers through those curls. Something he hadn't dared to do since he'd tried it when Zora was in the fifth grade. She made it clear he best *never* run his hands through a Black woman's hair again unless he'd been given *explicit* permission.

"The drink is a winner, too." He sipped it. "But I don't know that it's screaming orgasm good." He chuckled. "That's a pretty high standard."

"It's definitely better than ninety-five percent of the orgasms I've had that weren't self-induced." Zora sipped her drink.

Dallas sucked in a deep breath, inhaling some of the liquid. He coughed and sputtered, reminding himself of how embarrassing it would be if he choked to death and died with a raging hard-on caused by visions of his friend and her self-induced orgasms.

"Are you okay?" Zora reached out to pat his back.

"Yes. A little of my drink just went down the wrong way." He held out a hand, keeping her at bay and hoping she hadn't noticed his body's reaction to her words. He sank onto the sofa and changed the subject. "We won't be able to travel the world together and hang out all night drinking once you're a mom."

He'd said it jokingly, but he was struck by the aching realization that it was true.

"This is the end of an era for us, Zo."

Did he look as pitiful as he suddenly felt?

Zora juggled her drink, the cocktail shaker and another brownie, bringing them over and setting everything on the coffee table. She folded one leg beneath her and sat beside him, her thigh brushing his.

"I'm not *abandoning* you, Dal." Zora snuggled beneath his arm, draped over the back of the sofa. "But we all grow up eventually, Peter Pan."

"One of us is." He sullenly sipped more of his drink. "You've got your eyes on the CEO position at King's Finest. Now you want to become a mom." He paused, considering how he should phrase his next statement. "I'm surprised you want to do this right now, while you're making a case to be the next CEO."

"No one thought for a single moment that Blake becoming a father would hinder his ability to lead the company," Zora said indignantly.

He'd definitely hit a sore spot. Understandably so. "I'm not saying that, Zo." He rubbed her shoulder. "It's just that being a CEO and being a mom are two huge, life-changing, time-consuming endeavors."

"And I'm one hell of a multitasker." Zora winked, setting her glass on the table with a clang. She nibbled on more of her brownie. "Besides, Dad doesn't plan to retire for another few years. So the timing is perfect."

He gave her a weak smile and finished off his glass. "Like I said, you've really thought this through."

"I have," she assured him. "I know I can sometimes be a bit hotheaded and impetuous. But I'm done with that. I'm making good choices and careful decisions. Proving to my father and grandfather that I'm more than capable of leading the company and continuing their legacy. So don't worry. Everything will be fine."

"All right." Dallas poured the remaining cocktail into their glasses before holding his up in a toast. "May you get everything you desire and more."

"May *we* get everything *we* desire and more." Zora clinked her glass with his.

Not possible.

She wanted to start a brand-new life as a mother and a busy CEO who wouldn't have time for him anymore, while he wanted more moments alone with her like this.

So he would make the most of the next forty-eight hours. Because it might be the last time the two of them ever got to spend time together like this.

Six

Zora awoke to harsh sunlight spilling into the room. Which room and where she was, exactly, her brain didn't quite register. Her head was throbbing in response to the light filtering through her closed eyelids, so she had no desire to open them.

She sucked in a slow, deep breath, then cracked one eyelid open, followed reluctantly by the other. Her hair had fallen across her face and was blocking her vision. Which meant she probably looked a complete mess.

Zora swept the hair from her face and was greeted by sunlight gleaming off towering hotels on the Strip.

Las Vegas.

She was still in Vegas with Dallas. And she had some serious brain fog and one hell of a headache. Anything that had happened since the awards ceremony felt like a blur.

Zora honestly wasn't sure if she'd lost a few hours or a few days, which was disconcerting. Definitely not responsible, CEO/mom-in-the-making behavior.

She could already see her smug older brother Parker gloating about her being irresponsible and unworthy of running the company. Which meant she was never, *ever* telling him that she'd apparently drunk her weight in... God, she couldn't even remember what they'd been drinking.

Her head felt heavy, her tongue felt thick, she was too damned hot to be in an air-conditioned room and it felt like there was a weight around her middle. She needed coffee—lots of it—and an ibuprofen or four. And she wasn't sure what time it was, but she could do with a few more hours of sleep, too.

Suddenly, the bed shifted, and the weight around her abdomen tightened.

Zora screamed and tried to scramble away from the body invading her space and trying to spoon her. But in her inelegant attempt to create some space between her and her random hookup, she lost her balance and tumbled over the edge of the bed. Her limbs flailed, and her ass hit the carpet with a thud.

A thick ass and thighs apparently *did* save lives.

Someone should put *that* on a T-shirt.

Zora tried to spring up, but her wrist hurt when she put weight on it.

Great. She might've sprained her wrist, too. Well, maybe she only had one good wrist. But her legs worked just fine. So she was fully prepared to knee this dude in the family jewels if he didn't explain what he was doing in her bed.

Pronto.

The man suddenly shot up, as if he'd heard her scream on delay.

"Zora?"

"Dallas?"

They spoke simultaneously.

"What are you doing on the floor?"

"Why are you in my bed?"

Those words were spoken simultaneously, too.

"I'm not in your bed." Dallas winced, as if every word he uttered was reverberating around his skull. "This is my room."

She opened her mouth to object, but Dallas pointed to his army-green duffel bag on the floor, his favorite pair of cowboy boots leaning on the wall beside it. Zora glanced around the room. The two master bedrooms in the suite looked identical, except the furniture was oriented in opposite directions. Besides, none of her stuff was here.

Dallas was right; she was in his room and in his bed.

Zora glanced down, suddenly aware of the cold air chilling her mostly naked flesh. She was clad in a pretty, lacy, strapless and backless off-white bodysuit, which she didn't recognize.

Zora's confusion turned to panic, and her face suddenly felt hot. She glanced up to where Dallas had extended his large hand to her.

Despite his wince, he looked handsome. And her eyes couldn't help following the smattering of light brown hair that trailed down his bare, broad chest and disappeared beneath the sheet pulled up to his waist.

Zora swallowed hard, then put her hand in his and allowed him to pull her to her feet.

"Nice…uh…bodysuit." Dallas yawned, then tipped his chin toward the sheer, lacy garment that exposed more than a little of her hind parts.

"Very funny." Zora tugged at the sheet to wrap it around herself. She gasped when she uncovered her friend's morning wood—in all its naked glory. She quickly put the sheet back. "Dallas!" She shrieked. "Why aren't you wearing any clothes?"

"Again…my room." He gestured around the space. "I didn't realize I had company in my bed, but normally when I do, they don't mind that I sleep naked." He winked, then winced again, grabbing his head. "Ow."

"That's what you get." She folded her arms, then looked around the room. "Why am I in here and where are my clothes? Because, I assure you, this isn't mine." She pressed a hand to the fabric covering her belly.

"I kinda like it." He stretched, seemingly unconcerned about the disturbing situation in which they found themselves.

Dallas's laid-back demeanor was the perfect balance to her more…high-strung nature. Normally, she appreciated that about him and his ability to talk her off a ledge. He'd stopped her from doing a lot of ill-advised things over the years. But right now, when they had inexplicably shared a bed after a night of drinking and they were both in various states of undress, she wished her friend was experiencing at least a little of the panic that she was.

"I like this bodysuit, too," Zora said. "But that isn't the point. The point is that I didn't buy it, or at least I don't remember buying it." Zora pressed a hand to her throbbing forehead.

"It matches that." Dallas pointed to a garment thrown over a chair in the seating area by the window.

Zora walked over to the chair and picked up the backless little white minidress—just the kind of garment that would go well with the bodysuit she was wearing. But this dress didn't belong to her, either.

Did it?

She held the glittering, sequined dress against her body. It certainly appeared to be her size, though the hemline was shorter than what she'd typically wore. Zora sniffed the fabric and recognized her perfume.

There was no doubt about the fact that she'd worn this dress. She only hoped she'd purchased both garments new.

"My credit card." She turned back to Dallas, who was yawning and running a hand through his hair. "If I bought these items, they'll be on one of my credit cards. I just need to check them. Where's my phone?"

They both looked around the room. Dallas's phone was on the nightstand. But her phone was nowhere to be found.

Had she lost it?

"I'm sure it's here somewhere. Maybe out in the great room or in your room." Dallas picked up his phone. "I'm calling your phone now."

They both got quiet as they listened for "Castle on the Hill" by Ed Sheeran—Dallas's custom ring on Zora's phone. She heard the faint sound of music.

"While you find your phone, I'm just gonna—"

"Get dressed?" Zora asked, hopefully. She'd already seen her incredibly hot friend in the buff once, and it was starting to tax her already suspect self-control. The last thing they needed was a repeat of that kiss or...worse.

"Yeah." Dallas spiked his fingers through his hair. The muscles of his biceps bunched and flexed, as did his pecs.

Zora averted her eyes and whimpered quietly beneath her breath. Then she cleared her throat. "Awesome. Then we can talk about...whatever this was...over breakfast. I'm starving."

"Don't know if they'll still be serving breakfast." Dallas glanced at his phone again.

"Why? What time is it?"

"Almost two thirty," he said with a yawn.

"It's Vegas. I'm sure we can find someplace serving breakfast all day." Zora listened for the ringtone, but it had stopped. "Ring me again, please?" she asked.

Dallas nodded and yawned again.

Zora padded across to her room on the other side of the shared living space. She followed the sound of the music until she found her phone beneath a pile of clothing on her still-made bed.

Why had she taken out half the clothing in her luggage and strewn it all over her bed? At least that might explain why she'd purchased a new dress. Obviously, they'd done something for which nothing she'd brought seemed quite right.

Zora picked up her phone, which powered down in her hand. She groaned and plugged it into her charger. Then she glanced around the room for any sign of what had happened last night. There were several shopping bags in the corner.

Apparently, Buzzed Zora also enjoyed going on shopping sprees. Zora only hoped that her alter ego hadn't done too much damage to her credit cards and that everything she'd purchased—minus the killer bodysuit, which she *really* did like—was returnable.

Three of the bags bore the words *Bridal Shop* in fancy lettering. One was a garment bag, one contained an empty shoebox and another looked like the kind of bag that might be used for accessories.

Suddenly, it was hard to breathe. She dragged her hand through her hair, and a few strands of her tangled curls caught on her ring.

Ring? Zora squeezed her eyes shut, the hand stuck in her hair trembling.

She carefully unwound the strands that had tangled around the ring. With her eyes still shut, she sucked in a deep breath and pulled her hand from her hair.

Please, no. Please, no. Please, no.

She repeated the words in her head again and again, afraid to open her eyes and peek at the ring on her finger.

Zora slowly released a breath, then opened her eyes. She covered her mouth with her other hand to suppress the scream working its way up her throat.

She was wearing the pink sapphire engagement ring she'd admired in the jewelry shop the day before. The one the saleswoman had convinced her to try on.

The woman had been horribly wrong about there being no harm in dreaming. Because Zora was not only wearing the stunning pink sapphire and diamond engagement ring. She was also wearing a gorgeous diamond wedding band with alternating marquise and heart-shaped diamonds.

Zora clutched at her stomach, her hands shaking.

What the hell happened last night?

Seven

Was it possible that she and Dallas had…no. They couldn't have. They *wouldn't* have. She was sure of it. Because while she might tend to be a bit impetuous, Dallas was a rock-solid, sensible guy who always appealed to logic. So there was no way they could've possibly…

Zora couldn't bring herself to say the words, not even in her head. But there was one way to find out.

She found her sleep shorts and tank top and threw them on before making her way back across the suite toward Dallas's room. She tapped on the open door.

"Dal, are you dressed?"

"Almost. Gimme a sec," he called back. "All right. C'mon in."

Zora stepped into the room, forcing herself not to babble in a panic. There was probably a perfectly logical explanation for all this. Maybe they'd gotten completely lit last night, decided to crash some themed costume party, and she'd gotten too carried away with the props. Or maybe…

Zora took a deep breath, her head spinning and her stomach tied in knots.

Just calm down, Zora, and think.

She could do that. Focus on her breath. Slowly breathe in and out. But first, she had to see her friend's hand.

"Dallas, could you…can I see your hand?"

He raised his right hand.

"No, the other one." Zora pointed to his left hand hanging at his side.

He looked at her strangely but complied, raising the hand in question. That, apparently, was when he first saw it, too.

"Shit. Is that a—"

"Wedding band?" Zora stepped closer on wobbly legs, barely able to get the words out of her mouth. "It is. And this—" Zora held up her hand and showed it to her friend "—appears to be its match."

Dallas's eyes widened, and he slapped a palm over his mouth. Then he held her hand in his as he compared the two rings side by side. His was a handsome ring with five sparkling square-cut diamonds set in a channel aligned across the center of the ring.

"Are these gag costume rings?" His gaze met hers. "I assumed that the tiara in the bathroom was part of some costume."

"There's a tiara in your bathroom?" Zora's voice squeaked.

She hurried into the bathroom and retrieved the sparkly tiara from the counter. It had weight to it, and the vine design was intricate and beautiful. Those were Swarovski crystals; she was nearly sure of it.

Zora returned to the bedroom, where Dallas stood near the dresser holding a sheet of paper, staring at it and then the ring on his finger.

"Dallas, this isn't some cheap trinket." She held up the tiara, then held out the hand bearing the engagement ring and wedding band. "Neither are these." She pointed to his ring. "And I'm almost sure those are real diamonds set in platinum."

Her friend stared at his hand again, blinking, but not saying a word.

"My phone is charging now, but I need to check my credit cards. All of them. I have several bags in my room from a *bridal* shop. I think we honestly might've gotten—"

"Married." Dallas's voice was hoarse. He waved a piece of paper that he'd picked up off the dresser. "According to this document, we are now Mr. and Mrs. Dallas Matthew

Hamilton. Apparently, you've taken my last name. I honestly think that might be the most shocking part of all this."

"Let me see that." Zora took the paper from his hands and carefully read every single line. *Twice.* She handed it back to him and pressed a hand to her throbbing head. "No, no, no." She shook her head adamantly. "This isn't possible. We wouldn't do this. We wouldn't get…married." It was still difficult to say the word. "What would possess us to do this, and why the hell can't I remember any of it?"

Zora huffed, sinking onto the bed.

"Maybe this is just a bad dream," she said, more to herself than to him. "We'll wake up and everything will be just the way it was before we went to sleep. That has to be it."

Dallas pinched her arm, and she squealed. She slapped his hand.

"What did you do that for?"

"Just checking your dream theory." He grabbed a T-shirt out of his bag and tugged it over his head before sinking onto the bed beside her. "Besides, I doubt we'd both be sharing the same dream."

Zora groaned, dragging her hand through her hair, but being careful not to snag her ring on it this time. She turned to him. "What do you remember about last night?"

Dallas rubbed the back of his neck and sighed. "Not much." He shrugged. "I remember coming back here after the ceremony. We got in our pajamas for the night, and we were celebrating. You were making some drink with a whole lot of liquor in it. It had some crazy sex name."

"Right, I was making screaming orgasms," Zora said. "And then you told me that I should maybe slow down because the coffee liqueur was like a hundred proof or something. And we were stuffing our faces with those incredible little bite-size brownies your brother sent you. I know the drinks were kind of strong, and that would explain the killer hangover I have right now, but—"

"But maybe it wasn't the drinks or at least, not just the drinks." Dallas stood suddenly. "Are there any of those brownies left?" he asked.

"Are you really worried about snacks right now?" Zora asked.

"No, I just need to see the packaging." Dallas hurried into the other room with Zora on his heels. He rummaged through the baskets they'd opened last night until he found the one from his brother. He dug through its contents until he found the container. His head dropped and he groaned. "Well, that explains why Sam put a note on here not to open this basket until after the awards ceremony. These aren't *regular* brownies. They're edibles."

Did he just say...

"As in weed-baked-into-the-brownies edibles?" She walked closer, her arms folded.

"It appears so." Dallas handed Zora the packaging and took a seat on a nearby bar stool. "I'm sorry. I honestly had no idea my dumb brother would send me edibles in a gift basket."

Zora carefully read the label, something she wished she'd done the night before.

"This isn't your fault. You had no way of knowing. Besides, I opened the basket. I should've paid attention to the ingredients," Zora muttered, tossing the empty box back into the basket and sitting down on the stool beside her friend. "But remind me to strangle Sam the next time I see him. He owes us both an apology. And if I can't return all this stuff I bought last night, I'm going to be sending him a hefty bill. That ring alone was fifty grand."

"You're kidding." Dallas's eyes widened. He reached for her hand and studied the ring. Their matching rings gleamed. He nodded. "It's an incredible ring and it looks good on you."

"Too bad I can't keep it." She held her hand up and wriggled her fingers, admiring the way the light danced off the heart-shaped pink sapphire and the diamonds that flanked it. It was a truly lovely ring. And the color of the sapphire complemented her skin tone.

"Wait...you're assuming you purchased all this stuff," Dallas said. "But if, for whatever reason, we decided to get hitched last night, wouldn't I be the one buying the ring?"

"Traditionally, yes," she acknowledged. "But I can't imagine that you would've spent that kind of money for a ring. Let alone for a last-minute, drunken exchange of vows."

"You're saying I'm too cheap to have purchased that ring?" He frowned, pointing at her hand.

"No, I'm saying that you're frugal and sensible with your money," Zora squeezed her friend's shoulder. "It isn't an insult, Dal. I understand your insecurities around money," she said softly.

It wasn't something her friend liked to talk about very often, but she knew that he'd been traumatized by the sudden uprooting of his suburban life in a nuclear family in Nashville to live in the sticks with his grandfather in a rundown cabin. It had really shaken Dallas as a kid.

The sudden dissolution of his parents' marriage had done a hit job on his ability to trust and made him worry about money, even now that he had plenty of it. And though it wasn't something Dallas would ever admit, Zora was sure that it was part of the reason he always seemed to hitch himself to the wrong woman in the rare instances when he actually got seriously involved in a relationship.

He was afraid he'd be as shitty a husband and father as his own dad had been and still was. Douglas Hamilton was now working on his fourth marriage and second family. He and his much younger wife were expecting. Neither Dallas nor Sam were close to their father, though Sam did occasionally speak to the elder Hamilton.

"Again, not an accusation. Besides, we have bigger fish to fry. Like, going to the chapel listed on that piece of paper in there to find out if it's an actual, legal document. If it is, then we'll find out what we need to do to get it annulled."

"Great. I'm already following in the footsteps of my old man," he grumbled. "And I'm pretty sure this means I'll hold the family record for the shortest marriage in perpetuity."

"This doesn't count as a marriage. Both of us were obviously hallucinating or something. Shame on this cheesy chapel for marrying us in that state. The salesclerks should be ashamed of themselves, too." Zora propped a fist on her hip. "And it's not like we slept together…" She bit her lower lip. "I don't think."

"Believe me, Zo, if we had, you'd remember." Dallas smirked.

Zora couldn't help flashing back to the moment she'd pulled back the sheet earlier and discovered that her friend slept au naturel and that what he was working with was rather…*impressive*.

"I appreciate the big-dick energy, Dal—" Zora rolled her eyes when Dallas grinned "—but you're saying I'd remember…*that*…but not making the decision to *marry* you? Think about it." Zora shook her head. "And another thing—we're not going to tell anyone about this…*ever*. Like never, ever, ever. Not in this lifetime or the next. *Capisce?*"

"Fine."

Dallas had always kept his word to her. Still, his answer didn't sound very convincing.

"Pinkie swear?" She held up her pinkie finger.

"We're a little old for pinkie swears, Zo." Dallas tapped a finger on the counter of the bar. "But okay, fine. We don't tell anyone about the marriage—with the exception of our eventual spouses—and we get it annulled before we leave Vegas, if that's possible."

"God, I hope so." She hopped off the stool. "I need a shower and breakfast. Then we'll work all this out."

"I realize that the drunken marriage was a mistake, but you're not doing a lot for my self-esteem right now, Zo. Maybe tone down the I-can't-wait-to-get-rid-of-you thing just a tad." Dallas peeked through his thumb and forefinger.

"Sorry." Zora pressed a hand to her friend's cheek. "You're going to make someone an amazing husband one day. And she'll be incredibly lucky to have you."

"Just not you," he said solemnly.

"I…uh…" she stammered. *Is he serious?* Was he still hurt because she'd passed on his offer to be the father of her child?

"Because we're just friends. I get it. Give me fifteen minutes to shower. Then I'll be ready to go to breakfast." Dallas got up and walked away.

Zora hadn't meant to hurt Dallas's feelings. She was just being a little too honest. *Again.* She would work on that. *Really.*

Maybe she did have a lot more in common with Parker— who said just about every thought that entered his mind, completely unfiltered. Her brother was brilliant, but his people skills left a lot to be desired. Which was why she'd make a much better CEO than he would. She just needed to prove it to her father and grandfather.

A drunken, oops-we-made-a-mistake marriage? She might as well throw in the towel and admit that Parker had been right about her being an overemotional hothead who wasn't suited to run King's Finest.

Zora grabbed a bottle of water from the little fridge behind the bar and guzzled some of the liquid. She needed to stay hydrated and flush her system.

Hopefully, a hot shower and a fresh change of clothes would help clear her head. She needed to create a plan of action. Starting with packing up all the things that she'd purchased last night. Including that wedding dress that would've made her mother faint.

Duke and Iris Abbott would be horribly disappointed that their only daughter had gotten married in some Las Vegas chapel—probably by a jumpsuited Elvis impersonator with glued-on pork-chop sideburns. While wearing a tiara and a dress so short you could practically see her hoo-ha, as her mother would say.

Honestly, they were doing their families a favor by not telling them about their little Vegas adventure.

"Hey, Zo." Dallas was suddenly in the doorway of his bedroom, making his way toward her with his phone in his hand. "I'm pretty sure our deal not to tell anyone about our two-minute marriage is off."

"Why?" Zora set the bottle down and approached him. "Didn't we just agree it was best if they didn't find out?"

"That was before *this*." He handed her the phone.

There, in living color, was a video of the two of them, standing in a chapel. She was wearing the sequined mini-dress and tiara, and looking good, if she did say so herself. Dallas looked handsome in his tux, the same one he'd worn to the awards ceremony last night. They were in the middle of exchanging their vows during a surprisingly tasteful ceremony.

There was no Elvis impersonator—in a jumpsuit or otherwise. The chapel was tasteful and elegant. And neither of them behaved as if they were high off screaming orgasms and salted caramel brownie edibles. They just seemed... dreamily happy. She couldn't blame the officiant for believing they were simply a couple in love.

It was almost a shame that the ceremony wasn't real.

"So you took video." Zora shrugged, handing the phone back to him. "Erase it. What's the big deal?"

"The big deal is that I didn't take this video. You did.

And you uploaded it to your Instagram account," he informed her.

"I *what*?" Suddenly, her head was throbbing again. She gulped down more water, then set the nearly empty bottle back on the counter. "I'll delete it. My family hardly pays attention to my IG account, anyway. It's not like I posted it to the company account."

"Look again." He handed the phone back to her.

Zora looked at the video. It was posted to the King's Finest Instagram account and it already had thousands of likes and hundreds of well-wishing comments.

Shit. Her parents were going to kill her. *If* they'd seen it. Maybe they still hadn't. She could delete the video, and maybe they'd be none the wiser. She just needed to get to her phone. Hopefully, it was charged up enough for her to access the app.

But then Dallas's phone rang, and the face that popped up on the screen was her mother's. She juggled the phone as if it had turned to hot lava in her hands, and Dallas caught it.

He looked at the screen. "Shit. If your mom is calling me—"

"She's seen the video, and she's already tried calling my phone."

Zora sank back onto the bed. Now her family knew about her ill-advised MUI—marriage under the influence. Zora slapped a palm against her forehead, then winced at the pain reverberating through her skull.

Any aspirations she had of climbing to the top of the ladder in her family's business were clearly toast. After a public screwup of this magnitude, she'd be lucky to hold on to the position she already had.

Eight

Dallas stared at the phone ringing in his hand, still in a state of semishock.

He didn't do things like get drunk and get married. He was a laid-back, sensible guy. The one in the group who could always be counted on to appeal to reason. He'd talked his older brother out of breaking out the windows of an old abandoned farm when they were kids. And he'd convinced Zora not to take an ad out in a local newspaper declaring her ex a liar and a cheater.

So if he hadn't seen the video with his very own eyes, he honestly wouldn't have believed he was capable of this. In fact, he would've been more prone to accept Zora's joint dream theory or believed they were in *The Matrix* or some shit like that. Anything but the fact that he'd recklessly jeopardized Zora's chance to be named the future CEO of her family's distillery and sabotaged the deal he'd been working on for months with the Icelandic furniture company.

The stodgy, family-values CEO would not be amused when Dallas explained that he was as high as a fucking kite during his Instagram marriage to his best friend, which he was about to annul. So much for his trip to Iceland and the lucrative deal that would've gone along with it.

"I'm going to beat Sam's ass when I see him. He should have warned us about those brownies." Dallas huffed, thankful the phone had stopped ringing. He glanced over at Zora, sitting on the bed, looking stunned and miserable.

Just great. His descent into having the next broken marriage on his family tree was well on its way.

Dallas sighed and sat down beside Zora, draping an arm

over her shoulder. "You okay, Zo? Can I get you some more water? Or maybe some coffee?"

"Belgian waffles topped with strawberries and whipped cream and a side of bacon," she said absently. "And I don't care what time it is."

"You've got it." Dallas squeezed his friend's shoulder and chuckled. "I don't care what I have to do, I'll make it happen. And I'll fix this. I promise."

"How, Dallas?" She turned to him, suddenly more lucid. "What on earth can we possibly do to fix this situation? We're screwed."

"I don't know," he admitted. "But give me an hour to think of something. I'll put my phone back on Do Not Disturb. You leave yours charging in your room. We'll go to breakfast and work this out, just like you said. All right?"

Zora frowned, then gave him a reluctant nod before getting up and making her way back to her room.

Dallas watched his friend walk away despondent, as if the weight of the entire world had come to rest on her narrow shoulders.

Seeing his fierce, confident friend looking broken and beaten gutted him. Especially since he shared the blame for what had happened last night.

Zora's mother called his phone again. Dallas groaned. He wasn't sure which scenario would break Iris's heart more—the prospect of him and Zora having *actually* eloped or the fact that their short-lived marriage had resulted from reckless behavior.

Unlike his train wreck relatives, to the Abbotts, family was *everything*. They all still lived in their little town of Magnolia Lake. They all worked together in their family-owned distillery, with the exception of Zora's older brother Cole, who had become the premiere home builder in the area. Most of them lived within a five-mile radius of each other. And they sat down to Sunday dinner at Duke and Iris's house nearly every week.

So he had no doubt that her parents would be heartbroken that their only daughter hadn't had a big, formal wedding, surrounded by friends and family with her father walking his baby girl down the aisle. And they'd probably be even more disappointed to discover that neither of them remembered what had happened. That it had all been a big mistake and they were about to get the marriage annulled.

"Zora!" Dallas hurried out of his room to the other side of the suite, hoping to catch his friend before she stepped into the shower.

She was standing by the bed in her room, neatly folding the clothing spread out on her bed and putting it into her luggage. The bridal shop bags were on the bed, too.

"Yes?" She looked up from her packing.

"You aren't leaving?" He felt a slight sense of panic at the prospect.

"No, I'm just repacking all the clothing I apparently tossed on the bed last night. Why? Did you think of something already?" Zora raised one brow doubtfully, then turned back to fold another blouse.

"No...well, yes...maybe." Dallas spiked his fingers through his hair, his heart racing.

"Okay, that couldn't be any less clear." Zora chuckled dryly. "Why don't you just tell me what it is that you're thinking, then we'll go from there?"

He felt like their roles had been reversed. That was usually the line he used on her.

Dallas took a deep breath before meeting her gaze. "I was thinking that... I mean...why don't we just...*not* get this thing annulled?"

"What?" His friend peered at him as if he'd sprung horns and a tail. "Your solution is that we *pretend* to be married? Why on earth would we do that?"

Not the response he was hoping for. But Dallas stood a little taller, prepared to make his case.

"First, it wouldn't be pretending, Mrs. Hamilton." He grinned, then jerked a thumb over his shoulder in the direction of his room. "We *are* married, and we've got the marriage license and video to prove it."

"I realize that *technically we are* married." Zora folded her arms. "But it's not like we intended to be."

"We might not remember intentionally getting married, but we obviously went through a lot of trouble to stage this wedding." He gestured toward the bridal shop bags on Zora's bed. "And I think I know why."

"This I'd love to hear." Zora sank onto the mattress. "Did you find that on your phone, too?"

"No." Dallas sat beside her, leaving some space between them. "But I offered to father your child, and I know you rejected the idea—" he added before she could repeat her objections "—but at some point we must've decided to do it. That's the only reason I can imagine that we would've done this. And since we already have—"

"Maybe you're right, Dallas." Zora shot to her feet and paced the floor. He tried not to be distracted by the tiny shorts she was wearing or the fact that he knew what she looked like in the lace bodysuit he could tell she was still wearing beneath it. "But all the reasons I had for objecting to the idea are still true. And now you're talking about what…forgoing the whole in vitro route and actually…" She halted her steps and looked over at him, her cheeks and chest suddenly flushed.

Not much made Zora Abbott blush. Obviously, the thought of the two of them *together* had. That gave him the smallest bit of hope that he could convince her.

"Have sex?" Dallas chuckled when Zora's eyes widened. "Yes, Zora, that's what I'm proposing."

"I appreciate that you want to help me, Dal. And you

know that I love you as a friend." Her tone was apologetic. "I realize that I've chosen a non-traditional route to motherhood. But a small part of me wants to believe in the fairy tale. That one day the guy I'll fall head over heels in love with will come along. I don't want to settle for a partner because it's convenient. Not even one I care for as much as you. And as your friend, I want more than that for you, too. If we stayed married just so that you could do this for me…you'd come to resent me and our child."

Dallas walked over to her. "I could never resent you, Zora. You've been there for me, since we were kids. And you're the reason I have this business. You saw the vision long before I did. You encouraged me to take a leap of faith. And you backed me financially, even though I was determined not to take your money."

"I knew the investment would pay off." Zora shrugged, as if it were no big deal that she'd believed in him enough to arrange the financing for his start-up and invested a large chunk of her own savings in Hamilton Haus.

He'd paid every cent of it back, and then some. But the business could've easily gone down in flames. She'd stuck her neck out for him.

If Zora was truly opposed to the idea…fine. So be it. They'd have to deal with the consequences of last night's bender. But if she was turning down his offer because she was reluctant to accept his help, then he'd make it clear that he *wanted* to do this for her. Not out of a sense of indebtedness, but because she was his best friend, and he'd walk through a wall of fire for her.

"You stuck your neck out for me. Risked your reputation and your savings. So why is it so hard for you to let me do this for you?"

"I haven't been keeping a tally, Dallas," she said. "And I don't want you to do this to even the score or something.

I had the means, so I helped someone I really care about. It's that simple," Zora said.

"Then let me do the same." He squeezed her hand. "Or are you getting cold feet about having a baby?"

"No." She shook her head. "I've never been surer about anything in my life."

"Then let me help you, Zo. Because I *want* to make this happen for you, not because I feel obligated to."

She studied his face, her eyes welling with unshed tears as she chewed on her lower lip.

He knew his friend well enough to recognize that she was actually considering his proposal.

Nine

Zora took both of Dallas's hands in hers and met his gaze. Her friend had always been sweet, thoughtful, and considerate. And she'd always known that she could count on him for anything. But what he was now offering required sacrifice and long-term commitment.

She loved him all the more for it. But she needed to know that he'd really thought this through.

"Dallas, are you sure about this? Having a child together...we're talking about a lifetime commitment." She smiled. "That means you'll never truly be rid of me. Are you sure you're up for that?"

"I'm twenty-five years into this thing. No turning back now." He chuckled. "Besides, we were clearly going to outlive our spouses and become neighbors in one of those overpriced senior living centers where we'd play spades and dominoes all day, eat rice pudding, and complain about how our grandkids don't come to see us often enough." He shrugged. "We can still do that, only this way, we'll be talking about the same ungrateful grandchildren."

Zora burst into a fit of giggles, and Dallas laughed, too. But then an awkward silence filled the space between them.

Were they really considering doing this?

And if she was finding it awkward to have this conversation, how weird would it be when they actually decided to...*consummate* their marriage?

"There's one other thing." Zora's eyes drifted down to where their hands were connected. "I realize that we have a long history together, but as friends, not romantic partners. You're proposing that we actually have sex—for the sake of having a child," she added quickly. "But what if there's no—"

"Chemistry between us?" He chuckled quietly. "Maybe you've forgotten, but you kissed me a couple of years ago," he reminded her.

"That was also Buzzed Zora." A fresh wave of humiliation heated her cheeks, as she thought of Dallas's reaction to the kiss. "And that encounter didn't go so well, in case you've forgotten."

"I haven't." Dallas lowered his gaze and sighed. "That was completely my fault."

"No, it was mine. I tried to turn our friendship into something that it wasn't...that it *isn't*. And we'd be doing that again if we go through with this marriage."

"Because there's no attraction between us?" He raised one brow incredulously as he studied her face, his gaze lingering on her mouth.

Zora's heart raced, and she could feel her body reacting to the intense heat in Dallas's eyes.

This was new. Because Zora was reasonably sure her friend had never looked at her this way before: like he intended to devour her.

Dallas stared at his friend. Took pleasure in watching a crimson streak spreading across her cheeks.

"I didn't say... I mean...when I kissed you, you didn't..." Zora stammered, her espresso-brown eyes suddenly wide.

Zora Abbott never hesitated. She laid down demands with complete clarity. Was always clear about what she did and didn't want.

In fact, there were few moments in his life when he'd seen his opinionated friend truly speechless or even the tiniest bit vulnerable. Something in his chest warmed at being the reason Zora *Hamilton* stood in front of him now thunderstruck, trembling and a little nervous. It thrilled him that he had the power to give this incredibly strong woman pause.

Dallas leaned forward and took Zora's face in his hands. He glided his thumbs along her cheekbones, watching her eyes study his with anticipation as he closed the space between them.

Finally, Dallas did the thing he'd regretted not doing the night Zora had kissed him beneath the mistletoe. He pressed his open mouth to hers.

Dallas's eyes drifted closed at the pillow-soft sensation of Zora's lush lips meeting his. He savored the minty taste of her mouth, pushing his tongue between her lips when she opened them on a soft gasp. He swept his tongue over hers, then glided it along the ridges at the top of her mouth.

Zora wrapped her arms around him tentatively, her hands barely touching his back. As if she wasn't quite sure this was real. Slowly, she tightened her grip, her fingertips pressing into his skin through the soft cotton T-shirt. She leaned in closer, pinning his growing shaft between them.

An involuntary groan escaped Dallas's mouth at the sensation of his hardening length pressed to her soft belly. The feeling seemed to trigger awareness in every nerve ending in his body.

It opened the doors to the floodgates of desire for her that he'd long barred shut. Because Zora had always meant too much to him to risk their friendship for sex—no matter how badly he'd secretly craved her touch and her kiss. Now that it had been unleashed, his desire for her came stalking out of its dark, secret cave like a ravenous tiger in search of its prey.

His kiss became hungrier, more insistent than the tentative kiss he'd begun with, and Zora responded in kind. She gripped his shirt, her body cradled against his, as if she, too, ached for more contact.

Dallas dropped his hands to her waist, then cupped her

REESE RYAN 63

full bottom. It was something he'd fantasized about much more than he'd care to admit. The fabric of her shorts filled his palms, but his fingertips brushed the exposed skin just beneath the curve of her perfect ass.

He gripped the firm flesh, squeezing it and pulling her closer. Intensifying the sensation that already rippled down his spine, overwhelming his senses with a need he'd never allowed himself to acknowledge because the stakes were simply too high.

Suddenly, his phone rang again, bringing them both out of the daze they'd fallen into as they stared in the direction of the ringing phone.

"Guess you didn't get around to turning the Do Not Disturb back on." She gave him a soft, playful grin that made him want to toss her onto the bed amid the luggage and bridal shop bags and kiss every inch of her smooth brown skin.

"Guess not." Dallas silently cursed himself for forgetting. He stroked her cheek, bringing her attention back to him. "Well, does that answer your question?"

"Yes, I think it does," she practically whispered, then sighed quietly, taking a step away from him. She cleared her throat, both of them ignoring his cell phone as it continued to ring. "And if you really want to do this, then I accept your offer of help. But first, we need to establish some rules."

There was the confident, take-charge woman that he knew. The one who always felt a need to be in control.

"Yes, Mrs. Hamilton?" Dallas smirked, maintaining his loose grip on her waist, even though she had put some space between them.

Zora frowned but didn't object to his use of her new last name. "We need to outline the parameters of this 'marriage.'" She used air quotes. "That way we both know what to expect. So I'm thinking that there's really only a window of five or six prime days for ovulation, so we'd only need to have sex then. I have a double master, so we can maintain separate bedrooms, just like we have here. Then we'd only need to come together…you know…when necessary."

She started pacing the floor, thinking aloud, as he'd sometimes seen her do when working with her sales team at the distillery.

"Zora." He grabbed her arm gently. "I'm *not* your employee. I realize that the point of this exercise is to give you a child, but that doesn't mean that you're in charge of everything."

"Of course not." She frowned, clearly offended. But then she took a deep breath and released it. "I'm sorry if I gave you that impression. It's just that… I need things to be clear between us. And I don't want either of our feelings to end up being hurt. That's why it's best if we create an exit strategy *now*. So let's give this six months. Then we can tell our families we gave our marriage a try, but we're better off as friends."

"You really think six months is enough to convince our families that we gave this marriage our best effort?" Dallas asked, trying not to reveal his *already* hurt feelings.

Zora huffed, making her lips vibrate and her cheeks puff with air. "Right. We should make it at least a year. I mean…if you think you can maintain our sham marriage for that long," she said, her voice suddenly unsure. "I wouldn't blame you if you didn't. That's an awful long time for you to be off the market."

"Yes," he agreed. "We should plan to stay together for at least a year, but I submit that we should then reassess our feelings." His voice was firm as he maintained eye contact with her. "Because at the end of that year, maybe we'll discover that we don't want to go back to just being friends."

Zora inhaled sharply and blinked rapidly as she stared at him. "You're suggesting that we might want to make this a *real* marriage?"

"My one nonnegotiable condition for this agreement is that if we do this thing, it *will* be a real marriage. Same house. Same bed. Sure, we'll have sex during those optimal times, but also any time the mood strikes us."

"But—"

"Again, nonnegotiable." Dallas held up a hand, halting Zora midargument. "Nothing happens unless you want it to," he added for clarity. "But intimacy should never be off the table because of the calendar. Agreed?"

Zora tilted her head and folded her arms, resting her chin on one fist as she silently assessed him. As if she was seeing him in a totally new light.

He often allowed her to dictate when and how they spent their time together because, quite frankly, he didn't care what they did. All he cared about was spending time with her. But this was different. He loved his friend, but there was no way he was going to let her steamroll him on this agreement.

This was his opportunity to discover if there was something more between them than friendship. Something he'd often wondered about, especially since that kiss under the mistletoe.

"So you want to reserve the right to be spontaneous, but it's completely up to me?" she clarified.

"That pretty much sums it up." Dallas shrugged.

"Then I could only *want to* on those optimal dates," she pointed out with a smirk.

Whenever they negotiated anything, his best friend worked the hell out of that one year of law school she'd taken before she decided that she didn't want to be the King's Finest attorney after all. But then again, even as a kid, Zora had always been in active negotiation with the people in her life. She'd negotiated her allowance, chores, bedtime, curfew and the length of her skirts while in high school.

Dallas grasped Zora's tank top and tugged her closer,

dropping another kiss on her soft lips. His tongue searched for hers. He wrapped his arms around her, kissing her until he'd elicited soft murmurs of contentment, and her hardened nipples poked against his chest.

He wanted more. But he wouldn't push. Wouldn't take her farther than she was prepared to go. This was only about making a point.

She wanted him, too.

Dallas broke their kiss, staring down at her as she finally opened her eyes. He grinned. "I guess we'll see about that, Mrs. Hamilton."

"Fine." Zora shoved him away, and he couldn't help laughing. "Point made, and your terms are acceptable. Do we need to write any of this down?"

She went back to folding her clothing on the bed.

"I think I've got it." Dallas winked.

His phone rang again. He recognized the ringtone as his mother's. Dallas sighed. "If we don't answer the phone—"

"I know, I know. They'll just keep calling." Zora huffed, then ran her fingers through her hair, fluffing it. "Let's just get this over with."

"But how do we explain our sudden decision to get married?" he asked.

"Let's keep things as nonspecific—but as close to the truth—as possible. You know...minus the weed brownies and the blackout," she added.

"Come here." Dallas grabbed his wife's hand and sat in one of the chairs in front of the wall of windows that offered a view of the Las Vegas Strip. He pulled Zora onto his lap, taking her by surprise. Dallas wrapped an arm around her waist, then handed her the phone. "Ready?"

Zora sucked in a deep breath, then nodded.

Let the newlywed games begin.

Ten

Zora held her breath, her hands shaking as she sat on her friend's lap.

She'd shared tight spaces with Dallas plenty of times over the years. They'd shared tiny rental cars, a pop-up RV not much bigger than a soup can, and snug roller-coaster cars, to name a few. And they'd often sat close enough that she was *practically* on his lap. But *actually* sitting on Dallas's lap with his arm wrapped around her waist was a brand-new level of intimacy for them. One to which she would evidently need to become accustomed if they were going to pull off this temporary marriage of convenience for the next year.

But all this was a lot to take in.

Zora's head was swimming. Her heart was racing. Her body was overheating. Dallas's *impressive* man parts—the image of which she still couldn't get out of her head—poked against her bottom as he held her against him. Her lady parts were doing all manner of rogue things she'd much rather they not.

"You sure you're ready to do this?" Dallas asked.

The warmth and concern in his husky voice wrapped itself around her like a warm, soft blanket, assuring her everything would be all right.

"Yes. I'm ready." Zora sucked in a deep breath and slid her finger across the screen to answer the video call from Letitia Hamilton, whom everyone called Tish.

Zora and Dallas put on their biggest smiles.

"Hey, Ma." Dallas grinned.

"Hi, Tish." Zora waved awkwardly at the woman who'd

gone from being her best friend's mom to her mother-in-law in an instant.

Tension suddenly knotted her stomach. She'd always gotten along so well with Dallas's mother.

Would she be angry with her?

"Iris, Duke, the kids finally answered the phone. I'm looking at them now," she called excitedly, not bothering to respond to either of them. Zora recognized the paintings in the background. Tish was in the family room at Zora's parents' house.

This could all go very bad fast.

Finally, Dallas's mother returned her attention to the screen.

"I can't believe you two went off and got hitched without telling us. And yes, I realize that I hate flying, but I would've driven across the country for my baby's wedding," Tish said. A hint of sadness altered the upbeat tone that she'd begun the conversation with.

"Or better yet, you could've gotten married right here in Magnolia Lake so that we all could've been there." Zora's mother's head popped into the edge of the frame.

Dallas tightened his grip around Zora's waist. She took it as a silent reminder that they were in this together.

Zora sucked in a deep breath. She lifted her chin and deepened her smile. "I know, Mom. And I'm sorry. Dallas and I honestly didn't come to Vegas with the intention of getting married."

"And when exactly did you decide that you two were more than *just friends*?" her father asked from off-screen, the tension evident in his voice.

"The realization hit us so quickly, sir. It's all kind of a blur." Dallas jumped in when Zora didn't respond.

Oh, he was good.

"That's the only reason I didn't come to you first and ask for her hand," Dallas said.

Zora pursed her lips and bit her tongue, forcing herself not to remind all of them that she was a grown-ass woman who was nearly thirty-two years old. *She* was the only person who could give her hand away in marriage.

But since Tish looked sad, her mother seemed pissed and her father sounded dejected…it didn't feel like the best time to make her womanist speech. She put a pin in it to save that conversation for another day.

Her father grunted his response and said that he was going to the kitchen for a beer.

"I know your father is a little grumpy, but his feelings are hurt," her mother whispered loudly, squeezing her face closer to the phone. "You're his only daughter, Zora," she said, as if Zora wasn't well aware of that fact. "He's spent your entire life dreading the day he'd finally have to walk his baby girl down the aisle and give her away. But suddenly you're married, and he never got the chance to come to terms with it."

"I'm sorry, Iris," Dallas interjected, threading his fingers through Zora's and squeezing her hand, as if he sensed the tension knotting in her shoulders and back. "It's my fault. A whirlwind wedding here in Vegas was my idea. Once we realized how much we wanted to be together, we just got caught up in the emotions. We didn't want to waste another moment apart."

"Right." Zora glanced back at Dallas, flashing him a grateful smile. "Dal and I, we're both ready to settle down and start a family."

"So your father is right, you *are* pregnant." Her mother could barely restrain her excitement.

"No, Mom, I am *not* pregnant. I assure you," Zora said. "But Dallas and I are looking forward to becoming parents."

"That's so exciting." Tish beamed, sifting her manicured fingernails through her hair—the color of a brand-new, shiny copper penny. Her green eyes twinkled at the prospect. "And while you two haven't been answering the phone, hopefully working on making us those grandbabies," she added, causing Zora to stifle a cringe, "we've come up with a few surprise plans of our own."

Uh-oh. Zora did *not* like the sound of that.

"Um…okay." She glanced back at Dallas nervously. "What kind of plans?"

"We're going to have a formal wedding here at the barn. Nothing extravagant," Iris said quickly, before Zora had the chance to object. "Just a lovely little ceremony that both of our families can be a part of so your father can walk his little girl down the aisle, just like he always dreamed of doing."

"That sounds…really nice, Mom." Zora swallowed her objections. She hadn't intended to have the first wedding to Dallas. Now they were going to have a second, more formal one? "Right, Dal?"

"Sounds like a wonderful idea," he chimed in. "Thank you, Iris. Thanks, Mom. We can't wait to see you all when we get home."

Home. This still all seemed like some crazy dream she'd awaken from any minute now. But she and Dallas were married, and they were going to be living under a single roof as husband and wife for an entire year while they tried to make a baby.

"Zora—" Dallas squeezed her hand, bringing her out of her daze. "Your mother was saying how beautiful your rings are."

"Oh, thank you." She held up her left hand, showing off her new rings.

"My son has good taste." Tish grinned.

"He certainly does," Iris practically crowed. Then they both laughed.

"I couldn't agree more, Iris." Dallas grinned, his whiskey-brown eyes twinkling.

Zora sprang up from her friend's lap the moment she'd ended the call. She needed some space and a moment to clear her head.

"I'm going to finish straightening up this mess before the housekeeper comes in. Then I'm going to find out exactly how much damage I've done to my credit cards," she said. "I suggest you do the same."

He walked over to where she stood folding her clothing. "Are you sure you're okay, Zo? Hearing how disappointed your dad was about not getting to walk you down the aisle...that had to be hard."

"It was. And now they're planning to shell out real money for this wedding. I don't care what they just said. My mother is a Southern mama planning her only daughter's wedding. She's bound to get carried away. I can't let them waste money on an elaborate wedding for a marriage that isn't even real."

Dallas cupped her cheek. "I don't see the harm in giving them a chance to celebrate our marriage. But I'll do my best to make sure they don't get carried away."

"There is one other thing," Zora said.

"A prenup?" he asked.

"It's a little too late for that." A strike Parker would no doubt hold against her. "But before we start...you know... exchanging bodily fluids, we should both make sure that we have a clean bill of health."

"A fair point." Dallas chuckled. "I have no objections to that request. And since I have never had unprotected sex with anyone, I don't anticipate there will be a problem." He checked his phone, which was ringing again. "I need to take this call, do you mind?"

"No, but when you're done, can we grab something to eat?" Zora patted her belly. "I'm starving."

Dallas nodded and kissed her cheek, then answered his phone as he exited the room.

Zora sank onto the mattress and held up her left hand. She stared at her stunning new rings. The pink sapphire and diamonds sparkled in the sunlight.

A small part of her wished that all this was as real as Dallas seemed to want it to be. But they weren't two crazy kids in love who'd flown to Vegas to get married.

She loved Dallas as a friend, and yes, there was an attraction between them. But they weren't *in* love. Settling for anything less would eventually leave one or both of them feeling resentful. It wasn't a risk she was willing to take with a friendship that meant so much to her.

This marriage wasn't about love or attraction. It was about making a baby. Once they did, they'd go back to being friends who also just happened to be co-parents.

It was the right decision for everyone involved.

Eleven

Dallas stepped out of Zora's room, closing the door behind him. He cleared his throat and put on his brightest smile before accepting the call from the man he hoped to secure a deal with soon.

"Mr. Austarsson." Dallas made his way back to his room on the other side of the suite. "How are you, sir?"

"I am well, Dallas. Thank you." Einar Austarsson's thick Icelandic accent wrapped itself around every word he uttered. "But as I told you before, please call me Einar."

Right. Einar had made a point of explaining that in Iceland, they called each other by their first names—regardless of one's station.

"I am told by a member of my social media team that congratulations are in order for you and your beautiful new wife." The man chuckled with knowing laughter. "Why did you not mention when you introduced her that the lovely Zora was your fiancée?"

Because…she wasn't.

"We wanted to surprise our families… *Einar.*" Dallas made a mental effort not to call the man *sir*—a natural tendency as a man born and raised in the South.

"Well, I am sorry to disturb you on such a momentous day, but my plane leaves first thing in the morning. I thought it would be nice if you and I could sit down over a meal and discuss what a collaboration between our organizations might look like."

"I'd like that very much," Dallas said, grateful Zora had agreed to maintaining their marriage for at least a year. By that time, any agreement he and Einar came to should be signed and in progress. "My...wife and I were going to grab a bite to eat. But I could meet you right after that."

"How fortuitous!" the older man proclaimed. "Brigitta and I will join you. After our meal, perhaps our wives will excuse us to conduct our business?"

"I...uh...sounds great, Einar. Zora and I would love for you to join us," he said, hoping his new wife wouldn't mind.

Zora put on her brightest smile and greeted Einar Austarsson—a big man who towered over them wearing the warmest grin. He easily fit the bill of gentle giant.

Then she greeted his beautiful wife, Brigitta Werners-dóttir, who was the very definition of casual elegance. The stunning older woman wore a lovely, pale pink, cocktail-length chiffon dress with a sheer capelet that showed her upper back. And her makeup was flawless.

Zora had no doubt the woman awoke every day looking picture-perfect and put together. The very opposite of how Zora had looked when she literally rolled out of bed this afternoon.

Though she and Dallas had only been awake for a few hours, it was now early evening and she was still exhausted. Her mouth was dry and her head still hurt. Though thanks to an over-the-counter painkiller, it no longer felt like an African drum circle was being conducted inside her skull.

Still, she felt like roadkill, compounded by the trauma of discovering that—*Quelle surprise!*—she was now her best friend's wife. This was definitely not the way she'd intended to spend her pre-birthday weekend in Vegas. Nor was it what she had planned to be doing right now.

She'd been looking forward to a plate of Belgian waffles, dressed with fresh strawberries, doused in strawberry syrup, topped with a pile of fresh whipped cream and sprinkled with powdered sugar. And she'd intended on eating her decadent breakfast-for-dinner at some tacky, all-day buffet where she could wear a scroungy pair of leggings, a T-shirt, her darkest shades and a visor pulled down over her face.

But when Dallas had come to her and explained that Einar wanted to join them for dinner at the hotel's four-star restaurant… Well, how could she say no to playing the happy newlywed for the sake of his deal?

If she'd said no, Dallas would've understood. He wouldn't have complained or guilted her. And even if they hadn't been married, she would've done anything she could to help her friend nail this deal with the Icelandic furniture designer.

Still, the fact that she felt she *owed* Dallas because of the sacrifice he was making for her unnerved her. That was the feeling of obligation Zora didn't like hanging over her head. That made her chest feel tight and her skin itchy. She didn't like feeling beholden to anyone. As if she hadn't earned everything that she'd achieved in her life—despite her last name or the fact that she'd been born into a life of privilege.

Every day at King's Finest, she'd worked hard to prove that she was there because she deserved to be. As much as her father or any of her brothers. She realized that it was a personal hang-up that she needed to get over. And yet, in the back of her head, there was always the need to prove herself. To demonstrate to her grandfather, father and brothers that she'd earned her spot on that executive board.

Whenever she met with distributors and vendors, she carried a tiny chip on her shoulder. She was always prepared to put in check any man who made the mistake of believing she was just another pretty face. Or that she'd only been given the job because she was the granddaughter of Joseph Abbott, the founder of King's Finest Distillery.

But Zora was equally burdened with the concern that she'd come off as an angry Black woman for speaking her mind, doing her job, doing it well and not standing for any bullshit—as any male executive would be lauded for doing. So she'd learned to find that perfect balance between being a pretty face and the baddest bitch in the room.

So here she was, playing the part of devoted wife in full makeup, a fancy dress and heels that made her legs look amazing but pinched her toes. And she'd have to settle for a steak or some fancy pasta dish, which would probably be lovely—just not what she wanted.

Then again, she wasn't really playing a role. She was Dallas's wife now. A fact that still felt surreal. And she was his devoted friend who honestly would do just about anything to see this venture and his business succeed.

But tomorrow, Dallas owed her waffles.

The couples exchanged the requisite pleasantries until the hostess led them through the elegant restaurant to their table. Dallas pulled out Zora's chair and sat beside her, draping his arm over the back of it. His heat surrounded her, warming her skin—and *other* places. And his subtle scent tickled her nostrils, reminding her of how it had felt when he'd taken her in his arms and kissed her senseless—twice. When she'd momentarily forgotten that she and Dallas were just friends.

"How did you two meet?" Brigitta asked, smiling at them the way people often smiled at newlyweds.

Zora felt guilty for evoking such genuine emotions when their marriage had been the result of too-strong drinks and her failure to read the label on a brownie wrapper. Still, she smiled gratefully.

"We've known each other forever," Zora said. Her heart swelled and an involuntary smile curved her mouth, thinking of the day they'd first met. "In fact, we met on the playground in kindergarten, and we've been friends ever since."

"My wife is being too kind." Dallas chuckled, squeezing her shoulder. "I'd just moved to the area, and I was the new, shy kid in school. A couple of bullies tried to shake me down on the playground. Zora here, who was about half their size, blew in like a tornado, told both them off and promised that if they ever messed with me again, she'd sic all four of her older brothers on them. Needless to say, I never had a problem with them again, and she and I have been friends ever since."

Einar laughed so hard his forehead and cheeks turned bright red.

Brigitta pressed a hand to her chest and smiled. "That is the sweetest story I've ever heard."

"I'm pretty sure that was the day I fell in love with Zo." Dallas glided his hand lower, circling her waist and pulling her closer as he leaned in and kissed her cheek. "In retrospect, I'm surprised it took us so long to figure out that we were meant to be together."

Zora's cheeks flamed at the sweet, intimate gesture and the words—rooted in the truth—which felt so authentic. They were simply playing a role. The happy newlyweds. She realized that. But what he was saying and how his words affected her…it all felt so *real*.

When her eyes met his, Dallas had the most sincere smile. Her heart leaped in her chest, and her pulse raced. For a moment, she'd almost forgotten that Einar and Brigitta were sitting just across the table watching them like goldfish in a bowl. Oohing and ahhing like they'd just seen a baby take its first steps.

Fortunately, the server came and took their orders before she did something crazy, like climb on his lap and kiss him as though they were in their suite alone.

She ordered a seafood pasta dish, Dallas ordered a steak and Einar and Brigitta both ordered lobster. When the server walked away, Dallas excused himself to go to the restroom, leaving Zora alone with the couple momentarily.

"I know you're still newlyweds," Brigitta practically

cooed, "but it is just so wonderful to see a young man so very much in love with his wife. And you two have such an advantage, having been close friends for so long."

"Thank you, Brigitta." Zora smiled. "My sister-in-law always teased that we were like an old married couple. So I guess there's not much we don't know about each other." Zora sipped her water.

"But have you ever lived together?" Einar asked. When she shook her head, he and his wife both chuckled. "Believe me, Zora. No matter how well you know a person, you never *really* know them until you have to live with them. But I'm confident that you two will manage the adjustment."

It was something she hadn't considered before. She'd lived with all her brothers growing up. She was closest to Cole—her youngest brother. But when Cole had moved in with her for three months while he was renovating one of his homes several years ago, she'd been ready to strangle him by the time he'd moved out. So there was definitely some truth to Einar's words.

Dallas returned to the table and put his napkin on his lap. "What did I miss?"

"We were just talking about how different it is actually living with someone." Brigitta smiled warmly. "Speaking of which…will you two be moving into your home in Magnolia Lake, Dallas? Or yours, Zora? Or are you buying a new place altogether?"

"Mine," Zora said quickly.

Her eyes met Dallas's as she slid her hand into his beneath the table and threaded their fingers. He hadn't objected to moving into her place when she'd suggested it earlier. He'd only stipulated that they reside in the same house and sleep in the same bed. As their eyes met now, seated in such close proximity, with his large hand wrapped around hers, the thought of sharing a bed with Dallas sent an unexpected shiver down her spine. Made her body tingle in places she didn't want it to, especially not here and now.

"Right, but we might revisit the topic once we have kids." Dallas cringed the moment he'd uttered the words, as if he hadn't intended to say them.

"You're planning a family already. How lovely." Brigitta seemed thrilled by the news. "You're such a sweet couple. You'll be wonderful parents."

"I'll do my best. But I know that Zora will be a phenomenal mother, because she's an amazing aunt and an incredible woman." Dallas lifted her hand to his mouth and brushed a kiss across her knuckles. His action evoked another *aww* from Brigitta and made Zora swoon.

Einar shifted the conversation to business, and Zora and Brigitta talked about some of the shows Brigitta and her husband had seen while they were in Vegas and the Broadway shows she hoped to see next time they were in New York City.

The server brought out Einar's and Brigitta's lobster and Dallas's steak. But instead of the seafood pasta Zora had ordered, the server set a plate of large, fluffy Belgian waffles with strawberries and whipped cream and a side of bacon in front of her.

"My waffles." Zora pressed a hand to her chest. It was an elegant restaurant, and this was an important business deal. So she hadn't inquired about whether she could order an off-menu breakfast item for dinner, but apparently Dallas had.

"I promised you waffles." He winked, picking up his knife and fork.

She kissed his cheek, which made Einar and Brigitta smile approvingly.

Had her best friend always been so thoughtful and romantic, and she just hadn't noticed? Or maybe she was

just caught up in the fantasy that they were spinning for
the benefit of the man Dallas hoped to do business with.

This isn't real.

Zora repeated the words in her head over and over again.
At this rate, she'd be repeating them to herself a lot.

Twelve

Dallas could barely contain his grin as Zora held court, telling Einar and Brigitta an animated, sidesplittingly funny story about their adventures in Peru when they'd climbed Machu Picchu together. They'd been just out of college and determined to see the world but woefully ill prepared for the climb.

While he and Einar had sketched out some ideas for their proposed collaboration, Zora and Brigitta chatted like two old friends, trading stories and sharing laughs. Brigitta had shown Zora photos of the couple's four children, and Zora had shown off photos of Davis, Remi, Beau and Bailey. They lingered over the meal, chatting for nearly two hours.

Dallas was surprised the busy restaurant hadn't asked them to vacate their prime table.

Finally, Einar stood and declared that it was getting late. They had an early flight and needed to retire.

"It's been a pleasure to get to know you and your lovely wife." Einar beamed as he took Brigitta's hand. "I look forward to working with you in the future."

"Same here." Dallas shook the man's hand firmly, then his wife's. "Have a safe flight back."

"Zora, dear, it was such a pleasure to meet you. I'll email you that information about mentoring women for executive positions. You'd be perfect for it." Brigitta hugged her. "Congratulations again on your marriage. I know you two will be very happy together."

"Thank you." Dallas slipped an arm around Zora's waist, and she leaned into him, her hand pressed to his chest. He kissed her temple, his heart swelling for reasons he couldn't explain. "I'm confident we will."

He took Zora's hand in his, threading their fingers as they followed the older couple out of the restaurant, bade them farewell and headed toward the elevator.

They stood in the elevator car alone, her hand still firmly in his. He no longer had reason to hold Zora's hand. So why couldn't he let it go?

"We were in such a hurry to leave the suite, I didn't get the chance to tell you how beautiful you look tonight, Zo." Without thought, his gaze dropped to the neckline of the off-the-shoulder wrap dress Zora was wearing. The rust-colored fabric highlighted the reddish undertone of her skin.

"Thanks." She fiddled with the ends of the belt at her waist. Her cheeks had turned crimson again.

Dallas was starting to enjoy his newfound superpower: the ability to make the unflappable Zora Abbott blush.

They rode the elevator up in silence. When they got off, they were still holding hands.

"You were a star tonight, Zora," Dallas said as they made their way toward their suite. "My designs and awards brought Einar Austarsson to the table, but I'm pretty sure you sold him on working with me. You made me sound like a philanthropist design genius."

"Because you are." Zora stopped and turned to him. "And thank you for making the special request for my waffles. I didn't think eating breakfast for dinner at a fancy restaurant would be a good look for your big, important meeting. That's why I didn't ask for them myself."

"It's what you wanted." Dallas shrugged. "And I promised to make it happen."

"I appreciate it," she said. "After everything that's happened today, I needed the comfort of my favorite breakfast meal. I know that sounds silly."

"It doesn't, and it isn't. I understand," he assured her as they stood in front of the door to their suite.

Dallas was reluctant to release Zora's hand. To separate

himself from the warmth and comfort of the connection he felt with their palms pressed together and their fingers entwined.

In fact, what he wanted more than anything was to lean down and capture her mouth in a kiss again. This time, with no hesitation or interruptions. And he wouldn't stop with just a kiss. That was just the beginning of where he wanted to take things with her.

But they'd agreed to wait until they'd both had medical exams and he'd put Zora in the driver's seat. So he would honor their agreement, no matter how badly he wanted to take her to bed.

When he didn't make a move to retrieve the key card in his wallet, Zora waved her small purse in front of the card reader. The tumblers in the lock clicked, and the indicator light switched to green.

Dallas squeezed the handle, holding the door open for Zora. Once they were inside their suite, he slid off his suit jacket and toed off his shoes, eager to get into a T-shirt and a pair of shorts.

Zora kicked off her heels, then stooped to pick them up. "I'm going to get out of this dress and makeup. And I'm still exhausted. Would you be insulted if I turned in early tonight?"

"No, of course not. We've been through a lot today. Turning in early sounds like a great idea. I should do the same." Dallas hoped he'd managed to hide the disappointment he felt at the idea of going to their separate rooms. "Good night, Zora."

She nodded, then made her way to her room, closing the door behind her with a soft click.

Dallas got out of the shower, toweled off and pulled on the sweat shorts he'd brought to sleep in. The ones he'd started out wearing the night after the awards but had shed *after* his marriage to Zora.

It was still relatively early for a night in Vegas, but it had been an eventful twenty-four hours, and he was exhausted.

Dallas yawned and padded across the darkened room toward the comfortable bed that beckoned him. When he turned on the bedside lamp so that he could charge his phone, he was startled by movement.

"Zora?" Dallas ran a hand over his head. "I thought you were—"

"Same house, same bed. That was the deal, right?" she murmured, shielding her eyes from the light. "I, too, am a person of my word. Besides, I might as well get used to your snoring."

Dallas broke into laughter. He plugged the charger into his phone. "I do *not* snore," he countered. "I just breathe heavily. And you're on my side of the bed. Scoot over."

"Fine. *Anything* as long as you'll turn off that light. My head hasn't completely recovered."

Dallas turned off the light and climbed into the bed beside Zora, occupying the space that still retained her body heat. The pillow bore her signature scent. He lay on his back for a few minutes, staring at the ceiling before he finally turned on his side, his back toward her. "'Night, Zo."

There was a silent pause, and he wondered if she'd already fallen asleep. Finally, she said, "Sweet dreams, Dallas."

Dallas lay awake long after Zora had fallen asleep. A deep sense of longing filled his chest as he tried to keep his desire for his best friend at bay.

He was lying in bed beside the woman whose friendship meant more to him than just about anything in the world. But clearly, he felt something more than friendship for her, too.

Dallas closed his eyes and groaned. The words of his

jackass brother—with whom he'd spoken earlier and had shown zero remorse over the situation—still floated in his head.

Dude, you finally made your move on Zora. You're welcome. Now...do not fuck this up.

If only things were that simple.

Thirteen

Zora held her breath as Dallas turned onto the road that ran past the renovated barn where her mother was planning to hold their formal wedding. At the end was her parents' vast property and the home Cole had built for them.

Dallas had a tight grip on the wheel of his tricked-out GMC Sierra Denali pickup truck—one of the few luxuries her friend, who was now her husband, had splurged on. She could feel the tension rolling off his broad shoulders, too.

Still, he placed a hand over hers on the center console and squeezed it, offering her a confident smile.

Dallas pulled his truck into the driveway of her parents' home, already filled with the vehicles of her four brothers.

"Awesome. The entire motley crew is here," Zora muttered beneath her breath.

"If we stick to the plan, everything will be fine." Dallas pulled his hand away long enough to shift the gear into Park and turn off the engine. He squeezed her hand again reassuringly. "But I realize that this first day will be…uncomfortable. Believe me, I don't relish the idea of deceiving our families any more than you do. So if you'd prefer to just come clean and explain what really happened… I understand."

"No." Zora shook her head vehemently. In her head, she could already hear all the things that her parents and siblings would say. They'd use words like *reckless* and *irresponsible*. None of which described the future CEO of their company. "We came up with this plan for a good reason, and we should stick to it. For both our sakes. I'm a little nervous, but you're right. It'll be fine."

Dallas gave her a small smile, then nodded before hopping out of the truck. He went around to the other side of the vehicle to open her door.

Zora didn't move. Instead, she tugged on the bottom of her sweatshirt. Then she repositioned the scarf she'd draped around her neck to give her low-key look a bit of pizzazz.

She'd thrown on practically the first thing she'd seen when she and Dallas had arrived from Vegas and gone to her place to take quick showers and change their clothing. And now she was rethinking everything...including her outfit.

What did a person wear to a birthday dinner that had turned into a sorry-we-got-married-without-you party? She was pretty sure an old sweatshirt, distressed jeans, a pair of Timbs, and lip gloss wasn't it.

"You look beautiful, Zo. Stop overthinking it." Dallas's husky voice was as soft and comforting as the oversize sweatshirt she was wearing.

He was blowing smoke. Still, she couldn't help smiling. Zora ran a hand over her hair, slicked back and pulled tight into a low bun.

"That, sir, is a pity compliment."

He grinned, leaning in closer. His lips brushed her ear when he spoke. "You'd look amazing if all you were wearing was a potato sack, a pair of earrings and that heart-stopping smile of yours."

He stepped back and extended his hand.

"Thank you." Zora practically whispered the words as she accepted his offered hand. She stepped down onto the sideboard of the truck, then hopped onto the ground.

Dallas shut the door, then held her by the waist, pinning her in place as he gazed down at her. "Maybe we're still a little fuzzy on the details of our decision to get married," he said. "But we're staying married because you are a strong, confident woman who knows what you want." He stroked her cheek and smiled. "Don't let anyone get inside your head and make you lose sight of that. Not even the people you love."

Zora nodded, grateful for the pep talk. Dallas always knew what to say to talk her down off the ledge. And she loved him for it. She lifted onto her toes and kissed his cheek, one hand pressed firmly to his chest. "Thanks, Dal. For everything."

"For you, Zora?" He grinned. "Anything."

It was something he'd always said. She'd always taken it as sarcasm. Yes, she'd known that she could count on Dallas, and had suspected that he would've done her nearly any favor—even one as big as fathering her child. But she hadn't asked because she didn't want to take advantage of their friendship.

Over the past two days, Dallas had shown her that their friendship ran far deeper than she'd imagined. Reminded her how truly special it was. Confirmed that it was something she never, ever wanted to lose.

Those weren't just sarcastic words that Dallas had uttered. He meant them. And he was proving that here and now. She stared into the depths of his brown eyes, her hand still pressed to his chest.

If this "marriage" ruined their friendship, she would never forgive herself.

"You two planning on coming inside or are you just gonna make out with my sister out here for another fifteen minutes?" Cole stood on the front porch, his arms folded over his chest.

Here we go.

Zora grabbed Dallas's hand and threaded her fingers through his before turning in her brother's direction.

"*Really*, Cole? You're going all whiny-ass man baby on me right now?" Zora retorted as she and Dallas made their way toward the large porch of her parents' beautiful home.

"Nothing personal, sis." Cole huffed. "Some of us are hungry."

"Well, I suggest you eat a Snickers or something." Zora released Dallas's hand so she could hug her brother, despite the fact that Cole was being an asshole.

"Or you could just get your ass in here so we could eat." Cole chuckled when Zora playfully punched him in the gut. "By the way, happy birthday, little sis."

Her brother turned his attention to Dallas, the humor suddenly gone from his voice. "Dallas."

"Cole." Dallas nodded at her brother, his expression pleasant but unsmiling. He hadn't missed Cole's passive-aggressive swipe at him, and he was making it clear that he wouldn't be intimidated.

And damn if that didn't make her usually easygoing friend even hotter.

Zora slipped her hand into Dallas's again, and they followed her brother into the house. "Easy, tiger," she whispered. "Save a little of that big-dick energy. There'll be enough out-of-control testosterone in this house as it is."

He squeezed her hand but didn't respond otherwise. Dallas seemed to have his game face on, ready for whatever her brothers would throw his way.

Honestly, Zora was a little hurt and surprised by Cole's reaction. They were the closest out of the five siblings. Cole was the Abbott voted most likely to buck the system. After all, he was the only one of them who didn't work for the distillery. He'd taken a lot of heat for that, but she'd defended him vehemently to her brother Max, her father and her grandfather.

So she was more than a little irritated that Cole seemed pissed about her surprise marriage. He hadn't bothered to congratulate her and her new husband—a man he had always considered a friend. Zora took a deep breath and tried to put herself in her brothers' position. If one of them had secretly eloped and she'd had to learn about it from a social media post, wouldn't she be angry and hurt, too?

So she would try to maintain a cool head and keep that in mind while she dealt with whatever attitude they threw her way.

"Zora! Dallas!" Their mothers approached them as they came into the entryway of the house.

The space was decorated with mylar balloons in silver, hot pink, and black—her favorite colors. A *Happy Birthday, Zora* banner hung over the curved entrance to the dining room.

Her mother looked gorgeous in a dress with a festive, autumn-themed print. Iris Abbott's black hair, which hung to her shoulders in soft curls, was overcast with a burgundy rinse that camouflaged the few gray hairs she did constant battle with.

"I honestly don't know whether I should hug you or spank you both." Iris was smiling, but her eyes were misty. "You two gave us quite a shock."

Zora's mother hugged her, and Zora was relieved to sink into the comfort of her mother's warm embrace. "Sorry, Mom," she whispered into her mother's hair.

"I know, baby." Her mother squeezed her cheek as she studied her face. She glanced toward the living room, where her father and brothers and their significant others waited. "I know what it's like to be that much *in love*." She said the words in a teasing, singsong voice. "That kind of passion tends to get in the way of our better judgment. I was disappointed not to be invited to my only daughter's wedding, of course." Her mother sighed. "But I'm also very happy that you and Dallas *finally* figured out what Tish and I have known all along. You two were meant to be together."

Iris's smile deepened when she looked over at Tish, who was admiring Dallas's ring. Her new mother-in-law's green eyes locked with hers, and Zora froze, her stomach clenching in a knot.

Zora had always gotten along so well with Tish. Dallas's mother had often said that Zora was the daughter she never had. But that was when she and Dallas were just friends. Would she feel the same now that Zora had actually married her son?

After all, Cole had always had a warm and cordial relationship with Dallas. But in an instant, her brother's attitude toward the man who was now her husband had shifted.

Zora sucked in a deep breath as she mustered the strength to greet Tish and apologize for leaving the woman out of such an important moment in her son's life. But before Zora could utter a single word, Tish wrapped her arms around her and held her tight.

She'd received several hugs from Letitia Hamilton in the twenty-five-plus years that she'd known the woman. But never one as warm and lingering as the bear hug she was giving her now. Zora felt a sense of relief, but also a heightened sense of guilt for robbing Tish of a moment that must've been incredibly important to her.

"Zora, honey, I am thrilled that you're officially part of our family now. For so long, I've worried about my baby. That he would marry someone who wasn't right for him. Someone who could never make him happy." Tish pulled back and gazed at Zora, her eyes filled with tears as she cradled Zora's face. "I can't tell you how relieved I am to know that if anything ever happened to me, Dallas won't be alone. That he'll be with someone who loves him as much as I do."

"Thank you, Tish." Zora forced a smile, her voice trembling slightly. She'd been mentally preparing herself for negative pushback from their parents and older brothers. She hadn't expected such a genuinely warm and sweet reaction from Tish. "It means so much to hear you say that."

Zora's eyes welled with unexpected tears. Partly in re-action to Tish welcoming her into their family. Partly be-cause she couldn't help imagining how devastated Dallas's mom would be when they ended their marriage one year from now. Zora hadn't considered how important it must be to the woman that her sons didn't make the same type of disastrous match Tish had made when she'd married Dallas's father.

"I'm sorry you all couldn't be there," Zora repeated.

As far as their families were concerned, she and Dallas had made the conscious decision to exclude them from their wedding. Then they'd had the *audacity* to share their happy nuptials with complete strangers on the internet. And just for good measure, she'd posted it all on the King's Finest Instagram account.

No wonder Cole was being such a dick about this. They all believed she'd been a selfish, bratty princess, and she had no defense to convince them otherwise.

Her family was hurt that they hadn't been there. Hell, in a way, she and Dallas hadn't even been there. Not in any real way she could process at the moment.

"You two will make it up to us with this wedding we're planning," Zora's mother interjected, one hand propped on her hip. "In fact, I have some dates I want to run by you two."

"Can the wedding planning at least wait until *after* we've had dinner?" Zora's father appeared in the doorway, his arms folded.

Zora could see the pain and disappointment on his face. Her chest ached, and her gut wrenched.

Dallas gave her hand a quick squeeze. Then they walked toward her father.

"Hey, Dad," Zora said, her voice tentative.

She was a grown woman who was in complete control of her own life. She held an important position in their organization, where she had to make tough decisions every single day. But as she stood before her father now, she felt like Daddy's little girl. And she'd disappointed her father. Hurt him, even.

Zora and her father didn't always see eye to eye. But he'd respected her decisions because she'd been woman enough to come to him and tell him exactly what she intended to do and why, even when she knew he wouldn't approve. But this whirlwind marriage made her feel every bit the selfish brat her older brothers sometimes teasingly called her.

"Hello, Dallas. Happy birthday, Zora. Glad you two made it home safely," her father said calmly. "They're all waiting for you in the other room. Your mothers made sure your brothers didn't ambush you. Mostly because they wanted to ambush you themselves."

Iris and Tish glared at him.

"Thanks, Dad." Zora stepped closer to her father. "And I'm sorry. I—"

"Come here, sweetheart." Duke opened his arms.

Zora wrapped her arms around her dad, her cheek pressed to his chest as she inhaled the scent of his familiar aftershave.

"You don't owe any of us an apology. This is about dealing with our expectations for your life. And that's our problem, not yours. Your brothers might be a little miffed, but they'll get over it."

Her father patted her back, then extended a hand to Dallas, who gratefully shook it.

"Thank you for understanding," Dallas said. He took Zora's hand once her father released her. "We'd better head in there."

Zora was relieved by her parents' reactions, but she now braced herself for the backlash from her brothers.

"Zora! Dallas! Congratulations!" They were practically tackled by Savannah and Max's girlfriend, Quinn. She'd grown close to both women and considered them close friends.

"And look who's excited to see her auntie ZoZo." Savannah grinned, rocking baby Remi in her arms and nodding toward her nephew Davis, who was bouncing in his booster seat at the table, a wide grin on his face.

"Hey there, handsome. I missed you." Zora tickled her nephew's tummy and kissed his cheek. "Were you good for Mommy and Daddy while I was gone?"

The little boy nodded, enthusiastically. "I help Mommy take care of Remi."

"Good job, li'l man." Zora tweaked the boy's nose. Then she kissed her sleeping niece's forehead. She turned back to look at Dallas. "Isn't she gorgeous?"

"She's beautiful." He nodded, a soft smile curving the edge of his mouth as he slipped an arm around her waist. Dallas gently stroked the baby's arm. "Congrats to you and Blake on the sweet little addition to your family."

An involuntary smile crept across Zora's face and her heart swelled. She recognized that look in her husband's eyes.

He's imagining what our daughter will look like.

It was something Zora had often mused about as she studied Remi's sweet little face and stroked her soft curls.

Zora's heart melted. Until now, she hadn't considered that maybe Dallas was looking forward to parenthood, too. She'd believed he was only really doing this for her. But his warm gaze and genuine smile as he studied the sleeping newborn gave her a sense of hope that this arrangement would be mutually beneficial for them.

"No pressure, of course," Savannah said. "But maybe one day soon you two will have a little one of your own."

Dallas's smile almost looked shy. He nodded. "We hope so."

"Yes," Zora chimed in. "We definitely want kids...soon."

Kayleigh—her brother Parker's fiancée—came out of the kitchen with a glass in her hand. She smiled broadly, coming over to greet them.

"Congrats, you two. Happy birthday, Zora." Kayleigh gave them both a quick hug before she made her way to her seat beside sourpuss Parker.

Her brother's expression was dripping with the same condemnation he'd leveled at Zora when he'd implied that she was too emotional and irrational to lead the company.

Zora's free hand curled into a fist at her side as she stared her brother down. "Parker," Zora said, her tone daring him to say something out of line.

"Zora, Dallas." Parker's tone was measured. Kayleigh nudged her fiancé, not so subtly. He cleared his throat, then walked over to them. "Congratulations are in order, I suppose."

Parker extended a hand to Dallas, and her husband shook it tentatively, as if he was waiting for the other shoe to drop.

Zora didn't blame him. Without even trying, Parker had a way of putting his foot in his mouth and pissing people off. Even when he honestly believed he was being helpful.

"Thanks, Park. That means a lot." Dallas patted her brother's shoulder.

Parker stared at Zora strangely for a moment. He pushed his glasses up on the bridge of his nose. Then he did the thing Zora hadn't seen coming. He stepped forward and... *hugged* her.

Parker definitely wasn't a hugger. So Zora appreciated the effort, no matter how pained it was.

Zora returned the hug, and she could barely hold back a smirk as Parker gave her back an awkward pat, as if he were petting Kayleigh's dog, Cricket.

At least he's trying.

Which was more than she could say for her other three brothers, whom she'd have choice words for when she had

a chance to speak to them alone. She was honestly angrier
on Dallas's behalf than her own.

The Hamiltons had been friends to the Abbott family for
nearly as long as Zora could remember. They'd been there
for most of their birthday celebrations, holidays and more
Sunday dinners than she could count. So the fact that her
brothers were acting brand-new because she and Dallas had
chosen to get married made her increasingly hurt and angry.

She was about to read all three of them—telling them
exactly what she thought of their standoffishness—when
Dallas wrapped an arm around her again.

The intimate embrace seemed to relieve a little of the
tension in her back and neck.

"It's okay, Zora. We expected this, right?" he whispered
in her ear. "Don't let them get to you. Their feelings are
understandably hurt. Just give it a little time and this will
all blow over."

Dallas kissed her temple.

Zora leaned into him and released a quiet sigh. She nodded as the agitation simmering in her chest slowly died
down.

She and Dallas took their seats at the table.

"Blake. Max." She casually greeted her brothers, as if it
were no big deal that they were obviously angry with her,
and Dallas did the same.

Savannah and Quinn shot their respective partners a
look of disappointment. Each of her brothers responded
with his own brand of a *What did I do?* facial expression.

"Now that our entire family is here—" Zora's mother
beamed "—your dad has a few words he'd like to say."

Her father stepped in the room and stood beside her
mom, taking her hand in his.

"First, happy birthday, baby girl." Her father smiled and
everyone around the table echoed his birthday salutation,
for which she thanked them.

"Now, I know Dallas and Zora's sudden marriage came as a shock to all of us and that we're all feeling some kind of way about it—whether we're hurt or angry or a little of both," her father continued. "But let's not forget that your sister is a sensible adult, fully capable of making her own decisions, whether we agree with them or not. We need to respect that. Just as she's respected and supported the decisions that each and every one of you has made." Her father looked at her brothers in turn.

"And as for Dallas..." Duke turned toward him. "You've always been an honorary part of this family. You're a kind, respectable, hardworking man. The kind of man I always hoped my daughter would marry." Her father smiled warmly, his voice breaking slightly. He cleared his throat and nodded in Dallas's direction. "Iris and I are sincerely happy to welcome you as an official member of our family, son."

"Thank you, sir." Dallas nodded, obviously moved by her father's welcome speech.

Zora got up and hugged her father again. "Thanks, Dad," she whispered to him.

She was grateful her father had set the tone for her older brothers, even if her mother had likely put him up to it.

"Where's Grandad?" Zora asked. Her grandfather had had a stroke a few weeks before Remi was born. His recovery was coming along well, but he often pushed it, determined to recover more quickly. Zora couldn't help worrying about him.

"Grandpa Joe was a little tired today. He had an early meal and lay down for a nap. Hopefully, he'll join us later. But I don't want to wake him. He needs his rest." Her mother took her seat at one end of the table, while her father took a seat at the opposite end. "Now, are we ready to eat?"

"Yes!" Everyone at the table, including Zora and Dallas,

nearly shouted in unison. They all laughed, and it seemed to ease the tension a little.

Things got slightly less awkward as the night went on. Still, Zora couldn't help feeling bad for the hurt feelings her actions had caused.

After they'd had dinner and her mother's delicious, homemade birthday cake, Zora sat at the table with her and Dallas's chairs pulled close together and his arm draped around her chair. She leaned into him, enjoying the warmth and comfort of her new husband's embrace.

A part of her couldn't help wishing this was real. That she and Dallas truly were romantic soulmates destined to be together, as their mothers had always believed.

Fourteen

Dallas shrugged off his jeans and pulled his T-shirt over his head. He folded both and set them on top of the hamper in Zora's bathroom. Then he went back to her bedroom, where she was sitting in bed with her planner. A variety of writing utensils littered the bedspread.

"Sorry," she muttered, moving the pens and highlighters. "Not used to sharing my bed." Then Zora looked up at him, standing there in his black boxer briefs. "I...are you... is *that* what you're sleeping in?"

"Is this a problem?" Dallas spiked his fingers through his hair. They'd come straight to her place after her birthday dinner at her parents. All he had was his luggage from Vegas. So he didn't have a clean pair of shorts to sleep in. "If so, I'll have to go back to my place and grab a few things."

"No, of course not. I just...it...you surprised me, that's all." Zora tore her errant gaze away from his package, her cheeks crimson. "You're fine. After all, I've seen you in much less, haven't I?"

Dallas chuckled as he climbed beneath the covers. "You certainly have. And if we plan on having sex, as it's a key factor in procreation, I suspect you'll see me in a lot less again." He winked.

Zora rolled her eyes. "But not until after we—"

"Both have a clean bill of health," he chimed in. "I'm on it. I'll make an appointment before I leave for Chicago in a few days."

"You're going to Chicago?" She frowned. "When?"

"I'll be gone most of next week. I'll text you the dates

and add you to my business calendar. What about you? Don't you have some work travel planned?"

"Yes." She opened her planner and rattled off the dates for her scheduled trips to Atlanta and New York and an extended, two-week trip to four different countries in the European Union.

"Hmm...looks like our baby-making activities might require some coordination. Unless you'd like to come with me to Chicago," he suggested hopefully.

They tried their best to travel together at least once a year, when they weren't in relationships with other people. But even those trips had become more like working vacations. Both of them were attached to their phones and laptops, still responding to calls and emails. Still thinking about their respective businesses.

And though it was a business trip he was inviting her to join him on, he'd make sure that they found time to spend alone simply enjoying each other's company and planning for their future together.

"I can't just pick up and go to Chicago with you next week, Dal," Zora said. "I have a ton of prep to do leading up to my sales trips. Besides, I would only be a distraction to you."

"You're not a *distraction*, Zora. You're my wife." It still felt foreign to say those words to his best friend.

Zora looked at him peculiarly when he said them, so it was evidently still strange for her to hear, too.

"I realize that, Dal. But this marriage doesn't negate the obligations I have to our company or that you have to yours." Zora softened her tone and expression as she delivered the very direct words.

"Right. Of course."

He tried not to sound disappointed that his wife had made it clear, in no uncertain terms, that their relationship ranked several rungs below her career. In fact, her father had to insist that she take off the rest of the week as a sort of a staycation honeymoon. Even then, Zora hadn't acquiesced until Duke had threatened, only half-jokingly, to have security remove her from the premises if she came to work the next day.

"About tonight at your parents'. Are you okay?" Dallas asked. She hadn't said much about their visit since they'd returned to her house. "I know things with Cole were a little tense tonight."

"I know, but it's fine." Zora shrugged.

But Dallas knew better. He could tell by the subtle slump of her slim shoulders and the hint of sadness in her dark brown eyes. She was genuinely hurt that her brothers were being assholes because their little sister—who was a fully grown adult, capable of making her own decisions, and of running the company, if given the chance—had gotten married without their blessing.

"Blake's and Max's feelings are hurt because their little sister eloped. But with Cole...it feels like something deeper," he noted.

Zora frowned. "I know. I'll talk to him. *Eventually.*" She dropped the pens and highlighters into a pouch and zipped it, then put it and the planner on her nightstand. She turned out the lamp, shrouding her side of the room in darkness.

"I wouldn't have handled tonight well if you hadn't been there. Thank you for being my rock and the voice of reason. As always. And thank you for being patient with my brothers."

She leaned over to kiss his cheek, surprising him. He turned toward her suddenly, his lips crashing into hers. Zora pulled back, and studied him for a moment, neither of them speaking. Then she pressed a palm to his chest, leaned in and kissed him again.

She brushed her soft, sweet lips against his with a light,

feathery touch that made him wonder for a moment if the kiss was real or if he'd only dreamed it.

Zora leaned into him, and he allowed her to dictate the intensity of their kiss. But when she parted her lips on a gasp, he couldn't resist sliding his tongue between her soft lips and tasting the mouth he'd been craving.

Dallas cradled her cheek, tilting her head to give him better access to her mouth. Then he pulled her closer so he could feel her lush curves crushed against his chest through the thin tank top she'd worn to bed with another little pair of sleep shorts.

Her nipples beaded, pressing against him through the fabric. She murmured in response, and he kissed her harder, swallowing the erotic sound that made his cock swell. Needing to hear it again and again.

Zora climbed onto him, straddling his lap. Her sex pressed to his hardening length, making him groan with a growing desire for her.

Dallas gripped her bottom, pulling her closer as she kissed him, gliding her wet heat along his shaft through the barrier of their underwear. Making him crazy with need for her.

So many times he'd dreamed of kissing Zora. Of taking her to bed. Something he hadn't been proud of. Because crossing the line would jeopardize their friendship. Take them to a place they had agreed never to go. But he'd *wanted* to go there. And no matter how many times he'd chastised himself for thinking of Zora this way, his mind and body had other ideas.

Zora grazed his nipple with her thumb. An incidental touch that sent intense pleasure to his cock. He glided his fingertips up the soft skin of her back beneath the shirt, needing to have his bare skin on hers.

She broke away from the kiss, and his heart thudded in his chest, fearing that she was pulling away. But she kept her gaze on his as she tugged the shirt over her head and tossed it onto the floor, exposing her full breasts with their pebbled brown tips.

"Fuck, Zora." He whispered the words caught at the back of his throat. Dallas pressed a kiss to the base of her throat and another to her chest as he inhaled her sweet scent. He took one of the heavy globes in his hand, relishing its weight and size. She stroked his cheek, an intense hunger in her eyes as she arched her back. Her message clear.

Dallas's eyes drifted closed as he lowered his head, covering the offered morsel with his mouth. He savored her sensual murmurs and the way she dug her fingers into his hair as he teased her with little licks.

He rolled her onto her back and licked and sucked the hardened tip before moving to the other and doing the same. Then he kissed a trail down her soft belly and cupped her sex through the silky black panties shielding her wet heat.

Zora arched her back and groaned, tangling her fingers in his hair.

Dallas wanted to make love to her. More than anything. But Zora had just reminded him that they'd agreed to wait. He'd given her his word, and he'd honor their agreement, even if it meant he'd suffer from a killer case of blue balls for the rest of the night.

Dallas groaned, pausing for a moment to draw up the strength to tell her that they couldn't. Not tonight.

"Zora, I…" His eyes met hers.

"Oh God." She scrambled from beneath him, retrieved her shirt from the floor and put it back on. "I shouldn't have kissed you and I definitely shouldn't have…" She pressed a hand to her belly. "This one was definitely on me. I'm sorry."

"Don't be," he said gruffly, rolling onto his back on his designated side of the bed. "I wanted this, too." Dallas sighed. "But on the upside… When the time comes, lack of chemistry definitely won't be an issue."

A genuine smile spread across Zora's face and she dissolved into a fit of laughter. He couldn't help chuckling, too. It alleviated some of the tension in the room, like a pressure release valve had been opened.

Everything else between them felt so foreign right now. Sharing a laugh together was comforting and familiar.

Zora crawled back beneath the covers, clinging to the edge of her side of the bed. As if there was a chasm between them.

Dallas turned off the light on his nightstand and folded his arm beneath his head as he stared at the ceiling. "'Night, Zo."

"Good night, Dallas."

The disappointment was as evident in her voice as it had been in his. But after two years of musing about what it would be like to make love to Zora, he could certainly wait another week.

They would be together soon enough.

Fifteen

Zora parked in her designated spot in the King's Finest parking lot beside her brother Blake's luxury pickup truck. She sucked in a deep breath, grabbed her purse and the leather padfolio that held her iPad and bore her initials: ZAA. Only they weren't her initials anymore. Not according to the marriage license sitting on the desk in her home office.

She couldn't bring herself to display the document, but she couldn't bear to file it away, either. She'd looked at it every time she went into the office, as if she needed it there to remind her that she and Dallas were really married. If that hadn't convinced her, the fact that Dallas had spent every night in her bed since they'd returned home had made it quite apparent.

She'd arrived at the office an hour later than usual because she'd driven her husband to the airport for his week-long trip to Chicago. And after a week of literally sleeping together and nothing more, she'd been nearly ready to combust when he'd leaned in and kissed her before he hopped out of the car.

Zora glanced up at the window of her office and blew out a slow breath. Her family had been uncharacteristically quiet all week. No calls from her parents or grandfather. No text messages from her brothers. Even Quinn and Savannah had given her and Dallas their space. But she had the feeling that the Abbott radio silence was a temporary moratorium while she and Dallas were on their stay-at-home honeymoon. Now that it was over, all bets were off.

Zora stepped out of her black-on-black Mercedes E 450 coupe with dark tinted windows.

*No matter how nervous you feel inside, walk with con-
fidence. Shoulders back. Head held high.*

Zora could still hear her grandmother's sweet voice re-
citing those words to her when she was a slouching tween.
It was still good advice.

She wouldn't go slinking into the office with her tail
between her legs as if she was embarrassed by her hasty
wedding. Instead, she would own it.

Zora pushed her Peyton Coco and Breezy shades up the
bridge of her nose, tipped her chin and pulled her shoulders back as she strode toward the building in her caber-
net-colored power suit, a bold cheetah-print blouse and
cheetah-print booties.

The security guards at the gate congratulated her on her
marriage, confirming what Zora already suspected. Everyone in town and at the distillery likely knew about her and
Dallas's Vegas wedding.

Zora graciously accepted the congratulations of employ-
ees she encountered between the front door and her office.
She patiently stopped to chat with each person briefly as
they oohed and ahhed over the gorgeous pink sapphire engagement ring and diamond wedding band.

She spent a little more time chatting with her assistant,
Emily, who'd been holding down the fort in her absence.
The younger woman bounced on her heels excitedly when
Zora approached and wrapped her in a big hug. Emily was
genuinely excited for her, and the woman's enthusiasm was
contagious.

"Your rings are gorgeous, and Dallas is such a sweetheart. Plus, you've been friends forever, so you already
know everything about each other," Emily fawned. "You
two are so lucky."

"I guess we are," Zora said, an involuntary smile tightening her cheeks. "Thanks."

"By the way, your father wants you to meet with him in

the conference room at eleven. So we have some time to go over a few things first, if you'd like," Emily said excitedly.

"That'd be great, Em. Give me fifteen minutes?"

"Of course. And killer outfit… *Mrs.* Hamilton."

"Thank you, but Zora is fine, like always." Zora forced a smile and secured the topknot she'd pulled her curls up into, suddenly more conscious of the weight of the new hardware on her slim fingers.

"Zora, it is." Em could barely contain her grin. She sifted her fingers through her mermaid strands—dyed vibrant hues of purple, turquoise and blue. "Iced coffee?"

"Please," Zora said.

She'd gotten very little sleep during the past week. But for the opposite reason newlyweds were usually sleepless after their honeymoon. She and Dallas still hadn't had sex. Instead, she'd lain awake tossing and turning, her body thrumming with desire, knowing that her best friend— with his toned abs, hard chest and impressive package— lay just a couple of feet away from her wearing *very* little.

To add insult to injury, the last two nights she'd awakened cradled in his arms, the front of his hard body pressed to the back of hers. The first morning it happened, she'd freaked out a little. The second morning, she'd been slightly startled but had lain there until he awoke, enjoying the comfort, scent and warmth of him. Reveling in the affection he'd shown her, even unconsciously in his sleep.

Zora unlocked her office. "Emily, did my dad say what the meeting was about?"

"No. I tried to find out so you'd be prepared, but he was pretty tight-lipped about it," Emily said apologetically.

"Thanks for trying." Zora went inside her office and took a seat behind the desk.

The last two impromptu meetings she'd been called to were when her brother Parker had announced that he be-lieved that he should be named the next CEO of King's Finest, rather than her oldest brother, Blake, whom they'd all assumed would take up their father's mantle whenever he decided to retire. And then when her father and grandfather had announced that they would indeed decide on the successor to the King's Finest throne based on merit—rather than birth order.

It was the first time she'd ever given thought to the possibility of heading up the company.

Even as a little girl, Zora had insisted that her parents treat her equally to her brothers when it came to both privileges and chores. Her mother had been miffed. Her father had been impressed. And eventually, they'd both come to respect her request. So when the opportunity to lead the company was up for grabs, she'd insisted on being a candidate for CEO just like her brothers.

But since her grandfather's stroke—which occurred at that very meeting—there hadn't been much discussion among them about the succession plan. All their attention had gone to caring for her grandfather. Next, there was the revelation that Max and Quinn—who was heading up a new brandy initiative their company was rolling out— were indeed an item. Soon after that, Remi had been born.

The barrage of events had taken everyone's focus off the race to be the new CEO. Yet Zora doubted that any of them had taken their eyes off the prize.

She certainly hadn't.

So perhaps her father had called this morning's meeting because he'd made his decision. If so, she doubted that the timing was a coincidence. It could only mean that her hasty, surprise marriage had knocked her out of contention.

Zora did her best to shake off the negative energy.

Don't be a self-defeatist. Until Dad says otherwise, you're still a contender for this thing.

Suddenly, her phone alerted her to a text message.

Dallas.

He let her know that he'd boarded his plane and they'd be taking off soon. And he ended the text with a sentence that made her chest flutter.

Miss you already, Zo.

An involuntary smile lifted the corners of Zora's mouth, and without thought she pressed the phone to her chest. She missed him already, too.

Zora had enjoyed the time they'd spent together during the past week. She'd enjoyed chatting with her friend over coffee and working with him in the kitchen as they made breakfast and talked about their respective businesses.

The thing she'd avoided talking about was their plan to become co-parents. And admittedly, she'd taken her time scheduling the doctor's appointment she'd insisted on. Because while she was committed to the plan, she needed to be sure Dallas was, too.

She'd been pragmatic about sleeping with her best friend because she'd always been careful about her sex life. But she also wanted to give Dallas time to think about the commitment he was making with a clear mind. Without the mental haze and irrational thinking sex often precipitated.

So while Dallas was set and ready to go, her doctor's appointments were planned for the week while he was away. Then, if he returned and still wanted to move forward, she'd be ready. But until then, she was afraid to put too much of her heart into the idea of becoming a mother with Dallas. Because if the whole thing fell apart, she'd be heartbroken.

Zora sat behind her desk and reviewed Dallas's text message again. Then she typed her own reply.

Miss you, too. Call me when you land.

She resisted the urge to add XOXO. She'd often ended text messages that way in the past. But they were just friends then. Now they were something more. So signing the text message with hugs and kisses felt...different.

"Ready to go over my notes from last week?" Emily came bouncing into her office with her tablet, notepad and an iced coffee for Zora.

Zora dropped her phone, as if she'd been caught looking at an X-rated website on her work computer. She stood quickly, accepting the lifeline of caffeine.

Emily grinned at her, nodding toward her abandoned phone. "Got a text from hubby, huh?" She laughed in response to Zora's look of surprise, then answered the question she had yet to ask. "You're blushing and it's adorable. Y'all are so cute together."

Zora thanked the woman and flashed an awkward smile. "Now, about last week...what did I miss?"

Zora put on her game face and focused on what her assistant was saying. She shifted her brain from thoughts of buff best friends, bouncing babies and blown opportunities. Instead, she turned her attention to the thing she could control—her role in increasing the company's sales.

For now, everything else would have to wait.

"Zora, sweetheart, how are you?" Duke Abbott asked when she floated into the conference room about five minutes before their scheduled meeting.

But her father wasn't alone. All her brothers were there—including Cole, who rarely set foot in the distillery.

"Cole, what are you doing here?" Zora hadn't intended to ignore her father's greeting, but the fact that her brother was sitting in the chair typically occupied by her grandfather couldn't bode well. She glanced around the room. "And what's going on? If you guys say this is some kind of intervention, I swear to God—"

"Relax, Zo," Cole said.

"Zora, sweetheart, calm down," her father said simultaneously, rising to his feet.

Which, of course, only made her angry and more wary. In her experience, there was no better way to piss a woman off than to tell her to *relax*.

Zora set her padfolio on the table at her usual seat beside Max, but she refused to sit down. Instead, she folded her arms and stared around the table at each of them.

"Not until you all tell me what this is about."

"Zora, I'm sorry if you feel like you're being ambushed. That wasn't our intention." Parker cleared his throat. "We'd like to talk to you about a few things, that's all. No reason for alarm. Please, have a seat."

There was a soft, pleading look in her brother's eyes that threw Zora off her game. So now Parker was the quiet, compassionate voice of reason?

Zora pulled out her chair and took a seat, sliding away from Max, who had yet to speak.

Traitor.

"I have a lot to do today." She turned to her father. "So if someone could please tell me what this is all about?"

"Your brothers are concerned that in your haste to marry Dallas, you might've overlooked a few things. We just want to ensure that your interests and the family's are protected." Her father's expression was kind and his voice was as soothing as a warm bath.

"Why would you be concerned about me or the family's interests?" She glanced around the table. Cole and Max looked the most uncomfortable. Neither of them was giving her direct eye contact. So she went on the offensive, calling them both out. "Cole. Max. You two evidently orchestrated this whole thing. So don't act shy and delicate now. Let's hear it. Whatever you brought me here to say, *say it*."

"Look, brat, you know we all adore you," Max said. "But we can't stand by and not say anything when you've made an impetuous decision that could negatively impact you—"

"And us," Parker chimed in, his expression almost apologetic. "More importantly, Grandad's legacy." He gestured to the space around them.

"First, don't call me brat. I'm thirty-two fucking years old." She pointed a finger at Max. "Second, yes, our decision to get married was unexpected, but it was hardly a surprise to any of the *women* in our family. Third, how on earth would my decision to get married impact any of you? You didn't see me throwing a fit when any of you hooked up with your significant others." She glanced around the table accusingly.

"You're right," Max said, his open palms held up. "You're a smart, capable woman, and you've certainly outgrown the nickname, if you ever deserved it."

Zora relaxed a little and nodded at her brother. "Thank you."

"But c'mon, Zo, if any of us had gone to Vegas for the weekend and come back married, you'd be all over us about it," Cole interjected.

Fair.

"If it were some stranger you'd met at a blackjack table, maybe," Zora said. "Dallas isn't some stranger. He's an honorary member of this family. We've all known him since he and I were in kindergarten."

"Which is why we don't understand your sudden rush to get married." Blake's voice was calm and reasonable. "Especially since you've both always claimed that the relationship was platonic."

"It was." *It is. Kind of.*

"Then why the sudden marriage?" Max asked, his voice tentative.

"You told Savannah that you want to have kids. Is that because you're already pregnant?" Cole asked, his eyes finally meeting hers dead-on.

"No!" Zora responded immediately. She balled her hands into fists and counted to ten in her head. "But if I was pregnant, that would be *my* business." She glanced around the room at her brothers, all of whom looked varying degrees of uncomfortable. She pushed to her feet, her hands pressed to the table. "What? You don't believe me? Would you like me to pee on a stick for you, Cole?"

"That won't be necessary." Duke raised a hand, seemingly unnerved by the whole conversation.

Y'all started this.

Her grandmother had always said, "Don't start nothing, won't be nothing." It had been her motto in school when dealing with mean girls and bullies.

She'd tried to be nice to everyone and never started conflicts. But if someone else chose to initiate one, putting an end to the bullshit was her great gift.

"Look, I'm sorry." Cole sighed. "I was out of line. I'm just saying...this doesn't feel like you, Zora. Not at all. Hell, I half expected you to commission a tiara, a horse-drawn carriage and a release of doves for your wedding. So I don't get why you'd get married all of a sudden in Vegas without telling any of your family. Not even me." He seemed really hurt by that last bit.

Was that what this was really all about? Cole was upset because she hadn't confided in him about her "plan" to get married?

Zora heaved a quiet sigh and recalled how Dallas had pleaded with her to be patient with her family. To understand why they'd be so hurt by being left out of their wedding.

"Like I said before, we didn't go there intending to get married. This all just sort of...happened. But now that it has, it feels right and we're both happy. I wish you could be as happy for us as I was for each of you when you connected with your current partners." She shifted her gaze from Blake to Parker and then to Max. All of whom had the decency to at least look slightly ashamed of themselves.

Parker cleared his throat and spoke up. "We appreciate your support, Zora. And we… I *am* happy for you," he said after surveying his brothers' grim faces. "But since your wedding was spontaneous, I'm assuming you two didn't sign the prenuptial agreement we all agreed to use five years ago. The one designed to ensure King's Finest will always stay in our family instead of going to someone else."

Shit. Should have known that would come up.

If she'd married some random stranger, she'd be worried. But this was Dallas they were talking about. She trusted her friend. With her life, if need be.

"You're right." She slid into her seat. "We all agreed to use prenuptial agreements to protect KFD. But you're worried that we can't trust Dallas? Why would he try to take a portion of our company? He has his own and it's doing well."

"Dallas Hamilton is an upstanding, hardworking, successful young man, and I know he cares deeply for you, Zora," her father countered. "It isn't that we don't trust him, per se."

"Then what is it?" She glanced around the room, her heart thumping and her eyes burning with tears of anger that she blinked away.

"It's just better to be safe than sorry, Zo." Max clapped a hand over hers and squeezed it gently. "None of us are attributing bad motives to Dallas. But people and circumstances can change. It's something we can't predict. So it's better to cover all the bases."

"And since Dallas is doing so well, as you said, he shouldn't mind signing a postnuptial agreement to clearly delineate your assets," Parker noted. "In fact, it seems like it would be to his advantage, too."

"And the terms of the agreement are very generous," Blake reminded her. "So Dallas—or any of our former spouses," he added when Zora narrowed her gaze at him, "would still come out ahead. Not that we anticipate your marriage ending, Zora. Or any of ours, for that matter."

Zora stared at Blake, her heart beating rapidly. Maybe her brother really didn't believe that her marriage to Dallas would end any time soon. But given that she knew the truth about the temporary nature of their relationship, asking Dallas to enter into an agreement that would pay him a generous settlement on the dissolution of their marriage seemed unwise.

She pulled her hand from Max's and stood again. "No," she said quietly. "I appreciate your concern, but I'm not asking Dallas to sign a postnuptial. So if there isn't anything else, I have a lot of catching up to do."

Zora grabbed her padfolio from the table and left the room. She'd nearly reached her office when Cole caught up with her.

He stepped around in front of her and lowered his voice so no one else could hear him. "Is this about that Icelandic deal Dallas is trying to do?"

"What are you talking about?" Her eyes widened.

"Tish was telling us about it before you all arrived at Mom and Dad's last week. I looked up that guy Dallas is trying to collaborate with. Did you two enter a sham marriage because Dallas thinks he'll have a better chance of entering into a deal with the man if he's married rather than a bachelor?"

"That's ridiculous." Zora wrapped her arms around the padfolio and held it to her chest, hoping it dampened the sound of her raging heartbeat. She stood taller and tipped her chin, looking her brother squarely in the eye. "Seriously, Cole. Do you really think I would've given up my horse-drawn carriage and flight of doves for that?"

She started to walk away again, but her brother braced a hand on her arm and lowered his voice more.

"You're a good person and a loyal friend, Zora. And I know how much you care for Dallas. So, yes, I believe you'd make that kind of sacrifice for him. Just like you did when you helped finance his business."

"How'd you know about that?" Zora snatched her arm away from Cole's and frowned, her words a harsh whisper.

"I wasn't sure," Cole admitted. "But I've always suspected."

"Dallas never asked me for a penny. In fact, it took me months to convince him to accept my *investment* in his business." She stressed the word. "And as you can see, my gamble paid off. He paid every cent back with interest years ago. But please don't—"

"I won't say anything to anyone else about this," Cole assured her. "But you're my kid sister. I won't let anyone take advantage of your generous nature."

"Cole, I know you love me and that you're just trying to look out for me here but listen to me carefully. If you think my marriage is the result of some arrangement where Dallas is taking advantage of our friendship, you honestly couldn't be more wrong about him. Now please, have a little faith in me. After all, I've always had faith in you."

Before her brother could respond, Zora's phone vibrated in her pocket. She pulled it out, looked at the caller ID and smiled.

Dallas.

"That would be my husband calling to let me know he's landed safely. I assume we're done here?"

Cole sighed and nodded. "See you later, Zo."

Zora watched her brother head back toward the conference room. Then she answered the call.

She couldn't ever remember being happier to hear Dallas's voice.

Sixteen

The event Dallas had been scheduled to attend on Sunday morning—the last of his seven-day trip to Chicago—had been canceled. So he booked an earlier flight home.

Normally, Dallas would've used his windfall of free time to enjoy the city, sketch out design ideas, or read a good book. But from the moment he'd learned of the cancellation, he'd had just one thought: Zora.

So he'd paid the obscene fees to change his flight and taken a ride share back to his place to drop off his luggage, because he wanted to surprise his wife. Dallas grabbed some fresh clothes and a few other essential items. Just enough to get him through the next few days back at Zora's place. Then he slipped the letter from his doctor's office into the inside pocket of his matte black leather jacket with the word *Triumph* curved across the back in a barely visible, tonal print.

Dallas put the clothing in the saddlebags of his motorcycle—a Triumph Thruxton RS he'd treated himself to a year ago—and slipped on his black, matte Icon AirFlite helmet. Then he threw his right leg over the bike, settling onto the seat and placing his booted feet flat on the ground before turning the key in the ignition. After a few minutes warming up, he eased off the clutch, rolling the bike out of his driveway, before finally giving it some throttle once he hit the road.

It was early afternoon on a beautiful fall day. The sun shone through the trees, illuminating the vivid red, bright gold and glowing orange leaves still clinging to the branches. He loved riding at this time of year, the wind swirling around him as he reveled in the freedom of the road. But today he had a single focus: he had every intention of finally making love to his beautiful wife.

There was a churning in the pit of Dallas's stomach. He wasn't nervous about finally being with Zora. He'd been distracted all week by images of her naked beneath him in the bed they shared. The thing that unsettled him was the realization that this would change things between them forever.

His desire for Zora would come out of the shadows and be lain undeniably bare. Where neither of them could pretend it wasn't there. They'd agreed to go back to being friends at the end of a year. But what were the chances the genie would quietly return to the bottle?

The second thing that had been weighing on his mind was that he and Zora were about to embark on this journey toward becoming parents.

The enormity of what they were undertaking came into perspective the moment he'd lain eyes on Remi and stroked her soft skin. She looked so small and defenseless. And as he looked onto the baby girl's sleeping face, he couldn't help wondering what his and Zora's child would look like.

Would the child have its mother's bright smile and inquisitive eyes? His strong chin? Would her skin resemble her mother's gorgeous terra cotta brown skin or fall somewhere on the spectrum between Zora's rich, deep skin tone and his? Would she have her mother's fiery personality and infectious laugh or his laid-back demeanor and off sense of humor?

Dallas gave the bike more throttle as he hurtled toward Duke and Iris's house, where Zora would be along with the rest of her siblings and their mates. He'd like nothing more than to kidnap her, put her on the back of his bike and head back to her place, where he'd spend the rest of the day ravishing the body he'd been dreaming about in great detail.

He finally pulled onto the road that led past the barn and toward Zora's parents' place at the end of the street. Dallas parked the bike in his new in-laws' driveway, removed his helmet and made his way to the open side door.

As always, Iris Abbott's kitchen smelled heavenly. The scents of fresh-baked bread, savory meat, fragrant vegetables and enticing desserts teased his nostrils. But he wouldn't allow himself to be distracted by Iris's amazing food. Not now.

Making his way quietly up the few steps, he entered the kitchen where Zora, her mother, Quinn, Kayleigh and Savannah were gathered. Kayleigh and Quinn were busy making a salad. Iris was stirring a pot on the stove. Savannah sat on a bar stool, a blanket draped over her as she presumably fed baby Remi. Zora stood in front of her, a dish towel in her hand as the two women chatted.

Zora looked both sexy and adorable, her curly hair gathered in a messy bun. She wore a burgundy suede skirt that grazed her midthigh, a black turtleneck and black thigh-high boots that had him salivating.

Sitting through a meal next to Zora in that outfit, when what he really wanted to do was get her home and out of it, would be pure torture.

Dallas crept inside, walking as lightly as possible in the heavy black leather boots. He waved at Iris, but held a finger up to his mouth, imploring her to play along as he sneaked up on his unsuspecting wife. Iris grinned, as did Quinn and Kayleigh when they caught a glimpse of him. Savannah gave him the slightest head nod, so as not to tip off Zora.

In one smooth move, Dallas slipped his arms around Zora's waist and dropped a tender kiss on her neck.

Startled, she jumped but didn't scream. She turned around in his arms, her brown eyes gazing up at his. Her expression quickly shifted from surprise to genuine happiness at seeing him. Something about it made his heart dance.

"Dallas, what are you doing here? Your flight isn't scheduled to land until later this evening."

"I know." He tightened his grip on her waist, pulling her closer, his eyes not leaving hers. "I couldn't wait to see you, babe."

Dallas stared at his wife, unsure of how she would react to such a public display of affection. But she'd told him about how Cole doubted whether their marriage was genuine. What better way to prove those doubts wrong?

For a few moments, it felt as if time had slowed. The entire kitchen, which had been filled with chatter and laughter when he'd arrived, was suddenly silent. But Zora lifted onto her toes, looped her arms around his neck and dragged his mouth down to hers as she pressed a soft kiss to his lips. They were greeted by a chorus of awws.

Zora pulled back, glancing up at him. "Missed you, too. I'm glad you came home early."

"Speaking of home," Iris said, not so subtly. "Why don't you and Dallas head there? Your husband must be exhausted after his long week in Chicago without his boo."

Quinn, Kayleigh and Savannah all giggled.

"I can't skip out on dinner." Zora glanced over at her mother. "We haven't even eaten yet."

"Not a problem. I'll have your meals packed and ready to go in a few minutes. That'll give Dallas just enough time to go in and say hello to the boys."

Zora opened her mouth to object, but Quinn put a hand on her shoulder.

"Really, Zora, we understand," Quinn assured her. "Take your man and your meal and go home. There'll be plenty more Sunday meals with the family."

"Fine. We know when we're not wanted," Zora said.

"I'd love to have you all stay and have dinner with us, but I remember what it was like to be a newlywed," Iris said. "And with your busy schedules, you should make the most of every moment you two have to spend together."

"I agree." Dallas took Zora's hand and strode into the family room, where her father, grandfather, brothers and nephew were watching a football game.

Dallas greeted the men, shaking her father's and grandfather's hands. Parker, Max and Blake's greetings seemed warm and genuine, closer to what he was accustomed to from each of them. Cole nodded his greeting, but anger still brewed behind his dark eyes.

"We're not staying for dinner," Zora said sheepishly. "Dallas just landed, and he's had a really long week. Mom insists that I take him home to get some rest. She's packing our meals to go."

"Too tired to eat, huh?" Joseph Abbott snickered. "I wasn't always this old, you know."

"Leave the kids alone, Dad." Duke chuckled. He turned his attention back to them. "We understand. I don't think the world will end if Zora and Dallas miss a meal or two with us."

"Thanks for understanding," Dallas said to the two men.

"I was looking out the window at your motorcycle, Dallas," Grandpa Joseph said. "Mighty fancy bike you've got there. I remember when those café racers were popular. You restore that thing yourself?"

"No, sir," he admitted. "And this isn't a restoration. It's a brand-new bike made with the retro styling but all the modern bells and whistles."

"I like it." Zora's grandfather nodded approvingly. "And you certainly look the part, son." Grandpa Joe indicated his motorcycle jacket and boots. "You plan on whisking my granddaughter away on that thing?"

"Not today, Gramps," Zora said quickly. She squeezed Dallas's hand. "But maybe I'll let him take me for a ride, *eventually.*"

Dallas grinned. It was the first time Zora had ever shown any interest in riding on the bike.

"Seems dangerous," Parker offered. "You have life insurance and a living will, right?"

"Wow, Park. Way to kill the mood." Max chuckled.

"What?" Parker shrugged. "Have you seen the accident statistics for those things?"

Dallas and Zora spent some time showing Davis his bike through the window and answering the little boy's barrage of questions until Zora's mother appeared.

She handed them a cloth bag stacked with glass storage containers. "Got your food all packed."

Dallas released Zora's hand and accepted the bag. He leaned down and kissed his mother-in-law on the cheek. "Thank you, Iris."

"Of course." She grinned. "And no pressure, hon, but I wouldn't be opposed to you calling me Mom."

Iris's words simultaneously warmed his chest and broke his heart. His marriage to Zora would end in a year. He'd lose the privilege of calling Iris Mom nearly as quickly as he'd gained it.

"Thanks, Mom." Dallas smiled. Then he took Zora's hand and they said their goodbyes.

Seventeen

Zora pulled her Mercedes into her pristine, attached, two-car garage, and Dallas parked his bike in the empty space beside it. Then she hit the button to lower the garage door and stepped out of the car.

She glanced over at Dallas, and a shiver ran down her spine. The man looked incredibly sexy in a black motorcycle jacket, a matte black helmet that made him look mysterious and maybe even a little dangerous, and a pair of heavy motorcycle boots. The thought of him commanding all that power thrumming between his strong thighs…well, it was enough to make a girl go weak at the knees.

That was the reason she had never agreed to hop onto the back and ride with him when he offered. That and the fact that she was an unabashed control freak. It was hard enough to be the passenger in a plane or car. But sitting on the back of a motorcycle careening down a mountain road and taking hairpin curves with absolutely no say or control? It was an adventure she wasn't quite ready for.

Dallas engaged the kickstand and climbed off his bike, removing the helmet and hanging it on the back of the motorcycle. He dragged his fingers through his hair and grinned.

"You're a sight for sore eyes." His gaze roamed the length of her body, and her skin pricked with heat beneath his hungry gaze.

Zora sank her teeth into her lower lip and tried not to think about how delicious her husband looked.

"You can cut the act. We're alone now."

Yep, she was pathetically fishing for a compliment. Dallas Hamilton definitely had her off her game.

"It's no act, Zora." He stopped a few feet shy of her. "I told you, if we do this…it has to be real for however long we're together. I meant what I said." His whiskey-brown eyes had darkened and were hooded as he gazed down at her with a heated stare.

Her nipples beaded, and she could feel the dampness between her thighs. Zora swallowed hard, one hand going inadvertently to her neck. As if she needed to protect it.

"You called me *babe* earlier." She shifted her gaze from his increasingly intense one. "You've never called me that before."

"To be fair, we've never been married before. So there are a lot of things we haven't done." His lips curved in a cocky, half-grin. "Problem?"

"No," she whispered, shaking her head.

Dallas moved closer, so less than a foot separated them now. Yet he still hadn't touched her. And she couldn't help being disappointed by his restraint. But the promise he'd made when they first made their agreement in Vegas replayed in her head.

Nothing happens unless you want it to.

She wanted it to. God, did she want it. She thought of him often, her fingers gliding over the damp space between her thighs as she lay in the bed that felt so much emptier without him.

A heavy silence lingered between them, filled only with the sound of her breathing, growing shallower and more rapid by the moment.

"Got you a little something." Dallas retrieved an unopened envelope from the inside of his leather jacket and handed it to her, his eyes never leaving hers.

Zora glanced down at the envelope branded with the name of a local medical practice.

His all clear.

She had already texted him the results of the battery of

tests she'd taken. So there were no more excuses. No reason why she couldn't do the thing she'd wanted to do for the past two weeks. The thing she fantasized about a time or two long before they'd awakened married in Vegas.

"I guess we're all good, then." She handed it back.

"You don't want to open it?" he asked.

"I trust you, Dallas." Zora took a step backward, finding it more difficult to breathe with Dallas so close. The smell of his enticing cologne mingled with the scent of the crisp, autumn air was slightly intoxicating.

He stepped forward and she retreated again, her bottom pressed against the door of the Mercedes. "I appreciate the vote of confidence. But a deal is a deal, right?" He handed the envelope back to her.

Zora fumbled with it, ripping it open. She could barely focus her vision enough to make sense of the jumble of black letters on the pages. "Everything looks good." She handed the envelope back to him.

Dallas returned the letter to his inside jacket pocket. Zora's eyes were drawn to the way his Adam's apple bobbed when he swallowed and the scruff on his chin.

She wanted to kiss the same path her eyes had just taken along his skin. And she wanted to feel the slight burn of that scruff as he trailed kisses down her belly, as he had that first night in her bed when she'd lost control and kissed him.

Zora swallowed hard, her eyes meeting his again. Her heart raced, and her hands were shaking. Dallas was really and truly going to make her say the words. Be the one to ask for it. She could see it in his dark eyes. He wanted to hear her beg.

She honestly had no qualms about asking for what she wanted in bed, demanding it, even. But he was her best friend, and this all still felt so...strange. Still, she wanted him. More importantly, she needed him.

Dallas Hamilton had been the perfect fuel for her lust-

filled fantasies. But she needed something a little more…
solid…right now.

Zora allowed her hands to trail below his leather belt and
traced the ridge beneath the zipper of his jeans. A soft, almost tortured sigh escaped her friend's mouth, his breath
warm on her skin. A wicked little smile curved her mouth.
She was eager to elicit that same reaction again.

This time, Zora opened her hand as wide as she could
and gripped his stiff length through the thick denim. Her
fingers glided down the outline of his growing shaft,
and she cupped him at its base. Dallas made a sound she
wouldn't quite call a whimper, but it was pretty damn close.

"Fuck, Zora," he whispered, leaning into her hand, his
eyes drifting closed momentarily. Dallas placed his hands
against the car on either side of her.

It was exhilarating to be pinned between him and the
car. Yet it was empowering to know she was capable of
bringing her friend to his knees. Zora unzipped his black
leather jacket the rest of the way. Then she eased her hands
over his skin, beneath the fabric of his soft, brushed-cotton
T-shirt. She flicked his taut nipples with her thumb and
lifted onto her toes.

"Kiss me, Dallas," she whispered breathlessly. "Please."

He leaned down and covered her mouth with his own,
his thumbs caressing her cheekbones. This kiss wasn't tentative, as their previous kisses had been. It was greedy and
demanding. Intense and hungry. A side of himself Dallas
rarely showed.

Zora gripped his back beneath the shirt, hoping her short
nails wouldn't leave marks. She lost herself in the kiss, her
body aching with need for him. Her keys had fallen out of
her hand and onto the garage floor long ago.

She didn't care. All she cared about was getting naked
and letting her husband make love to her.

Zora fumbled with Dallas's belt, finally unbuckling the

stubborn item as they continued their kiss. She slipped her hand beneath the waistband of his boxers. This time they both groaned with satisfaction as she fisted his heated skin.

"Fuck," he muttered as she glided her palm up and down his rock-hard shaft. "God, I wish this was anything but your fancy-ass Mercedes. I'd lift you onto the top of this thing, spread you open and have the only meal I care about right now."

She halted her movement, the vision sending a shudder down her spine, making her knees weak and her sex weep.

Zora swallowed roughly. She was just about to tell him that the dent in the hood would be totally worth it when he backed away.

"We'd better get this food into the house," he said, his chest heaving. "And I'm going to grab a shower. Then I plan to pick up *exactly* where we left off."

Zora nodded as Dallas opened the door, reached in and grabbed the bag of food her mother had packed, his perfect ass on display.

Yes, she was *definitely* going to enjoy this.

Dallas shrugged his clothes off onto the floor and stepped into the steaming-hot shower in the other master bedroom. He typically showered and shaved in this bathroom, since Zora had everything in hers neatly arranged. Every spot was filled with some kind of facial cleanser, foundation, eye shadow or mascara.

The fact that there wasn't enough room for him and his things in Zora's bathroom was a perfect metaphor for his concerns about their relationship. She was the only person in his life who hadn't needed him in one way or another.

Even now, she didn't really need his help. She had the situation all planned out and she had the means to execute that plan on her own.

The neat little box he'd fit into in Zora's life was as her

friend. Did a woman as self-reliant as Zora have room for him in her life?

After sudsing his entire body, Dallas stepped beneath the spray to rinse himself off. Then he pressed a hand against the cool tile, stuck his head beneath the spray of hot water to rinse the shampoo from his hair and sighed.

Suddenly, the glass shower door opened, ushering in a gust of cool air and releasing the steam.

"Zora." He could barely get the word out of his throat. His friend stepped into the shower. Every inch of her glorious brown skin was exposed, leaving him speechless.

Dallas looped one arm around her waist. He trailed the other over the curve of her ass as she leaned into him.

"Thought you might like some company." Her dark eyes glinted as she flashed an impish smile. "Then there was that thing about picking up where we left off." She shrugged. "I got a little impatient."

Dallas brushed his lips along her temple, then pressed a kiss there. He pressed another on the shell of her ear. "You are so incredibly beautiful, Zora," he whispered. "And I can't wait to make love to my wife."

He nibbled on her ear and she giggled.

"Your temporary wife?" she asked. "I think she's looking forward to this, too."

"I prefer to think of you as my wife, *full stop.*" Dallas cupped her cheek, his eyes meeting hers. He needed her to see that he meant what he was saying. "Not my temporary wife. Not my future ex. Just my wife, who also happens to be my best friend."

"I like that," she whispered, leaning into him and wrapping her arms around his back, her short nails digging into his skin.

He kissed her, exploring the sweet taste of her mouth as he sucked her lower lip between his own. His hands explored her smooth skin and delicious curves, which he appreciated all the more for seeing them in their full glory.

Dallas trailed kisses down her neck, then took one of the heavy, brown globes in his hand, kissing and sucking the pebbled tip as Zora squirmed and moaned quietly, her back pressed against the tiled wall. He trailed his hand down her belly and over the small patch of thick, dark curls between her thighs. He moved his fingers back and forth over the bundle of nerves, kissing her mouth again to swallow her quiet whimpers. Then he plunged one finger, then another, inside her.

"God, Zora. You are so wet for me," he whispered in her ear. "But I think we can do better than this."

Dallas dropped to his knees on the hard tile floor, his hands on her hips. Zora stared at him wordlessly, her eyes wide, as he eased her bottom onto the edge of the black tiled bench and gently pressed her knees apart, widening the space between them. Then he dipped his head and tasted her there.

Zora released a breathless whimper and spiked her fingers into his hair. Her moans grew louder, more desperate, as he licked and sucked her sensitive flesh. The escalation of her encouraging commands and desperate little pleas made him as hard as steel. He added two fingers inside her as his tongue continued to work its magic.

She arched her back. Her feet flexed, lifting onto her toes. Her body tensed and her legs shook. The way she whimpered his name made him want to take her right there in the shower with her hands splayed against the wall and one foot propped on the tile bench.

But this would be their first time together, and he wanted to take his time with her. Show her just how good things between them could be, if only she gave them a chance.

Dallas stood and turned off the water. He drew Zora into his arms and kissed her. Slowly and tenderly, at first. But the fire and passion between them built. Her kiss became hungrier, and his was downright greedy. Because he honestly didn't think he could ever get enough of her.

He wrapped his arms around her waist, pulling her tighter against his painfully hard dick. Dallas ached with his desire to be buried balls-deep inside his ridiculously sexy wife. The woman he hadn't been able to stop thinking about for the past week.

Maybe their marriage was only temporary. But he was still a lucky bastard, getting to come home to this gorgeous woman each night and share a bed with her.

With the hot water turned off, the temperature around them cooled and Zora started shivering.

Dallas tore his mouth from Zora's plump, kiss-swollen lips just long enough to get them both toweled off and over to Zora's bed at the opposite end of the upstairs hall.

They climbed beneath the luxurious white duvet and soft Egyptian cotton sheet, their naked bodies still damp from the shower.

"May I?" Dallas indicated the band that held Zora's hair back in a messy bun. When she nodded, he took it off, releasing the loose ringlets that had been stretched by the tension. Dallas sifted the soft, silky curls through his fingers, as he'd imagined doing so many times before.

"You are so beautiful, Zora." Dallas grazed her cheek with his callused thumb as he stared down into those hypnotic brown eyes.

Dallas captured her full lips in an intense kiss. As the heat between them built to a fever pitch, he gripped his shaft, pressing it to her slick entrance and slowly penetrating. He reveled in every ounce of pleasure that rolled up his spine as he inched inside her until he was fully seated.

Dallas kissed her again, forcing himself to take it slowly as he moved inside her. Determined to savor every moment.

But as their kisses grew more intense, so did the power and speed with which he moved his hips.

"Oh God, Dallas. Yes. *Yes.* Just like that. Don't stop. *Please.*" Zora's fervent pleas escalated as their bodies, now damp with sweat, moved together. Each of them hurtling closer to the edge.

He repositioned her leg, lifting it over his hip and changing the angle of impact.

She responded immediately.

Panting and breathless, Zora cried out his name.

Her hair was wild, and beads of sweat trickled down her forehead and neck. But Zora was sexier than he'd ever seen her before.

Her sex pulsed, tightening its grip on his shaft. Dallas rode the waves of Zora's pleasure until he'd hurtled into a sea of bliss. One he hoped to revisit again and again.

His back arched and his muscles strained as he spilled every ounce of himself inside her. Finally, he tumbled onto his back, his chest heaving.

Zora propped one of the many pillows on her bed beneath her bottom, presumably to allow gravity to get his little swimmers where they needed to go.

They both lay there, breathing heavily as they stared at the ceiling in silence.

Finally, his breath slowed. "That was—"

"Weird…right?" she offered.

"Definitely not the word I was going for." Dallas chuckled, turning onto his side and sweeping loose curls away from her face. "I was gonna say fucking amazing."

"Sorry, I totally should've led with that, because yeah, it was *definitely* that." Zora gave him a quick kiss. "But also…weird, right? Because it's us. But then, maybe that's what made it so amazing, too."

"Always wondered what this would be like. The moment certainly didn't disappoint." He kissed her neck.

"You thought about this *before*? Like before we woke up married?" She pressed a hand to his chest, halting him from going in for another kiss.

"And you haven't?" He hiked an eyebrow.

"Not the point, Hamilton." Streaks of crimson kissed Zora's cheeks and dotted her chest.

"What is the point?" He nuzzled her neck with his nose and flicked one pebbled brown nipple with his thumb.

"Round two." She whispered the words roughly. "But after we fuel up in the kitchen."

Dallas surveyed her mischievous smile, his own grin deepening. He chuckled. "I definitely like the sound of that."

Eighteen

Zora strolled into the kitchen, dressed for work in a casual navy pantsuit and a white blouse, unable to shake herself from her blissful haze. Dallas had already brewed a pot of coffee and the aroma of sizzling bacon made her mouth water.

She'd awakened that morning wrapped in Dallas's arms, as she had many nights before. But this time was different. They were both still naked after a night of making love and getting acquainted with each other's bodies. And when she'd tried to ease out of his grip and make her way to the bathroom to get ready for work, she'd inadvertently roused him from his sleep.

He'd blinked drowsily for a moment before he'd gained clarity. But then he'd greeted her with the most adorable smile.

Dallas always had a way of smiling at her when they'd seen each other again for the first time in months that made her feel...special. As if she were the most important person in his world. But the look in his eyes that morning had practically made her melt into a puddle of goo, like some old-school cartoon character.

"Hello, beautiful," he'd murmured gruffly.

What was the proper morning greeting for your best friend who also happened to be your temporary spouse and future baby daddy?

A fist bump? A kiss on the cheek? Maybe a peck on the lips?

"Good morning, Dal. Sorry I woke you, but I need to get ready for work."

"Or you could ditch work today and stay in bed with

me." He'd nuzzled her ear and gripped her waist with seemingly no intention of releasing his hold. "I promise to make it worth your while."

"I…umm…" She'd cleared her throat, unable to string together a coherent sentence. "Em and I are leaving in a couple of days, so—"

"Which is why you should stay in bed with me today." He'd nibbled on her ear and grazed her nipple with the roughened pad of his thumb.

"I took nearly a week off for our honeymoon. That was just two weeks ago," she'd objected half-heartedly.

"But we weren't having sex then, which is kind of the point of a honeymoon," Dallas had said as he trailed kisses down her neck.

"Is it, though?" Zora had tried her best to seem unaffected by his touch. "I thought it was to destress from the wedding by spending time alone together."

"And having sex." He'd kissed her chest, his sensual mouth pulling into a flirtatious smirk. "Lots of it."

When he'd nuzzled her neck and feathered kisses over her heated skin, that was all it took for her to settle right back into bed with him.

"Hey, babe." Dallas leaned down and kissed her neck, bringing her out of her erotic daze.

He was shirtless and wearing a pair of jeans commando, slung low on his hips. Zora's eyes went immediately to the light brown trail of hair on his stomach that disappeared below the waistband of his jeans. Suddenly, memories of the shower they'd taken together that morning—where he'd taken her again, up against the shower wall—flashed vividly in her brain.

She shut her eyes against the image and cleared her throat. "Hey. I see you made breakfast," she said.

Dallas chuckled, as if he could see the naughty images flashing in her head. "It was the least I could do after throwing you off schedule this morning. I know you like things just so. Have a seat."

He indicated one of the stools at the breakfast bar as he arranged four slices of bacon on each of their plates.

Zora was going to object. It was already later than she usually arrived at the office. But Dallas had gone to all the trouble of making this breakfast for them while she got dressed and put on her makeup. It seemed rude to turn it down. Besides, banging like a couple of horny teenagers apparently made you voraciously hungry.

It suddenly became quite clear why Blake, Parker and Max had started coming into the office later and leaving earlier than they had before they'd gotten into relationships.

"Thank you." She slid onto the stool and took a sip from the glass of orange juice he'd set in front of her. "This was sweet of you. But you didn't have to do this. I could've grabbed something on the way to the office."

"Then I wouldn't have had the pleasure of having a meal with my wife," he said, sliding scrambled eggs onto their plates.

"You like saying that word, don't you?" Zora set her glass down.

"What word? *Wife*?" Dallas glanced at her curiously, then smiled sheepishly when she confirmed as much with a nod. He shrugged. "I hadn't thought about it, but I guess maybe I do."

Dallas spread some of his mother's homemade strawberry preserves on a slice of toast.

Zora refrained from asking the question that burned on the tip of her tongue.

Why?

All this was designed as smoke and mirrors to conceal the less-than-romantic truth from their families—that they'd gotten high as two kites in a windstorm and gotten married in a Vegas chapel. That they'd stayed married because she wanted to have a child but wasn't willing to wait for a theoretical spouse to give her one.

But pretending as if this was truly a marriage *here*, when they were alone, felt like a dangerous game with the potential of consuming them, leaving one or both of them hurt. And despite the crazy circumstances in which they found themselves, the last thing she wanted to do was to hurt her friend.

Dallas Hamilton was a rugged man who loved the outdoors. He made the most gorgeous furniture with his beautiful, intricate brain and his talented hands. But he was also sensitive and sweet in a way that most men she knew weren't.

He protected that soft underbelly by being careful about whom he let in. It was the reason none of his past relationships had been serious. He was still fiercely protecting the heart of that little boy who'd been crushed when his father walked away.

She would do everything in her power to protect that kind, loving little boy, too. So it was up to her to keep them both on track. To remind them of the plan whenever they began to veer away from it.

"What's on your agenda for today?" Zora asked brightly. "Are you working out of the Hamilton Haus offices or your personal workshop?"

Dallas slipped onto the bar stool beside her and bit into his toast. "I thought I'd work out of your home office. Try to work up a few designs to present to Einar. You don't mind, do you?"

"Of course not. This is your home, too," she said, meaning it.

Dallas had been gracious enough to move into her house, despite the fact that his office and personal workshop were back at his place. That meant he had to commute there now rather than just traveling a few feet away from his bed when he arose in the morning.

"Will you be home for dinner?" Dallas sipped his coffee.

Okay, maybe it did still feel a little weird that this was now Dallas's home, too. That she had to share her personal space and navigate her way around his things—like the clothing he'd fold and lay on top of the hamper.

"Yes, dear." She flashed him a teasing smile. "I'll be home in time for dinner."

Dallas arranged the ingredients on Zora's kitchen counter to make his spicy chili and sweet jalapeño cornbread—a meal he knew Zora loved. He'd made it for her a few times when she'd come to his place for a movie night or to watch college basketball during March Madness.

He'd spent all morning at a secondary desk in Zora's home office, working on a few design ideas to present to Einar. However, the real point of the project was for Dallas to immerse himself in Icelandic life for several months and allow the place, the people and their furniture aesthetic to inspire him to create something fresh and new. Designs that represented a true blend of cultures.

This deal was important to him. He wanted to show Einar Austarsson that he was serious about the project and ready to set the wheels of the deal in motion. These kinds of projects typically took six months to a year of planning before he got on a plane and ventured abroad to what would be his temporary home.

Much like this one.

Dallas glanced around Zora's kitchen. It was sleek and modern with every fancy countertop appliance one could imagine: a spiralizer, an air fryer, an electric pressure cooker and a stand mixer. It was the exact opposite of the simple kitchen back at his cabin, once owned by his grandfather.

His place was small and dated. The kitchen was less than half the size of Zora's with limited usable counter space. But the cabin reminded him of his late grandfather and all the things the old man had taught him: like how to make five-alarm chili and how to design and build furniture. Growing up, it had been a hobby into which he'd poured his anger and frustration. It had evolved from a calling that brought him peace and satisfaction to a livelihood for himself and the people he employed here in Magnolia Lake and around the world.

Dallas rummaged through the cabinets in search of a pot suitable for making chili. He groaned quietly as he thought of his and Zora's conversation earlier that morning.

You like saying that word, don't you?

It obviously still made Zora uncomfortable for him to refer to her as his wife, though that's exactly what she was. He, on the other hand, felt a little thrill every time he said the word.

Zora Abbott Hamilton was his wife. And he'd been enjoying every minute of it. From the moment they'd awakened in bed together in that hotel in Vegas to talking about their plans for the day over breakfast that morning.

He loved that, at least for a little while, he got to share a life and a bed with this beautiful woman who had always meant so much to him and always would. So hell yeah, he liked calling Zora his wife.

He'd offered to father Zora's child because his friend desperately wanted to be a mother, and she meant the world to him. So he wanted to make motherhood happen for her. But his perspective had taken a sharp turn when he'd held Remi in his arms for the first time. Then, just to seal the deal, little Davis had offered to become Uncle Dallas's new best friend.

Dallas smiled fondly, thinking of the kids. That was the night he'd realized that he, too, longed for a family. But he hadn't allowed himself to dwell on the thought before. Because marriages and relationships in the Hamilton family didn't seem to last.

So Dallas hadn't been eager to get married or have children. One failed relationship after another only confirmed his suspicions that he was better off as a bachelor. As long as he'd had Zora in his life, the fleeting nature of his romantic entanglements hadn't really mattered. But what he hadn't considered was that he and Zora were in a long-term relationship. One that was solid and had stood the test of time.

Why should their marriage be any different?

They loved each other, enjoyed each other's company, wanted the best for each other and were clearly sexually compatible. Having a child together would only strengthen the bond they already shared.

So why not make it permanent?

Dallas should've been unnerved by the idea of making this marriage a permanent one. But the idea had been building in his head and his heart from the moment he'd found that marriage certificate on his dresser at the hotel in Vegas.

He'd long wondered if the friendship that he and Zora had could become something more. And now he believed that it could—a thought that was thrilling and terrifying.

If it worked, they'd have the best of both worlds, being friends and lovers. If it didn't, he'd lose the woman who meant everything to him. It was the reason neither of them had wanted to risk getting involved. But now that he had a taste of what life could be like for them as lovers and friends, he couldn't imagine them not being both.

Dallas set a Dutch oven on the stove and rubbed at his chest. The thought of walking away from Zora a year from now caused an ache deep in his chest. Because he did love his best friend. And because they belonged together.

Now he just needed to figure out how to convince Zora of that.

Nineteen

Zora lay in bed with Dallas on Sunday morning, her cheek pressed to his chest and one arm wrapped around his waist. She'd returned from her trip to Atlanta on Friday afternoon, and from the moment he'd picked her up at the airport, she'd been in heaven.

The kiss he'd greeted her with had turned her inside out and left her knees quivering and her body aching for him. As soon as they'd arrived back at her place, he'd been all too happy to oblige.

They'd spent the weekend making up for lost time, since Dallas would be leaving the next day for a trip to London.

Zora's phone suddenly began to play "A Song for Mama" by Boyz II Men—the custom ring for her mother.

She groaned, snuggling closer to her husband. Zora's muscles felt warm and languid. Too relaxed and loose for her to reach all the way to the nightstand where her phone was perched.

"I'll call her back as soon as we get up," Zora murmured into his chest. Since neither of them seemed to have plans to get out of bed any time soon, she had no idea when that might be.

"Good, because I'm not done with you yet." Dallas grinned, rolling over onto her and kissing her mouth, his hardened length pressed against her.

Boyz II Men started to sing again.

"Ugh." Zora huffed, exasperated. Why hadn't she turned on her Do Not Disturb mode? "If I don't answer the phone, she'll think we're having sex."

"Good." Dallas trailed kisses down her neck. "Because we are."

"They don't need to know that."

"I'm pretty sure they already do." He chuckled, the sound of his voice warm and soothing, like warm honey poured over her skin. "We're newlyweds. It's safe to assume that they expect us to be fucking like rabbits."

"How very poetic." She jabbed him playfully in his hard belly.

Dallas kissed her neck. "You know I love your family, right?"

The muscles in Zora's back tensed. No conversation with a lover that began with that line ever ended well.

"Yeah?" Zora knew that Dallas loved her family. Still, the word came out as more of a question. "But?"

He gave her a knowing smile, his brown eyes twinkling. "You've only been home a few days, and I'm leaving tomorrow morning."

He brushed the hair from her face and pressed his mouth to hers in a lingering kiss. Then he kissed her ear before whispering in a gruff, sexy voice, "So I'd much rather spend my last few hours here, making love to my wife."

He caressed her back and nibbled on her ear.

Zora shivered, her nipples stiffening as electricity traveled down her spine and settled into the damp, warm space between her thighs.

"Your *fake* wife," she murmured. Because, of course, she couldn't help herself. The moment between them felt so damn perfect and too damn *real*.

Dallas pulled back and studied her face. A devious smile curved one edge of his mouth. "But the orgasms I'm going to give her will be very, very real."

Let the church say amen.

She swallowed roughly, her heart racing. Her sex throbbed with the memory of how real every orgasm that he'd given her thus far had been.

Hell yes, she wanted more of that. But she also didn't want to seem too eager. To come off as desperate.

"This isn't just about my family. It's about your mom, too. Tish misses you. More than she's willing to admit." Zora stroked his cheek, his whiskers tickling her hand. "And it's just a few hours. We won't stay long. I promise."

"Okay." Dallas sighed. Despite the tiny smile he managed, there was a look of defeat in his brown eyes. He kissed her palm.

Dallas's romantic gesture made her heart flutter. She buried her cheek in his chest again, cradling her body against his. Zora had never felt so safe and content in a relationship. She could be herself with Dallas without judgment. She loved it, and she loved him. Still, none of this was the way she'd imagined finding and falling in love with the man she'd spend forever with.

There had been no stars in her eyes, no moment when they'd glanced at each other and realized they were hopelessly in love. Zora had been waiting for her epic love story and breathtaking romance her entire life. She wouldn't settle for this thing with Dallas because it was comfortable for both of them.

She wanted fireworks, and Dallas deserved them, too. Because he was an incredible man who would one day make someone a fantastic husband.

She wouldn't take that moment away from either of them. Nor would she risk losing her best friend forever when one or both of them eventually realized that they were better off as friends.

"Zora, Dallas, hello. I'm glad to see you two, because Tish and I have a million questions to ask you about the wedding," Zora's mother said as she and Dallas walked into her parents' kitchen, hand in hand.

"The wedding?" Zora repeated the words as if she hadn't heard them. A stalling tactic she'd used since she was a kid.

"Yes, Zora. The wedding we're planning for you here. You know, the one where your families actually get to attend." Her mother exchanged a look with Tish, not bothering to hide the bite of sarcasm in her voice.

They were definitely still not over the hurt of being absent from her and Dallas's wedding.

Dallas squeezed Zora's hand. "Of course, Ir—" He quickly shifted in the middle of saying her mother's name when the woman pointed at him, one brow raised. *"Mom,"* he said instead with a soft smile. "You two have been very patient, giving us time to acclimate to married life these past few weeks."

"But we need to ask you to be patient for just a little while longer," Zora interrupted, rubbing her husband's arm. "Dallas is leaving for London in the morning. We'll probably head out soon after dinner—so that he can get packed," she added quickly when both women cackled deviously.

Zora's cheeks heated. It wasn't as if her mother wasn't fully aware that she was a grown woman with a healthy sex life. Still, it felt odd hearing their mothers imply they were leaving dinner early expressly to have sex. Especially since it was true.

"I think the travel should slow down for both of us in a couple of weeks…at least for a bit," Dallas volunteered, filling the awkward moment. "Then we'll all sit down and plan everything out."

"Fine." Tish pointed a finger at the two of them. "But let's not put this off so long that your first child ends up being the flower girl at the wedding."

"Amen." Zora's mother laughed. "Now Dallas, why don't you join the boys in the den? Zora, Quinn stepped away for a minute, but she insisted on handling the cooking today. I'm sure she'd love your help preparing the fruit salad."

"Absolutely, Mom. I'll be right back."

Zora walked with Dallas toward the den.

"You all right, babe?" He stopped suddenly and settled his large hands on her waist, leaning down to give her a quick kiss on the lips.

Zora reminded herself that this was all one big show. As much for themselves as for her family. But damn if it didn't feel every bit as real as the solid chest her hands were pressed against and the soft, firm lips pressed to her own.

"I'm fine. But I promised you we wouldn't stay long, and I intend to keep that promise." She smacked him on his jeans-clad bottom. "You should go ahead. I'll be in later to say hello to everyone."

Dallas nodded, reluctantly releasing her after planting another kiss on her forehead.

Zora sucked in a deep breath, her eyes drifting closed for a moment.

"This isn't supposed to feel so…real," she whispered to herself. But she'd evidently said the words louder than she'd thought.

"What isn't supposed to feel real?" Quinn asked, emerging from the guest bathroom.

"Uh… I…" Zora swallowed. "Nothing, I was just talking to myself."

She quickly turned on her heels and returned to the kitchen with Quinn, her heart racing. Zora washed her hands at the sink, then dried them.

"Where do you want me to start?"

"Help me make the potato salad first?" Quinn asked.

"Of course." Zora stepped aside while Quinn drained the potatoes.

As they worked together in the kitchen, her friend was unusually quiet. Once the potato salad was finished, Quinn laid out pineapples, mangoes, apples, strawberries and blueberries for the fruit salad.

"Is everything okay, Quinn?" Zora asked. "Did something happen between you and Max?"

"No." Quinn waved a hand. "Max and I are fine."

"But something is bothering you," Zora hedged.

Though their grandfathers had been close friends for decades, Zora and Quinn hadn't become friends until Quinn had come to work on a project for their family's company. And she couldn't be more thrilled that Quinn and her brother Max were together now. They were perfect for each other.

Quinn turned toward her. "I just wondered…this whole deal with you and Dallas…is this about—" Quinn looked around the space and stepped closer, lowering her voice "—that thing we talked about at the Magnolia Café that day. You know, when we ran into Sloane, Benji and the twins?"

Shit.

Zora gritted her teeth, groaning quietly. Other than Dallas, Quinn was the one person Zora had told about her interest in having a child on her own. At the time, Quinn and Max hadn't even been dating and she honestly didn't even know Quinn that well. But Quinn had been kind and easy to talk to, and the honest admission had just slipped out.

Zora had made the other woman promise not to say anything to her brother or anyone else about it. She'd obviously kept her word, or Max would've confronted her about it the moment he'd learned that she and Dallas were suddenly married.

"I don't want to lie to you, Quinn." Zora grabbed one of the pineapples, turned it on its side and picked up the chef's knife. "But I don't want to put you in a position where you're forced to either lie to my brother or—"

"I get it." Quinn held up a hand. "Enough said." She started peeling one of the mangoes. They worked in silence for a few moments before Quinn spoke again. "And you should know that I'm absolutely not judging here. Dallas is a great guy, and I've always thought you two behaved like a couple anyway. So you getting together didn't surprise me, Savannah, Kayleigh or either of your moms."

Zora stopped slicing the pineapple and turned to Quinn. "Why do I feel like there's a big fat *but* coming?"

Quinn shrugged. "It's not a *but* exactly. It's just something to keep in mind. That's all."

"Okay. I'm intrigued. Let's hear it." Zora put down the knife and wiped her hands on a kitchen towel. "What's wrong?"

"I don't know what arrangements you two have made, how permanent this thing is or if you're even really married—"

"Trust me," Zora said, "we definitely are."

Quinn returned to peeling and slicing the mango, her eyes on the cutting board.

"I couldn't help noticing the look on Dallas's face when you two are together." Her mouth curved in a soft smile. "There's no faking that kind of adoration, Zora. Whatever this is to you, to Dallas, this is plenty real."

Zora's cheeks tightened with an involuntary smile. "We've been best friends since we were kids," she said. "I adore him, too."

"No, sweetie," Quinn said in a distinct bless-your-li'l-heart voice. She set down her knife, dried her hands on the towel and put a hand on Zora's shoulder. "I'm talking head over heels in love here."

Zora cleared her throat. "Of course, we love each other. We've been best friends forever. But that's not the same as being *in love*."

"What do you think being in love is, Zora? To me, it's friendship with someone who truly gets you. Someone who always knows just what to say to make you smile when you've had a horrible day. Sex and attraction...that's the easy part. For some people it happens right away.

For others, it happens so gradually you hardly realize it. But the friendship, mutual respect and really *knowing* each other…that's the hard stuff. That's what the rest of us struggle with. But you and Dallas already have that. You've had it nearly your entire lives."

"If my best friend was a woman, would you think we were soul mates?" Zora tipped her chin defiantly.

"If the two of you were as into each other as you and Dallas are…*absolutely*," Quinn said without hesitation. "Love is love, sweetie. And what you two have is *definitely* love."

Zora wrapped her arms around herself as she considered her friend's words.

"I know how important Dal's friendship is to you, Zora. So just make sure that you're both honest about your expectations for this marriage. Friendships like the one you two share are rare and worth saving." Quinn huffed, as if relieved. "That's it. That's all I wanted to say, and now that I have, I feel much better."

Quinn returned to slicing up the mango, and Zora went back to cutting the rough, spiky skin off the pineapple.

Great.

At least one of them felt better. Because now all Zora could think about was whether Quinn was right.

Was Dallas in love with her?

And if he was, what would happen to their friendship once their arrangement came to an end?

Twenty

It had been two months since Dallas had awakened in Vegas to discover that he was now married to his best friend. Yet it barely seemed that long. And the whole thing felt more like an elaborate game of tag than a marriage.

If they were lucky, they got to spend a few days together before one or both of them had to jet off on some business-related trip. Most of the trips had been planned long before they'd gotten married and decided to start trying to have a baby. Still, he hated that they spent so much of their time apart. Zora had only agreed to stay married for one year, and he'd been silently building a case for making their marriage a permanent one. Trying to show her how much better their lives were now that they were together.

But whenever it seemed that Zora might be more open to the proposal, she'd say or do something to remind them both of the temporary nature of their relationship.

Dallas rubbed the last of the ebony stain into the cherrywood of the chaise longue he'd been working on for the past week. It was the final piece of a collection that he'd been inspired to create since he and Zora had been together. Initially, Dallas had hoped to design a few pieces to present to Einar. But instead he'd been inspired to create a line of sleek, modern furniture with a little bit of an edge. A series of pieces that lived comfortably in the space between masculine and feminine. The perfect compromise between his and Zora's styles.

He'd been inspired by the design of her office with its mix of masculine and feminine pieces and a dramatic black accent wall dotted with bright pops of white in floating shelves and matte-framed black-and-white photos of land-scapes and of her family. There were even a few photos of the two of them on their many travels together.

None of this had been in his plans. But once the idea had seeped into his brain, he hadn't been able to stop ob-sessing over it. He'd made two different headboards, a bed frame and an office desk so far. But this chaise, which he envisioned as the perfect piece of furniture for the foot of Zora's bed, was the pièce de résistance of the entire line. And he couldn't wait to show her.

Dallas wiped his hands on a rag and stood back to ad-mire his work. One more coat of the stain, plus a top coat to give it a shine. Then he would show the piece to his wife—the woman who'd inspired it.

His phone rang, and he glanced over at it on a nearby work surface. He was hoping it was Zora, but he quickly remembered that she'd taken his phone and set up a cus-tom ring for herself. Dallas chuckled thinking of it. It had been something she'd tried to get him to do for years and he'd never bothered. But now, as his wife, she'd grabbed his phone one night and set up custom rings for herself and for his mother.

He had to admit that it was damn useful. Since it was neither Zora nor his mother, he started to ignore the call. But when he stepped closer, he recognized the name on the lock screen.

Einar Austarsson.

Dallas's muscles tensed. Things had been crazy for Dal-las the past few months. He and Einar had exchanged peri-odic emails about the project, but the man's slow responses had left Dallas wondering if Einar had changed his mind about collaborating.

He picked up the phone and answered, and the man greeted him cheerfully, as if they were old friends who'd lost touch. Einar explained that he'd been preoccupied with renovating their main warehouse after the roof collapsed during a particularly hard snowfall.

"But enough about that," Einar said cheerfully. "I'd like to accelerate our plans for collaboration. When can you join us here in Reykjavik?"

Dallas had anticipated this call for months, but he hadn't expected Einar to want to move so quickly.

His life had changed completely in two months. Dallas and Zora were married and actively trying to have a baby. And he was in a race against time.

He had ten months to convince the woman he loved that their marriage wasn't just a fluke. That they belonged together.

Zora got into her car and made her way out of the parking lot. She'd left work a few minutes early on a dark winter afternoon, eager to get home to her husband. Over the past few months of being married, both she and Dallas had floated in and out of town, making the most of the few days here or there that they got to spend together.

She and Dallas had yet to get pregnant, though certainly not for lack of trying. And while they'd both thoroughly enjoyed this new physical aspect of their relationship, they also just really enjoyed each other's company and this deeper level of intimacy. Even if all they were doing was sitting together in her office working on their respective projects or lying in bed binge-watching a show on Netflix.

As friends with busy lives, they'd gotten accustomed to not seeing each other for weeks or months at a time. But now Dallas's absence from her life, and from her bed, left her with a deep sense of emptiness and loss. This marriage was a friends-with-benefits deal with an expiration date—set by her. Dallas had dropped not so subtle hints that he'd be *content* to continue their arrangement.

Honestly? She was flattered—even thrilled—whenever

Dallas joked that maybe they should just stay married. But what Dallas hadn't ever said was that he *loved* her or that he was *in love* with her. Being content with each other wasn't enough to sustain a marriage. They'd eventually come to resent each other the way his father had come to resent his mother. Because it seemed obvious that Douglas Hamilton hadn't ever really wanted to be married or have children.

What if their marriage, entered into in a hazy stupor neither of them could recall, turned out the same way?

The prospect of losing the friendship they'd nurtured since childhood broke her heart.

As Zora waved good night to the guard at the gate, the opening notes from Ed Sheeran's "Castle on the Hill" rang from her purse.

Dallas's custom ringtone.

"Hey," she said. "I was just about to call to see if I should grab dinner on the way home."

He chuckled. "Is that your way of asking if I've cooked dinner?"

Zora couldn't help laughing, too. "Busted. I'm sorry, but you've spoiled me with the delicious meals you make whenever you're home. I think I'm going to miss that most," she teased.

"Oh, it's my cooking you're going to miss the most, huh?" He laughed. "Then maybe I need to step up my game tonight."

"Ooh." The word slipped out of Zora's mouth before she realized it. Her nipples beaded at the prospect. "That sounds…promising. I can't wait to get home."

"Good." Dallas's rich, husky laugh rang throughout the car. "But first, can you make a detour and come to the cabin? I want to show you what I've been working on the past few months."

"Tonight?" She hadn't intended to sound so whiny, but it

was a Friday night at the end of what had been a long week, and she was physically and mentally exhausted.

"It'll be worth it. I promise." She could hear the soft smile in her husband's voice. "Got a surprise for you."

"Really?" Zora perked up, thoroughly intrigued.

She'd spent the past few hours dreaming of a hot bath and a warm meal—even if it was just a cup of ramen noodles heated in the microwave. This cold winter night was made for her warmest pj's and a pair of fuzzy pink slippers. But Dallas sounded so excited.

How could she possibly say no?

He'd rearranged his entire life to give her the child she so desperately wanted. The very least she could do was stop by his workshop to see whatever it was he wanted to show her.

"On my way," she confirmed with a smile. Zora was unbelievably grateful to Dallas, but also a little uneasy with how quickly she felt a sense of obligation.

A few minutes later, her phone rang again. Zora answered it.

"*Gott kvöld,* Brigitta. *Hvernig hefur þú það?*" Zora used the limited Icelandic her friend had taught her to wish the woman a good evening and ask how she was.

Zora hadn't spoken to Brigitta in some time, but they frequently exchanged emails. And over the past few months, Zora had done some speaking engagements and mentored women with the potential to be future business executives. All of which had been coordinated by the international women's organization Brigitta sat on the board of.

It had been Dallas who'd championed her to Brigitta as a potential speaker and mentor. Zora knew firsthand that there was a dearth of women in high-level positions in corporations. Still, she'd been reluctant to take on a volunteer role with the organization at first.

Dallas had encouraged her with stories of the fulfilling work he'd done with native artists around the world. Many of whom were women who were the primary earners in their families. Dallas reminded Zora that she could have a powerful impact on those women because she understood how tough it could be for women who did manage to achieve executive-level positions.

Zora was glad that she'd taken on the challenge.

Her volunteer work through Brigitta's organization had given Zora a deep sense of joy and renewed purpose in her work. It was something she hoped to do more of. And it had her thinking deeply about ways to expand King's Finest's community involvement.

"I am well," Brigitta said, the usual lilt absent from her new friend's voice. "But I think that there is something you should know."

Zora heaved a sigh, trying to put the uneasiness of her call with Brigitta out of her head for the moment. She drove down the narrow road that led to Dallas's cabin and pulled into the long driveway.

The cabin itself was modest. Dallas had done some basic updates but had yet to give the place the renovation it needed. However, he had renovated the space that meant the most to him—the large barn on the property. That was where he spent most of his time when he was home.

She got out of the car and made her way toward the barn. Dallas slid the door open and greeted her with *that* smile. The one that lit his eyes and animated his entire face. The smile that instantly made her feel better. Appreciated. *Loved.*

In that moment, all of the doubt, fear and hesitation she had about being married to her best friend seemed to fade away. Maybe he hadn't said the words explicitly. But for the first time it seemed so very clear. He loved her, and not just as a friend.

"Hey, beautiful." He kissed her. "How was your day?"

"Better now that I'm here with you." She returned his smile.

The moments they spent together made her incredibly happy. But it wasn't just her day that was better by being with him. Her life was so much better with Dallas Hamilton in it as her husband.

An involuntary grin slid across Dallas's face. Zora's words filled him with an indescribable sense of satisfaction. Because his days and nights were better with her in them, too.

He could stand there all night with his gorgeous wife in his arms, but the temperature had started to drop and despite the wool coat that Zora was wearing, she was shivering.

Dallas rubbed his wife's arm, then escorted her inside his workshop, sliding the barn door back into place behind them.

Mostly, it was a place of peace and creativity for him. Designing and building each piece of furniture was a form of moving meditation for Dallas—as yoga was for some people. And he was surrounded by memories of his grandfather, who had taken him under his wing and taught him the art and craft of building unique furniture that reflected the place from which it came and the people he was building it for.

"So many memories here." Zora squeezed his hand as she glanced around the space. "I miss your grandfather."

It was as if she was somehow inside his head, as she so often was. Because she understood him more than any other person on this earth. And he understood her, too.

Dallas nodded, breathing through the emotions that choked back his words.

"So…you wanted to show me something?" Zora asked brightly.

"Yeah." Dallas shoved his hands in his pockets, his stomach suddenly taking a dip, as it did on those damned roller coasters his friend loved so much.

He swallowed hard, nervous to show her what he'd been working on. Dallas had always shared his work with his friend at every stage of production. He valued her feedback on his projects, even if he didn't always agree. But this collection felt more personal than anything he'd created before.

If Zora hated it, the rejection would cut much deeper this time. Because he'd poured his heart and soul into each piece.

"It's over here." Dallas led Zora to a far corner of the workshop. He indicated the sleek, black leather chaise that he'd finished earlier that day. It was the final piece of the new collection that he'd designed. He tipped his chin in the direction of the piece and shoved his hands in his pockets. "What do you think?"

"Oh my God, Dallas." Zora ran her fingertips over the buttery-soft leather—a material he hadn't often incorporated into his designs. "This just might be the sexiest piece of furniture I've ever seen in my life." Zora walked around the chaise, her hand never leaving its surface. "You know I love everything you make. But this is stunning. It's my absolute favorite piece that you've made."

"I'm glad you like it, Zo." Dallas sighed in quiet relief, his heart expanding in his chest. "Because you were my inspiration."

"Me?" Her eyes widened as she looked at him, then returned her attention to the chaise, as if seeing it for the first time.

"Yes." Dallas glided a hand over the surface, but his gaze was on Zora. "It's bold and sleek. Contemporary with a bit of an edge. Curvy, sexy as hell and…"

"Unapologetically Black?" She grinned, her eyes sparkling.

Dallas chuckled. "Actually, I chose the color because it's one of your favorites and it fits with your current design scheme."

"You made the chaise for me?" Zora pressed a hand to her chest.

After all the intimate moments they'd shared, it was *this*—revealing how much she moved and inspired him—that made him feel most vulnerable. "I thought it would look nice at the foot of your bed. Or maybe it could replace the chair you hate in the seating area near the window."

"So there'd be room for both of us to sit and read?" Her eyes glistened when she met his gaze.

"Something like that." He smiled.

"Thank you, Dal. I love it. It's beautiful."

"So are you." He cradled her wet cheek and grazed her lower lip with his thumb before claiming her mouth with a kiss.

Zora smiled sheepishly, tucking her hair behind her ear. "And what about these?" She indicated the bed frame, dresser and bedside table nearby.

"Initially, it was just the chaise that came to mind." Dallas rubbed his neck. "Then I decided to make a few pieces to go with it. Do you like them?" Dallas ran his hand over the high-gloss finish of the cherrywood stained ebony.

"I do. They're a perfect complement to the chaise. It's a little bit of a departure from your usual style, but I love it, Dallas. Are these pieces prototypes for Einar?"

"No." He shifted his gaze from hers. They'd talk about that later. He cleared his throat. "I'd started out with that intention, and then it just morphed into something that felt too personal for a collaboration." Dallas shrugged. "I'm adding it to the Hamilton Haus lineup. I'd like to call the collection Zora."

Her gaze snapped to his and she blinked. "You're naming the collection after me?"

"If you're okay with it." Dallas dragged a hand through his hair, suddenly feeling self-conscious. "I thought I should run it by you fir—"

Before he could finish his sentence, Zora had stepped forward and cradled his face in her hands, her eyes drifted shut as she pressed her mouth to his.

Dallas slipped his arms around Zora's waist beneath the tan coat and pulled her tight against him. He relished the sensation of the generous curves that had inspired him as Zora's body melded into him, her lush lips gliding over his. He tilted her head back, slipping his tongue inside the warm cavern of her mouth—minty and sweet.

Despite the chill in the winter air outside, Dallas's face burned, and a fire ignited in his belly as the heat built between them, consuming them. Making him hungry with desire for the incredible woman who'd been his wife for the past two months.

Maybe their marriage had been the result of a series of mistakes and questionable choices, but he was damn glad it had happened. That he got to be Zora Abbott Hamilton's husband. That she was wearing his ring and—at least for now—had appended his last name to hers. And he would do whatever it took to show her that the marriage wasn't a mistake.

It was destiny. Written in the stars the moment they'd encountered each other on that playground twenty-five years ago.

As their kiss grew more intense, his body ached with its need for hers. Zora was so incredibly sexy. Something that he'd tried his best to ignore for the past ten years. But now he didn't have to pretend not to notice what a beautiful goddess his best friend was. Or that she had a body that could stop traffic. And there could be no more convincing himself that they were better off as friends.

But he was on the clock. He needed to convince Zora that they belonged together, even if it was a ridiculous fluke that had brought them to this point.

Without breaking their heated kiss, Dallas slipped the coat from Zora's shoulders, dropping it onto a nearby bench. She yanked up his T-shirt, and he helped her tug the garment over his head, tossing it onto the floor. It was quickly joined by her suit and blouse and his jeans. Finally, they stripped each other of their underwear, which joined the quickly growing pile on the floor.

Dallas broke their kiss, leading Zora to the chaise and bending her over it, preparing to enter her from behind. It was one of the positions Zora had identified as being ideal for conception. But his wife turned to him, an impish glint in her eye as she pushed him down onto the chaise and climbed onto his lap, facing him.

Zora wrapped her legs around him, locking them behind his back and she looped her arms around his neck.

"I like it," he murmured between kisses. "But I thought we were focusing on positions ideal for conception."

"I know." Zora stroked his cheek, her eyes searching his. "But tonight… I don't want it to be about us trying to get pregnant. I just want this to be about…us."

Dallas nodded, his heart squeezing in his chest at the implication that Zora was finally admitting what he'd already known for months. That what they shared went deeper than their temporary arrangement or even their wish to have a child together.

Dallas wrapped one arm around Zora's waist as he pulled her closer, the slick space between her thighs gliding along his hardened length.

Zora murmured with pleasure at the sensation of the stiff bundle of nerves grinding against his steely length.

Her breath came in short, throaty pants, both of them gasping for air at the feverish kiss.

He gripped her hips, his fingers digging into her soft flesh as he lifted her, guiding her onto his aching member. He was desperate to be inside her again, as if they hadn't made love earlier that morning. She reached for his hardened dick, pumping it with her hand before guiding it inside her. Zora glided down onto him, and they both groaned with pleasure.

"Fuck, Zora." He whispered into her hair, "Babe, you feel so damn amazing."

Zora kissed him, her thumbs pressed to his cheeks as her lips clashed with his. Her hips moved slowly at first. But as the intensity of their kiss escalated, the movement of her hips mirrored their frantic kiss.

Zora cried out his name, her body going stiff as she held on to his shoulders tightly, as if she needed his support. He tightened his grip on her thighs, hoping he wouldn't leave bruises as he moved against her.

His body was suddenly racked with the deepest, most intense pleasure. He wrapped her in his arms and buried his face in her hair, which smelled like some sweet chocolate confection.

"Zora, I love you." His voice was low, the words barely more than a whisper. Words Dallas had wanted to say for months. But he could never seem to find the right time to say them.

Zora didn't move. Didn't speak. It felt as if she was barely breathing.

The silence between them rang in his ears, as loud as the circular saw of his grandfather's he'd used to make the chaise they were on. Dallas shut his eyes closed and sighed.

The awkward silence loomed over them like some invisible monster that had climbed from beneath the chaise

the moment he'd opened his stupid mouth and told her he
loved her.

But it was true; he did love her. And not just as a friend.
It had never been clearer to him. But he suspected that his
sudden declaration of love had freaked Zora out.

Zora climbed off him, stepped into her shearling-lined
suede boots and slipped on her coat. She wrapped it around
her, as if she needed a shield between them. She quickly
stooped to gather her clothing.

"Bathroom," she called over her shoulder as she hurried in that direction.

Dallas sighed, a knot twisting in his gut.

That didn't go how I'd hoped.

"Meet me over at the cabin, Zo. I'll order something for
dinner. Then we can…talk," Dallas called after her.

Zora stopped in her tracks, as if she'd suddenly run into
a wall. She glanced back at him over her shoulder and nodded before resuming her retreat.

Dallas shrugged on his jeans and shirt and grabbed up
his belt and underwear, not bothering to put either on. Then
he stuck his feet into his boots without tying them and
headed to the cabin to order dinner and shower.

His wife had evidently been unsettled by his admission
of love. But he meant every word, and he was certain she
felt the same.

Dallas groaned, feeling temporarily defeated, yet determined to make Zora see that what they had was real and
worth fighting for.

Twenty-One

Zora shut the bathroom door behind her, instantly furious at herself for running away like a child. Awkward moments like this were exactly why she'd been so terrified of taking on marriage and parenthood with her best friend.

Did she love him? *Hell yes.* But before Vegas, it had been so easy to delineate the *type* of love she had for Dallas.

Zora had always admired that the ancient Greeks understood how truly complicated love was. They had four words for it: *agape* was love of mankind, *storge* was the love parents had for their children, *philia* was love between friends and *eros* was passionate, erotic love.

BV—in the time Before Vegas—it had been clear that the love they shared was a love between friends, pure and simple. And she'd really, *really* intended to keep it that way. Even after they'd agreed to have a child together. But little by little, things had been shifting between them over the past few months. Their marriage was starting to feel less and less like an arrangement and more like it was real. Like the love they shared was so much deeper than friendship or even just sex.

Had she fallen in love with her best friend? Was he in love with her, as Quinn believed? Zora had been wrestling with all those thoughts in her head, but she hadn't wanted to say them out loud—not even to herself. So she hadn't been ready to hear them coming from her best friend.

Zora plopped down on the cold toilet seat. She was an accomplished exec who mentored other career women, a candidate for CEO of her company and on the precipice of beginning the journey into motherhood. So she needed to

have a grown-up conversation with her husband about what
he'd said and her growing, complicated feelings for him.

She would clean up, put on her coat and traipse over to
the cabin to have the conversation she'd been terrified of
having for the past few weeks.

Zora's keys jingled in her pocket as she clutched her
clothing in one hand and pulled the tan wool coat tightly
around her naked body with the other. She set her things
on the counter and surveyed the space.

While Dallas had overhauled the barn, he'd only made
a few improvements to the cabin. Still, what he'd done had
been a dramatic improvement to the dark, dank space it
once was.

A stunning billiard table that Dallas had built himself
dominated the sparsely furnished open area in the center
of the cabin. The hallway on the left led to the master bedroom. The hallway on the right led to Dallas's office and
a small guest room.

Dallas had brought Cole's company in to open up the
back wall of the cabin and install large windows that let in
lots of light. Her brother had also revamped and modernized
the small kitchen so it could accommodate a dishwasher,
a beer fridge and a full-size, state-of-the-art refrigerator.

Dallas had crafted the gorgeous slab of wood that served
as the island countertop himself. Made from salvaged, old-
growth redwood with a live edge, it served as the breakfast
bar and provided the kitchen's only real food prep work-
space.

Still clutching the coat closed with one hand, Zora made
her way to the master bedroom, where she could hear the
shower running. She sucked in a deep breath, dropped her
clothing and the coat onto Dallas's bed, toed off her fur-
lined boots, and padded into the bathroom.

Dallas stood beneath the shower, rinsing shampoo from

his hair. Zora opened the glass door and stepped inside, startling him momentarily.

He cocked his head and a slow smirk lifted one corner of his sensual mouth. "So the shower crashing, that's your thing now, huh?"

"Maybe." She shrugged, reining in a smile. "Is it a problem?"

"Hell no." Dallas wrapped an arm around her waist. "You can shower with me any time, Mrs. Hamilton." He leaned down and kissed her mouth.

"That's Ms. Abbott-Hamilton." Zora kissed him again. "But because you're cute and you're definitely packing—" she pressed her body against his steely length "—I'm gonna let it slide."

Dallas chuckled, his laughter bouncing off the tiled walls.

"Are we all right, Zo?" He studied her face as he held her in his arms. "You seemed pretty upset about me saying "

"I know, and I'm sorry." She cut him off before he could repeat the words. The muscles in her neck and back tensed as warm water beat on their bodies. "I was just…stunned to hear you say the words."

"I meant what I said, Zo." He caressed her cheek, his gaze soft and warm. "I love you, and not just as a friend. I love being your husband. Love the prospect of being a father to our kids. I love that you're both my best friend and the woman who has my heart and always will."

Zora furrowed her brows, her heart breaking. Dallas wasn't making what she had to say easier. Zora swallowed hard, the words caught in her throat. She tucked wet curls behind her ear.

Her voice was shaky. "Dallas, I—"

"I love you, Zora," he said again. "And I want to be with you. Not just for a few more months. What we have… I want this forever, and I know you do, too."

She did. Zora realized that now. But she also realized that this arrangement wasn't fair to Dallas. Maybe they were meant to be together. But perhaps it just wasn't the right time in their lives.

"Dallas, I don't think that—" Zora tried to drop her gaze, but he maintained his light grip on her chin, as if this connection between them was a lifeline he was holding on to at all costs.

"It's true, Zo. This isn't me getting caught up in my feelings because the sex is amazing. It's how I genuinely feel. I might've been under the influence when I recited my wedding vows in that Vegas chapel. But, baby, I meant every single word. I love you, Zo. I think I always have." His voice wavered a little.

Zora closed her eyes, her eyelashes wet with tears. His sweet words and the emotion with which he delivered them made her heart squeeze in her chest.

She wanted to tell him the truth—that she loved him and wanted to be with him, too. But that wasn't what she'd come here to say. Because it wasn't what was best for the man she adored.

"Dallas, I love you, too," she said, tears streaming down her cheeks. His expression instantly went from joy to trepidation. Because he knew her well enough to know that she was gathering the strength to say something that pained her. "But this arrangement… I didn't realize how unfair it is to you."

"Shouldn't I be the one to decide whether or not I feel like this is unfair to me?"

"You're a good friend, Dal, and you've been an amazing husband—"

"I've *been* an amazing husband?" Dallas cocked one brow. "As in past tense?"

When fat tears rolled down her cheeks in response, his frown deepened.

Dallas turned off the water and stepped out of the shower. He handed her a towel, then grabbed one for himself before stalking into the bedroom.

Zora followed him into the other room, drying her wet skin with the soft white towel he'd handed her.

She sat at the foot of his bed, unsure of what to say.

Dallas rummaged through his drawers in silence before finally grabbing a pair of boxers and slipping them on. He turned to her and sighed, dragging a hand through his hair.

"You're asking to end our marriage *now*, aren't you?"

"Yes." She whispered the word, her heart breaking.

"Why, Zo?" He sat beside her on the bed. "It clearly isn't what you want, and it isn't what I want either. What we've built…it means *everything* to me." He covered her trembling hand with his.

"It means everything to me too, Dal. But I'm scared." Zora wasn't accustomed to admitting her fears and weaknesses; not even to herself. They were emotions she stuffed deep down. Something to be overcome. Dallas intertwined their fingers and tightened his grip on her hand. Zora instantly felt a sense of comfort.

"I know that the prospect of us making this a real marriage makes the stakes much higher. And yes, that does seem terrifying, given what we have to lose," Dallas admitted. "You're not alone in that, Zo. I don't know exactly what this next chapter of our lives will bring, either. But I know that as long as we're together, it's going to be amazing, and that together we can get through anything."

"I want to believe that, Dal. I do, but—"

"I'm not asking you to believe in some fairy tale, Zo. I'm asking you to climb down into the trenches with me and fight for it, because this friendship is too important to us. Our past failed relationships couldn't compete with our jobs or our families. But you, Zora, are my priority. Your love, your friendship and the family that we're trying to make…they mean everything to me. For you, sweetheart, I'm willing to make sacrifices."

"Like your decision to pass on the collaboration with Einar Austarsson?" she asked.

Dallas's eyes widened. "How'd you…" He rubbed the back of his neck and sighed. "Brigitta told you."

It wasn't a question, so she didn't bother confirming what he clearly already knew.

"I didn't pass on the project," Dallas hedged. "I requested that we put it on the shelf for now."

"But why, Dallas?" She cradled his cheek. "You've worked so hard to put this collaboration in motion."

Dallas turned his head and kissed her palm. He sighed. "I thought we'd be moving forward on this in a few months, maybe a year. But he wanted me to come to Reykjavik as soon as possible to set things up. It would take about three months. I told him I couldn't commit to that right now because we're trying to start a family."

"What did he say?" Zora asked.

"He'd assumed you were coming, too." Dallas rubbed his chin and chuckled bitterly. "I reminded him that my wife is an executive who can't just pick up and move abroad for three months. So I passed on the deal for now and asked him to keep me in mind. Perhaps we can collaborate in some way down the road."

Her eyes filled with tears, and she squeezed his hand. "Honey, I can't believe you'd give up this deal for me. I know how important it is to you."

Dallas shrugged as if losing this opportunity, which could make his company millions and further expand his brand and reach, was no big deal. "Now you know that you're more important to me than working with Einar Austarsson or anything else."

Zora's heart felt full and as if it were ripping apart at the seams. "I appreciate the sacrifice you're willing to make for me, Dal. But I didn't and would never ask you to make such a sacrifice. I want what's best for you. I want you to be happy," she said. "All you've talked about is how much you wanted this."

"True." He squeezed her hand as he peered into her eyes. "But that was before I realized that I want to be with you. To make babies with you. To build a life with you right here in Magnolia Lake." A soft smile kissed his lips.

Dallas was saying all the right things. Pushing all the right buttons. Giving her *everything* she could ever ask of him.

At the expense of himself.

She couldn't let him do that.

"You didn't consult with me on this. You didn't even ask if I'd consider coming with you."

"And would you have, Zo?" he asked pointedly, then sighed, running a hand through his hair. "We both already know the answer to that."

"So you just decided for me?" She was genuinely hurt and angry.

"It's one project, Zora. Hamilton Haus is doing fine. This isn't the end of the world."

"These immersive projects you do every few years are an integral part of your brand. It's what makes Hamilton Haus so unique. More importantly, those projects make you immensely happy, Dal. And they do so much good for the native artists you feature from all over the world. I can't take that away from you."

"Marriage is about sacrifice, Zora." Dallas slipped his hand into her hair and stroked her cheek. "I'm willing to sacrifice that aspect of my business or at least adjust it."

"Marriage is about compromise," Zora countered. "Both sides have to give a little to find a happy medium. If only one person is making all the sacrifices, the relationship won't work. It'll cause resentment. I don't want that for us, Dal."

"So what are you saying, Zo?" The pained look on her husband's face broke her heart.

Tears started to flow down her face again. "I'm saying that as much as I want this, I'm not sure how to make this work for both of us."

"Zo, sweetheart, please just tell me what you want. Ask me anything." He leaned down, pressing his forehead to hers.

Zora sucked in a deep breath and closed her eyes. Then she opened them, forcing a smile, even through her tears, as her eyes searched his.

"Two things. First, tomorrow I want you to call Einar and tell him that you've changed your mind." She stroked his cheek.

Dallas nodded sadly, his eyes filled with the same pain she felt. "All right. What else?"

She loosened the towel, letting it fall away as she climbed onto his lap and pressed a kiss to his lips. "Make love to me."

Dallas kissed her and made love to her as if it was the last time they'd ever be together.

The possibility that it might be tore Zora apart.

But she loved Dallas too much to let him give up this opportunity. Regardless of what it might mean for the two of them.

Twenty-Two

Zora stood at the front of the boardroom before her grandpa Joe—whose recovery from his stroke was going well; her father, Duke; and her brothers Blake, Parker and Max. She'd just laid out her case for establishing the King's Finest Foundation and proposed that she be the one to spearhead the project.

Dallas had been in Iceland for nearly two weeks. She'd spent many of those nights in tears as she lay alone in bed, staring at the ceiling and wishing her husband was there. But she'd spent some of her time productively, developing the proposal she'd just presented to her family.

Her father and grandfather liked the idea of starting a foundation that would do good in underserved communities, strengthen the KFD brand and cement their legacies. But her father had an expected question.

"If you're shifting your focus to establishing the foundation, who'll run sales?" He frowned, rubbing his whiskered chin. "I don't need to tell you how important your work here is, Zora."

"Thanks, Dad." She smiled. "My assistant, Emily, is smart and ambitious. She's been critical to the team since I hired her right out of college six years ago. Her talents are being vastly underutilized in her current role," Zora admitted, returning to her seat beside Max.

"In my volunteer work, I'm giving women the knowledge and tools to ascend the career ladder. Charity begins at home. I'm not suggesting Emily can take over for me. But I've given her increasing responsibilities, and she's exceeded my expectations every single time. I'm proposing that I only retain the highest-level tasks while dividing the rest between Emily—in a newly minted role with a commensurate title and salary—and two other members of the team who are also ready for more responsibility."

Zora folded her hands on the table and surveyed the faces of her family, who were also the company's executive board.

"Excellent plan, Zora." Her grandfather beamed. "I'm proud of you for putting this together. Inspired by the race to be CEO?"

"Actually, about that… I've given it a lot of thought, and I'm committed to the success of the foundation and to maintaining our forward momentum in sales. So I'd like to withdraw my name for consideration and endorse Blake."

The faces of everyone in the room conveyed various levels of shock. Not surprising. After all, she was the most competitive person at the table.

"This isn't a democracy and Blake isn't a political candidate, Zora," Parker pointed out. He looked especially agitated.

"No, it isn't," her father confirmed. "But family always comes first here at King's Finest. So your grandfather and I certainly care what you think. You'll be the nucleus of this company, working together long after we're gone. Your wishes carry weight."

"Good," Max said. "Because I've been doing a lot of thinking about this, too. Would I like to be the CEO? Sure. But I honestly do believe Blake is best suited for the position. So, I'd like to endorse Blake, too. Not because he's the firstborn. Because his knowledge, work ethic, temperament and the respect he's earned from everyone here at the company recommend him as the *logical* choice." Max smirked at Parker—Mr. Logic—when he stressed the word.

Parker twisted his mouth and groaned. "To be clear, I'm *not* withdrawing myself from consideration," Parker said.

"But I acknowledge the logic behind your arguments. So if Blake is the person designated as the next CEO of King's Finest, I believe he'll represent the company well. And I'll do my part to support him."

Her father exchanged a look with their grandfather, who nodded.

"I'm glad you've come to this conclusion on your own," Duke said. "Because your grandfather and I agree that Blake should be the next CEO of King's Finest Distillery. You all put the interests of this family and our company ahead of your self-interests. And I couldn't be prouder." He beamed.

"Good job, brat." Max turned to Zora when the meeting ended. "By the way, I'm sorry I wasn't more receptive when you returned from Vegas married. You took us all by surprise, but you and Dallas are right for each other. Marriage looks good on you, Zo."

"Thanks, Max." Zora forced a smile. Their families knew that Dallas had gone to Reykjavik for business. They weren't aware that their relationship was in limbo. She'd gone to Sunday dinner, put on a brave face and updated their families on her husband's trip, based on their daily, early morning phone calls.

The only two people who seemed to truly realize how devastated she was over her separation from her husband were Cole and Quinn. But she hadn't confided the truth to either of them.

When she rose from her seat, Blake was there.

"Thanks, Zo." He hugged her. "That was unexpected, but I appreciate your confidence and support. How's the wedding planning coming?"

Zora groaned. "The moms are driving us crazy. But with Dallas in Reykjavik right now, I'm hoping they'll back off a bit."

"Be patient with them. They're over the moon about

you and Dallas finally getting together," Blake said. He smiled. "We all are."

Great. Now her knucklehead brothers wanted to be supportive of her marriage to Dallas?

Figures.

"Hang in there with the wedding stuff, Zora." Parker patted her shoulder. "Besides, the more they're focused on your wedding, the less they're bothering Kayleigh and me about ours." Parker flashed a rare grin, and Zora couldn't help laughing, too.

It was the end of another long day, and she felt more than a little fatigued. She just wanted to go home, crawl under the covers, and think about how amazing her life had been those first months they were married. Wishing there was a way to make this marriage work for both of them.

Twenty-Three

Zora stood in her mother's kitchen before Sunday dinner, staring out the window onto the backyard where her father manned the grill. Her heart ached and all she could think of was the last time Dallas had been here with the family.

She missed him more each day. So much that it felt like she was making herself physically ill. She was pretty sure she was coming down with something. Her mother had felt her forehead and informed her that she had a serious case of missing her man.

Zora was not amused.

She looked out the window at her mother, most of her siblings and their spouses, who'd donned jackets and braved the crisp late fall air to sit around the fire pit and keep her father company. Savannah and Kayleigh were in the family room with Remi, who was now three months old and getting bigger every day.

Maybe she was feeling especially somber because she and Emily were leaving the next day for their weeklong trek across Europe to meet with distributors in Belgium, Finland, Sweden and Germany.

Zora was startled by the slamming of the fridge. She hadn't even heard Cole arrive.

"You plan on mooning over the dude the entire three months he'll be in Iceland having the time of his life?" Cole twisted the cap off his beer.

"That's it." Zora turned to her brother, one fist on her hip. "Everyone else in this family has accepted my relationship with Dallas. But you   the one person I *expected* to have my back—you've been a total jackass about it."

"Look, you don't need to get so upset about me razzing your little boyfriend—"

"Dal is *not* my boyfriend, Cole. He's my *husband*, and he's been practically a member of this family since we were kids. You two have always gotten along fine."

"I know," Cole said gruffly, then sipped his beer.

"Then what the hell is your problem?" She poked a finger into Cole's shoulder. "Why are you suddenly treating Dallas like the enemy? He isn't. He's the same amazing guy who's always been a friend to all of us." Zora's voice broke. Tears clogged her throat and stung her eyes. Wetness streaked down her cheeks, which made her furious with her brother and with herself.

Zora never wanted to be babied by her brothers. She wanted them to recognize that she was as smart and as tough as they were. So she'd learned long ago never to let them see her cry.

She was breaking her own code and she was livid about it.

Cole set down his beer and grasped her arm. "Zo, I'm sorry. I didn't mean to hurt your feelings."

"My feelings aren't hurt." Zora yanked her arm from her brother's grip and propped a fist on her hip. She tipped her chin, leveling her angry gaze at him. "I'm *furious*. You've never treated anyone else's spouse or partner this way. In fact, you adore Savannah, Kayleigh and Quinn. So why are you being so shitty to Dallas?"

Cole wrinkled his brow, picked up his beer and swigged it. He shrugged his shoulders in response to her question, which only infuriated her.

"That's bullshit, Cole. There has to be a reason you're behaving this way. What could possibly have changed in the few months since Dallas was here for Mom and Dad's anniversary and for Benji and Sloane's wedding? You two got along fine then."

"You really want to know?" Cole asked.

"Obviously." Zora glared at her brother.

"He lied to us." Cole set his beer down again. "He's always sworn there was nothing going on between you. Then suddenly, you two elope. That didn't come out of nowhere, Zora. Evidently, there was a lot more than friendship between you."

"*That's* why you're upset?" Zora could barely restrain a laugh. "Because you think we've been hooking up all this time and he lied to you about it?"

Cole folded his arms. His expression indicated that he didn't see the humor in the situation.

"First of all—" Zora pointed an accusatory finger at her brother "—it's none of your damn business who I have or haven't been sleeping with. Second—" she held up two fingers "—Dal didn't lie to you. We were never together before we got married." Zora relaxed against the kitchen counter, shrugging her shoulders. "Our decision to get married was spontaneous. It was as much of a surprise to us as it was to all of you. But it felt right and we were happy—"

"*Were*?" Cole raised an eyebrow. "As in you aren't anymore?"

"Are," she said. "I meant we *are* happy." But her eyes wouldn't cooperate, and tears spilled down her cheeks. She sniffled. "Why can't you just be happy for us, bucket head?" She shoved her brother's shoulder again.

Cole hugged her, despite her objections. Her tears and makeup were getting all over his dark shirt.

He pulled her away from the window so their family wouldn't see her crying.

"You're right. I was a jerk. But something about your story just wasn't right, so I was concerned. You're my little sister and my closest remaining friend," Cole said. "Guess I didn't take the sudden news of losing you, too, so well."

Zora wiped her face and stared at her brother.

His closest remaining friend?

Suddenly, the real issue became clear. Why hadn't she recognized it earlier?

"This isn't so much about me and Dal as it is about you and Quinn, right?" Her voice was tempered with compassion.

"I don't know what you're talking about." Cole averted his gaze from hers. He gripped the bottle and took a swig.

"Yes, you do," Zora said softly. She glanced around the kitchen to ensure no one else was around. Then she lowered her voice and stepped closer. "You're not as okay with Max and Quinn being together as you pretend, are you?"

Cole's frown deepened, his expression stony. "They're happy, and I'm happy for them."

"Then why do you look so wounded?" Zora placed a hand on her brother's arm. She studied his expression, though his eyes wouldn't meet hers. This wasn't simple jealousy or even resentment. "The friendship you and Quinn struck up... For her, it really was just that. But for you... what...did you think that after you'd gotten done sleeping your way across the South you two would eventually end up together?"

Cole glared at her. "I'm feeling a little bit judged here, Zo."

"No judgment intended." She held up her hands. "But if that's how you really felt about Quinn, I understand the loss you must feel. But at least you two are still—"

"Friends?" He laughed bitterly, draining his beer. "Right. Because I can call her up and say, 'Hey, let's spend the weekend at my place in Charleston,' and Max would be totally okay with that," he said sarcastically, his brows drawn together.

"Right." Zora nodded. "And now that Dal and I are married, you feel like you've lost your two closest friends all at once." She sighed softly. "I get it."

"I doubt it," he said.

"No, I do," Zora insisted. "It's kind of how I felt whenever Dallas would get involved with someone else. They were suddenly taking up this space in his life that had always belonged to me. And they, of course, felt threatened by our friendship."

"Since you two are married now and planning on having your own little brood, I'm pretty sure the feelings of his ex-girlfriends were pretty damn justified." Cole smirked as he rinsed his bottle out in the sink. He dropped it in the recycling bin.

"Point taken." Zora grinned. "Guess I owe them an apology."

"And I owe you and Dallas one." Cole placed a hand on her shoulder. "I have been an ass ever since you two got back from Vegas, and I'm genuinely sorry, ZoZo."

He hugged her, and she sank into the warmth of her brother's embrace, grateful that they'd called a truce. Until Savannah, Sloane, Kayleigh and Quinn had come into her life via her brothers and cousin, she hadn't had many female friendships. And she and Cole had formed a bond early on. So aside from Dallas, he'd always been her next closest friend.

Zora could understand the pain her brother must be feeling. Everyone else in his life seemed to be moving on, leaving him behind. Which must've added to the isolation of being the only member of their family not involved in running King's Finest.

"We good?" he asked, letting her go and tweaking the high topknot she'd pulled her hair into.

Zora slapped his hand away and patted her hair back into place. "You know better than to touch a Black woman's hair."

"Bet you ain't tellin' ol' boy that." Cole raised an eyebrow and chuckled.

"Shut up." She poked her brother, her cheeks hot as she thought about the way Dallas had first taken down her hair and run his fingers through it. Zora pulled another beer out of the fridge and handed it to her brother. "Now that we're friends again... I do have a confession to make. Can we talk upstairs?"

Cole nodded, his expression laced with concern. "Of course. Let's go."

They went to the sitting room upstairs and settled on the couch.

Zora told her brother the truth. About her and Dallas's wedding in Vegas. About her decision to have a child on her own. And that she now realized that she was in love with her best friend.

Her brother listened patiently. Then he reassured her that their secret was safe with him before giving her a final word of advice.

"You're an Abbott, Zo. If I'm being honest, you're the toughest and most determined one of all of us. So are you going to hang around here pouting about missing Dallas, or are you going to find a way to make this work? Like you said, Dal is a good guy. Plus, he gets you. Let's face it, you might never find a combo like that again." He smirked.

"Very funny," Zora said.

Cole chuckled, then sighed. "Seriously, Zo, the guy really loves you. Anybody can see that. Dallas has already proved how much he's willing to sacrifice for you. The question is, what are *you* willing to sacrifice to make this work?"

Zora laid her head on her brother's shoulder and sighed.

That was the question she needed to answer.

Twenty-Four

Dallas parked the Range Rover Velar in the attached garage of the villa in Vogar, Iceland, where he'd been staying for the past few weeks. Both the car and the villa had been graciously provided by his host, Einar Austarsson.

The spacious villa was a forty-minute drive from the Austarsson factory in Reykjavik. The all-glass garden house, equipped with a hot tub, provided an impressive view of Keilir—a hyaloclastite mountain created during subglacial eruptions during the Ice Age. In the distance, he could see Snæfellsjökull—a 700,000-year-old glacier-capped stratovolcano.

Sitting in the hot tub and taking in such awe-inspiring scenery was a lovely way to end the day. Under normal circumstances, such natural beauty would spur countless ideas for new designs. But instead, he'd spent most of the time that he wasn't actively working on the project thinking of Zora.

Sometimes, he could still hear her voice in his head. Encouraging him. Being an adorable smartass. Finally admitting she loved him and wanted to be with him.

To say he missed Zora was an understatement. He'd agreed to move forward with this project and his residency here in Iceland. But he had no intention of giving up on their marriage.

Would it be a challenge to coordinate their busy schedules and demanding work lives so they could spend more time together and provide a stable home for any children they brought into the world? *Yes.*

Would it be worth whatever sacrifice that Herculean task required? *A thousand times yes.*

For now, he had to settle for video calls and text messages. But as long as Zora was willing to try to find a way to work all of this out, Dallas remained hopeful.

Dallas turned the knob and entered the house. He halted immediately, scanning the room. Two familiar scents lingered in the air. The first was his grandfather's five-alarm chili. The second was...

"Zora?"

There was no answer.

He walked into the quaint kitchen with its stunning black cooktop island. The style of the island and gold accents gave it the feel of an Old World piece of furniture. A huge Dutch oven simmered on the stove. He lifted the lid and inhaled.

Definitely his grandfather's chili.

Dallas replaced the lid and turned around, and his heart nearly leaped out of his chest. He swallowed hard and stared at the woman before him, but he couldn't open his mouth to speak.

He'd thought of Zora incessantly. Dreamed of her each night. Had his brain conjured her into existence?

"Zora," he said again finally, whispering her name.

"Yes, babe." She smiled, inching closer. Her voice trembling. "It's me."

"But I just spoke to you this morning. You...you were in Berlin on your business trip," he stammered.

"I was." Zora stepped closer, her grin deepening. "But I'm here now. With you. And baby, there is no place in this world I would rather be."

Dallas's heart overflowed with an amalgam of emotions: surprise, joy, relief. He regarded his beautiful wife, through the haze of emotion that blurred his vision. She was gorgeous with her hair worn in long, thick glossy twists, half of which were pulled up into a high topknot.

He closed the space between them, cradling Zora's face

in his hands. Dallas pressed his mouth to hers, capturing her soft lips in a passionate kiss.

Zora wrapped her arms around him, her fingers clutching the fabric of his wool sweater.

He'd missed the comfort of her arms. The sweetness of her kiss. The contentment of being in her presence. And now that he held her in his arms again, he honestly didn't think he'd ever be able to let her go again.

Zora squealed when Dallas lifted her suddenly, sweeping her off of her feet and carrying her to his bedroom.

"The chili," she reminded him. "Your mom gave me your family recipe, and I don't want to screw it up."

"It'll be fine. It's on simmer," he muttered, carrying her to the bedroom where he'd slept alone every night for the past few weeks. Wishing she was there.

Dallas made love to his wife, determined to make up for every moment they'd missed. Hoping he could convince her to stay.

Dallas lay in bed holding Zora in his arms, her cheek pressed to his chest. He'd left her just long enough to slip on his underwear and pad across the heated floors to turn off the chili.

"Zora, you have no idea how much I've missed you." He kissed her forehead, damp with perspiration.

"I think I do." Zora raised her head. Her espresso-brown eyes sparkled, and the smile on her face made his heart dance. "I missed you, too. *Desperately.*"

"How long can you stay?" He twirled one of the loose twists around his finger. "Hopefully until my flight home for Thanksgiving."

"Yes." Zora was barely able to contain her grin. "And if you don't mind having a roommate, I plan to return here with you after Thanksgiving. I'll make this my base until your project ends."

"You're kidding?" His heart beat wildly in his chest. "How? I mean…what about your bid to be CEO?" He sat up with his back against the headboard.

Zora sat up too, pulling the blankets up around her. "We all agreed that Blake should be KFD's next CEO."

"And you're okay with the decision?"

"I am. At this point in my life, the prospect of running the company doesn't give me the kind of joy and fulfillment I'd always imagined it would."

"What would?" Dallas asked, stroking her cheek.

"Being a wife and a mother." Zora smiled softly. "But also spearheading the creation of KFD's new charitable foundation. There are so many projects and causes I'm passionate about. So much good we could be doing in the world. While I'm here with you, I'll work on making that happen."

"That's wonderful, Zora. But you didn't do this just because—"

"My family has discussed starting a foundation a few times over the years. No one took up the cause, so we always kicked the can down the road. Now feels like the right time for me to do this. And yes, it would give me more flexibility while our children are young."

A huge grin slid across Dallas's face.

"What is it?" Zora asked, smiling, too.

"You said our *children*. Does that mean—"

"That I love you, and that I want to be your wife forever and ever?" She smiled, tears streaking down her face. "Yes, Dal, it does."

"Then there's one more thing I need to do." Dallas slid to the floor on one knee and took Zora's hand in his. His mouth was suddenly dry and there was a fluttering in his gut.

"I apparently said this before." He chuckled. "But I need to say it again, because I don't ever want you to doubt it."

Dallas drew in a shaky breath and his smile widened. His eyes welled with emotion.

"I love you, Zora Abbott. I have since the day I first met you on that playground. You've been in my corner since we were six years old. I loved you then, and I love you now. I have been waiting for this moment my entire life. I want to spend the rest of my life being your best friend, your lover, and the father of our children." His voice broke slightly. "Please say that you'll *stay* my wife forever."

Salty tears spilled down Zora's cheeks as she bit her lower lip and nodded, "Yes, Dallas. Nothing in the world would make me happier than to spend the rest of my life with you."

Epilogue

Dallas lay in the bed he and Zora now shared in Vogar, Iceland. They'd returned home to Magnolia Lake to spend Thanksgiving with their families. Much to his surprise, Zora and their mothers had planned a simple but elegant wedding ceremony for their families that Saturday. They'd returned to Iceland a week later after a proper honeymoon in Costa Rica.

They would board their flight back to Magnolia Lake for the holidays tomorrow morning. Dallas was content to lie in bed with his wife, her warm, soft body melded to his as they lay together naked.

Zora kissed his bare chest, then lifted her head. Her hair, which she now wore in loose curls, was wild because he'd run his fingers through it when he'd made love to her. Her hair partially covered her face. But he couldn't miss her smile. His wife practically glowed with happiness.

"I got you an early Christmas gift." He suddenly remembered the gift-wrapped package he'd picked up in Reykjavik earlier that day.

Zora grinned. "I've got something for you, too."

Dallas climbed out of the bed to go find his bag and retrieve the gift. He presented it to her, and she opened the prettily wrapped box with its shiny, gold ribbon, pulling the merino wool sweater dress out of the box and grinning.

"I love it. It's gorgeous." She beamed, thanking him as she leaned over to kiss him. Then she retrieved a small box from the drawer of the bedside table and handed it to him. "Here's yours."

Dallas loosened the ribbon that tied the box and opened it. He stared at his gift. His eyes widened and his heart thudded in his chest. For a moment, he was unable to speak. He stared at the little white and blue stick with a single word on its digital screen: *Pregnant*.

"Is this...are we..."

"Yes." Zora laughed softly, placing a hand on her belly. "We're pregnant."

Dallas's heart raced and he couldn't stop smiling. He took his wife in his arms and hugged her.

"How long have you known?"

"I suspected as much last week, so I took a few different tests. I visited an OB/GYN earlier today. She confirmed it," Zora said. "You are happy about this, aren't you? Because I am hopelessly in love with you, Dallas Hamilton. And I can't wait to raise this baby with you. You're not only my best friend, you're the love of my life." Her eyes were wet with tears.

"I love you so much, Zo. And I could not be happier." He leaned down and kissed her belly, then pressed another to her lips.

Dallas had been granted everything he could've ever wished for. He could receive no greater gift. And it was worth whatever sacrifices they'd have to make to build a life together.

* * * * *

HOW TO LIVE WITH TEMPTATION

FIONA BRAND

Thank you, as always, to my wonderful editor, Stacy Boyd.

To the Lord: Father, Son and Holy Spirit. Thank You!

"The Lord bless thee, and keep thee: The Lord make his face shine upon thee, and be gracious unto thee . . . and give thee peace."

—The Aaronic blessing, *Numbers* 6:24–26

One

Allegra Mallory checked the rearview mirror of her gorgeous new convertible as she made the turn off Miami's Biscayne Boulevard onto Sixth Street. Her heart sped up as the glossy black truck that was following her, and which she was almost certain belonged to billionaire tycoon Tobias Hunt, cruised up behind her.

Tobias. Six foot two inches of grim, muscled male, with wintry gray eyes, cheekbones to die for and a rock-solid jaw. *The man with whom she had spent one passionate night with two years ago.*

Irritation, and a tension she had no interest in identifying, made her fingers tense on the steering wheel. The last time she had seen Tobias had been at her great-aunt Esmae's funeral just days ago. It went without saying that she had avoided him, which had been easy because a great many people had attended the church service, and then afterward had filled Esmae's beautiful old Hacienda-style beach mansion. However, when her aunt's lawyer's office had called to give her a time for the reading of the will, which would also be attended by Tobias, who happened to be Esmae's step-grandson, avoidance was no longer an option.

Allegra braked for a set of lights. Another glance in her rearview mirror confirmed that he was still on her tail and, out of nowhere, unwilling memories surfaced.

The fact that she had done the one thing she had always promised herself she would never do, have a one-night stand, *and with the last man on the planet she should ever have gone near*, still annoyed her.

Not that she had thought it would be a one-night stand.

At the time, she had been silly enough to think that, because she'd had a crush on Tobias for the last four years, *he was the one* for her, and that this could be the beginning of something deep and real. The kind of relationship her parents had, and which she had always thought would automatically fall into her lap because she was a good person and absolutely deserved to be loved.

The black truck nosed in close behind her in the gridlocked traffic, further dwarfing her car and making her feel distinctly herded. Allegra frowned at the tinted windows that obscured the identity of the driver but, before the truck had gotten too close, she had caught a glimpse of the license plate in her rearview mirror. The legend, *Hunts*—wordplay on Hunt Security—had made her stomach tighten and sent a sharp, unwanted little thrill down her spine.

Not that Tobias was hunting her, she thought firmly. Normally, they were very good at avoiding each other. The only reason he was behind her was that they were both driving to the same place, because they both had to be at the reading of Esmae's will.

Unable to resist, Allegra glanced in her rearview mirror yet again. This time she caught movement and the flash of Miami's hot, morning sun glinting off dark glasses. Another sharp little zing went through her, because Tobias was now looking directly at her, which meant he knew she had been checking him out.

Suddenly aware of how visible she was in her convertible, while Tobias was concealed behind the badass gangster glass, she looked doggedly ahead at the sea of midmorning traffic.

The tension that was still gripping her, and the odd little darts of adrenaline, were simply a product of having to deal with Tobias after the grief of losing Esmae, and her natural apprehension about the will. One thing was certain: she was *not* attracted to Tobias, and she definitely wasn't turned on by him.

Following their one night together, and the fact that, just a few days later, Tobias had been photographed with gorgeous heiress Francesca Messena, her mom—worried that the rejection was making her actually feel *inadequate*—had paid for her to get some professional counseling. To complete her healing, Allegra had also signed up for a number of alternative therapies to purge the memories and release her anger.

One of those therapies, centered on forgiveness, had involved writing forgiveness statements and burning them. The politically correct words had been difficult to write, but the flames had been fun. By the time she had finished, she had also succeeded in doing some helpful research for her spa business, and she had achieved her goal: she was no longer attracted to Tobias.

The light turned green. Allegra accelerated smoothly through the intersection, enjoying the purr of the car's engine while she tried to concentrate on following the verbal instructions of her navigational system, which was speaking to her in a distractingly sexy British accent. Problem was, she enjoyed listening to the deep, male voice so much, she kept forgetting the instructions. Luckily, she had twenty-twenty vision and saw the turn she needed to make directly ahead. Seconds later, she swung into the underground parking garage of the high-rise that housed Esmae's lawyer's ultra-expensive law firm.

Aware that Tobias was, once more, practically tail to bumper with her, she braked at the barrier to take her ticket then accelerated just a little too fast in the vast, dungeon-like lot as she began looking for a space. Because it was downtown and midmorning, and the building contained a busy events center, of course, it was packed.

Allegra caught movement off to the right. She didn't know if a vehicle had gone into a space or was leaving but, on the off chance that it was exiting, she took a right hand turn into the next lane. The payoff for that was that Tobias cruised on straight ahead, so he was no longer tailing her.

But Allegra's relief was short-lived because, seconds later, a pretty woman and her young daughter, who was dressed in a hot-pink leotard, her hair piled on top of her head and glittering with diamantés, exited the car, which had obviously just parked.

On the drive in she had seen the billboards advertising the junior beauty pageant that was taking place at the center, so it was a good bet that the little girl was a contestant. The pretty picture the little girl made spun her back to her days on the beauty pageant circuit, which she had quit when she was sixteen, mostly because she refused to wear pink and rhinestones: not even if she was dead. And if anyone dressed her in pink and rhinestones when she was dead, she would come back to haunt them.

But then her mother had dangled a collegiate pageant that was offering a chunk of cash that would go a long way toward her university costs, plus a car and diamonds. Allegra had mulled it over for a whole five seconds. Should she go for it?

Does a hungry lion lunge at a steak?

In the end it had been a no-brainer, so she had gotten the cash, the car *and* the diamonds. She wasn't so hot on the silver-and-crystal crown, but on down days, sometimes it was nice to wear it.

Frustrated at the seemingly full parking garage, but relentlessly positive, she continued searching for a spot. Her mother, at this point, would ask God to get her a parking space, but that was where she and her mother parted company. Paige Mallory was the pampered only daughter of an old Louisiana family, the Toussaints, an ex–Miss Louisiana beauty queen and a real piece of work. The way Allegra saw it, God was way too busy fixing the mess people had made of the world to park her car for her, so she lifted that burden from His shoulders and did it herself.

There would be a space in here; the ticketing machine wouldn't have let her in otherwise.

She just had to find it before Tobias did.

When she was almost at the end of the lane, she caught the glow of taillights down to the right. Since she didn't think any new cars had entered the building in the last few seconds, that could only mean someone was leaving. At the same time, she caught a second flash of movement off to the left. She frowned. Tobias had also noticed that the car was leaving, and now his muscular black truck was heading straight for the space.

Adrenaline pumped. She came from a family where rules were rules and manners were important. Her father and her four older brothers opened doors for women. Invitations were sent in the mail, not texted; dinner was eaten at a table, with cloth napkins; and important conversations were conducted in a civilized way, face-to-face.

She should do the right thing, wait politely and let him take the space.

But two years ago, Tobias had not done the right thing by her. He had turned their night of passion into a meaningless encounter, then, a couple of days later, had made it even more meaningless by breaking up with her *over the phone*.

Her jaw tightened.

Then, before she could veto the action, her foot jammed down on the accelerator.

Tobias Hunt braked hard as a white convertible, with the name *Madison Spas* emblazoned across its side, made a fast turn out of the lane just ahead, cutting him off then slotting neatly into *his* space.

Even if he hadn't recognized the showy white convertible as he'd driven into town, he would had to have been blind not to recognize the distinctive head of silky chestnut hair piled into a messy knot, the delicate cheekbones and faintly imperious nose half-hidden by a pair of oversize sunglasses.

Allegra Mallory.

A former beauty queen, tagged by prominent social media influencer Buffy Hamilton in her list of "Who's Going to Marry a Billionaire," at a hot *#2*, right behind Buffy, who had listed herself at *#1*.

Maybe that isn't a piece of information that a burned-out-Special-Forces-operative-turned-CEO-of-a-security-conglomerate should know, he thought bleakly, but it was a fact that he'd had significant encounters with both women.

Buffy, clearly intrigued by his rise into the billionaire stratosphere six months ago, when his family trust had finally released his inheritance, had invited him aboard her father's luxurious yacht. He had declined the weekend party for two.

In stark contrast, Allegra, who had strolled into his life six years ago, had never invited him anywhere. All she'd had to do was arrive in Miami with her cool dark gaze, rich list style and Southern stroll to utterly disrupt his life.

As he cruised past, Tobias caught a glimpse of long tanned legs and sexy high heels as Allegra stepped from the car. The sharp visual of her in an emerald green dress and snazzy little jacket that clung to her figure and provided a tantalizing hint of shadowy cleavage, nixed his frustration that he was now going to be late for the reading of Esmae's will.

Jaw taut, he attempted to clamp down on the now-all-too-familiar sharpening masculine interest and the humming tension that Allegra always inspired, as if an electrical current was coursing through his body.

For over half a decade he had worked hard to suppress the potent attraction that had blindsided him when Esmae's niece had first arrived in Miami, just weeks after he had moved in with his longtime girlfriend, Lindsay. An attraction that still seemed as disruptive and all-consuming as it had two years ago when, after breaking up with Lindsay, *because he couldn't forget Allegra*, he had finally given in to temptation and spent one passionate night with her.

In doing so, he had been aware that he had crossed a line. He had become like the father he had spent most of his life trying to forget.

James Hunt hadn't been able to settle into either a good marriage or a bad affair. He had destroyed Tobias's mother's life by leaving her alone and dangling, while he had moved from liaison to liaison with a never-ending string of A-list party girls. Fifteen years ago, he had finally died in a car accident, leaving them to pick up the pieces. Although, it hadn't been soon enough for Alicia Hunt, who had developed a heart condition and passed away just six months later.

Tobias had read the medical reports; he knew the jargon, but that didn't change the fact that his mother had died of a broken heart.

He continued to cruise, but memories of that night kept distracting him from his search for another parking space.

A clear, hot night, the sky brilliant with stars, the French doors of Esmae's beach house flung wide to admit the cooling sea breeze. The sound of waves breaking on the shore, and Allegra Mallory, even more gorgeous naked, sleeping like a baby in the rumpled bed they had shared.

Fingers tensing on the steering wheel, he dismissed the too-vivid images that reminded him that he had done the one thing he had promised himself he wouldn't do. He had stepped into the well-worn tradition of Hunt men, thrown away the rock-solid relationship he had committed to and gone after a glitzy socialite on the make.

And the mistake he had made had had repercussions that still haunted him, because Lindsay, unbeknown to either of them, had been pregnant. As it turned out, she had lost the baby the day after he had slept with Allegra. Although she had been at pains to absolve him of guilt, Tobias was acutely aware that if he had stayed with Lindsay, if he had ignored the attraction to Allegra, the baby, *his child*, might have lived.

Two years ago, weighed down with guilt, sick to his

stomach at the damage he had caused, he had controlled the desire to plunge into a liaison with Allegra that he was well aware could only be based on the magnetic pull of the Hunt billions, and had cut all ties. Their one night together was old history. What really concerned him now was the fact that she was here for the reading of the will.

She was here to collect.

An incoming call distracted him from brooding on exactly what Hunt possessions Esmae had left to her only niece. Tapping the glowing icon on the truck's touch screen, he answered the call from his ex-military buddy, JT. "I know I'm late," he growled. "My flight was delayed. Stall Phillips until I get there."

Damned if he would miss any part of this meeting. Esmae had held shares in Hunt Security. With five percent of the multibillion-dollar firm his family had painstakingly built from nothing up for grabs, and the aristocratic Mallory family's notorious history of swindling and conning his once-dirt-poor family, it was a nobrainer. He had to be there.

JT didn't bother to hide his impatience. "You don't seriously think Esmae left the shares to Allegra? After all, they are *Hunt* shares—"

"That fell into Esmae's hands, because my grandfather neglected to make a new will after he married her, then had the bad luck to die suddenly in a boating accident."

But the real slippery dealing had gone back a generation further than that, to his great-grandfather Jebediah, who had once worked as a ranch hand for Alexandra Mallory until he had gone shares with her in a land purchase. Three years later, in the middle of a drought, and a hot affair with Jebediah, Alexandra had disappeared into the sunset. The lawyer who had cut the ranch in half had somehow managed to give Alexandra the piece that, soon after, became one of the richest oil fields in Texas. Meanwhile, Tobias's family had ended up with a dust bowl that had almost driven them broke.

He clamped down on his impatience. JT was a shark but, as long as their friendship was, he was a newcomer to the firm and hadn't had time to absorb all of the nuances of the Hunt/Mallory saga. "If Esmae was going to play nice with the shares, she would have accepted my father's offer to buy them twenty years ago, but she refused. The only saving grace was that my grandfather had the foresight to sign over ninety-five percent of the business to my father a couple of years before he died, otherwise Hunt Securities would be Mallory Securities."

"But Esmae did give you an undertaking before she died—"

"That was when I was the only beneficiary of Esmae's will. Then, two years ago, Allegra moved to Miami full-time, the will got changed and Esmae decided to keep the new will under wraps." Tobias's gaze broodingly skimmed the ranks of cars. "Esmae made changes she knew I wasn't going to like. Why else keep them a secret?"

His pulse rate lifted as he caught a glimpse of Allegra stepping into an elevator. Her head turned; her gaze clashed with his. A split second later, the doors closed, and the fiction that she hadn't noticed she had cut him off and stolen his parking spot died a death.

Tobias negotiated another tight turn and took the ramp up to the next level, which looked as packed as the one he had left. "The Hunt Security shares should come to me," Tobias said bleakly "but it's a fact that I'm not blood kin to Esmae, and Allegra Mallory is. And, when a Mallory is in the picture, all bets are off."

His great-grandfather Jebediah had known that better

than anyone. "Don't forget, Esmae bankrolled Allegra's spa business, and it's a fact that Allegra has been at Esmae's bedside for a good few months now."

There was a small silence. "You really think Allegra's likely to pull something like that? I've read the online hype, but, hey, let's remember who's writing it. Buffy Hamilton. I mean, *seriously*...?"

Tobias found himself controlling his temper with difficulty, which was unusual, because he never lost his cool, and especially not with JT. They'd spent a tour of duty in Afghanistan together. If there was one person he trusted to have his back, it was JT. "You dated Buffy, so I guess you should know."

"You're beginning to sound like Julia. I spent a weekend on her father's yacht," JT muttered. "There's a difference."

Julia was the girlfriend with whom JT had recently broken up. Tobias frowned. "You didn't tell me that was the reason for the breakup."

"It wasn't. Let's just say there were...other factors, but Julia managed to bring Buffy into the picture."

"You mean there *was* someone else."

Which was no surprise. JT was tall, tanned and blond, with the kind of muscular beach-boy good looks women seemed to find irresistible. He was also the son of a megarich Florida real estate tycoon, so he had no lack of "next" girlfriends.

"Not...exactly. My point is that the *someone else* I was interested in wasn't Buffy."

"Back to the will," Tobias said flatly. "Six months ago, Esmae made Allegra a beneficiary of her *secret* will. That means Esmae's done something I'm not going to like, and whatever it is, Allegra's in it up to her neck."

"I get it that Esmae's been secretive. I just don't think

Allegra's the type to leverage benefits from a dying relative."

Tobias stiffened. The last time he had discussed the will with JT, they had been on the same page. Now, it sounded like JT had joined the Allegra Mallory fan club. "I didn't know you'd met Allegra." *And fallen under her spell.*

There was a brief silence. "As it happens, we, uh, did meet a couple of times. Julia was a client at her spa, used to swear by her herbal wraps and mud baths. And we might have had her over for dinner along with some other friends."

Tobias's jaw tightened. That was an "affirmative" on JT falling under Allegra's spell.

He gave up on the upper-level parking and cruised back down to the lower deck, scanned the rows of cars and finally caught some movement. "I'm guessing that was before you split with Julia."

There was a small, stiff silence. "I'm hardly likely to have had Allegra over for dinner otherwise."

"No," Tobias said softly, "because that would be a date."

JT and Julia had split up a month ago. Tobias now had to wonder if Allegra was the reason JT's relationship had foundered. If she was running true to the online hype, she could be angling for JT to be her next wealthy lover.

Grimly, he accelerated toward the area he had seen the car leaving. "There's only one reason I asked you to be present at the reading of the will, and that's because something's up. I wouldn't have needed you, otherwise. I'll see you in a few minutes."

Tobias terminated the call.

JT and Allegra. He had not seen that coming.

And it would be happening over his dead body.

As luck would have it, the vacant space was just two down from where Allegra's stylish convertible was parked.

He checked his watch. His annoyance shot up another notch when he noted that he was now a good ten minutes late. Exiting the truck, he locked it, strode toward the elevators and punched in the number of the floor. As the elevator sped upward, he remembered the last interview he'd had with Esmae, who, even at ninety-two, had been strong-willed, imperious and just a tad manipulative.

All recognizable Mallory traits.

From odd things his step-grandmother had let drop, Tobias knew that Esmae had done something out of the ordinary with the will. The fact that she had kept it secret, and that he had not had access to a copy of it, was the final confirmation.

Allegra's presence at the reading guaranteed that the changes involved Esmae's great-niece.

The doors slid open. He strode into the plush offices of Esmae's lawyer's law firm and was directed to her lawyer Phillips's office. As he stepped through the door, his gaze automatically settled on Allegra. Her dark glance clashed with his. Despite bracing himself for the moment, every muscle in his body tightened.

Not for the first time it occurred to him that, usually with women, he could walk away clean. When it was over, it was over. But when it came to Allegra, the usual rules hadn't applied.

Neither had time and distance, or the guilt that had gnawed at him, worked their magic. Despite searching out and dating other women who should have been perfect for him, just as his ex Lindsay had been, he still wanted Allegra Mallory.

Join the club with who-knew-how-many other men, including JT.

A little grimly, he refreshed himself on the past record of Mallory and Hunt liaisons.

Alexandra Mallory had slept with Jebediah, then scammed him, making herself even richer in the process. That was strike one.

Seventy years ago, Esmae had escaped the financial crash that had nixed the fabled Mallory fortune and solved the family's poverty problem by jumping on his grandfather Michael Hunt's newly minted money train. Strike two.

Esmae had been beautiful, but Allegra, with her rich hair, delicately molded cheekbones, firm jaw and wide mouth, was next-level gorgeous.

Even so, there was no way in hell he was going to let Allegra Mallory carry on the family tradition with him.

There was not going to be a strike three.

Two

Allegra dragged her gaze from the brooding, magnetic challenge of Tobias's, as if in taking the parking space *he* had wanted, and making him a good fifteen minutes late for the appointment, she had thrown down a gauntlet.

And he had picked it up.

Guilt that she had behaved so aggressively, and other less distinct and more disturbing sensations that coiled in the pit of her stomach, was almost instantly replaced by fiery irritation. She couldn't help thinking that it was not a bad thing that, for once in his life, Tobias hadn't gotten something he wanted just because he had wanted it.

Taking a measured breath, she smoothed out her expression. But maintaining any level of calm was difficult, because when Tobias stepped into the room, with his broad shoulders, cool gray gaze and that palpable air of command, he took up all the air.

Her fingers automatically went to the simple-but-classy diamond bracelet at her wrist, which had been part of that last prize package she had won as a beauty queen. Wearing the diamonds had been a conscious choice for this meeting, not just because diamonds went with *everything*, but because the jewelry reminded her that she was successful and goal oriented, and that her life was not defined by others' mistakes.

And, it was a fact that in the last two and a half years, following a fake scandal that had ended the high-flying business career in San Francisco that she had sweated blood to attain, she'd had to forgive a lot of those kinds of mistakes.

Determinedly ignoring Tobias and his smooth-talking lawyer, JT, she directed a cool glance at Phillips. "Perhaps we should start? I have an appointment at twelve that I don't want to miss."

The appointment was with a funky little vegan café that made her favorite herb-and-nut salad, and chocolate bliss balls that were to die for, but no one here needed to know that.

"And we wouldn't want you to be late," Tobias said in a soft, curt voice that made her stomach clench.

Doing her best to control the flush that warmed her cheeks, Allegra kept her gaze firmly on Phillips, who was looking at her in a measuring way as he handed her a copy of the will. After six months with a finance firm that had seemed filled with men who, apparently, hadn't yet grasped that women could look attractive and still have schedules and priorities that did not include them, she had gotten used to that look.

Apparently, because she had inherited the chestnut Mallory hair and her mother's dark eyes and traffic-stopping figure, men found it difficult to take her seriously. That was their problem, totally, but she was a helpful person and usually, in a business setting, she did her best to tone down her appearance.

However, today, with Tobias in the mix, she hadn't been inclined to tone down *anything*. The dress she was wearing discreetly hugged her curves, revealed a hint of cleavage and was short enough to showcase her long legs, which were possibly her best feature. The matching bolero jacket gave the outfit a more business feel while at the same time emphasizing the way the dress cinched in at her waist and that her bust size—courtesy of her mom—was a "don't mess with me" 36C.

Instead of a sophisticated French pleat, she had gone for a looser, messier knot, which looked great with a pair of diamond Chanel earrings that had been a graduation gift from her father. As a gift, the earrings had been a little over-the-top. Her brothers had been annoyed because they had only gotten watches, but what could she say? She was Daddy's girl.

In any case, the dress and the jacket—besides giving her the pampered, high-end look she needed in her business—were by the newest, hottest designer in the business: Francesca Messena.

Maybe it might seem strange that she would wear clothing made and designed by the woman she had learned had slept with Tobias both before *and* after he had slept with her. But the way Allegra saw it, buying Francesca's clothing was a clear sign that she had healed and moved on, and that the stinging sense of betrayal when Tobias had ditched her in favor of Francesca had been utterly banished from her psyche.

And, of course, it went without saying that, as part of her recovery process, she had forgiven Francesca. It had taken a while—she had burned a whole ream of forgiveness statements before the job got done—but she had kept reminding herself that Francesca was basically a good person. She simply hadn't known how big a rat Tobias was. Besides, why should she be denied the clothes she wanted to wear just because Tobias had been briefly included in both of their lives?

To not wear the Messena brand was to say that Allegra lived in a universe where Tobias controlled what she did and did not wear, and last she heard, Tobias was *not* the ruler of the universe.

As Phillips started reading, Allegra skimmed the first page, aware that, somewhere within the document, there was going to be a surprise she was not going to like. That surprise could only have to do with Madison Spas, because the only reason she was here was that Esmae held fifty percent of the shares.

Too late to wish she hadn't let her aunt invest, and that she had done what she had originally planned and taken out a loan with her own bank.

Just four months ago, when Allegra had learned Esmae was terminal, she had even offered to buy out the shares, but Esmae had said there was no need, since she was leaving them to Allegra in her will. That would have been all well and good, except that Esmae had then point-blank refused to let Allegra see a copy of the will.

Now she was braced for a worst-case scenario. She could be about to lose control of the business she had started, and which she loved with passion, to Tobias Hunt!

Extracting her reading glasses from her handbag, she slipped them on and attempted to concentrate on the legalese. Normally, she was very good at speed-reading and picking out the main points, courtesy of a master's degree in finance, but with Tobias pacing Phillips's overlarge office like a large, caged cat, it was difficult to concentrate.

By the third page in, she was beginning to relax, then Phillips delivered the kind of punch line that had her re-reading the clause.

Live in Esmae's beach mansion, for a whole month with Tobias, or she would lose the shares in her business?

She went hot, then cold, then hot again. She reread the clause, just in case there had been a mistake.

There wasn't, and in that moment, a mistake *she* had made came back to haunt her.

After spending that one night with Tobias, she had been indiscreet enough to tell Esmae what had happened. The words had practically burst out of her because she had been so confident that she was on the brink of the kind of deep, life-altering relationship with Tobias that she had secretly hoped would be in her future.

Predictably, Esmae had been reserved. Even though she had married a Hunt, she knew that if there was one man Allegra shouldn't have slept with, it was Tobias, because the acrimony that had existed between the Hunts and the Mallorys for a good three generations was, apparently, still alive and well.

Too late to regret telling Esmae her deepest, darkest secret. A secret her aunt had promised not to tell.

Now, it was suddenly looking like the past wasn't buried after all, because it seemed that Esmae was attempting to matchmake from beyond the grave.

Of course, there was a thin possibility that this might not be about matchmaking. Esmae, the only Mallory who had ever actually married a Hunt—a second marriage to Tobias's grandfather—could simply be trying to help the two families reconcile their differences. Although that didn't make sense since, now that Esmae was gone, there was literally nothing to tie the two families together.

Allegra frowned. Two years ago, when she had confided in Esmae, had she been silly enough to speculate that marriage might be in their future?

An embarrassing, too-vivid memory surfaced. That would be a *yes* on mentioning the marriage word.

She drew an impeded breath, abruptly aware that Tobias was standing, arms folded across his chest, gun-metal-gray eyes trained on her, as if he believed the "living together" clause had been her handiwork.

As if she had manipulated Esmae into changing the will because she still wanted Tobias.

A slow, deep flush warmed her cheeks. *As if.*

JT, whom she knew on a casual basis because his ex-girlfriend Julia used to be a regular client at Madison Spas, seemed more relaxed, but there was no mistaking the same cold, incisive gaze.

Mortification aside, the combined presence of Tobias and JT, in theory, should have made her feel embattled, like a small animal cornered by a powerful and efficient wolf pack. But it was a fact that she had grown up with four very large older brothers and, by the time she had turned five, that tactic hadn't worked for them, either.

Taking a deep breath, Allegra forced herself to relax. She was doing exactly what her therapist had advised her not to do: overstressing. The problem was she liked to be in control, and ever since Esmae had died, everything had been distinctly out of control.

She took another slow, deep breath and closed her eyes for just a second as she attempted to center herself by using a visualization recommended by her Christian meditation instructor. Unfortunately, the calming image of a limpid, moonlit lake seemed to have developed a roiling whirlpool right at the center.

Her lids flickered open; Tobias's gaze locked with hers before dropping to her mouth. Another one of those stomach-clenching electrical tingles ran through her, as if, deep down, at some primitive level, her body couldn't help but respond to Tobias.

But that couldn't be, she thought, briskly, since she was over him. They were *over one another*.

It would be a chilly day in hell before either of them would willingly choose to share personal space.

Although, it was looking like there was no way to avoid it.

Tobias said something short and flat under his breath, "So, there's no way out of this."

Annoyed at the way his statement mirrored her own thought, her gaze clashed with his again, which was a mistake, because another jolt of tingling heat set her even more on edge.

Tobias moved so that his broad shoulders blocked a good deal of the hot sun streaming through the window of Phillips's office. He pinned Phillips with that remote, unnerving gaze, and suddenly the stories about Tobias's time in the military as some kind of Special Forces ghost seemed to gather force.

"Let me get this right. If I don't share the house with Allegra, I lose shares in *my* business."

The edge to Tobias's statement underlined his annoyance that there was a lot more at stake for him than for Allegra, courtesy of the fact that he was the CEO of a multibillion-dollar security firm. She was also aware that the shares that Tobias's grandfather had left to Esmae several years ago weren't just ordinary shares, they were a crucial chunk of voting shares. That meant that whoever held them had the right to vote on matters of corporate policy.

She had no idea how much they would be worth. Although, given Tobias's bread-and-butter security products like house and car alarms, his extremely expensive detective agency and VIP security service, and other whispers about military contracts and satellites, she guessed the figure could be in the millions.

Phillips, who had an ex-military look himself, with a short crisp haircut and a square jaw, flipped a page, as if he had to refresh himself on the type of clause that no lawyer was likely to forget. "That's correct."

Allegra coolly redirected Phillips's attention back to her. "And if I don't live in my great-aunt's house for a month, I'll lose shares in *my* business to Tobias?" She wasn't worth millions, or even billions like Tobias. Her net worth was more in the six figures range, if you counted her mortgage, but even so… "Madison Spas is important to me, and it's not, exactly, worth peanuts—"

Philips gave her the kind of politely disbelieving look that signaled that, at some point in the proceedings, he had joined Tobias's wolf pack. "The terms set for both sets of shares are there in black-and-white Miss Mallory, clause 16 C."

Tobias, who had moved to prop himself on the edge of the lawyer's enormous mahogany desk, crossed his arms over his chest. "I'm not exactly interested in picking up shares in your beauty business—"

"It's *not* a beauty salon." Aware that her voice was just a little too clipped, she forced herself to do a silent count to five.

When it came to dealing with strong alpha males like Tobias, responding in emotional ways was a complete waste of time. Knowledge and logic were what counted but, according to her mother, there was another, even more effective, tactic. It contained no logic whatsoever: you just looked for an opportunity to say *no*.

She met Tobias's gaze squarely and tried to ignore the

fact that his expensive masculine cologne was having an annoyingly distracting effect on her. "As I'm sure you know, Madison Spas is an exclusive spa and retreat center specializing in de-stressing therapies and holistic living."

"Which is exactly my point. It's not, exactly, my line of business."

"I'm glad you made that point," Allegra said smoothly, "because producing homogenous boxes of car alarms and door locks doesn't exactly interest me, either."

There was a brief silence. "Hunt Security does more than make locks and alarms."

"Oh, I forgot…you also have some kind of a detective agency."

JT made a muffled sound, somewhere between a cough and a laugh.

A gleam of something close to amusement surfaced in Tobias's gaze. "I guess that's one way of describing Hunt Private Investigations."

Allegra suddenly realized that fighting with Tobias was just a little too…exhilarating. The last thing she needed was to open the door on a dangerously addictive attraction that was officially stone-dead.

She sent him a chilly smile. Tobias might be rich and powerful now, but her family, despite being cash-strapped for the last couple of generations, had once been wealthy and successful, too.

JT, who, until that moment, hadn't taken any part in the conversation, caught her eye, which was startling, because for the past twenty minutes, despite the fact that he had been quite friendly to her in the past, he had studiously ignored her. "Maybe you should give Allegra a break, Tobias. You know what Esmae was like…headstrong, unpredictable—"

"If you're trying to suggest Esmae might have had

dementia," Phillips interceded, "forget it. She had a test just a few months ago to confirm that she was of sound mind, just in case anyone tried to overturn the will."

JT frowned. "If she didn't have dementia, why write a will like that?"

Allegra didn't miss the implication. If Esmae was of sound mind, then someone else had to have applied pressure on her to write those crazy, eccentric clauses into the will. And, since Tobias would never willingly choose to share a house with her, of course, she had to be the culprit.

Over the innuendoes and veiled insults, she returned her glasses to their case and tucked it in her bag, then rose smoothly to her feet. If there was ever a time to deploy her mother's "no" tactic, and get some power back, this was it. "Contrary to what you all seem to believe, I don't know what on earth possessed my aunt to put that clause in the will, because she *knew* chapter and verse that I'd rather be stranded on a desert island than spend one night under the same roof as Tobias."

She shot Tobias a chilly look, just to make sure he had gotten the *no* message. That not only that she didn't want him, but that she would *never* want him. "Literally, wild horses couldn't drag me. Ever."

A heated, distinctly sexual tingle shot through her when she noted that his gaze was narrowed and glittering and fixed on hers. As if somehow her complete denial had had the complete opposite effect she had intended. That instead of being offended, he had *liked* what she had said.

As if her total, utter rejection had turned him on.

Three

Tobias frowned. "If Esmae knew there was no point putting us in the same house together, why bother?"

It was the wrong question to ask. Two years ago, Allegra had been vulnerable and off-balance after what had happened in San Francisco, and too trusting of Tobias. Now, she was older, smarter and a whole lot more ticked off. "Maybe Esmae put that clause in her will for your sake, not mine."

He folded his arms across his chest. "Okay, I'll play. Why did Esmae think I needed to live with you for a month?"

"Francesca Messena," she said succinctly. "And her twin, Sophie…although, not so much."

It occurred to her that Francesca Messena had been relaxed, vivacious, the kind of woman men were naturally drawn to and loved to date. On the other hand, Sophie had had a reputation for being distant and controlled, more interested in business than men. *More like herself.*

The sudden thought that Tobias had never truly been attracted to her because, like Sophie Messena, she was *not his type*, made her feel even more annoyed. If she was not Tobias's type, that meant the one-night stand they had shared had been even more meaningless than she had thought.

Tobias pinched his nose. "Why are we talking about the Messena twins?"

Jaw tight at the conclusion she had just drawn, that Tobias had slept with her without even liking who she was, Allegra plowed on. "Do I have to paint a picture? You pursued both of the Messena twins—"

"I wouldn't call it pursued, exactly."

"We can split hairs all day long," she said coolly, "but the point is that, just a few months ago, both sisters got hitched in a double wedding to *other* men."

"I recall the wedding, since I was a guest."

"Which is exactly what I'm getting at. Not to put too fine a point on it, but Esmae knew that your love life had, shall we say, hit a downward slope. Clearly she was concerned that you were having trouble finding someone—"

"So she decided to give me a little help."

She rewarded Tobias with the same kind of professional smile she gave her spa clients when they reached a fitness milestone. "Just a theory."

Phillips cleared his throat, the noise punctuating the tense silence that had descended on the room. "As riveting as all of this is, you can't leave yet, Miss Mallory. There's, uh…more."

Allegra blinked, for a moment she had been so consumed with correcting Tobias that she had forgotten about the will. Even worse, she had done the one thing she had promised herself she would not do—she had become emotional.

Adrenaline still humming through her veins, she sat down.

Almost immediately, Phillips began working his way through the fine print of the will, dealing with special bequests. The Hunt jewelry, apparently a massive haul of soulless diamonds that were kept in a bank vault, went to Tobias. When Phillips mentioned a box of Mallory keepsakes, and a painting of Alexandra Mallory, Esmae's mother and Allegra's great-grandmother, she frowned.

She hadn't known a painting existed. Neither had she thought anything was left of Alexandra's life, because the family fortune had been wiped out. "Are these keepsakes also in the bank vaults?"

Phillips consulted a separate page sitting on his desk. "No, they're not. I assume the items are memorabilia and of no particular value, because your aunt stored them in the attic of the beach house."

As fascinating as it was to hear that Esmae, who had been Alexandra's only daughter, had preserved some memorabilia, the final dry clause made her stiffen.

Esmae had, of course, left her five-star resort, the luxurious Ocean Beach Resort, which she had built with Hunt money, to Tobias, with a catch. Unless he personally managed it for the first month, *the exact time she and Tobias had to share the beach mansion*, ownership, in full, was transferred to her.

For a moment, Allegra was too stunned to react. The "living together" clause had made it look like she was trying to trap Tobias into marriage; this one made her look like a scheming gold digger on the make.

She was abruptly spun back two and a half years, to the moment her financial career had crashed and burned because two executives at the firm she had just started at had both accused her of trying to trade sex for money, promotions and even jewelry, and all because she had gotten tired of the usual singles dating scene and had made the fatal mistake of trying an online, "executive" dating site.

Admittedly, she had dated one of them, Halliday, *once*. She hadn't known that he was an executive of the firm that had employed her, because he had been away from the San Francisco office for a number of weeks setting up the new San Diego branch, *and* he had been using a fake name. Even though he was married, *to the boss's daughter*, he had been trolling online, pretending to be single. Annoyed when she had uncovered his true identity and then had said an absolute *no* to an office affair, he had then made a preemptive strike to protect his career and his marriage by claiming on social media that she had offered to sleep with him to get a promotion.

If that wasn't bad enough, another executive of the same firm, Fischer, a close friend of Halliday's, and a nephew of one of the partners, who was also married and using the same dating site, had then cornered her and propositioned her in her office. When he had refused to take *no* for an answer, because, apparently the fact that she was an ex-beauty queen meant that *no* didn't mean *no*, she had been forced to fend him off with a large stapler.

Unfortunately, the glancing blow to his jaw had left a bruise and drawn blood from his lip. To make matters worse, he had reeled back, tripped over a chair and ended up on the floor. At that point, maybe he would have slunk away and said nothing, but another new intern had walked in on them. Face red with embarrassment, Fischer had stormed out, then proceeded to also smear her online, claiming that she had attempted to seduce him and had wanted expensive jewelry in payment.

As a result, she had been hauled before the firm's disciplinary committee. Even though their findings had been "inconclusive," *because there was no evidence*, apparently the scandal had made her position at the firm a "problem." She was pretty sure the "problem" part of her employment had been locked in when she had used the forum to give the managing partners a piece of her mind.

Maybe she should have zipped it, but she didn't like injustice, and the reluctance of her bosses to actually investigate, because of nepotism, had been the last straw. If they lied and covered up for their own executives, she could not recommend that anyone trust their money to them. Using that same logic, she could no longer entrust her career and her talents to them, either, so she had quit.

Unfortunately, her victorious exit had been somewhat marred by the manifestation of a mysterious medical condition called SVT, supraventricular tachycardia. That was a complicated term for the fact that, every once in a blue moon, her heart would pound out of control and, if it didn't naturally regulate itself, she needed medical intervention to bring it back to its normal rate. It was a condition that had started up when she had been in college and which her doctor had told her was probably due to the fact that she was a type A personality. In layman's terms that meant she had control-freak tendencies and didn't handle stress well.

She registered that Tobias had said something short and flat, and that JT was lodging his protest with Phillips in succinct lawyer-speak. But, in that moment, she wasn't concerned about either Phillips or JT.

Her gaze clashed with Tobias's. "There's a simple solution. I'll get *my* lawyer to draw up a document that relinquishes all rights—"

"Take a look at clause C," he said. "If you give up your rights to the hotel, and then if I fail to manage it for the next month, it goes to the eldest of your next of kin who is, I believe, your brother, Quin."

She read the next clause, and her stomach sank. There was no way Quin, who already owned a very successful boutique hotel in New Orleans, would release Tobias from the clause. He would take the Ocean Beach Resort in a New York minute.

She fixed Tobias with a level look. "I have no idea what's going on here. The only conversation Esmae and I had was about the shares she held in Madison Spas, and that was because I wanted to buy her out four months ago—"

"So the whole thing about living together wasn't your idea?"

She froze in the middle of refolding the will. "Hmmm, let me see… Go and live in an isolated, overstuffed mansion with the last man on earth I would ever want to share any personal space with?"

She rose to her feet, hooked the strap of her handbag over her shoulder and checked the sleek white smartwatch that encircled her wrist, which indicated she had missed an incoming call from Janice, her receptionist. "That would be no, and no."

Tobias didn't bother to hide his disbelief. "In other words, Esmae thought this up all by herself?"

"Yes." Out of nowhere, her heart began to pound and her stomach tightened around a cold, hard lump of dread that, once again, her reputation was going to be shredded for something she hadn't done. That the lies and deceit that had destroyed her financial career would somehow taint her new business enterprise and destroy that, too.

Although, that wasn't likely to happen, she thought crisply. She was her own boss. This time no one could pressure her to leave.

Although, Tobias could refuse to renew her lease.

That would create difficulties, because she would have to relocate the spa. She was currently looking at new premises for a second spa, but that would take months to set up. If she had to move the business in the next few weeks, she wouldn't have anywhere to go.

Taking a calming breath, she did a slow, internal count to three. If she could retain her current premises, that was definitely the best option, which meant she needed to correct Tobias's false assumption.

She pinned Phillips with a cool glance. "Have you ever seen me before?"

He froze, as if he was under cross-examination. "Uh, not that I can remember."

"That's right, because we have never met. And why would we? You were my aunt's lawyer dealing with her private, personal affairs. Things that have nothing at all to do with me."

Tobias's brows jerked together. "The fact that you didn't meet with Phillips doesn't prove a thing."

Allegra transferred her gaze to Tobias. "You think I took advantage of Esmae while she was on her sickbed and influenced her to change her will. But, if that was the case, why didn't I ask for more, and outright? Like the house and the diamonds, for example? Very expensive assets that she left to you.

"And, before you ask, no, I don't want the house, and I definitely don't want the diamonds—I'm quite capable of getting my own—and I don't need to prove anything about the will. Maybe you should start remembering that I've lived in Miami for just over two years. During that time we've been in the same room, maybe, five times total. Two of those occasions have happened within the space of the last few days—at Esmae's funeral and now.

If that's your idea of pursuit, then your love life must have flatlined."

She shoved her copy of the will into her handbag.

Maybe she should have ignored what Tobias had said, but his statement that she was pursuing him had cut too close to the bone because she *had* pursued him, past tense, and been rejected.

On top of that, this whole situation, of being in a room with men who seemed to view her as a woman prepared to use her sex to get what she wanted, was an unpleasant reminder of what she had gone through in San Francisco.

She started for the door, but Tobias reached it first and held it open.

The gesture reminded her that, even online, Tobias had a reputation for being honorable to a fault, and a gentleman. Not that she had experienced that side of his personality.

She sent him a fiery glance and tried not to notice the mouthwatering cut of his cheekbones, or the intriguing hollows beneath, the scar that ran across the bridge of his nose, as if he'd been caught in a bar room brawl or, more likely, been involved in some form of hand-to-hand combat. Unbidden, her stomach tightened at the thought of Tobias in warrior-mode. On the heels of that, a vivid memory of lying in bed with him, their limbs entangled, sent heat flashing through her. Then, she pulled herself up and she was *back*. "You're pointing the finger at me, but maybe *you* were the one who influenced Esmae?"

"Okay, I'll bite," he said mildly. "Why would I want to have you living in my house for a month?"

"Because you're secretly in love with me, can't resist me and, last I heard, it's the only way you'll get a date!"

Stepping through the door, she closed it in his face.

* * *

Tobias stared at the smooth mahogany of the door, his attention riveted.

He had tried not to notice the faint sprinkling of freckles across Allegra's nose that reminded him of the windblown young woman who used to hang out at the beach, and the warm flush that had extended across her cheekbones as she'd stared at the scar on his nose.

Or his sudden conviction that Allegra still wanted him.

The knowledge tightened every muscle in Tobias's body, which did not please him one little bit, because Allegra wanting him was the one reason that made sense of Esmae's crazy, manipulative will.

The crack about his difficulty getting a date made him frown. The past couple of years, up until his uncle had retired as the CEO of Hunt Security, he'd been focused on learning the financial side of business. He had spent six months with Gabriel Messena and *had* dated the Messena twins, as it had turned out, on a strictly friend-zone basis.

He had been aware of social media comments around the fact that both Sophie and Francesca Messena had ended up with other guys. But the plain fact was, that as gorgeous as Sophie and Francesca were, they had felt more like sisters than girlfriends.

Now, suddenly, the fact that Allegra had been his last serious date in more than two years struck him forcibly.

Up until that point, he hadn't thought about the lack in his love life, but now his reaction to Allegra, *and hers to him*, was pressing alarm bells.

It was a fact that the reason he had dated Francesca Messena, before and after he had slept with Allegra, was that he had wanted to, once and for all, nix the attraction he felt for Allegra. *And close the door on the "almost" relationship that had caused Lindsay so much pain.*

Unfortunately, the tactic hadn't worked. Dating Francesca hadn't made him stop wanting Allegra.

All she had to do was walk into a room and he reacted—

Phillips, who at some point had gotten to his feet, was also staring at the door. "You going to be all right for the next month? She's, uh…fiery."

"I'll survive."

Even though she'd gone, Allegra's light, flowery perfume seemed to float in the air. Normally, details like the perfumes that women wore went straight over his head, but with Allegra he had trouble forgetting the details. Like the freckles, and the fact that she was wearing the exact same fragrance she had worn when they had made love.

It was a salient reminder that, two years ago, despite all of the reasons he should have left Allegra alone, he *hadn't* been able to resist her. He had abandoned his usual cool reason and had allowed himself to sink into the kind of whirlpool of passion from which it had been difficult to extract himself.

It had taken a bitter phone call from Lindsay, to make him do what he should have done all along, and run a basic online check of Allegra. When he had done so, he had discovered that she had recently been involved in romantic liaisons with at least two West Coast millionaires. The guilt Tobias had felt aside, he had concluded that the one night he and Allegra had shared, as intense as it had been, had been nothing more than another casual liaison.

Plan to have Allegra live with him for a month?

It hadn't been his idea. Maybe Esmae had inserted the clause for the hell of it, to make his life difficult one last time? But, whether Allegra had had a hand in the will or not, the very fact that Esmae, who had doted on her niece, had inserted those clauses, implied that she had done so because she knew Allegra wanted him.

Tobias's pulse rate lifted at the thought.

And there was his problem, he thought grimly. For reasons he couldn't fathom, he still wanted Allegra. There was no logic to it, just a knee-jerk desire that had stayed with him for six years. A desire he had doggedly ignored in the hope it would peter out.

Unfortunately, ignoring what he could only term a fatal attraction hadn't worked.

As he stepped out of Phillips's office, with JT hard on his heels, it occurred to him that maybe it was time to try the tactic he should have used all along.

Let the attraction play out over the next month and die a natural death, like every other attraction to date.

After all, living with Allegra for a month according to the terms of Esmae's will didn't mean anything more than just that. They were sharing a house. If they shared a bed that hardly constituted a relationship, or the marriage for which Esmae was clearly angling.

His whole body tightened at the thought of Allegra back in his bed.

Just one month, and then it would be over.

He didn't know why he hadn't thought of that solution before. Maybe if he had, he would already be free of the inconvenient attraction that to date had nixed every relationship he had attempted to form in the past six years.

He caught sight of Allegra at the end of the corridor as she waited for the elevator to empty. She glanced his way, as if she had sensed him behind her, her gaze clashing with his.

JT, who was in the process of checking his phone, lifted his head. "Maybe she'll hold the elevator for us."

And hell might freeze over.

Given the way Allegra had cut in front of him to take the parking space that morning, then closed Phillips's door in his face, it was a given that she would shut them out.

His jaw compressed as the steel doors glided closed, but at the same time, he felt a fierce jolt of satisfaction, because Allegra hadn't just shut him out; she had also shut out JT. Clearly they weren't as close as JT thought.

Tobias hit the call button on the only other elevator. As he checked the numbers flashing over the door, it occurred to him that the eye contact with Allegra as the elevator doors had closed was an almost-exact replay of what had happened down in the parking garage. That confirmed that she had known he had tailed her into the parking garage and then had deliberately cut him off.

Perversely, the fact that she was boldly crossing swords with him in a way no other woman had ever done, ignited something primitive in him; the urge to answer the challenge when, if he was smart, he would just wait out the month and let her go.

But, even as he formed the thought, he knew he wouldn't do it.

Despite what Allegra had said, he wasn't convinced that she hadn't had a hand in Esmae's will, but the fact that she wanted him seemed to override even that consideration.

The thought of her lying naked in his arms once again made every muscle in his body tighten.

Suddenly, the next month didn't seem like such a prison sentence.

Four

Allegra watched with satisfaction as the floor numbers flashed while the elevator descended to the underground garage.

The moment she had seen Tobias exiting Phillips's office with JT directly behind him replayed. Adrenaline had pumped as Tobias's eyes had locked with hers. That in itself had been annoying, but not as annoying as the fact that, evidently, he had expected her to *want* to stay eye-locked with him as he had strode toward her.

As if she was some kind of Barbie doll robot just waiting for him to activate her.

No way was Tobias even remotely that important in her life, so she had stepped into the elevator and hit the close door button. It was a small act of revenge but, after the scene in Phillips's office, there was no way either Tobias or JT should expect to share an elevator with her. Happily, she had timed things nicely, so they hadn't even been close when the doors had snapped shut, sealing her into blissful isolation.

On the way down, she checked her hair and makeup in the mirror. Despite all of the turmoil, she looked almost as smooth and composed as she had when she'd left home. That was thanks to the beauty pageant circuit, which had taught her that, no matter what went on in the dressing rooms, you stepped out on the stage with a smile on your face.

Humming beneath her breath, she found her ear pods, put them in her ears and dialed up some soothing music on her phone, then spent the remaining seconds watching the numbers flash over the door until the elevator came to a halt. A few seconds later, an elderly man sporting a cane, who was cute and kind of reminded her of her granddad, trundled in the door and peered at the numbers, as if he was confused.

A quick conversation, and the press of a button, and she had him sorted out. As the elevator lurched into action again, she realized she was still breathing a little too fast. Technically, she was hyperventilating, which was not good. She needed to breathe deep and slow.

The elevator stopped for the old guy to get off, and while she waited for the doors to close and start speeding down again, she checked the heart rate app on her watch. The last thing she needed was another SVT event, because those attacks, as easy as they were to fix, were *scary*.

Just over two years ago, when she had ended up in the ER, following the "interview" with the partners at Burns-Stein Halliday, she had listened to her doctor's advice then consulted the oracle—that was her mom—before deciding to make some changes in her life.

Both of her parents had wanted to bring charges

against Burns-Stein Halliday for sexual harassment in the workplace. Her mom had even threatened to "go over there," and that was some scary stuff. But Allegra definitely hadn't wanted the stress of a court case, which could have landed her back in the hospital, or worse.

The last thing she had wanted was to *die* or end up in some clinic somewhere, making baskets, all because BSH was a horrible employer. The way she saw it, she owed it to her parents, and the world at large (not BSH, she didn't owe them anything) to stay happy, and stay alive.

Once she had made the decision not to sue BSH, it had been an easy step to embrace a career that was founded on the two things she knew she was good at: money *and* beauty.

A few weeks holiday with Esmae in her private beach mansion had given her the inspiration she needed to start up her own retreat spa.

Esmae, who had been something of a risk-taker and adventurer in her younger days, had offered to back her, mostly because she was tired of being treated like she was old and washed-up, and so Madison Spas had been born. The name *Madison* had seemed appropriate, because that was a second name they both shared.

The spa had been up and running for almost two years now, and, in that time, she had expanded to offer a number of beauty and pampering treatments. Lately, it had become something of a destination for burned-out celebrities needing to recharge, hence her need to open a second retreat, this one in a more remote location.

She had already earmarked a possible property. Once she got past the hurdle of the next month, she would be able to have a conversation with her bank manager and arrange the finances she needed to expand.

In the meantime, Esmae's will had literally locked her and Tobias together for the next month.

Logically, she had known that the resort would go to Tobias, because the place had been built on Hunt money. She just hadn't thought he would turn up in person to take over as manager.

Now, not only was her life totally ruined for the next four weeks because she had to share a house with Tobias, but Esmae had also managed to throw them together in their working lives!

The terms of the will had left zero doubt that Esmae was attempting to matchmake from beyond the grave. And, to make matters worse, Allegra was pretty much sure it *was* all her fault, because, somehow, Esmae had gotten the mistaken idea that she still wanted Tobias.

The elevator doors opened to the darkened underground garage.

Strolling at a moderate pace, because her shoes were too high for anything more than a sedate saunter, and still listening to the soothing music, she made a beeline for her car. The sound of the second set of elevator doors opening behind her, which she could still hear quite well because the ear pods were the expensive kind that let you hear everything else as well as the music, sent tension humming through her. Despite the temptation to speed up her pace, she kept her gait smooth and even. So what if it was Tobias? He didn't scare her—

"Allegra."

Despite her confidence, the deep, curt tones of his voice made her stomach tighten, but she kept her pace smooth and unaltered. After all, she had *ear pods* in; chances were she hadn't heard him.

The sound of footsteps sent tension humming through her. As tempting as it was to speed up, she kept her languid stroll, but took out her phone for good measure, so Tobias could see she was doubly busy.

The next second her phone rang. It registered an unknown caller, but she knew exactly who it was.

She hit the accept call button. "How did you get my number?"

Tobias's deep, curt voice filled her ear. "You gave it to me two years ago."

Wrong answer. "I took it back."

"Then I guess I must have forgotten to delete it."

"What do you want?"

"Turn around and find out."

Stabbing the disconnect button, she threw a seemingly confused look over her shoulder, as if she hadn't understood that Tobias, accompanied by JT, had been behind her all along. "Oh, it's…you."

She made a show of removing the ear pods. "Sorry. Were you trying to talk to me?"

Amusement surfaced in Tobias's gaze. He dangled a key. "You're going to need this."

Allegra instantly recognized the pretty beaded key chain, because it was the same one she had used when she had lived with Esmae, before she'd found her apartment.

Taking care not to brush his fingers with hers, she took the key but, as she did so, emotion welled up. It was still so hard to believe that Esmae, who had made her feel so at home in Miami, was gone.

She met Tobias's gaze squarely, suddenly glad she had decided to wear such ridiculously high heels, otherwise she would have had to tip her head back to do so. "Thanks. Although, for the record, I do not want to live with you—"

"We won't be *living* together."

Her gaze narrowed. The knowledge that, despite everything she had said in Phillips's office, Tobias really did think she was after him, and was scheming to trap him, settled in.

She had always wondered where the impulse to hit someone came from. Now, she knew.

JT offered Allegra a good-ole-boy smile. "Honey, I think Tobias knows you don't want to *live* with him. I mean, you've already said why, chapter and verse—"

"Don't call me Honey." The words flowed out, cool and crisp, cutting JT off, so that he stared at her, surprised.

Allegra hadn't meant to offend JT, who was an occasional client, especially not when he had been defending her. But he hadn't exactly been her friend in Phillips's office, and, since the horrible events of San Francisco, she'd developed a zero tolerance for that kind of casual intimacy.

Tobias slanted JT a pointed look. "You should stay out of this."

JT backed off a step, his expression wary. "No problem. Not my fight—"

"That's right."

"Okay. Well…" JT shrugged. "I'm on my way back to the office."

JT's footsteps echoed through the garage as he headed for his car, but, now that they were alone, the tension between her and Tobias was suddenly thick enough to cut.

Tobias frowned. "You've done something to your nose."

Taken off guard by the change in tack, Allegra automatically touched the side of the bridge of her nose, which had once been marred by a small bump. The bump had only been discernible from certain angles, but after being ditched by Tobias, the imperfection, which came from the Toussaint side of the family, had seemed to glare back at her every time she looked in the mirror. "I had surgery to fix it. It wasn't a big deal."

Tobias gaze shifted. "And you've changed your hair."

She blinked, for long moments transfixed by the color of his irises, which seemed softer and darker than she remembered, fringed as they were by inky lashes. She dragged her gaze free, breaking the moment. The problem was, she didn't know whether to feel pleasure that Tobias had noticed the surgery or her hair color, or irritated for the same reason.

She shoved the house key in a zip pocket in her handbag, along with her ear pods, while she tried to figure out why on earth he was almost complimenting her. When she couldn't, because there was no way he could be trying to sweet-talk her into a date, she decided to keep things neutral and treat him with politeness, like she would a client. Who knows? The politeness might even rub off on him. "Thank you for noticing. I haven't changed anything—that's my natural color. I *used* to color it with blond streaks, but since the spa provides natural therapies and detoxification regimes, it wouldn't look good if I showed up for work as a bottle blond."

But, underneath all of her annoyance with Tobias, she couldn't quite suppress the warm, fuzzy feeling of pleasure that he had noticed the changes she'd made.

Then a horror-filled thought nixed the pleasure. Now that she *had* to share a house with Tobias, could he possibly be thinking that she would be open to sharing his bed, on a strictly casual basis, of course?

Suddenly, the month with Tobias seemed even more fraught. Two years ago, she had fallen for him and thrown caution to the winds. If he seriously set out to seduce her now, would she be strong enough to resist him?

Out of the blue, a solution settled into place. It was

the perfect answer to a situation that seemed to be getting way out of hand.

Digging her car keys out of her bag, and sticking with the business owner/client synergy, she plastered a neutral smile on her face. "As I was saying...one of the reasons I don't want to share a house with you is that..." She drew a deep breath and crossed the fingers of one hand behind her back. "*My fiancé* won't exactly be happy if I move in with you."

The slam of JT's car door and the cough of his car starting echoed through the cavernous space.

For a weird moment, Tobias's face looked like thunder, and she actually got the impression that he was going to argue with her, then his expression cleared.

He glanced at her left hand, which was, of course, bare. "I didn't know you were engaged."

Allegra still had the fingers of her right hand crossed behind her back. She had lied, and she *never* lied. But, even though she hated having to do that, she had to continue with the charade now. "Why would you? We're not exactly friends."

JT's car cruised toward them, heading for the exit. Tobias stepped out of the lane, closer to the vehicle they were both standing next to, and lifted a hand as JT went past. When he produced a key, a small shock went through Allegra, because she realized they were standing right next to his black truck. Somehow, he had managed to find a space just two down from where her convertible was parked.

The lights of the truck flashed as he unlocked it. "Strange that Esmae didn't mention your engagement."

Allegra kept her cool, professional smile on her face, but her mind was going a million miles an hour. She was going to have to find an actual fiancé now, which was problematic, since lately she'd been so busy with plans for the new retreat property she had even stopped dating. She didn't know if she even knew anyone who could fill the role.

"Esmae didn't know," she said smoothly, "because it's…only just happened."

Tobias's gaze seemed to laser through her. "Interesting. So when, exactly, did you get engaged? At the funeral?"

Allegra suppressed the urge to snap that it was none of his business. But now was not the time to lose her cool. Besides, she was struck by how irritable Tobias was, even more annoyed than he'd been in Phillips's office. He had been short with JT, now he was needling her, as if her engagement had somehow added to his aggravation, which didn't make sense.

He should be dancing in the street. Unless it mattered to him that she was engaged.

Unless he was jealous.

She instantly dismissed the notion. There was just no way, because, if Tobias was jealous, that meant he cared for her, and pigs would fly before that happened.

Thinking quickly, she tried to come up with a believable date for getting engaged. "We got engaged—the day before the funeral."

"You worked the day before."

Her gaze narrowed at his knowledge of her schedule and the way he kept questioning her, as if he didn't believe she could be engaged. With an effort of will, she kept her smile in place. "I'm a woman," she said flatly, "I multitask. Besides, I don't work twenty-four hours of every day. When the spa closes I have…a life."

His gaze pinned her in place, before dropping to her mouth, sending tension zinging through her. She was even getting a weird feeling low in her belly, as if she were actually just the tiniest bit turned on, which *couldn't* be.

"So, who's the lucky guy?"

Her phone rang. Talk about saved by the bell, because her mind was utterly blank on the subject of who could possibly be her fiancé.

She extracted her cell phone out of her handbag just as the call, which was from one of her suppliers, was transferred to voice mail. But the fact that it was a work call provided her with the inspiration she needed.

She had recently employed a gym instructor and personal trainer, Mike. A part-time model and actor waiting for his big break, Mike was tall, muscled and blond, and looked like a Norse hero. He wasn't exactly the brightest person on her team and he had an offbeat humor and a narcissistic streak that could be challenging, but he *was* gorgeous. He was also cash-strapped and had recently asked her for more hours.

That, along with his acting training, made him perfect for the part.

Allegra tried to look as if she'd just remembered Tobias's question. "His name's Mike, uh—" she was so used to calling Mike by just his first name that, for a second she had trouble remembering his surname "—*Callaghan*. You'll meet him soon enough. Although," she said smoothly, "I shouldn't have said anything, since we haven't announced it yet."

She checked her watch, as if she was suddenly in a hurry, which she was, now that she had an engagement to organize. "How soon do I have to move into the house?" She could not quite bring herself to say *your house*.

Tobias crossed his arms over his chest. "Today, if you want."

"Great. The sooner it's over the better, because I'd like to have some privacy to be with my fiancé."

Something heated flashed in his gaze. "I'll be moving in this afternoon, as well."

She busied herself sliding her phone back in her bag. "Naturally, Mike will be helping me. Maybe he can also give you a hand if you need it? He's really strong."

A glint of humor surfaced. "I don't need a hand. It's not as if I'm staying out there more than the month."

She offered him the kind of distant smile she used to end conversations with people she had not wanted to talk to in the first place. "Just one month and we'll both have what we're entitled to, and then we can go our separate ways."

The amusement disappeared from Tobias's gaze. "Spoken like a true Mallory."

The way he said it stung. Of course, he had known that Esmae had backed her financially, but her assistance hadn't been necessary. "For your information, I tried to buy back those shares from Esmae four months ago."

"I'd believe that if she hadn't written her new will around the time she went into partnership with you."

"So you think I made the offer already knowing Esmae was giving me the shares?"

Something snapped. Before she could stop herself, she stepped close enough to Tobias that she could feel the heat blasting off his body and smell the clean scents of soap and whatever that cologne was, and jabbed a finger at his chest. "You make it sound like I'm dishonest, which is entirely your business, but it's a fact that I'm entirely capable of raising my own finances, which is what I would have done if Esmae hadn't been so set on wanting an interest in Madison Spas."

She glared at him. "And, for the record…neither is my

family, either past or present, dishonest. The Mallorys have had their share of luck, good and bad, just like the Hunts. And, before you say it, I know the story about Jebediah and Alexandra and, quite frankly, I'm over it. If you ask me, the reason Jebediah went so sour on Alexandra wasn't because he ended up with a piece of land that didn't have an oil well on it. It was because Alexandra rejected him and found *someone else*. Someone who was probably a whole lot nicer."

She could say more. The way Tobias's family told the story about Esmae's marriage to Michael Hunt was equally objectionable. As far as Allegra was concerned, the implication that Esmae had been a scheming gold digger was utterly ridiculous, because Esmae Mallory had been gorgeous enough to marry anyone she chose. What's more, Allegra had the pictures to prove it. "And let's talk about the elephant in the room. The Hunt family is hugely successful and rich. You could buy and sell the oil well Alexandra ended up with, *out of sheer good luck*, a million times over and still have change. So why don't we just park the whole story and move on!"

"This is why," he muttered.

Tobias's hands landed at her waist, his head dipped and his mouth landed on hers. As kisses went it was light, almost tentative, or would have been if she hadn't swayed off-balance and gripped the lapels of his jacket.

His arms came around her waist, and all the breath went from her lungs as he pressed her close enough that she could feel the hard wall of his chest, the pound of his heart and the riveting fact that he was aroused.

At that point, a hot little pang shot through her, and her knees went as limp as noodles. Dimly, she was aware that the strap of her handbag had slipped off her shoulder and the bag was now on the concrete floor. But she couldn't

worry about that, it was all she could do to hold on to Tobias's shoulders, as she angled her jaw to deepen the kiss.

Tobias muttered something else under his breath,
that sounded suspiciously like a swear word. His hands
cupped her bottom and she was hauled even closer, then
upward, so that her feet were left dangling. She wound
her arms around his neck and hung on. A split second
later, she felt the cold solidity of metal behind her, as he
settled her against the cold steel of the truck.

The sound of the elevator doors opening made her
stiffen. Heat flushed through her as she realized what she
was doing, what she had allowed. They were practically
making love against the side of Tobias's truck. Embarrassed at the way she had clung on to him, she wriggled
free and smoothed her dress, which had hiked up, back
down around her thighs.

Dragging in a breath, she stepped back, then had to
grip the edge of the truck because her legs still felt un-
steady. "That shouldn't have happened."

Tobias straightened his tie, which she must have
dragged loose. "Because you're engaged?"

Allegra's cheeks warmed. She had almost forgotten
that part. *"Yes."*

A middle-aged man with a briefcase walked past them,
an interested gleam in his gaze.

It was at that point she realized that a button on her
bodice had popped open, exposing more than just a hint
of cleavage. Fumbling in her haste, she rebuttoned the
bodice, then bent down and retrieved her gorgeous Messena handbag, which was now covered in dust smudges.
Tobias retrieved a lipstick and a vial of perfume that
had rolled beneath the truck. Feeling flustered because
she had kissed Tobias back, she snatched back her personal items.

She rummaged in her bag and found her car keys. "That can't happen again."

"You're the boss," he growled.

She sent him a fiery glance. She wasn't sensing any regret, in fact, just the opposite. There was still a heated gleam, right alongside the bad-tempered attitude, and then she finally figured it out. There was no way a guy could fake arousal, and she had been plastered against Tobias, so he hadn't been able to hide the fact that he was aroused, either.

Tobias wanted her.

The problem was, he wanted her *against his will*, which was more than a little insulting, and brought back the hurt and humiliation of Tobias ditching her two years ago.

As far as she was concerned, in behaving that way, Tobias had committed *the* cardinal sin: he had trivialized her.

She didn't need a crystal ball to know that he had bought into the fake news propagated by Halliday and Fischer on their toxic social media pages.

He was probably, even now, making some kind of superficial value judgment about her but, thankfully, because she had such a kickass attitude, what Tobias thought would absolutely *not* affect her. One of the reasons she hadn't dated a lot in high school or college, and had made the mistake of going to an executive dating site, was that very reason. Usually, she could spot the kind of guy who was going to make shallow assumptions about her a mile off. The second she figured it out, she walked because, newsflash, she was just not interested in spending time with a guy who only saw her as a cliché.

Turning on her heel, she stalked toward her car. She needed to think, and fast, because now she had to figure a way to get through a whole month with a Tobias who wanted her.

Then she remembered Mike. Duh.

Opening the driver's-side door, she placed her bag on the passenger seat, slid behind the wheel and closed her door with an expensive *thunk*. She was just about to start the car when Tobias walked around the rear, leaned down and placed both hands on her door, preventing her from backing out of the space.

"Just so we make one thing clear. Your *fiancé* can help you move in, but that's where it ends. He can't stay."

Allegra could feel the color rising in her cheeks, not just at Tobias's dictatorial manner, but at the way he had said *fiancé*, as if he didn't really believe she had one.

She pressed the starter button of the car. The engine purred to life, which was a handy way of letting Tobias know that the conversation was over.

The fact that he clearly didn't believe her, besides being insulting, made her all the more determined to employ Mike for the role. She didn't know what she would have to pay him, but if she had to empty her personal bank account, she would do it.

It was bad enough that she was going to have to live in Tobias's house for a month, but his high-handed manner in laying down the rules about her seeing her fiancé— even though Mike wouldn't really be her fiancé—burned.

By the time she moved into Esmae's—*Tobias's*— house, her fake engagement had to be fully operational.

Tobias released her door, but she wasn't quite ready to leave.

Tilting her head back, she gazed at Tobias from beneath her lashes. She had practiced that look in the mirror and while doing selfies until she had perfected it, and she knew it was crazy hot.

Maybe goading Tobias at this point wasn't the smartest choice, but the last time she had taken orders she had been three. And, even at that age, she had known that last order had been reasonable, because if she had eaten all of the cookies in the cookie jar she *would* have been sick. "Are you trying to tell me that I can't have sex with my fiancé?"

Something dangerous flashed in Tobias's eyes, as if she had finally pushed him over the edge of a precipice she hadn't known was there. Out of nowhere a hot thrill shot down her spine.

"Not in my house," he said softly.

Their gazes locked with a laser intensity she was having difficulty breaking, probably because Tobias's eyes had a magnetic, mesmerizing quality, which, somehow, made all brain function stop.

Approximately ninety seconds ago, she had figured out that Tobias wanted her. Now, she had another vital piece of information.

He didn't want Mike to have her.

Which meant he *was* jealous.

Another hot thrill, this one going all the way to you-know-where, practically welded her in place. "Oh good," she said, injecting a brisk, businesslike note into her voice. "For a moment there I thought you were saying I couldn't have sex with my fiancé at all!"

Before she could become completely paralyzed from the hypnotic effect of Tobias's gaze, *and agree to sleep with him again*, she put the car into Reverse, backed out of the space, then shot toward the exit. She was almost at the turn into the exit ramp when another vehicle reversed into the lane.

Braking, she waited, fingers tense on the wheel. A faint tingling at the back of her neck had her checking the rearview mirror. Tobias's truck glided in behind her, once again dwarfing her small car.

She should have waited for him to leave first, because now she was stuck with Tobias behind her until she could get out of the building. Like the drive in, his big black truck was making her feel distinctly herded, which was a feeling she had never experienced until Tobias.

In the past, there had been occasions when guys had deliberately followed her to get her attention, but the most she had felt was irritation. She had literally batted them off like flies.

The SUV in front finally achieved some forward motion. Relief washed through Allegra when she finally turned onto the city street. The little café where she was buying lunch was on the coast, and Tobias's office was in the center of town, so he would have to turn in the opposite direction.

When he did so, she relaxed a fraction more, but the feminine tension that had spun out of control when they had kissed was still keeping her on edge.

Annoyed at the way she was still reacting, she shifted in her seat and rolled her shoulders to try and relax her muscles, but vivid flashes of what it had felt like to kiss Tobias and be pressed close against him, kept ratcheting up the tension.

She braked for a light, then checked her mirror. Another hot pang shot through her when she spied the rear of Tobias's truck, even though it was at a distance.

A car horn blared. Depressing the accelerator, she drove through the intersection and, just in time, remembered to take the lane that led toward the beach.

The problem was that, for reasons she couldn't fathom, she was turned on. The feelings had sneaked up on her, but this time she would not be caught off guard.

After months of therapy and graduating from a series of online relationship empowerment classes for women, she was now equipped with a degree of emotional intelligence she hadn't possessed when she had made the mistake of sleeping with Tobias.

Despite still wanting him, she now knew exactly what she was coping with: a fatal attraction. What's more, she had the tools in place to resist Tobias.

She was forewarned, forearmed and she was "engaged."

The fact that Tobias had kissed her after he had learned she had a fiancé made her frown. The only reason that explained his total lack of respect for the fact that she was pledged to another man, was that he hadn't believed in the engagement.

Just like he hadn't believed her when she had told him she wasn't trying to trap him into marriage.

That meant that, despite her efforts to prove that she didn't want him, he was still convinced that she did.

That meant she *definitely* had to have the engagement visible, and in Tobias's face, by this afternoon.

Five

Tobias strode into his downtown office and lifted a hand to Jean, his indomitable, indispensible PA, before stepping into the inner sanctum of his office.

Tossing his briefcase on a leather chair, he walked to the huge wall of glass that offered spectacular views out over the cityscape, with glimpses of Miami Beach, and out to sea. Although, for long seconds the view didn't register at all, because he was back in the darkened underground garage, with Allegra Mallory winding her arms around his neck and stretching her taut, curvy body against him as the first kiss had turned into a second and then a third.

He had come close to losing it. He knew it, and so did Allegra. And all because she had dropped her bombshell about having a fiancé, a piece of information that should have filled him with relief but which, instead, had had the opposite effect.

The fiery tension that had burned through him when she'd announced her engagement was still humming through him.

Allegra, engaged?

Not if he had his way.

Allegra Mallory was his.

The thought settled in with a curious inevitability. Why, exactly, he wanted Allegra was unclear. He knew plenty of beautiful, intelligent, charming women. Over the past two years he had done his share of dating, specifically to cure himself of whatever it was he felt for Allegra.

Six years ago, it had hit him like a bolt from the blue. Two years ago, it had resulted in his breaking up with his fiancée, Lindsay. The power of the attraction had been strong enough that, even though he was certain the stress of the break-up had contributed to Lindsay's miscarriage, he hadn't been able to forget Allegra.

Every time she walked into a room, despite the guilt that still gnawed at him, every muscle in his body tightened—

His door popped open. JT walked in, with a pizza box and a box of doughnuts balanced on one hand, a bottle of soda in the other. He lifted a brow. "Peace offering? Didn't realize I was...you know, stepping on your toes."

Tobias met the other man's gaze for a long moment. He had been short and to-the-point, but he didn't regret it. JT had needed to know that Allegra was off-limits. "If it helps," he said grimly, "*I* didn't know it until right then." He checked out the pizza and the doughnuts and shook his head. "Lunch?"

"More like two glorious works of art." JT put the pizza, the doughnuts, the soda and a small stack of napkins on his coffee table. He helped himself to a seat and opened the lid on the pizza box. "Double cheese with fennel sausage *and* prosciutto. And the doughnuts are salted caramel with vanilla cream."

"You are going to die."

"And go to heaven." JT loaded a slice of pizza onto a napkin. "Now that you've apologized, you can have some pizza."

Pizza wasn't exactly his lunch of choice, but since he hadn't actually eaten today, apart from the coffee on the red-eye flight from New York, Tobias accepted a slice. But he was still too wound up to sit.

When he'd finished, JT passed him a napkin. "So... you and Allegra. I guess I should have remembered that you, uh, slept with her."

Tobias's brows jerked together. "How did you know about that?"

"I was at Esmae's ninetieth birthday party. I just happened to see you two down on the beach."

"That was two years ago. Times have changed." Tobias wiped his fingers with the napkin, then tossed it into the trash. "Apparently, she's engaged."

JT stopped dead, a slice of pizza part way to his mouth. "You're kidding. That's the first I've heard of it and, in this town, I hear *a lot* of stuff." He set the pizza down, underlining the gravity of the moment. "I mean, with Allegra looking the way she does, she's not exactly invisible. There are a lot of guys who would *happily*—"

"Stop right there, JT."

"Yeah. Uh—sorry." JT wiped his fingers with a napkin and tried for a rueful smile. "Well, I guess if she's engaged that means she's probably not dying to get her hot hands on you, after all. Although..." He closed the lid of the empty pizza box and zeroed in on the dough-nuts. "What if the engagement's just a ploy, and she's trying to make herself more attractive? You know, make out she's—" he sketched quotation marks in the air "'—unavailable.'"

"Allegra's been in Miami, living less than a mile from my apartment, and successfully avoiding me for two years, so the availability theory doesn't exactly hold up."

Shrugging, JT selected a doughnut. "So the engagement's real. That sucks. Wonder who the lucky guy is?"

Tobias found himself controlling his temper with difficulty. "Someone called Mike Callaghan."

"Thor? No way." He took a bite of the doughnut and chewed reflectively. "Not that he's actually the Norse god of thunder—he's the personal trainer at the spa. Julia did a couple of sessions with him, just before we broke up. At least that explains it. He's some serious eye candy, *and* they work together."

Tobias's jaw tightened. Up until that moment, Callaghan hadn't seemed entirely real. In fact, Tobias had gotten the distinct impression that Allegra had pulled a name out of a hat.

And, as it happened, Tobias had made it his business to know whom Allegra was seeing. The surveillance hadn't been exhaustive. Mostly, he had checked out her social media sites when he had a spare hour in the evenings. The overriding impression was that she had only dated on a casual level. Two, maybe three dates, was all she ever committed to with one guy, and he couldn't recall ever seeing Callaghan's name.

But the fact that she worked with the guy changed things, because that meant she saw him on a daily basis. Suddenly, the thought of Allegra in bed with Callaghan didn't seem like such a stretch.

The tension that was coursing through him was oddly clarifying. He realized he was grimly, burningly jealous, but at least the feelings clarified what he had felt in Phillips's office and in the parking garage.

He wanted Allegra.

He didn't know for how long he would want her. Despite the complication of the will, and the mistakes of the past that still haunted him, his feelings for Allegra were, as they had been all along, curiously black-and-white.

He just wanted her, period, and he knew that, even though wild horses wouldn't drag it from her, that she wanted him, too.

He was also aware that, with Callaghan now firmly in the picture, if he didn't claim Allegra now, *today*, he could lose her completely.

When JT finally left, Tobias looked at the carnage of his office, the overflowing trash can, the soda spills and the clouds of powdered sugar that seemed to have settled on every available surface. Not for the first time, he thought about what life would be like without JT, then, almost immediately, dismissed the thought.

He had known JT most of his life. They'd gone to school and through BUDs together. As annoying as he could be, JT was the closest thing to a brother that Tobias had.

On impulse, he dialed his PA's number. Even though he'd eaten a slice of pizza, he still felt hungry and, since he was moving into Esmae's house straight after the Ocean Beach meeting, it made sense to get something now.

There was a café on the ground floor of the building that Jean liked. If he wanted to eat in, she usually got them to send up sandwiches and salads.

When he gave her his request, she was silent for a beat. "You don't want beef?"

"I'd like to try something—different."

"How different?" she said cautiously. "There are at least a dozen vegetarian dishes."

Tobias frowned. "What do you like?"

"Me? I usually have the vegetarian stack, or sometimes lentil patties or a wild rice salad." She paused. "Maybe you should have fish. They have a very nice salmon quiche—"

"I'll try all the things you listed."

An hour later, Tobias finished sampling the variety of vegetarian dishes the café had delivered. They weren't bad; there was nothing he disliked. The problem was he was still hungry. The only thing he'd really enjoyed had been the coffee. Whether it was psychological or not, the food he'd eaten had failed to satisfy.

Like his love life.

He checked his watch. In less than an hour, he had to drive to the Ocean Beach Resort for his meeting with the manager, Marc Porter. Over the next month, like it or not, he was going to have to come to grips with running a luxury resort, something he knew very little about.

The only positive was that Esmae had had a talent for surrounding herself with young, highly qualified staff, and the present manager was a case in point. The biggest issue was Allegra's spa. He didn't have access to those figures. All he had was a copy of the lease agreement with the resort, which expired in two month's time.

It made sense not to renew the lease. The way he saw it, Esmae's passing meant he could once-for-all sever his connection to Allegra, *and remove the temptation she posed from his life*. But the fact that he wanted Allegra back in his bed had changed things somewhat.

Madison Spas still had to go. Allegra wouldn't be happy, but he would make it up to her. He could even soften the blow by finding her alternative premises before he terminated the lease.

Whatever the issues were, they were solvable.

But *after* he had gotten her back in his bed.

Allegra parked her car in its space at the Ocean Beach Resort and strolled into the premises that housed her spa. Not for the first time, her heart swelled with pride at what she'd achieved.

Ocean Beach was a luxurious resort, which catered to the affluent and those wanting a beach holiday. Her spa offered the beach vibe as well, but she had gone out of her way to create secluded gardens and quiet spaces where solitude could be enjoyed. Most of her clientele stayed at the resort proper, and came for various treatments or half or full-day packages, but she did have secluded cabins for clients who wanted the privacy and quietness of a retreat stay.

Once she reached her office, she checked the schedule of activities, specifically to find out where she might find Mike. Gym classes were finished for the day, but he did have one client booked for a personal training session, which was set to finish any minute.

She walked through to the gym, which was airy and light and outfitted with the latest state-of-the-art equipment, as well as a mirrored wall for dance classes. Mike was presently leaning against a weight-lifting frame, stopwatch in his hand, while his client, a plump, Asian executive-type Allegra recognized as one of their most faithful regulars, attempted to do lunges.

Mike directed an amiable grin in her direction, hit the stopwatch app on his smartwatch and clapped his client on the shoulder. "Better live to fight another day, eh James? Hit the showers, and I'll see you at six in the morning for that run on the beach."

James was aghast. "Six?"

Mike slung a towel around his neck and picked up his gym bag. "Unless you want to go earlier?"

"Arrgh... Six is fine."

Allegra waited until the executive staggered through the door that led to the showers before opening what was going to be an awkward conversation.

Mike, who refused to wear glasses while he was working, pushed a pair of horn-rimmed glasses onto the bridge of his nose as he ambled toward her. "Hey. What's up, boss?"

Allegra gave him her best professional smile. "Last week you asked me for more hours. At the time, I didn't have any extra work, but something's cropped up."

Mike gave her a distracted grin as he dug in his gym bag. "Sounds like that could be promising for me." He found his phone. "Did you decide to run with my proposal for a cage-fighting class in that bit of jungle down by the beach?"

"Not exactly. Most of our clients come here to wind down, so I can't really see how something like that is going to work." There was no easy way to say it. "The extra hours would be more in the line of *acting* than physical training."

"Acting? Cool." Mike frowned as he flicked through something on his phone. He peered at her over the top of his glasses, which were clearly for distance, not close reading. "How did you know I was looking for an acting gig?"

Allegra frowned. She did not exactly see the fake engagement as a "gig." "You told me. In the interview."

"Phew, that's a relief! Because when I get my big

break, I'll be gone." He made a sudden, swooping plane-like movement with his hand, then went back to flicking through texts. "I've been waiting for my agent to contact me about a part in a new daytime soap. Some kind of *Baywatch* meets aliens and zombies thing."

Allegra took a deep breath and determinedly put her irritation to one side. "In the meantime, like I said, I do have an acting job of sorts for you." She mentioned a figure.

Mike looked up from his phone and grinned. "Who do I have to sleep with to get that?"

"You won't be sleeping with anyone," Allegra said frostily. "The job is strictly window dressing." She drew a deep breath, but there was no point in beating around the bush. "I need a fake fiancé for a month."

Mike stared at her as if she'd just grown an extra head. "Why would you want a fake fiancé?"

"It's…complicated."

He frowned, as if he was having trouble getting his head around the concept. "So, you need an *escort*? I mean, I did it for a while, but I hated the hours and the bars. Kind of messed up my fitness routine. Then there was the whole cougar thing…"

Allegra's brows jerked together. "Do I look like a cougar?"

Mike blinked. "No, ma'am. You look like my boss."

"Exactly." Allegra was beginning to think she had made a major mistake in asking Mike. From what she could remember of his curriculum vitae there had been a lot of detail about his personal training, modeling and acting abilities. There had been no mention that he had ever worked as a male escort. "I don't need an escort. I need an *actor*."

Mike frowned, then nodded, as if he had finally gotten it. "So all I have to do is *pretend* to like you."

"Pretend to be my fiancé," she corrected. Then, because she was beginning to think Mike had gotten his wires crossed over what the job entailed, she clarified, "This does not involve sex in any way, shape or form."

"And you still want to pay all that money?" He grinned, and, for a minute, she thought he was actually going to try and high-five her. "Cool."

When she got home that evening, Allegra changed into a cotton dress that was airy and easy to move in, because she would be doing a lot of lifting, and slipped on a comfortable pair of sneakers. She packed two suitcases with everything she would conceivably need over the next month, then did a tour of the bathroom, gathering up toiletries.

She had made sure to include some evening wear, because she had planned a schedule of dates with Mike to cement the fact that they were an engaged couple. She had also packed her jewelry case, which was filled with an assortment of significant jewelry she would not feel comfortable with leaving in an empty apartment, as well as some cheap and glitzy pageant bling. If she had forgotten anything, it would be an easy enough matter to call back to her apartment.

She wheeled the suitcases to her front door. Normally, she would have carried them out to her garage and loaded them into her car herself. However, because Mike had agreed to meet her at her apartment, she figured that, as part of his role, he could take care of her baggage.

She did a quick check of the apartment to make sure the windows were locked, then grabbed a shopping tote and emptied perishables from the pantry and the refrigerator. Esmae used to have a couple live in with her, but since she'd been in the hospital, she had switched to having them just call in to look after the grounds and check the house. That being the case, there wasn't likely to be any fresh food at the house. She set the tote next to her suitcases, then checked her watch, noting that Mike was ten minutes late.

Feeling a familiar sense of irritation at Mike's casual attitude toward time, she made a start on loading the bags herself. After all, the important part of Mike helping her move was that he *unloaded* everything and carried it to her rooms while Tobias watched.

Getting the bags into her little convertible was a mission, courtesy of the fact that it was a two door. With difficulty, she managed to wedge the smaller one in the space behind the front seats and prop the largest bag in the passenger seat. The bag of perishables went on the floor, along with her handbag.

Feeling on edge, she walked back into the house and did a last check that she hadn't forgotten anything, ending up in her cool, stylish bedroom with its white-on-white decor and pretty little terrace. On impulse, she checked her appearance, since the last thing she wanted was to turn up at Tobias's house with smudged makeup or messy hair.

Her mineral-based foundation, which, naturally, was the same brand her spa sold, looked smooth and perfect. Her eye makeup was subtle, but smoky, making her eyes look even darker. On impulse, she rummaged through the drawers, found extra hairpins and fastened the knot in her hair more securely.

When Mike eventually arrived in his beaten-up truck, which sprouted rusted fishing rod holders, it was a good twenty minutes past the time they had agreed, and the sun was sinking low on the horizon. Keeping her irritation in check, because it would have been so much easier to have loaded the bags into his truck than squeeze them into her convertible, Allegra gave him a copy of the schedule of dates she had formulated that afternoon and instructed him to follow her to the mansion.

Twenty minutes later, she drove through the gorgeous wrought iron gates that guarded the driveway to the Spanish-style mansion and pulled up in the circular area of gravel outside the front doors. Her heart thumped against her chest when she saw Tobias's black truck already parked, indicating he was in the process of moving in.

Allegra pushed her door open and climbed out, just as Mike's truck pulled to a halt behind her. Walking around the sleek exterior of her car, she opened the passenger-side door, unfastened the seat belt, then began wrangling the suitcase, until she remembered Mike was supposed to do it.

Feeling exasperated, she abandoned the case. For some reason, Mike was still sitting in his truck. The reason became evident when she discovered that he was intently reading the dating schedule.

She knocked on his window. "You're supposed to be helping me."

He wound down his window and pointed to the first sentence of the schedule. "You want me to do this first scene, right now?"

For a moment, she was actually speechless. "It's not a scene, Mike. It's real life."

"Oh…yeah!" Grinning, Mike climbed out of his truck and folded and jammed the pages of the schedule into the back pocket of his jeans.

Allegra drew a deep breath and attempted to relax.

"Don't forget, you're supposed to be pretending to be my fiancé." A little grimly, she noted he had his glasses on, which was not ideal, because he looked far more impressive without them. She was about to tell him to take them off, put them in the truck and leave them there, but then the front door to the mansion popped open.

Tobias strode down the front steps, looking more muscular than she remembered in faded jeans and a T-shirt that molded his broad shoulders. His gaze immediately went to Mike, who was in the process of hauling her luggage out of the front seat.

"You must be Allegra's fiancé."

Mike set the suitcase down on the gravel. For a moment, he looked utterly blank, and Allegra wondered if her scheme was going to unravel before it even got off the ground, then he grinned and stepped forward to grip Tobias's hand. "Yep, that's me. Uh... Mike Callaghan's the name."

Tobias seemed ultra-relaxed. "The personal trainer. I saw you at the resort when I called in this afternoon."

A little shocked that Tobias knew Mike worked for her, when she was hoping that he would remain a mysterious figure, Allegra inserted herself into the conversation. "Mike doesn't work for the resort, he works for me. That's how we met."

She wound her arm through Mike's, and did her best to look as if she was happily relaxed and content to snuggle into her new fiancé's side. The situation was made all the more difficult by the fact that she was Mike's employer and, while he had agreed to act as her fiancé for money, the last thing she wanted to do was cross a line when it came to physical contact.

Tobias directed his next question at Mike. "How long have you worked at the spa?"

Mike froze like a deer in the headlights, and Allegra's stomach sank. She had briefed him extensively; she had just not thought he would need an actual script.

She smiled brightly. "He's been with the spa for a few weeks, isn't that right, Mike?"

"Uh—yeah. A few weeks."

Allegra kept the smile on her face. "It was a whirl-wind…relationship." She could not quite say *engagement*.

Tobias crossed his arms over his chest. "Must have been." His gaze seemed to pin her in place. "I guess con-gratulations are in order. So, when is the happy day?"

Allegra glanced at her watch, in an effort to convey that she really did not have time for this chitchat. "We haven't gotten around to thinking about that just yet."

"Just like you haven't gotten around to getting a ring?"

Six

Allegra stiffened. Tobias's voice was neutral, but she knew him well enough to know that, when he was quiet, he was at his most dangerous. He had used that same kind of flat tone when he had ditched her. She had also heard it when he had queried Esmae's medical bill, which had sprouted one more zero than it should have had.

She had hoped to slide by without the necessity of a ring. Firstly, she could not really afford to buy one. After she paid Mike, her discretionary spending was gone for the next two months. Secondly, for Allegra, an engagement ring had always signified the promise of true love. It was bad enough that the engagement was a facade, she did not want to deepen the dishonesty of what she was doing by wearing a ring.

As loath as she was to give Tobias any information at all, she was left with no choice. She had planned for Mike to meet her in town tomorrow so she could pay him the first installment of his fee. She had also planned to get a ring. With any luck, she would be able to source a ring from the keepsakes Esmae had left her. Failing that, she could always use some of her own collection of fake and real diamonds, and have a ring made, but that would probably be almost as expensive as buying something new.

"As a matter of fact," she said smoothly, "we're planning on getting a ring tomorrow."

Feeling more cheerful, she released Mike's arm and tried not to look as relieved as she felt. "If you don't mind, we need to get on with moving my things into the house. I'm guessing I can use my old room?"

"Marta's already gotten it ready for you."

For the first time in days, a warm wave of pleasure washed through Allegra. Obviously, Tobias had kept on Marta Gomez, who had been Esmae's housekeeper and cook for a good thirty years, and her husband, Jose, who had looked after the grounds.

A burst of rap music made her start. Mike extracted his phone from his back pocket, and turned away to take the call. Long seconds passed as he strolled a few paces, then leaned against his truck, evidently in deep conversation.

Working to keep her expression smooth and unruffled, as if it didn't matter that her "fiancé" was now completely ignoring her, Allegra bent down into the car and dragged out the smaller of her two cases, which was wedged behind the seats. As she set it on the gravel and closed the car door, Tobias picked up the heavier case, which Mike had abandoned.

"Looks like your boyfriend's busy for a while. I'll show you to your room."

Following in Tobias's wake, Allegra walked into the

familiar cool interior of the Spanish mansion, which his grandfather had built for Esmae. Classic blue-and-white mosaic tiles flowed into vaulting rooms. The dark, ornate furniture that Allegra remembered from her teen years was long gone, and in its place were rustic dressers and coffee tables, low couches upholstered in neutral linen, gorgeous chandeliers that looked as if they were made of translucent shells and thick comfortable floor rugs in neutrals and deep blues.

She followed Tobias up the long, sweeping staircase, with its soft white walls lined with Hunt family portraits. When she realized that he probably wouldn't deposit the bag at the door of her room, but would carry it in, a sudden tension gripped her.

Maybe she was being too sensitive now, but during the next month, her bedroom would be the only part of the house that was off-limits to Tobias. It would be her sanctuary. The last thing she needed was for him to invade her very private haven, so that every time she was in the room she had to fight off memories of his presence there.

She sped up, but he reached the doorway before her.

"Thanks very much for the help," she said briskly, "but you can leave my case in the hall——"

"While you wait for lover boy to carry it in?"

Ignoring her completely, Tobias strolled into the room and placed her suitcase at the foot of her bed.

To compound matters, as Allegra set the case she was carrying down, he walked over to a set of French doors, opened them and stepped out onto the balcony, which overlooked the drive. Jaw taut, she followed him, intending to order him out of her room.

Her stomach sank when she saw Mike below, still leaning on his truck and talking on his phone, a relaxed grin on his face, as if he had totally forgotten he was supposed to be helping her move in. As if he was enjoying talking to whomever was on the other end of the phone more than he enjoyed being with her.

Tobias lifted a brow. "Looks like Callaghan's still busy."

Probably with his real girlfriend.

That was a little detail Allegra had not yet had time to address. The first opportunity she got, she would make sure Mike understood that while he was employed as her fiancé, he could not have a girlfriend on the side.

Tobias's gaze shifted to her. "That's just as well, since I would prefer it if he didn't come upstairs into your bedroom."

"*You're* in my room."

"I'm not your lover."

And, suddenly, the air was alive with tension. Allegra was burningly aware that, if she'd thought Tobias had forgotten the night they had spent together, she was wrong.

He closed the gap between them, until he was close enough that she could feel the warmth of his body, smell the fresh scent of some expensive cologne. His gaze locked with hers. "Damn, I wasn't going to do this. Not yet, anyway."

She knew she should move. Alone with Tobias on the balcony, it was the perfect moment to take a stand and demonstrate that the old attraction that had held her in thrall for so long was now as dead as a doornail. The only problem was that, like the moments in the parking garage, knowing that Tobias still wanted her had done something crazy to her body. She felt frozen to the spot, yet burning and melting inside; she couldn't have moved if her life depended on it, because deep down, she realized that she didn't want to resist him. Just for once, she wanted to have what she wanted, and right now, that was Tobias.

She tilted her chin back and met his gaze boldly. "And what is it that you shouldn't do?"

"Kiss you," he ground out. "Not with him here."

Warm, calloused hands cupped her face, sending further fiery shivers of sensation through her. The calluses reminded her that Tobias was not just a high-powered executive running a multi-national empire. Apart from his time in the military, he had always spent a lot of time in and on the water. When she had vacationed with Esmae, she had used to watch him obsessively as he had sailed yachts in the bay.

Tobias's mouth closed over hers. White heat burned through her, and she found herself going up on her toes, her arms automatically looping around his neck as she fitted herself against his body and melted into the kiss.

This shouldn't feel so familiar, she thought breathlessly.

And it shouldn't feel so good.

Tobias groaned, which sent another hot thrill through her, lifted his head, then settled back down for a second, deeper kiss and memories she had suppressed for two long years flooded back.

The brazen way she had thrown caution to the winds and virtually seduced Tobias.

She had found the spare key to Esmae's beach house, which was kept under a potted plant, and they had stumbled into the darkened hall. Switching one light on, and leaving the rest of the house in dimness, she had taken Tobias's hand and led him to the stairs. Several long, drugging kisses later, they had located a bedroom. As they undressed and fell together on a muslin-swathed four-poster bed, moonlight had flooded through the French doors, investing what they were doing with an other-

worldly romanticism that had added to the sense that what was happening wasn't quite real.

But the sharp memory of what had happened just two days later put the lovemaking in context. It had been casual sex. Nothing more, nothing less, and that was exactly where this was heading.

Aware that they had been brazenly kissing on the balcony, in full view of Mike, she jerked free of Tobias's hold. Not that Mike had noticed. At that precise moment, he finally finished his call, looked around, then up, and grinned and waved.

If ever there was a moment that Allegra reflected on why she didn't feel the slightest attraction for Mike, that was it. If she had any dragons to slay, he just wouldn't be there. He would be phoning one of his girlfriends or talking to his agent, and she would have to take care of business herself.

Feeling suddenly annoyed beyond belief and *suspicious*, she met Tobias's gaze squarely. "Why did you kiss me?" She lowered her voice, just in case Mike could hear. "No, don't answer, because I *know* why. You wanted to see if I was here to seduce you into a marriage that neither of us in our most insane moments would ever want. I would just like to reiterate that, despite the kiss, which was totally inappropriate and dishonorable on your part because I am *engaged*, I do not want you."

Tobias folded his arms across his chest, his gaze oddly brooding. "I wasn't testing you."

"Then what were you doing?"

A knock on the door brought the conversation to an abrupt halt.

Marta poked her head around the door, her expression openly curious. "I'm just about to leave now, but I've left dinner for you. All you need to do is serve yourselves."

* * *

Half an hour later, after Mike had driven away, Tobias walked downstairs and out onto the drive to lock his truck. He was on his way back to the house when he saw a set of folded papers where Mike's truck had been parked. He picked them up. He wasn't interested in snooping, but in this case, he didn't need to be, because the sheets were folded in such a way that the words were on the outside, and clearly visible.

Dating Schedule.

Tobias gave up any idea of discretion and perused both printouts, which were produced in a spreadsheet format. There were a series of preplanned dates, instructions on where to meet, what to wear and, several times the bolded command that Mike was not to pick Allegra up in his rusted old truck, because she would be doing the driving.

Apparently, when it came to dating, Allegra liked to take the lead, and Mike didn't just need direction, he needed micromanaging, even down to instructions on what to wear for specific dates.

He ran his eye over the dating schedule, which was top heavy on activities that centered on the Ocean Beach Resort and seemed to have more to do with Callaghan cleaning out some shed filled with old gym equipment than with actual romantic interludes. Tobias was pretty sure that the other address that figured prominently was the site for Allegra's second proposed spa property. Those dates seemed to involve a tape measure and meetings with an engineer. There was no mention of the kind of romantic dates that would be paramount for an engaged couple except for one sketchy date that was simply labeled, *I get the ring. Lunch, Atraeus Mall, twelve sharp.*

He presumed that was about getting the engagement ring. Although, it sounded like Allegra was providing her own ring, and Callaghan was turning up, as ordered, for lunch. And nowhere was there any mention of meetings with either Allegra's or Callaghan's families.

While he knew that her family was based in New Orleans, he knew nothing about Callaghan except that he worked for Allegra. *Although that would soon change*, he thought grimly.

Refolding the schedule, he carried it with him into the house. When he reached the library, which housed his grandfather's collection of rare books, an enormous carved mahogany desk and a couple of leather chesterfield couches that looked like they'd come off of a period movie set, he slipped the papers into a drawer.

The portrait of his great-grandfather, Jebediah Hunt, with his granite features and straight black brows, seemed to stare down at him. Not for the first time, Tobias noted that he looked stern and unlikeable, not the kind of character he would want to meet in a darkened alley.

Allegra's words about Alexandra leaving Jebediah, because she had just not liked him, came back to haunt him. It was a fact that his great-grandfather had been a tough and difficult man.

Tobias had to wonder if Allegra saw *him* in the same light. His grandfather had used to tell him he was a chip off the old block, referring to Jebediah as the "old block." Now Tobias was beginning to think the words had been a criticism, not a compliment.

But, for all his faults, Jeb had not lacked character. When things had gone south with Alexandra and the ranch, he had walked off the land and started again, this time as a Pinkerton agent. A few years later, he had started his own detective agency, which had been the beginnings of Hunt Security.

Tobias walked to the French doors that opened onto

a patio. The view of the Atlantic Ocean from the high point the mansion commanded was impressive, although it barely impinged on his thoughts.

Ever since this morning, when Allegra had told him she was engaged, he had been tense and on edge, but now he was almost certain her engagement was fake. Especially since the fiancé she had produced out of the blue was an employee. But he was also aware that he couldn't risk making that assumption.

He slid his phone out of his pocket and made a call to the head of the Miami branch of Hunt Private Investigations. Tulley picked up almost immediately. Minutes later, Tobias terminated the call.

If Allegra had hired Mike to play her fiancé, Tobias had to assume she had done so to either make it look as if she hadn't influenced the will and was an innocent party in Esmae's machinations, or she was trying to protect herself from him.

Given that Allegra had no compunction about putting him in his place, he did not think the second reason applied.

Of course, he couldn't rule out the possibility that he had gotten the situation completely wrong, and the engagement was real.

Although, he didn't think so.

Just the thought of Allegra with Callaghan made his jaw tighten. Every instinct told him that, despite the engagement, they weren't lovers, yet.

The dynamic did seem more employer-and-employee than lovers, but he couldn't take the risk.

He had given Tulley twenty-four hours to investigate Callaghan, but whatever the PI uncovered, Tobias was already decided.

Callaghan had to go.

Seven

Allegra closed the door of her bedroom behind her and leaned on it, her heart racing.

She touched her mouth, which was still faintly swollen and tingling. She couldn't believe she had let Tobias kiss her, *in full view of Mike, while he had been taking a call down on the drive.*

If Mike had turned his head by just an inch or two and looked up, he would have seen them, then the whole engagement scenario would have become...complicated.

A flashback to the moment Tobias's mouth had come down on hers made her tense. Suddenly, it seemed unbearably hot, the air humid and close. Pushing away from the door, she walked through to her en suite bathroom and splashed cold water on her face. After blotting her face dry, she hung up the thick, luxurious hand towel and checked her appearance in case she had smudged her mascara, which she had.

Using one of the cleansing pads Marta always kept the bathrooms supplied with, she cleaned away the dark smudges and took stock. Unfortunately, her mouth still looked faintly swollen, and there was a small red mark on her jaw, as if Tobias's five-o'clock shadow had grazed her skin.

Awareness tightened her stomach as she remembered the shiver of pleasure that had gone through her when he had done just that. To add to the picture of wanton abandonment, her neatly coiled hair had come loose to the point of collapse, and tendrils were wisping around her chin and clinging to her neck.

Dimly, she noted that was probably because Tobias's fingers had slid through her hair as he had cupped the back of her head while he had kissed her.

While *they* had kissed, she corrected bleakly. Tobias had moved in on her, but she couldn't forget that she had kissed him back with enthusiasm.

As if she couldn't get enough of him.

Forcibly tamping down her thoughts about Tobias, she returned to the bedroom, unzipped her case, and found her makeup case and the waterproof bag that contained her hair and skincare products.

Setting the cosmetic bags down on the beautiful oyster marble bathroom counter, she systematically unpacked, taking a simple pleasure in stocking the bathroom with all of the signature products of Madison Spas. Storing the empty cases in the vanity cabinet, she dragged the pins from her hair, brushed it out until it was smooth, then redid the smooth coil at her nape.

After dabbing concealer over the red mark, she smoothed on a tinted moisturizer, then touched up with a hint of blusher. A coat of mascara on her lashes and a quick colorless gloss on her lips finished off the transformation.

Walking back out to the bedroom, she unpacked her clothes, a process she hoped would normalize being in the same house as Tobias.

Unfortunately, feeling normal, when she had kissed him, not once, but *twice* in one day, was proving difficult.

The dire warnings one of her counselors had given her about the dangerous flaws inherent in burying what had happened between her and Tobias with an organized list of therapies, as if, cumulatively, they guaranteed a cure, came back to haunt her.

In a moment of clarity, she realized that the problem was that, underneath it all, she *liked* the challenge Tobias posed. He was exactly the kind of tall, muscular, brooding alpha guy she naturally gravitated toward. The second she stepped into the same room as Tobias, her heart sped up and adrenaline pumped.

The plain fact was, she had been brought up with wolves, and she had gotten used to running with them. If she had been able to wind Tobias around her little finger, she would have lost interest in him, the way she had with other men.

She took a deep breath and let it out slowly.

The thought that she might weaken and give in to the attraction that still drew her to Tobias, and which seemed just as powerfully at work in him, briefly transfixed her.

It wouldn't happen, she reassured herself. That was precisely why she had a fake fiancé.

Allegra grabbed a fragile, filmy dress in a vibrant jungle print with a plunging neckline—another extremely expensive Messena original—and shoved it on a hanger.

All she had to do was manage her time so that she did not spend it with Tobias, and stick to the engagement program.

A great way to stay away from him tonight would be to look for the keepsakes Esmae had left her, and see if there was anything that remotely resembled an engagement ring. According to Marta, the antique trinket box her great-aunt had reserved for her was labeled with her name and stored somewhere in the attic of the beach house.

Returning to the bedroom, she transferred the remaining clothing into drawers and the gorgeous walk-in closet. The final item was her jewelry case. However, as she lifted it out of the suitcase, she realized that the steel catch had gotten caught in the stretchy webbing, which had secured her suits. The net result was that the box, which was *heavy*, slipped from her fingers and hit the floor. The lid sprung open and diamonds and pageant bling for Africa spilled across the floor.

Muttering beneath her breath, she returned all of the items to the box, taking care to store the genuine diamonds in their own special compartment. However, when she tried to close it, the lid wouldn't fasten properly, because the catch was now broken. She would either have to buy a new box, or get this one repaired.

She placed the jewelry case on a shelf in the closet, then neatly stored her cases away in there, as well. Her few dresses and outfits looked sparse and insignificant on their hangers, but that was a welcome reminder that her stay here would be short.

All she had to do was sleep in the beautiful king-size bed, eat the delicious meals that Marta left and locate the personal belongings that Esmae had stored in the beach house.

As heart-wrenching as it would feel to go through her aunt's personal things, she could not contain a certain buzz of excitement. The mysterious "keepsakes" aside, there was a painting of Alexandra Mallory, the interesting and mysterious ancestor Allegra had only ever heard about, but never seen.

Dinner was brief, and oddly anticlimactic. Allegra had expected that Tobias might try to engage her in conversation, so she had pointedly been busy on her phone. However, aside from an initial greeting, Tobias had practically ignored her, eating the fresh crab appetizer followed by one of Marta's spicy steak salads in between calls. Allegra had just found the cold dessert Marta had left in the fridge when Tobias had taken yet another call.

As he got up from the table, Allegra heard the name, Francesca, and froze.

Closing the fridge door, she walked out to the gorgeous dining room, which opened onto a terrace. She slapped the chilled bowl of dessert down on the solid oak server that ran along one wall as Tobias walked out onto the sun-washed terrace to take the call, in private.

Allegra spooned a small amount of the fresh fruit salad into a glass bowl, all while trying to convince herself that he couldn't possibly be talking to Francesca Messena.

Correction, Francesca Atraeus, because she was now married. But when she moved closer to the terrace, ostensibly to look at the view, she heard Tobias mention the name John, Francesca's tycoon husband, and all doubt evaporated.

An odd pastiche of emotions gripped her. Shock, and a sinking feeling that Francesca was *still* in contact with Tobias despite choosing and marrying someone else, followed by burning outrage.

How could Tobias kiss her *twice*—and both times it

had been a whole lot more than a kiss—then have a private, intimate chat with his ex-lover?

And what did Francesca Atraeus think she was doing? Wasn't one man enough for her?

The burst of anger gave way to a hollow feeling in the pit of her stomach that she recognized all too well, because she had felt the same empty feeling when she had found out that Tobias had gone straight from her bed to Francesca's.

She stared at her dessert. As tempting as the jewel-bright fruits looked, she was no longer hungry. Walking back to the table, she set the bowl, and her dessert fork, down. A sip of water relieved some of the tension in her throat but didn't shift the churning sensation in her stomach.

Two years ago, when she had learned that Tobias had gone back to Francesca, she had done some research and discovered an interesting fact, courtesy of his lover's social media pages. Francesca liked men, plural, and had gone through boyfriends like a hot knife through butter. But most of her exes were still in contact with her.

Either Francesca was the nicest person alive, or she enjoyed the power of keeping men on a string.

The low, clipped timbre of Tobias's voice grew louder, signaling that he was strolling back in the direction of the dining room. If she didn't know better, she would think it was a business conversation, but, as far as she knew, Tobias didn't have any business connections with Francesca, who was a fashion designer. That pointed to a possibility that made her jaw tighten: that Francesca, despite her marriage, still wanted Tobias.

When Tobias came back to the table, Allegra picked up her fork and tried to look interested in the fruit salad. "Business call?"

His expression was remote as he took his seat directly opposite her. "I thought you didn't want to talk."

She knew she should leave it, but somehow the fact that Tobias was talking to the woman he had dated before and after he had slept with her, *less than an hour after he had kissed her on the balcony*, was infuriating. It underlined the fact that, when it came to Tobias, she had always been in the shadow of another woman.

Picking up the dessert fork, she stabbed a piece of melon and attempted the smooth, professional smile she usually reserved for difficult clients. "I thought I heard the name Francesca."

"Francesca Atraeus. That's right. She's arriving on a flight tomorrow."

Allegra froze "She's coming *here*?"

"Is that a problem?"

Allegra abandoned the fork with its mangled piece of melon. "It is if she's coming to stay at this house, since I wasn't allowed to have Mike stay."

Tobias frowned. "Francesca's not staying here. Why would she, when she can stay at her husband's hotel?"

Allegra blinked. In the heat of the moment, she had forgotten that John Atraeus owned one of the swankiest hotels in town, so Francesca could stay there any time she liked. Not to mention the fact that she also had family in town.

The problem was, the instant Tobias had mentioned Francesca's name she had felt a weird sense of déjà vu. She had kissed Tobias, twice. That morning they had come crazily close to making love, *so of course Tobias was going to sleep with Francesca again.*

She took a deep breath and tried to think, although thinking was difficult when all she wanted to do was reach across the table, snatch up Tobias's phone, fling it over the terrace and watch it break into pieces.

With an effort of will, she dialed back on an anger that, after two years of counseling and calming therapies, should not exist. The kind of explosive anger she recognized all too well because she had felt it once before, when Tobias had left her bed and gone back to Francesca's.

She was jealous. Burningly, crazily jealous.

Allegra stared at the tough line of Tobias's jaw. She needed to go somewhere quiet and bang her head against something hard, something that would hurt. Somehow, she had once more allowed herself to become entangled in the old fatal attraction: she was back to wanting Tobias, again.

"So, why, exactly, is *she*—" she couldn't bring herself to say Francesca's name "—coming to Miami?"

Tobias, who had resumed eating his beef salad, as if nothing momentous had happened, paused. "Does it matter?"

Allegra kept her expression smooth and neutral with difficulty. "I wouldn't have asked if it didn't matter."

He set his fork down. "Her twin was interested in installing one of their boutiques at the Ocean Beach Resort. Since Sophie now has to be out of town for a couple of weeks, Francesca agreed to come and check the resort out."

Allegra took a sip of water while she tried to come to terms with the fact that Francesca could be a regular visitor at Ocean Beach. A regular part of Tobias's life, even though she was married. "The resort doesn't have space for another clothing boutique."

Then a horrifying thought occurred.

She pinned him with a fiery glance. "Unless you're planning on not renewing my lease when it expires in two month's time."

And of course, she suddenly knew that was *exactly*

what he was planning. She had been so absorbed with navigating the terms of the will, and getting through this month with Tobias, that she'd sidelined the issue of the lease. But, if he wanted to get rid of her completely, she couldn't think of a more perfect way.

"The reason the Messena twins are looking at the Ocean Beach Resort is that they know we're looking at expanding."

Allegra frowned, aware that Tobias had failed to answer her question about the lease, but she was now sidetracked by this new issue. "That's the first I've heard of it."

"That's because nothing's decided yet. At the moment, expanding the resort is at the planning stage."

Even though she knew she was overreacting, she couldn't seem to stop herself. "But you had time to tell Francesca."

Tobias's cool glance seemed to laser through her. The intensity of it made her suddenly aware that she had been just a little too transparent about the other woman; that she could even have made the mistake of letting him know she was jealous.

Just as quickly, she dismissed the notion. They were talking about the resort; she was worried about the future of her business. There was no way Tobias could know that she was becoming more and more annoyed about his relationship with Francesca.

"As a matter of fact," he said quietly. "Esmae had had tentative plans to expand, which she'd put on hold when she got unwell. Her banker, Gabriel Messena, brought up the project at the funeral. I gave him permission to mention that there could be retail premises becoming available in the next year to his sisters. Is that a problem?"

Allegra plastered a smooth, professional smile on her face. "Why would it be a problem?"

Briskly, she pushed to her feet. Picking up her dessert dish, she aimed a neutral look in Tobias's general direction, as if everything was perfectly fine. "If you'll excuse me, I'm going to have a look in the beach house attic while it's still light out. According to Marta, that's where Esmae stored the items she wanted me to have."

As Allegra walked up the stairs to her bedroom, she acknowledged that the fact that Francesca Messena was still in Tobias's life, and still wanted him, shouldn't be a problem.

But, now that she had acknowledged that she wanted Tobias, it was a *big* problem.

Until Allegra received evidence to the contrary, she had to assume that Francesca, despite her marriage to John Atraeus, had once again set her sights on Tobias.

Two years ago, Francesca had gotten Tobias, and Allegra had let him go. But that would be happening again over her dead body.

It occurred to her that she could not go after Tobias and keep her fake engagement to Mike.

She would have to choose.

A fake fiancé who was extremely expensive and who had to be cued at every turn? Or a frustrating, elusive, battle-scarred tycoon who was making no bones about the fact that he wanted her in his bed, at least for now?

And she would have to make her choice before Francesca landed in Miami.

Eight

Allegra took the path down the hill to the beach house as the sun finally set and the long, extended twilight settled in. Flicking on her phone light, she negotiated the final set of steps and climbed onto the deck of the beach house, which was located on a steep bank that overlooked the beach. She found the key to the back door, which was concealed beneath a potted plant, and paused for a moment, because it had been so long since she had ventured anywhere near the beach house. Unlocking the door, she stepped into the small hall.

Wrinkling her nose at the stuffy heat, she flicked on a light to relieve the gloom, and left the door open to let fresh air circulate through the house. Sliding her phone into a handy pocket in her dress, she did a quick walk through an equally hot-and-stuffy kitchen, dining and sitting room area, and decided to open a set of French doors to allow the sea breeze to flow through.

For once, she was unable to appreciate the breathtaking view of the ocean stretching to a hazy horizon and, off to the right, the pier, with its dinghy floating off a rope at the end. If it was this stifling downstairs, the attic would be like an oven. Taking a last deep breath of fresh air, she headed upstairs, flicking lights on as she went.

Despite her every effort, her heart sped up as she walked past the master bedroom, with its wrought iron four-poster bed—draped in filmy mosquito netting—dark floorboards and bleached woven rugs. Two years had passed since she'd spent the night with Tobias here. She had expected it to look different but, disorientingly, it all looked exactly the same.

Dragging her gaze from the bed, she flicked on a hall light, dispelling the sense of being caught in the past, and entangled in memories that were still too vivid. However, as she started up the narrow flight of stairs that led up to the attic, the wall sconce made a suspicious buzzing sound, flickered, then died.

She muttered beneath her breath because, when she had switched on that last light, it must have been too much for the antiquated system, and now she had blown a fuse, plunging the entire upstairs into darkness. Reaching into her pocket, she found her phone. Moments later, she activated the flashlight app again and a reassuring beam of white light illuminated the door to the attic.

She had only ever been up here once before, when Esmae had asked her to bring down a box of clothing she had wanted to donate to charity. As she stepped into the dusty, vaulted room, striped with shadows, courtesy of the window shutters, a curious sense of expectation assailed her. Even though she was a Mallory, and knew the basic story of what had gone wrong between Alexandra and Jebediah, actual facts were sketchy. And, while she had seen sepia photos of her grandparents, she had never glimpsed a picture of Alexandra or her husband, James Walter Mallory, who had died before Alexandra had left England.

She flicked a light switch. Of course, nothing happened.

She beamed the light from her phone around the room as she picked her way through old tea chests and broken furniture. Dust made her cough as she brushed past furniture that had probably not been touched for decades. She found the catches of the shutters and, systematically, opened them to allow the last natural light of the day to lighten the gloom, and took stock.

Apparently, Esmae's personal family items, for convenience, were situated close to the door. Almost instantly, Allegra spotted an old dresser shoved up against the wall. A small wooden box sat on top of it.

In order to reach the dresser, she had to skirt a broken armchair and clamber across what looked like an ancient travelling trunk. The second she touched the box, which had a small white label on it bearing her name, a small pulse of excitement went through her.

She brushed her palm over the smooth surface of the lid. As she cleaned the dust off, the nascent gleam of the letter *A* inset in mother-of-pearl in the fine, dark wood, sent another small thrill through her. This must have been Alexandra's personal jewelry box.

Out of nowhere, emotion washed through her, strong enough that she even felt faintly teary, which was unusual since she hadn't expected to feel much of a connection. After all, she had never met Alexandra Mallory, and most of what she'd learned had left a conflicting impression.

She hefted the box, which was surprisingly heavy, and

decided to carry it downstairs where she could clean it up, wash her hands, then examine the contents in the light.

Several minutes later, she set the box down on the kitchen counter. After washing the dust from her hands, she checked out the kitchen cupboards. Esmae had always kept the kitchen fully stocked with cleaning products and basic items, just in case someone came to stay, so there was no problem finding paper towels and hand wash.

As she wiped away the remaining dust that coated the box, the quality of it became clear. Allegra couldn't be sure, but the dark, swirling wood looked like rose-wood, and the mother-of-pearl inlay wasn't just confined to the letter *A*, but was used as a decorative edging and for a delicate filigree of flowers that encircled the *A* and flowed around the box.

Throwing the soiled paper towels in the trash, she unlatched the silver catch and opened the lid. She didn't know what she expected to find, but the faded diary sitting on top wasn't it.

She removed the diary and found a series of worn black velvet bags. She opened the first one and a fiery necklace flowed into her palm. She was no expert, but from the color shooting off the clear crystals, she was pretty sure they were diamonds. Although, she couldn't really tell in this light. She would have to examine them in the morning, and get them properly assessed by a jeweler.

If they were diamonds, that just didn't make sense. She knew how the story went. Alexandra and Esmae were both supposed to have been broke.

Who lost everything but held onto the family jewels?

The remaining bags contained matching earrings, a brooch, a bracelet and a stunning ring. There were also simpler, prettier pieces, comprised of pearls and garnets, that looked like they belonged to an older time, the gold heavy and gleaming, the settings blurred.

Feeling more than a little confused, because she hadn't known that this jewelry even existed, and Esmae had never breathed a word, Allegra carefully replaced all of the items. She could only assume that her aunt had inherited the jewelry at some point but, because she had married an incredibly wealthy Hunt, she had stowed it away rather than wear something that might be contentious.

But that still didn't explain why Esmae had never spoken about it, or why it had all been left up here, to molder in a dusty attic.

Leaving the box on the counter, she made her way through the dim house and climbed back up to the attic to see if she could locate the painting of Alexandra. She was in the middle of clambering across an old sofa when a scraping sound made her freeze. Her first thought was that she had disturbed rats, in which case she was leaving *now*; then the low, gravelly timbre of Tobias's voice registered.

"Damn, what's happened to the lights?"

Allegra stepped on something that shifted under her foot, a moldering pile of magazines. Luckily, she was still holding onto the back of the sofa, so she kept her balance. "I think I blew a fuse when I switched on the hall light."

A beam of light briefly pinned her. "When you didn't return to the house, I thought something must have happened. I'll check out the fuse box in the morning. If it's still the old, antiquated system my grandfather had put in, the whole thing probably needs replacing." He swept his phone light around the room. "Damn, didn't Esmae throw anything away?"

"Apparently not. And neither did anyone else." She

held up what looked like an ancient cattle whip. "I'm thinking this didn't belong to Esmae."

"Let's hope not."

She caught the gleam of a wicked grin, quickly gone, and for a moment, her heart stopped in her chest. She had seen Tobias laugh and smile before, but it had always been for others, never for her.

Tobias dragged the huge old horsehair sofa she had just scaled aside. The next obstacle was a large and hideous armchair that was leaking stuffing.

He hefted the chair as if it weighed nothing, propping it on top of an old mattress. "About time most of this stuff went in a dumpster."

Dust swirled in the air, making her sneeze, but at least he had cleared a path. "Thanks, I think." She found herself smiling in Tobias's direction, which was faintly shocking, because in all the years she had known him, she didn't think they had ever shared this kind of light banter.

"No problem. Looks like Esmae stored a good three generations of junk up here. It's going to take weeks to clear it all out."

Tobias beamed his phone light into the corner. "Is that what you're looking for?"

Allegra glimpsed the outline of a painting, covered by a sheet and propped against the wall. Her heart sped up. If she didn't miss her guess, that was Alexandra's portrait.

"That would be four generations of junk," she said softly.

Dragging the dustcover aside, she shone her light on the painting and caught her breath. Apart from the fact that Alexandra's skin was pale and her hair was darker than Allegra's—and the time period was Victorian—it was eerily like looking into a mirror.

Her great-grandmother had clearly been painted when she was young, possibly before she had married. Her smile was warm and faintly mischievous, as if she was on the edge of dissolving into laughter, and there was a sparkle in her very direct gaze. Allegra hadn't expected to feel any kind of a connection with her ancestor, but the painting was so lifelike and vivid that it seemed to bridge the gap of years.

Allegra checked out Alexandra's hands in the painting. There was no ring, so she was definitely painted before she had married. She also noted that while Alexandra was wearing some of the older, more ornate garnet-and-pearl jewelry from the box, there wasn't a diamond in sight.

Tobias's phone light joined with hers, bringing out the Titian glow of Alexandra's hair, the gleam of her eyes and the exotic cut to her cheekbones, as if somewhere along the line she had Italian blood flowing through her veins. "She's beautiful,"

An unexpected glow of happiness flooded her as Allegra attempted to lift the painting up, in order to move it closer to the attic door. If Tobias thought Alexandra—who looked remarkably like herself—was beautiful, then, by definition, he must also think that she was beautiful.

"I'll get that." Tobias lifted the heavy painting from her hands as if it weighed almost nothing and propped it by the attic door. "No wonder Jebediah wanted to marry her."

Allegra frowned. "That's the first I've heard of that."

Tobias made his way across the attic to the nearest window. He yanked at a catch that had stuck, and eventually got the window open. A cooling breeze relieved the heat. "They were sleeping together, and he had plans to marry her. That was the reason he went into business with her."

Indignation rose in Allegra. "Last I heard, sleeping with a man isn't part of a business contract, unless—"

"She agreed to the marriage," Tobias said bleakly. "Then, practically the next day a city lawyer turned up and Alexandra and her two children disappeared. No explanations, no goodbyes. The lawyer wrote from New York to terminate the business relationship and the rest is history."

Suddenly, the animosity between the Hunts and the Mallorys was beginning to make more sense. It hadn't all been about the oil well; it had been *personal*.

Allegra stared at the fresh-faced portrait of a young lady with a firm chin and a remarkably steady gaze. Allegra hadn't dwelled overmuch on the conflicted history of the Hunts and the Mallorys, but in her opinion, Alexandra didn't look anything like a gold-digger. "It sounds like we have two different stories. Mine says that my great-grandmother who was left on her own after her husband died, brought up two children who turned out to be successful, functional human beings. When the money ran out, she died poor and still alone. I don't know what happened between them, but Jebediah must have gotten it wrong." But, even as she said the words, she couldn't forget the cache of diamonds in the jewelry box downstairs.

"Whether he got it wrong or not," Tobias said on a flat, hard note, "it was Jebediah who got hurt."

Her gaze clashed with his. "But he clearly recovered and married, while Alexandra never did. Explain that. And, if she was so beautiful and so focused on the bottom line, why go to bed with a ranch hand? For that matter, why go into business with him? It doesn't make sense. The obvious solution for a woman who wanted riches was to marry someone with a fortune."

"Is that what you would do?"

The words seemed to drop into the well of the night, and suddenly the conversation was deeply, unbearably personal. Years of hurt coalesced into a hard bands across her chest. She had lost count of the times men, in general, had seen her as on the hunt for a rich husband, or trivialized her because she was a woman and attractive. For Tobias to do it was the last straw.

"That would be no and no." Dragging in a deep breath, she tried to dial down the tension that was humming through her. It registered that half the problem was that it was so hot and humid and dusty in the attic that it was hard to breathe. Deciding to leave the painting where it was and get it another day, she stepped through the door and started down the pitch-black stairs, her trusty phone with its light beaming ahead of her.

She was aware of the click of the attic door closing, Tobias's tread on the stairs behind her, and suddenly she was sick and tired of being treated like a cheap opportunist, and spoiling for a fight. When she reached the hall landing, she spun and jabbed a finger at his chest. "I don't know how you can make a comment like that. You don't know the first thing about me. I didn't get a business degree because I wanted to sit at home doing my nails while some man goes out and provides for me. I prefer to create my own business opportunities and make my own money."

Something flashed in Tobias's gaze. "And keep your men controllable. Like Mike."

Her brows drew together. There was something fundamentally wrong with the conversation. First she was some kind of cliché gold-digger looking for a man to take care of her. Now, apparently, she was domineering. "What makes you think Mike's controllable?"

"He is your employee."

"And you think I'd hold that over his head?"

"It's not the kind of relationship I'd be aiming for."

"Now I'm interested," she shot back. "Tell me what the perfect relationship looks like, since, clearly I haven't stumbled across it yet."

Tobias's hand landed on the wall beside her head. Suddenly, he was close enough that she could smell the clean scent of his skin and the subtle hint of an expensive aftershave. "You need someone who won't take orders."

"Last I heard you're not even close to a love doctor." She drew a lungful of air and lifted her chin, but that was a mistake, because it brought her mouth closer to his. "Got someone in mind?"

Something heated and unbearably familiar flashed in his gaze. Wrong question. She had practically issued an invitation.

"Now that you mention it," he said flatly, "that would be me."

Nine

Heat flooded Allegra, almost welding her to the spot. She met Tobias's gaze boldly. "I thought you didn't want a relationship."

"It's more that I don't want to want one," he ground out.

"That makes it worse!"

His head dipped, and she felt the edge of his teeth on one lobe. Sensation arced through her. The passionate moments on her bedroom balcony replayed through her mind. She needed to move, *now*. The conversation had gotten too personal and, when it came to Tobias, her will-power wasn't good. This close, she was reminded of the night they'd spent together, of how good it had felt before everything had gone so horribly wrong.

She drew back. "What makes you think I still want you?"

"This." He brushed his mouth across hers.

She drew an impeded breath. "That's not fair."

Tobias picked up a strand of hair and wound it around his finger, tugging lightly. "Believe me, if I could control whatever it is that happens to me when you're around, I would."

That wasn't what she wanted to hear, that she was someone he was unwillingly attracted to, rather than someone he could have a genuine relationship with. But, along with the hurt, there was a glimmer of light at the end of a long, dark corridor. "But you do want me."

And, ever since they'd first slept together, he hadn't been able to stop wanting her. It wasn't much, it wasn't enough, but it was *something*.

"Six years now, and counting."

Her breath came in. She had expected him to say two years, not six.

Six years ago, she'd had her first holiday in Miami. It had been a gift from Esmae to celebrate the successful completion of her first year at Stanford. It had also been the start of her crush on Tobias, who, at that point, had used to keep his yacht moored off the end of Esmae's pier. Allegra had used to sit on the beach with her sunglasses and a magazine and try to pretend that she wasn't fascinated and a little heartsick that Tobias always had his beautiful blond girlfriend in tow.

Her aunt had been kind enough to invite her back during subsequent summer breaks. In all of that time, Tobias, who had always been cool and distant, had barely seemed to notice her. Until they had ended up sitting on the same log at a beach party that had followed the more formal birthday party Esmae had thrown.

She planted her palms on the warm, hard muscle of his chest. "Then why did you walk away after our night together? Don't tell me it was because of the Jebediah and Alexandra thing."

"To be honest, that never entered my mind—"

"Because it doesn't apply to us," she said fiercely "It never has."

He pulled her close, and she let him, suddenly needing to feel that the wanting was real.

"I'd broken up with Lindsay a couple of weeks earlier—"

"The tall, blond girl you were engaged to?"

And, suddenly, she got it. He had said six years, which meant he had wanted her *while* he had been in a relationship with Lindsay. She frowned, because that meant she had been the "other woman" for Lindsay, which wasn't cool. Not that she had known it! "And you felt guilty because you wanted me."

"Something like that."

She registered that there was more that he wasn't telling her, but it was hard to concentrate on what that could be when she was so thrilled that he had genuinely wanted her for *six* years. She was on the verge of probing into what, exactly, that *more* could be, when he leaned down and kissed her and the question dissolved.

Lifting up on her toes, she angled her jaw to deepen the kiss, looped her arms around his neck and fitted herself more closely against him. His instant response sent a wave of heat through her.

She registered his hands on her waist, then they were moving, one step backward, through a doorway. Even though it was dark, and the phone lights were not much help, if she didn't miss her guess, this was the bedroom they had made love in last time. Two more steps, and she felt the soft but firm outline of a bed at the back of her knees.

Tobias lifted his head, but she pulled his mouth back to hers and kissed him again, long enough that she felt she was drowning in sensation. His hands settled at her waist, then glided up her back. She felt her dress slacken as her zipper glided down. Flimsy cotton puddled around her feet on the floor. By the time she had stepped out of it, Tobias had dispensed with her bra.

She dragged at the buttons of his shirt and found naked skin, and the intriguing roughness of the hair sprinkled across his chest. With an impatient movement, he finished the job, shrugged out of the garment and let it fall to the floor. His hands closed around her breasts, sending heated sensation zinging through her. He dipped his head and took one nipple into his mouth, and time seemed to slow, then stop, as heat gathered and coiled tight.

"Oh, no you don't," he said huskily.

A split second later, the room went sideways as he swung her up into his arms. Dimly, she registered that one of her sneakers had slipped off her foot, while the other was still on, then the coolness of the linen coverlet sent a faint shiver through her as he set her down on the soft expanse of the daybed.

Outside, the wind, which had picked up, sent rain scattering against the windows. But in the darkened room, illuminated only by their phone lights, it still felt close and overly warm.

Feeling suddenly vulnerable and exposed, despite not quite being naked, she toed off her remaining sneaker and watched as Tobias peeled out of his pants. Light and shadow flowed over his broad shoulders, tiger-striping his muscled torso and narrow hips, and her breath came in at his raw, masculine beauty. Dimly, she registered that Tobias had just sheathed himself with a condom. The fact that he carried condoms on him made her go still inside. Maybe he was just careful, and they were not for anyone specific. But the fact that he had them on hand pointed out the obvious, that Tobias was a sexually active male.

The thought that the condoms could be for Francesca Messena made her stiffen. If she'd had any doubts about making love with Tobias, they were gone in that moment. Francesca might have plans for Tobias, but right now, he was *hers*.

Six years ago, Allegra had taken one look at Tobias, her mind had gone blank and her body had reacted. It had been chemistry, pure and simple, and the plain fact was she had never fully recovered from it.

Somehow, despite all of the work she had done to move on, the attraction had lingered and she had become ensnared by it again.

But then, so had Tobias.

The bed dipped as Tobias came down beside her. She wound her arms around his neck and snuggled close, her breath coming in at the intimate heat of skin on skin.

A long drugging kiss later, and she lifted her hips so he could strip her panties down her legs, then there was no time to think. She grasped his shoulders as he slowly entered her. Then, she shifted a little, trying to ease the pressure, because it had been two years since they had made love. Two years, during which she hadn't wanted to be intimate with anyone.

And before that? Well, she just hadn't been intimate with anyone. She had been too driven, too busy and too annoyed with the expectation that she should have sex with a guy just because *they* wanted it. Consequently, the experience was still weirdly new.

His gaze locked with hers as he seated himself fully inside her. "Are you okay?"

She grasped his shoulders and braced herself, every cell taut and tingling as he began to move. "I'm fine."

She drew an impeded breath. "You're wearing a condom, which is good, because I do not want to be an unwed mother. Just...don't stop."

And, right there, he stopped.

She caught the gleam of a wry smile. "Do you always like to be in charge?"

"Of course, I like to be in charge," she muttered. "I'm from Louisiana."

This time he definitely grinned, as if it was cute that she was from Louisiana. He should meet her mother. She frowned when he still didn't move. She wriggled a bit closer. What *was* the holdup?

Inspiration struck. She had read *a lot* about nipples. Apparently, you could control men when you touched them. So, she touched them.

He made a sound somewhere between a strangled groan and a laugh, but at least he started moving.

She clung to his shoulders, and it was all she could do to contain the intense waves of sensation and emotion that broke through her. It had been so long since they had last made love, since she had felt truly desired. She had never thought of herself as a particularly sensual person, but when she was with Tobias she felt acutely sensitive and, somehow, more alive. Pleasure zinged through her and, when he touched her, she practically purred. And, until this very moment, she hadn't realized how much she had *missed* Tobias despite the hurt, despite everything she had done to surgically remove him from her life.

Tobias found her mouth and kissed her then, suddenly, there was no containing anything as heat coiled and built unbearably, then splintered into the night.

Long minutes later, her eyes flipped open. She thought she had closed her eyes for just a few minutes, but in that time the phone lights had died, so she guessed it must have been an hour or more.

Outside, the wind was now gusting, and a light rain was still pattering on the windows, which meant the weather was blowing in off the sea. The air temperature had dropped, but she was toasty warm because Tobias's arm was wrapped around her waist, as if he wanted to keep her close, even in sleep.

Turning her head on the pillow, she tried to see his face, but it was now so dark, she couldn't make out actual features, so she consoled herself by snuggling in a bit closer. Although it was hard to relax, because she had loved making love with him, more than she could have imagined, and she wanted to do it again. And, now that she was awake, she didn't feel one bit tired.

The rain stopped, and there must have been a break in the clouds, because the room lightened. Propping herself on one elbow, Allegra stared at Tobias. Moonlight shafted more strongly through the French doors, illuminating his clean-cut profile and rock-solid jaw, the inky crescent of his lashes.

She had an almost overwhelming urge to reach out and trace the line of his jaw, wake him up and kiss him. Anticipation was already humming through her at the prospect of being in his arms again, but that gave her pause.

The giddy happiness welling up inside, the desire to throw caution to the winds and live in the moment, made her go still inside.

What if this was just an attraction that was finally working its way toward a dead end and, after the month was up, they would both be over each other?

Or, maybe, just maybe, it was the real thing.

Her heart beat a little faster at the thought of settling

down with Tobias, of a real relationship, maybe even marriage.

But she couldn't forget that the last time she had imagined a future with Tobias, he had ditched her.

That meant she had to start thinking, and not just feeling. Tobias was a challenge: used to command, and with a quiet, seasoned toughness that she knew stemmed from his years in Special Forces. And she couldn't forget that there had been no words of commitment, or love. Just the off-the-register attraction that had bound them together for six years.

As much as she wanted to reach out and touch him, to snuggle in close and rouse him with a kiss, she was suddenly certain that if she wanted to win Tobias, she would not do so by giving in and having sex with him again.

They had already made love, and nothing had changed.

Tobias had finally opened up about Lindsay, but getting information out of him had been like getting blood out of a stone. And the fact that he had left his fiancée because he had wanted her still niggled. Something about his confession just hadn't added up...then it finally came clear.

If Tobias had been fighting an attraction to Allegra for years, why had he gotten engaged to Lindsay in the first place? And why *stay* engaged, when he knew that he wanted someone else?

Then there was the fact that, when he had finally broken things off, he had not tried to start a relationship with her. He had just spent one night with her and walked away.

As if he didn't consider her relationship material.

As if he saw her the way some guys at university had, as some kind of clichéd beauty queen, who was only good for a casual fling. And, suddenly, a whole lot of other things fell into place.

They had been at each other's throats at the lawyers. Then, suddenly, he had wanted sex with her in the parking garage. Almost as if he had decided that, since she was in his house for the month, why not have sex with her, *and get her out of his system*?

The more she thought about it, the surer she became.

She was certain that if she did continue to have sex with Tobias, which would be the easy option, he would be only too happy, because it would confirm the image he had of her and make it easy to walk away at the end of the month.

And just like that, she was *back*.

Now, hopping mad, she moved carefully, so she wouldn't wake Tobias, who she no longer wanted to touch, and slipped from the bed. Her bare feet landed on cool, marble-smooth floorboards. She straightened, becoming aware of the faint stiffness that went with making love when she was unaccustomed to doing so, a stiffness she had only ever experienced once before.

That small fact made her even madder. The fact that she had only ever made love with Tobias was…worrying.

Since she liked it so much, why hadn't she slept with anyone else?

Tiptoeing around the room, she found her phone, picked up her clothes and sneakers, then went to the bathroom to freshen up and change.

As she zipped up her dress and pulled on her sneakers, she noted that one of her key problems was that she'd never had a casual approach to sex, because that just wasn't how she was wired. For starters, she was naturally suspicious of intimacy; she just didn't like people close when she didn't know them very well. And, after the "problem" in San Francisco, she had gotten even more hard line.

And yet, she had made love with Tobias, and made herself vulnerable to him in ways that he hadn't seemed to notice.

For a start, she had been a virgin.

Another thought occurred to her. Tobias had made a point of letting her know how important his engagement to Lindsay had been. Apparently, his attraction to Allegra had been a betrayal that Lindsay had not been able to forgive. But Tobias had not at any point asked her about her own engagement to Mike.

Her brows jerked together. She wondered how Tobias could not care that they were both, supposedly, betraying Mike in an even worse way?

Of course, the engagement wasn't real, but he didn't know that.

She briefly considered that Tobias had gotten swept away by passion and had simply forgotten she was engaged.

Or maybe he hadn't forgotten the engagement at all, *but saw making love to her as a legitimate way to cut Mike out and claim her for himself.*

She drew a slow breath as she examined the possibility. Tobias behaving that way made a curious kind of sense. His actions had not been above board or even honorable.

What they had been was *alpha*.

Ten

Allegra tiptoed downstairs, wincing when a floorboard creaked beneath her bare feet. When she reached the kitchen, she grabbed the jewelry box from the counter and let herself out the door onto the deck. Minutes later, sneakers on her feet, she was walking along the moonlit path back to the main house. At the top of the hill, the brightly lit windows of the mansion were like a warm beacon.

She checked her watch. It felt like hours had passed, but it wasn't quite midnight. She had only been in the beach house for just over three hours. Having some of the best sex of her life, and for only the second time in her life, *with the same man.*

As she climbed onto the terrace, she paused for a moment to take in the view, which was breathtaking. The sky was filled with ragged clouds. Despite that, the moon was full and had turned the sea to molten silver, and etched the sweep of lawn with the jagged silhouettes of trees and the pitched roofline of the beach house.

She had left the fascinating painting of Alexandra behind, but she would retrieve that tomorrow. The main thing was that she had the jewelry, and she couldn't wait to get to her room so she could clean up the ring she had discovered and see if she could use it as a fake engagement ring.

Anxious to reach the sanctuary of her bedroom before Tobias caught up with her, she stepped inside and hurried through the dark corridor and up the stairs. She was well aware that she did not have a good track record with Tobias. If he caught up with her now, she would probably not be able to resist him. They would make love again, and that could be fatal.

In order to reverse the mistakes she'd made, she needed to move forward with the relationship strategy she had already put in place, otherwise what they had might stall and die. That meant no sex until Tobias was ready to use words like *love* and *commitment*.

She continued up the sweeping elegant stairs. Once inside her room, she closed the door, set the jewelry box down on her bedside table and flicked on the bedside lamp. She also remembered to put her phone on charge, since using the flashlight had drained the battery.

Shivering slightly, because the rainy weather had definitely dropped the temperature, she drew the curtains.

She found fresh underwear, and the soft T-shirt and cotton shorts she liked to sleep in, and walked through to the bathroom. After quickly showering and washing her hair, because she wanted to leave super early in the morning before Tobias got up, she toweled herself dry. Once she was cozily belted into a light cotton bathrobe, she strapped her watch onto her wrist. That had gotten to be a habit, because she still liked to keep an eye on her heart rate. She then stood in front of the mirror as she combed out her hair and dried it.

As she did so, her gaze was drawn to a red mark on her neck, and another on her jawline. Small abrasions that were probably caused by the five-o'clock shadow on Tobias's jaw.

She drew a swift breath as heated memories surfaced. Tobias kissing her neck, nuzzling her jaw, biting down delicately on one lobe…

A soft click made her start. The sound had come from downstairs and was probably a door closing, which meant Tobias had walked back to the house. Instantly, her heart sped up.

She quickly switched off the bathroom light, then walked through to her bedroom and killed the bedside lamp, plunging the room into darkness. Maybe she was overreacting, but if Tobias knocked on her door, she didn't trust herself not to let him in. If he saw that her lights were off, chances were he would just go straight to bed.

Long seconds later, she heard his footsteps as he walked past her room, then the sound of his door closing.

Contrarily, she felt annoyed that he hadn't even so much as paused at her door. Feeling her way in the dark, she found her bed and sat down, keeping an eye on her watch, which glowed in the dark. A minute or so later, she heard the sound of a shower then, a few more minutes later, a door closing. When a further five minutes had passed without any sound, she flicked her lamp back on.

Hefting the jewelry box, she set it down on the bed. It looked even richer and more beautiful in the soft glow of the lamp. After she had removed the diary and set it down on the bedside table, she began emptying the velvet bags onto the white coverlet.

White wasn't the best background color to view the jewelry, and she wasn't a jeweler, so she couldn't be sure—maybe they were just paste—but the "diamond" jewelry looked breathtakingly real. She picked up the ring, which stood out as being different from the other pieces because it was smaller and plainer. With its cushion-shaped diamond and simple gold band, it was quite definitely an engagement ring.

Feeling almost as if she was trespassing on someone else's memories, she slipped the diamond ring onto her ring finger. It was too tight, which was a shame, but it looked pretty. She would have to get it resized before she could wear it.

Slipping the ring off, she returned it to its velvet bag. She then collected up all of the other jewels, placed them back into their velvet bags, then stowed them all in a zipped pocket in her handbag. She would take them into her favorite jeweler, Ambrosi, first thing in the morning. Hopefully, they would be able to assess the "diamonds" for her and resize the ring. Luckily, Ambrosi was in the Atraeus Mall, where she had arranged to meet Mike for their "getting the ring date," so that would save her some time.

She put the antique jewelry box away in the walk-in closet, then checked her phone, which was now showing some charge. She texted Mike, to give him a heads-up to check the schedule she had given him, because he needed to meet her at the Atraeus Mall tomorrow at twelve p.m. sharp.

Dragging back the coverlet, she climbed into bed and switched the lamp out, but just as she was finally sliding into sleep, inspiration struck, and she sat bolt up-right in bed.

Eighteen months ago, a girlfriend had treated her to an online seminar called *How to Get Your Alpha Man*. It had been run by Elena Lyons-Messena, who was a psychologist and something of a spa guru.

Pulled from Elena's own personal experience, it had been blunt and to the point. You didn't get your alpha man, who was a natural leader of the pack, by being soft and doing whatever he wanted you to do.

You got him by taking charge, by being opinionated and even difficult, because alpha men liked a challenge. If they thought you were just going to sleep with them and be all soft and cute, you could kiss the relationship goodbye, because they would be doing what alpha men did, looking for the next challenge.

From memory, there had been two key tactics, both based around availability.

Firstly, you had to make it clear that you would not always be available to him, but that you would fit him in when you could.

Secondly, make it clear that your schedule included *other men*. Once an alpha knew that you were available to other men, and that those men found you intensely desirable, it was a game changer.

Elena had been firm on the point that the strategy worked, because it catered to the alpha's natural instincts to fight for the woman they wanted, and to win her. As ruthless as the tactics were, she had suggested that the strategies could actually be viewed as a form of kindness toward your alpha male, because you got him through the whole pursuit-and-choice thing quickly, and then everyone could relax.

She had also noted that, if none of the strategies

worked, you needed to save yourself and leave him. At this point, the best-case scenario was that the alpha would wake up to what he had lost, come after you, and propose. Worst-case scenario: you would discover that you had gotten it completely wrong, and you could then get on with the rest of your life.

Now, thoroughly awake, Allegra flicked on her bedside lamp and found the book that went with the workshop. She flipped to the chapter on commitment. The first paragraphs seemed to leap off the page.

Warning: Sleeping with an alpha before they have committed is risky, because they can view the sex as "the prize," and you could end up being the victim of a one-night stand. If you have slept with your alpha too soon, you need to quickly find a way to reject him.

With alphas, "no" is a good word.

Shades of her mom!

According to the book, she had already committed the cardinal sin with Tobias, *twice.*

She had given him the prize of sex, and he hadn't had to pursue her to attain it, because both times she had practically seduced him. If there was a hunter in their "relationship," it was her.

That had to change.

She didn't know what the result of tonight's lovemaking would be but, given their track record, and the fact that Tobias was meeting Francesca some time tomorrow, she did not think Tobias had commitment in mind.

If she still wanted Tobias, that meant *she* had to change the way she behaved right now.

Uncannily, she had already made a start on Elena's strategy by trying, to make herself "unavailable" to Tobias, and signaling that she was available to another man, by getting "engaged" to Mike.

She was taking a risk by continuing with the charade, but the way she saw it, she had no choice.

She could not commit herself to a man who might never reach the point of committing to her. If Tobias didn't fight for her, it was a no-brainer. She needed to follow Elena's advice and walk away from a relationship that had already consumed six years of her life.

Just the thought of playing that kind of game made her heart beat faster, because a part of her just wanted to cling to Tobias and build on what they had.

But that would only result in her getting ditched again.

Eleven

The sun was attempting to diffuse a dawn glow through sullen, dense clouds as Allegra dressed in a gorgeous, short turquoise skirt with a matching camisole top, and a sheer white blouse that went over top. The gauzy blouse tied in a knot at hip-level, giving the whole outfit a sharp, but groovy, holiday vibe. As a final touch, she secured the Chanel earrings through her lobes, then slipped into a pair of strappy turquoise heels. She checked her watch, noting that it was almost seven, a whole hour earlier than she normally left for work, and shoveled her purse, makeup and phone into a white tote.

Her hair was still loose, and she hadn't put on any makeup, but she would do all of that when she got to work. Her main concern was to get out of the house before Tobias got up because, at a guess, he was going to be annoyed that she had walked out on him last night, and would want to know why. That was a conversation she didn't want to have right now.

The way she saw it, it was imperative that she move forward with her "engagement" to Mike, and it was entirely possible that Tobias, being the alpha that he was, would demand that she get rid of Mike while she was sleeping with him.

If Tobias was masterful enough, and gave her that look that made her knees melt, she could not guarantee that she wouldn't weaken and agree to "give up" Mike. If she did that, she would be throwing away the only leverage she had.

She didn't know how long she would be able to keep up the charade. At an optimistic best guess, she had a day, because by tonight Tobias would be totally ticked off and, if all went according to plan, he would demand a conversation.

At that point, he would realize the danger: that he was about to lose her to another man and, hopefully, would be galvanized to fight to win her back.

So, first off, she needed to get out of the house without Tobias seeing her. Second, she needed to move forward with making her "engagement" to Mike look more convincing than it currently did. Her plan was to take a nice pic of them having a romantic champagne lunch together to use as a screen saver on her phone. Tobias would then see it, because she would casually place her phone near him. Third, she would wait for Tobias to initiate a conversation about how he couldn't bear for her to marry Mike, because he had realized he couldn't live without her.

Before she left her room, she did a quick check of the jewelry, frowning when she noted that one of the old velvet bags had actually split open. Rummaging in her drawers, she found a portable jewelry case, emptied out the pretty selection of costume jewelry and dropped that in her tote. Once the jewelry had been assessed, she would toss the shabby old velvet bags and store the pieces in the case.

She grabbed a light rain jacket and tossed it over one arm. Apparently, there was some kind of storm system heading their way, so the weather was going to get worse, not better. After a last check of her appearance, she walked to the door and paused to listen. When all seemed quiet, she turned the ornate brass knob but, a split second before she opened the door, she heard the sound of footsteps and the low tones of Tobias's voice, as if he was talking on his phone.

Her heart slammed against her chest. Tobias was already up. She drew a deep breath and waited long seconds, just in case he was about to walk down to the kitchen. When she didn't hear anything further, she opened the door a crack. She could hear his voice in the distance, so he was obviously still on a call, but the hall was empty.

Breathing a sigh of relief, she stepped out into the hall and gently closed her door behind her. She made her way downstairs and cut through the kitchen, which were closest to the garage. When she reached her car, she delved into her tote in search of her keys. When she didn't find them, her stomach sank.

With all the turmoil of moving into Tobias's house, *and the kiss in her room yesterday afternoon*, she hadn't returned the keys to her handbag as she usually would. She had a vague recollection of setting them down on one of the bedside tables. That meant that when she had transferred items from one handbag to another this morning, she had not stowed her car keys, because they were still on her bedside table.

Dropping her tote and the rain jacket in the passenger seat, she jogged to the kitchen, then started up the grand, curving staircase, listening intently as she went.

Her pulse pounded when she heard a door pop open. She froze. Luckily, she was just far enough around the curve of the staircase that she wasn't visible to anyone in the hall. Although, if Tobias was walking toward the stairs, she was busted.

A few seconds later, she heard the click of a door closing. Straightening, she walked as quickly and quietly as she could to her room, ducked inside and found the keys.

She was tempted to brazenly stroll out of her door and down the stairs, but an innate caution made her pause. The sound of footsteps in the hall confirmed her decision. She waited for Tobias to walk past her door. He was clearly on his way to the kitchen so, once he was safely there, she could sneak down the stairs and leave via the front door.

His footsteps slowed, then stopped directly outside her door. She froze, certain he was about to knock. A split second later, she heard an audible vibration, then Tobias's low, curt tones as he answered a phone call. His voice receded, signaling that he was walking away as he took the call.

She made herself wait one more minute, then quietly opened the door and stepped out into the hall. Taking a deep breath, she walked as quietly as she could down the stairs, checked that Tobias was nowhere in sight, then tiptoed across the grand front foyer. Moments later, she was outside and walking around the side of the house to the garage. Luckily, none of the kitchen windows overlooked the garage, so she should be free and clear.

Tobias strolled through to the study to collect his briefcase, which, in all the confusion of moving in yesterday afternoon, he had left there.

He kept his phone to his ear as Tulley, the private investigator he had tasked to check out both Allegra and Mike, ran through a dry list of facts about Allegra. Facts that he already knew and that provided details of the scandal that had unfolded in San Francisco, but which did nothing to further illuminate what had happened.

Tobias had hoped Tulley might find evidence of coercion or financial pressure that would explain what his gut told him didn't fit, because the more time he spent with Allegra, the more discordant the online stories seemed.

And, after the couple of hours they had spent together in the beach house last night, he had been forcibly struck by something he should have seen before. Allegra was gorgeous, confident and mouthwateringly sexy, but she was also ultra-organized, assertive and direct.

Those qualities didn't sit easily with claims made by social media sites that she was an ambitious party girl using her looks and sex to snag a wealthy husband. Added to that, Tobias had found that, when it came to sex, if anything, Allegra was slightly awkward, even a little shy, almost as if she was unaccustomed to intimacy.

He frowned as that thought brought back a memory of the first time they had made love, two years ago. At the time, as unlikely as it had seemed, it had passed through his mind that Allegra could have been a virgin. But then he had read the online scandal around her and decided there was no way. Then Lindsay had miscarried, and he had done the only thing he decently could, and broken with Allegra completely.

His jaw tightened as a hot flash of the way Allegra had pressed against him last night sent a wave of heat through him. If she was not the free-and-easy party girl that certain social media accounts made her out to be, but the focused-and-professional businesswoman she appeared to be in Miami, then that made sense of her walking out on him last night. From her point of view, his behavior had been self-centered and insensitive *for the second time.*

As he picked up the briefcase, a flash of movement caught his eye. He glanced up in time to see Allegra, in a short turquoise skirt and a filmy white blouse and wearing high heels, jog across the gravel drive in the direction of the garage.

Dropping the briefcase back on the couch, he curtly told Tulley he would call him back. Terminating the call, he strode toward the kitchen. The throaty purr of her convertible starting broke the morning silence as he went through the door that opened onto a covered walk. Two strides later, he stepped into the garage.

Allegra was in the process of backing out. He called her name and was almost certain her gaze locked with his as she braked. Although, it was difficult to tell, because she was wearing sunglasses. A split second later, she spun the wheel and disappeared down the drive.

Jaw taut, he found her number and rang her. The call went straight through to voice mail.

He left a brief message, then slid his phone back in his pocket.

There was definitely a problem. He didn't know what, yet, but he would find out.

As far as he knew, Allegra never went anywhere without her phone. She was either on it, or she was listening to music, but there was no way she didn't know he was calling her. She just hadn't chosen to answer.

His jaw tightened as he returned to the sitting room and hit redial on Tulley's number.

It occurred to him that he had been asking the wrong questions.

Online social media platforms were notorious for twisted stories and outright lies. He had been the victim of a few himself. Four months ago, social media influencer, Buffy Hamilton, had, entirely by chance, been snapped with him at the same charity event. She had then implied they had spent the night together. JT had been on his case for weeks.

When Tulley picked up the call, Tobias told him to email him a copy of the report, then tasked him to do a second investigation, this time on the two wealthy guys, Fischer and Halliday, who had claimed that Allegra had slept with them for expensive gifts, and to further her career.

"I want to know everything," he said curtly. "And I want the report yesterday."

"Uh…before you hang up, I think you might want to hear what I found out about Mike Callaghan."

Tobias frowned. He had almost forgotten about Callaghan. "Go ahead."

"Aside from being employed by Miss Mallory as a yoga instructor and personal trainer, the guy's an actor. Apparently, he's waiting to see if he's got a part in some online-streaming daytime soap based in Hollywood, and once he's got that, he's out of here. And, get this…he's got a girlfriend. That is, someone other than Miss Mallory. And, apparently, he and Miss Mallory don't seem to have ever dated. In fact, my source, who works with them both, didn't even know they were a couple. Furthermore, she was pretty sure Miss Mallory was over Callaghan as an employee, and was on the verge of firing him."

Until she found a further use for him.

Satisfaction relaxed the tension that had gripped Tobias ever since Allegra had announced that she was engaged.

It was official. The engagement was fake.

In all likelihood, she had chosen Callaghan for the role *because* he was an actor. If that was the case, she had to be paying him. Given that her finances were stretched with starting a new business, and that she was looking to expand, that was something she probably couldn't afford.

The only reason that made sense of the fake engagement was that Allegra wanted to make it clear she'd had nothing to do with the clause in Esmae's will.

But then she had given him the exact opposite message by sleeping with him.

Tobias pinched the bridge of his nose. He couldn't believe it, but he was actually beginning to lose track of what was happening. It was a far cry from his days in tactical military intelligence when he had used to track down terrorist cells. But those were days when one plus one equaled two. And, with Allegra, apparently, that equation could add up to almost any number, depending on what she wanted. If she had been a spy, she would have run circles around the CIA, the KGB, Mossad…hell, everyone.

A little grimly, he noted that it was time to step away from a situation that was getting more and more entangled by the day. The only problem was, after last night, he didn't want to step away.

He wanted her back.

The decision settled in. There was no logic to the decision, just pure, unadulterated desire. Despite the red flags, he found Allegra to be quirky, challenging and fascinating. Making love with her was nothing short of addictive. After years of what had devolved into something less than a friendship with Lindsay, followed by the superficial relationships that had filled the gap since then, keeping Allegra in his bed was a no-brainer.

Fake engagement or not, he didn't want out.

And, if Allegra thought she could walk away from him without at least an explanation, she could think again.

He found the dating schedule he had picked up off the driveway yesterday and unfolded it. Two years ago, he had left Allegra cold. Now, he had to consider that he had made a mistake. He had hurt her, but he would make it up to her, if she would let him. But, first, they needed a conversation, and that was going to happen at… He found the date with Callaghan, which was scheduled for today, at the Atraeus Mall. At twelve, sharp.

Tulley cleared his throat. "Do you still want me to, uh…keep an eye on Miss Mallory?"

A flash of Allegra jogging across the drive, clearly trying to avoid him, played through his mind. She was up to something. His jaw tightened. Hell, yes.

In a clipped voice, he gave Tulley his orders. Keep an eye on Allegra's movements for the morning. "If she and Callaghan leave the resort together, call me."

Terminating the call, he walked through to the kitchen to make coffee. As far as Tobias was concerned, now that he and Allegra had made love, Callaghan should be out of the picture, but there were no indicators that that was happening.

He found grounds and started the filter machine. He should have made sure Callaghan was gone last night. The only problem was, he hadn't been exactly interested in conversation until he had woken up to find Allegra gone.

He had walked up to the house and noted that Allegra's light was on but, by the time he had reached the door of her room, her light was out.

He had considered knocking. Maybe it was just a co-incidence that her light had gone out just seconds before he had gotten there, but he didn't think so. She had been avoiding him.

That notion had been confirmed just minutes ago when he had watched her accelerating down the drive.

Frowning, he went over the sequence of events that had led to their lovemaking, then the encounter itself. From memory, there hadn't been a lot of conversation. In point of fact, his interactions with Allegra were the exact opposite of those he had with every other date he could remember.

But then, what he felt for Allegra was a whole lot different to what he'd felt for any other woman. It was a fact that his feelings were knee-jerk and intense and, he had to admit, his manners were mostly absent.

Normally, he was methodical and controlled in most areas of his life—in business, and especially in relationships. One of Lindsay's criticisms of him had been that he had been too locked down, too reserved. But, when it came to Allegra, he could not even seem to control his responses.

The rich fragrance of coffee filled the kitchen. Tobias filled a mug, but, before drinking it, he spread the two-page dating schedule out on the counter.

The crisp organization inherent in every neatly formed box was impressive. It confirmed that Allegra was take-charge and detail-oriented, even when it came to her personal life, and that, evidently, Callaghan did take orders.

Despite his frustration over Allegra neatly avoiding her last night, and this morning, he grinned at the thought. Even if he hadn't known Callaghan was a fake, the way she ran him around was clear evidence that he was all wrong for her. She would be bored with him in ten seconds flat.

Tobias studied Allegra's bolded instruction that she

would organize a ring. The word was clearly code for the fact that Allegra would be providing the ring.

His jaw compressed at the thought that she was going to the expense of buying a ring when she couldn't afford to do so.

On impulse, he retrieved his phone and opened up the email with the attachment of the report Tulley had just sent through.

He had never thought overlong about Allegra as a businesswoman—he had been too busy focusing on nixing the attraction that sizzled between them—but now that aspect of her was brought sharply into view.

He knew she had a business degree from Stanford, but Tulley had clarified that it was actually a master's in Finance, which was a considerably more prestigious, longer and more difficult degree. To add to the picture, apparently she had been a driven student, because she had graduated with distinction, with a grade point average of 4.7, which was crazy good.

Suddenly, the picture of Allegra as a good-time girl in search of a wealthy husband didn't even come close to panning out.

If that was her goal, and with her looks, she could have married at eighteen and spent her life shopping and lunching. Instead, she had gotten into Stanford, which was no easy task. Then, she had worked for five years for a degree that fitted her out for a high-flying career in the financial fast lane, earning six figures just to start.

One of the top West Coast financial firms, Burns-Stein Halliday, had recruited her. Just months later, her reputation in shreds, she had walked away from the firm and her career.

Almost six years of hard work and focused ambition

gone, because she had, apparently, decided that sex was a priority.

He set his coffee down, suddenly annoyed. He didn't think so.

To the best of his knowledge, Allegra had seldom dated at all. If she had one obsession, it was her business. And, in the two years she had been living in Miami, he only knew of one guy she had slept with, and that was him.

For the first time, he seriously considered that Allegra had been set up.

Tulley had made brief notes about the two men with whom she was supposed to have had wild extramarital affairs. They were both connected with the firm, one an executive who was married to the senior partner's daughter, the other an executive who was the nephew of one of the other partners. That instantly raised a red flag.

Why would Allegra risk sleeping with either of them, when she had to have known it could cost her the career for which she had worked so hard?

Tulley had included pictures of the two men. They were both now in their forties and fifties with the typical lean, tanned look of players. One of them even sported a diamond stud in one lobe. Neither of them was married now, but they both had been when the alleged scandal had happened.

He sat back in his chair. Adrenaline was running through his veins. He was beginning to feel the way he had before he had gone on a mission, coldly focused, ticked off and on edge.

If it turned out that one, or both, of those men had lied, probably to protect their own reputations in business, he would make it his business to expose what they had done.

And, if they had cost Allegra her career, they could pay for it.

Pushing to his feet, he finished his coffee, rinsed the cup and put it in the dishwasher.

Retrieving his briefcase, he walked through to the garage. With any luck, since he would be at the Ocean Beach Resort today, moving in as manager, he might even run into Allegra.

But, he wasn't betting on that happening.

Which was why he would make it a priority to be at the Atraeus Mall when she was supposed to be meeting with Callaghan.

Placing his briefcase on the passenger-side seat, he swung behind the wheel. But before he started the truck, he made a call to JT, who had connections in Hollywood, and instructed him to offer a large cash contribution to the production Callaghan had auditioned for, on the condition that they hired him *today.*

Forty minutes later, en route from his Hunt Security office to the Ocean Beach Resort, he took a call from JT. Callaghan had verbally accepted the contract offer.

Satisfaction eased some of the tension that gripped him.

When it came to Allegra, he was fiercely, uncompromisingly possessive. He'd spent six years trying to deny the attraction, because he just hadn't seen her as relationship material. She was almost too gorgeous and terminally high maintenance, with a stream of guys constantly vying for her attention. Then, when Lindsay had miscarried, the guilt that had hit him had underlined that giving in to temptation where Allegra was concerned had been a serious mistake.

But, two years on, he was beginning to realize that he had misread Allegra, and how much he *liked* her: the sass and the challenge, her sharp business mind and fierce independence; the fact that she ran rings around most men, including him. And the more he uncovered about the *real* Allegra, the more strongly he was attracted to her.

The plain fact was, he didn't just want her in his bed; he was beginning to want a whole lot more than that.

The thought of Callaghan placing an engagement ring on Allegra's finger, even as a sham, made his jaw lock.

That would happen over his dead body.

Twelve

Allegra drove into the underground parking garage of the Atraeus mall at eleven thirty, which would give her plenty of time to pick up the ring from the jeweler's before Mike arrived.

Hooking the strap of her tote over her shoulder, she took the elevator up to the ground floor and stepped out into the fabulous foyer, with its marble floors and glittering high-end boutiques.

Because she had wanted to avoid Tobias until she had the ring on her finger, she had deliberately absented herself from the spa. As it happened, she had put her time to good use, with meetings with her banker, then the real estate agent who had listed the property she was hoping would be her new spa. Now, all she needed was for Mike to turn up at twelve, as instructed.

She glanced around the mall, just in case Mike was early. He wasn't, so she decided to use the time to get a bunch of roses from the florist. The plan was simple. Buy the flowers, get the ring and install it on her finger, then snap some pics of herself looking vibrant and happy with Mike looking like a handsome, devoted fiancé. When that was done, she would install the pic as a screen saver and go back to the resort.

The heady scent of flowers wafted around her as she walked past buckets of cut blooms and beautiful bunches of roses. Automatically, she chose a dozen red roses, because they shouted romance *and* they would look totally striking against the turquoise and white of her outfit. She paid for them and strolled back out into the mall. As she did so, she glimpsed a tall, dark guy in a suit as he disappeared into an elevator. She stopped dead, her heart pounding, because she had been almost certain that was Tobias, although it couldn't be. She knew for a fact that he was spending the day at the resort with Marc, because she had checked.

She had a sudden flash of the annoyance on Tobias's face as she had backed out of the garage. Happily, she had thought to put her sunglasses on, so she had been able to pretend that she hadn't noticed him.

When she decided she had space in her day for him, he would see the ring and the flowers and understand that, just because they had slept together, that didn't mean she was happy to fall in with his plans to have casual, uncommitted sex with her for the next month.

She checked her watch and studied the bustling traffic, which was predominantly female. Mike was tall and distinctive; he would be easy to spot. Her gaze snagged on a small guy with blond hair who was standing, quite still, amid the milling shoppers, a phone in his hand, and who, at that moment, just happened to be looking directly at her.

It was a little creepy, but she instantly dismissed him as a husband who had been abandoned in the mall, and who was probably waiting for his wife to emerge from a boutique.

Juggling the flowers, Allegra extracted her phone from her tote and checked to see if Mike had texted or called. He hadn't. She tapped his number and waited while it rang. When he didn't pick up, she left a voice message.

She decided there was no point hanging around waiting for him, so she strolled toward Ambrosi, a fabulous designer jeweler that had started out life as a pearl house on the Mediterranean island of Medinos. Ordinarily, she would be excited to just walk through those doors and breathe in the romance of a store that had started out life in antiquity and was gorgeously decorated to reflect that past. But, after last night, romance was off her list. Today was all about getting on track with her new agenda, which was to drive Tobias crazy with jealousy.

To that end, first thing that morning she had brought the ring in to be resized, and the other jewelry to be cleaned and assessed. The sales clerk had promised they would be ready by twelve.

As she strolled toward the glass doors, her reflection bounced back at her. With her hair piled up in a messy knot, the red roses against her white shirt, and the vivid turquoise mini and high heels, she definitely looked sharp. Just as she was about to step through the doors, she glimpsed the little man who had been looking at her before, directly behind her. This time his phone was up, and he was definitely taking a photo.

Her jaw tightened. Before she had left San Francisco, a guy who had probably been inspired by the lies posted about her, had used to follow her around, take pictures and share them online. She had put the cops onto him, and he had been stopped. Since then, she had developed a zero tolerance for being stalked. If this creep was still hanging around when she left the store, she would take *his* picture and let him know that, if she ever saw him again, it would be sent to the police.

The store assistant, a young, beautifully groomed woman called Fleur, produced the ring, which now sparkled with an eye-catching brilliance. "Just wait one moment, and I'll get the other jewelry you brought in. I think Clark has almost finished buffing it."

Allegra set the bunch of roses down and picked the ring up off the black velvet pad the store assistant had placed it on. She slid the ring onto the third finger of her left hand, but, as she did so, her mood, which had been upbeat, bottomed out and a curious sense of disappointment assailed her. She had been so busy with her plans to ramp up the fake engagement, she hadn't thought about how wearing the ring would make her feel.

Brought up with parents who had been in love and totally devoted to each other, she had always imagined that she was destined to experience the same kind of nurturing, protective love. That, when an engagement ring went onto her finger, it would be an emotionally loaded moment, shared with a man who would swear to love and honor her. That the ring on her finger would symbolize the beginning of their shared life of love and intimacy.

Instead, she had a fake engagement, a fake ring, a fake fiancé who would probably not even keep the appointment she had paid him to keep and a stubbornly addictive attraction to a man who only wanted her for sex.

Swallowing against a sudden tightness in her throat, she wrenched the ring off. As she did so, Fleur returned with a tall, gaunt man in a pristine suit, who looked more like an undertaker than a jeweler.

He placed the shabby pile of black velvet bags down on one side of the counter, then set down a large, signature Ambrosi box. He flicked the lid open with a flourish and extracted the necklace. A quick glance at Fleur and she scurried to produce a black velvet pad. With solemn, reverential movements, he arranged the necklace, which had developed a fiery glow beneath the dazzling LED lights.

Allegra's breath caught, despite knowing that the necklace, like most of the other jewelry, had to be fakes. Why else would Esmae, who had loved wearing the Hunt diamonds, have shoved them in a box in a dusty attic?

Clark produced an envelope and extracted two sheets of paper, which he spread out on the counter. "I've done a quick assessment, but if you like I can get you a more detailed second opinion from someone who deals in antique jewelry for insurance purposes—"

"What do you mean, insurance purposes?"

Clark gave her a transfixed look. "You don't have either the Faberge diamond necklace and earrings, or the Van Cleef and Arpels bracelet and brooch, insured?"

Feeling distinctly shell-shocked, Allegra walked out of Ambrosi with the roses and a small fortune in diamonds in her tote: rare, designer diamonds with the kind of provenance that would guarantee sky-high values. Jewelry that Esmae had never mentioned, and that Allegra's own family knew nothing about.

Because she knew so little about the jewelry, she wasn't prepared to call any of it hers. They could be Hunt jewels, perhaps belonging to Tobias's natural grandmother. Although, if that was the case, why had Esmae possessed them? And why had she kept such fabulously expensive jewels separate from the Hunt diamonds, which were cataloged and stored in a bank vault?

The other thought that had occurred, and which was much more likely, was that they were some kind of second Mallory skeleton in their scandal-ridden closet; that they had been hidden because they were *stolen*.

Either way, before she did anything with them, *and ended up in prison*, she needed to know more. She needed to read Alexandra's journal.

Lost in thought, Allegra made a beeline for the restaurant where she and Mike were supposed to have their engagement date. As she strolled, she checked her phone again. Mike hadn't acknowledged her text, and he still hadn't made any attempt to call her.

Keeping the phone in her hand on the off chance that he would actually call, she lengthened her stride. The café was just around the next corner. A split second later, just ahead, a familiar set of broad shoulders and the back of a well-shaped head registered.

Tobias.

He was casually striding, his phone held to one ear.

So, it had been him she had seen earlier. Shocked that he should turn up here, now, she spun on her heel and walked briskly back toward the main foyer. Mike wasn't here, so why go to the café at all? The last thing she needed right now was to have to deal with Tobias.

Stepping past a beautifully dressed couple, she almost ran down the same little man she had seen taking her photo earlier. "You!"

Clearly, he wasn't used to being confronted, because he froze like a deer in the headlights.

Holding up her phone and almost dropping the roses, which she now wished she had never bought, she snapped his photo. "There's no point pretending you aren't following me," she said coolly. "Tell me your name, or I go straight to the police."

"His name's Tulley," a deep, curt voice said, from behind her. "He works for me."

Allegra spun, adrenaline pumping as her gaze clashed with Tobias's. "Doing what?"

Although she already knew. Tulley who seemed to have an unhealthy zeal for sneaking around spying on people, probably belonged to Tobias's over-priced detective agency.

"Tulley's a PI."

The confirmation that Tobias was having her watched, *investigated*, sent a searing dart of hurt through her. It meant that he hadn't believed a word she'd said about her innocence, that he didn't trust her, *and that he had slept with her anyway*.

But, if he thought she was going to crumble, he could think again. "At least spying is marginally better than stalking. But if you truly believe all of the lies that have been written about me online, then we're done."

Shoving her phone in her tote, she turned away, but Tobias stepped ahead, blocking her.

"I don't believe them," he said quietly. "Babe, the reason Tulley's been following you is because I wanted him to keep an eye on you until I could get here. We need to talk."

Her jaw tightened against her automatic delight that he had called her *babe*, and the utter relief that he had finally seen that she wasn't a shallow party girl those social media accounts had made her out to be. But the fact that he had sicced Tulley on her meant that, at some level, he still didn't trust her.

Deliberately, she checked her watch. "Will it take long?"

"I guess I deserved that." He was silent for a beat. "After you ran out on me this morning—"

"I didn't 'run out' on you. I drove to work."

His gaze, the icy-hot one that set her on edge and turned her on all at once, drilled into her for long moments. "After you *drove to work*, I asked Tulley to keep an eye on you because the hell I was going to let Callaghan near you before we could have the conversation we should have had last night."

Conversation? For a long drawn-out moment, it was difficult to absorb the heart-pounding possibility that Tobias might, finally, be falling for her. That her strategy had worked even faster than she could have imagined. "What conversation, exactly, would that be?"

"This, for a start." Tobias produced a folded-up document she instantly recognized as the dating schedule she had given to Mike the previous day. "According to the schedule, you and Callaghan are getting a ring today."

Cheeks warming, she snatched the paper out of his hand. "That doesn't belong to you. Where did you get it from?"

"Callaghan dropped it on the drive yesterday."

That figured. As of that moment, Callaghan—*Mike*—was fired as her fiancé.

She dropped the crumpled schedule into her tote. "Last I heard, getting a ring is an entirely normal thing for an engaged couple to—"

"You can't be engaged to Callaghan," he said flatly. "Not when you're sleeping with me."

A heated surge of emotion practically welded her to the spot. Tobias's statement that she was sleeping with him, the narrowed, glittering glance, as if he was Tarzan and she was Jane, was unequivocal and possessive enough to send chills down her spine.

Tobias definitely wanted her.

She registered that Tobias's abrupt declaration—the alpha male equivalent of staking claim—was what she had wanted from him two years ago, and what she had absolutely needed from him last night.

It wasn't flowery; it did not contain the word *love*, or anything at all about emotion or commitment. It was irritable and bad-tempered, even dictatorial, but that was what made her heart sing, because it was evidence that Tobias felt something real for her and that, finally, he was prepared to fight for her.

Then, she registered the ultimatum. Because she had slept with Tobias last night, she couldn't be engaged to Callaghan—that is, *Mike*, she corrected herself, irritated that she was starting to think like Tobias. "You're hardly in a position to give me an ultimatum when you've made it crystal clear that *you're* not interested in a relationship."

"I am now."

Allegra stared at the visible pulse beating along the side of Tobias's jaw. Dimly, she was aware of a cluster of teenage girls drifting past, giving him interested looks, and that, at some point, Tulley had left. Dimly, she registered that the bustling sounds of the mall, the hum of conversations, seemed to have fallen away. For long seconds, it was as if they were enclosed in an intimate bubble, where only the two of them existed.

She met Tobias's gaze squarely. "I won't sleep with you just because it's convenient for the month."

"Convenient?" His brows jerked together. "Believe me, sleeping with you has nothing to do with *convenience—*"

Tobias's hand closed briefly around her upper arm as he moved her out of the path of a motorized wheelchair. In the process, the top of her head brushed against his jaw, one palm landed against the solid muscle of his chest, and she caught the heady scents of soap and clean skin and cologne.

His gaze locked on hers. "Damn, I wish we weren't—"

"*Tobias!*"

Allegra stiffened. Tobias frowned and let her go.

Francesca Messena-Atraeus had just strolled out of the opulent jeweler they just happened to be standing next to and which was, ironically, Atraeus Jewels.

For a split second, Allegra was so shocked to see the beautiful fashion designer that she didn't notice what she was wearing. Then, the silky, turquoise mini and camisole top, the filmy white shirt and high, strappy turquoise heels registered.

Had she mentioned that her outfit was an ultra-expensive Messena design?

Her stomach sank. There were some moments that got impressed indelibly, and damagingly, on a person's psyche; she was pretty sure this was one of them, because there was a *rule* about women wearing the exact same outfit.

And it didn't stop there. Even their hair was done the same, *and* their nail color matched. They could have been a mirror image of each other, the only difference being that Allegra's hair color was darker than Francesca's, which was currently a tawny blond.

And, as Francesca strolled toward them, a truth she just hadn't seen hit her forcibly.

She had seen buying Francesca's line of clothing, handbags and shoes, as a sign that she had healed, that she didn't hold a grudge that Francesca had stolen her man, and that she had moved on. But now, she understood exactly what she had been doing. She had made herself over *as Francesca*, so that Tobias would fall for her.

The sick feeling in her stomach was a confirmation she didn't want, but which she needed to face.

Two years ago, her hair had been long, with luxurious waves. Now, it was still long, but layered, so that it swung sexily around her face, a virtual mirror image of Francesca's current cut.

She had also changed her normal low-key colors on her nails to flamboyant pinks and, instead of lower more comfortable shoes, she had begun wearing gorgeous high heels that were more about looks than practicality. Again, just like Francesca.

She had even bought a range of silk lingerie that Francesca had said was her favorite on one of her social media sites. The cost had been astronomical, and now she knew why she had splurged on something she would not normally have bought.

Another horrifying thought struck. She had to wonder if the reason Tobias had showed a renewed interest in her was that she looked a whole lot more like Francesca than she had two years ago? That the reason he had made love to her was that he saw her as some kind of Francesca substitute?

Her mother had been right, she thought blankly. Somehow, she had allowed Tobias's rejection of her to affect her at a deep, bedrock level, to the point that she had even lost confidence in her own attractiveness.

But that wouldn't be happening any longer.

And, if Tobias thought that she was going to continue to be some kind of Barbie-doll substitute for the woman he couldn't have, he could think again.

Francesca jogged the last few yards, went up on her toes, wound her arms around Tobias's neck, hugged him close and kissed him on the cheek. But it was Tobias's reaction that commanded her attention. When his arms went around Francesca, he grinned, his teeth white against his tanned skin. Feeling increasingly miserable, she registered that he wasn't just attracted to Francesca, he *liked* her.

Francesca pulled free, but kept her arm around Tobias's waist, as she waved at a tall, blond friend who had just stepped out of a nearby boutique. She introduced the woman, whose name was Clara, to Tobias with the gleeful announcement that this was the gorgeous guy who was taking her out for dinner that night.

Allegra froze, for long seconds, stunned, then thoughts and emotions cascaded. She knew why Francesca was here; it was a business visit. But this didn't look or feel like business, *and Tobias was taking her out to dinner.*

She wished it didn't matter. But it did, because, for a few moments, she had thought that she and Tobias were finally on the brink of something special.

Now, the fact that Tobias had never taken her out for dinner, or even asked her for a coffee, struck deep. Just like he had never thought to buy her flowers or to give her any of the small gifts that were part of courtship.

She blinked, feeling like a sleeper just waking up. The way he was with Francesca suddenly seemed to point out all the lacks in their relationship, the huge abyss between what Tobias was offering and what she wanted.

And what she wanted wasn't so outrageous. They were ordinary, everyday dreams that shouldn't be so hard to attain, like a man of her own, a home they could share and, sometime in the not-too-distant, misty future, babies to love. All of the things a lot of women of her acquaintance had already, and which they took for granted, but which had, so far, eluded Allegra.

The problem was, trying to be in a relationship with Tobias was like hitting a brick wall. All they shared was sex.

Despite trying to appear casual and unaffected, *as if meeting the other woman in Tobias's life barely impinged upon her*, Allegra's face felt frozen as introductions were made.

Happily, Francesca breezed past the fact that they were dressed like twins by complimenting Allegra on her great taste in clothing. Despite feeling embarrassed by the clothing issue, and deeply hurt at the way Tobias had failed to court her in any way, Allegra briefly acknowledged that, if Francesca wasn't after Tobias, they would probably be friends.

When Tobias mentioned Madison Spas, the transfixed look on Francesca's face gave Allegra the distinct impression that Francesca had suddenly placed her, and not in a good way. That meant she knew about the scandal in her past.

She didn't come across that reaction so often these days, especially not in the spa business, which was so far removed from her previous career it could be on another planet. But, every now and then, the past did jump out to bite her.

Allegra managed a polite, professional reply, then Francesca surprised her by asking specific questions about her spa treatments. Normally, she would be in her element talking about mud wraps and their super foods menu, but relaxing was difficult because every time Francesca touched Tobias's arm with a small, intimate gesture, she felt miserable and increasingly tense.

Because despite the hurt of the past, despite her strategy and the caution she had thought she was exercising, she had fallen for Tobias, hook, line and sinker.

Again.

Thirteen

Allegra's phone trilled. Relieved to have an excuse not to look at the gorgeous couple Francesca and Tobias made, she fished it out of her tote.

The call was from Mike. She had been so distracted that she had completely forgotten about him. "Where are you?"

"Uh… MIA."

Her brows jerked together. *Miami International Airport?*

Aware that Tobias could hear what she was saying, she walked a few more steps away and tried to keep her voice smooth and pleasant. "I need more details, Mike."

"Uh…sorry about breaking the news to you like this but, you know I was trying out for that soap? Well, thing is, someone put in a good word for me, and I got a part. Not the lead, but who knows? Now that I'm in, the *sky's* the limit—"

"*Mike.*"

"So, yeah. I need to be in LA tomorrow—"

A feminine voice cut Mike off, followed by a loud rustling, as if Mike was attempting to cover the speaker end of the phone.

Although muffled, Allegra distinctly heard his muttered, "Felicity, babe, just give me some space for a minute? I'm talking to, you know, *her*."

Felicity. That would be one of the girls Mike shared an apartment with and who Allegra had thought was just a good friend. Clearly, they were a whole lot friendlier than he had let on.

"Let's cut this short," Allegra said crisply. "You've got some kind of acting part. Now, you're flying somewhere with a *friend*—"

"Felicity, yeah. We're leaving for LA. Like, right now."

Allegra frowned, sudden suspicion gnawing at her. Mike was broke, he had told her so, and she hadn't yet paid him for being her fake fiancé. That was one of the things she was going to address this afternoon. So where did he get the money to pay for flights to LA, not only for himself, but for Felicity? It was possible the production had paid him an advance, but it was a small part, and he had only just heard this morning. Added to that his departure was so sudden, and *organized* when, normally, Mike couldn't organize his way out of a paper bag, that she didn't see how any of it was possible.

Suspicion coalesced into knowledge. Mike had failed to make their date; instead, *Tobias* had turned up. "When, exactly, did Tobias buy the tickets?"

There was a small horrified silence. "How did you *know*?"

Allegra's jaw tightened. "The same way I know he was the one who 'put a good word in for you,' probably with one of the financial backers. So, when? Yesterday, or this morning?"

The timing made a difference, because, if Tobias had arranged to get rid of Mike last night, before they had slept together, that would make his actions in sleeping with her even more calculated.

"This morning. He got in contact with someone in LA. An hour later, the production manager offered me the part. Tobias was totally cool. He paid for our tickets, even arranged accommodation—"

"And your job at the spa?"

A final boarding call echoed in the background, cut through by Felicity's terse statement that she was boarding now, even if Mike wasn't.

"Yeah, sorry about that," Mike mumbled. "I sent an email, like, ten minutes ago. Look, I gotta go—"

The call terminated.

Allegra flicked through to her emails and opened Mike's resignation, which barely extended to two lines, one of them being, *Hi, Ms Mallory.*

She closed the email and slipped her phone back into her tote. Grimly, she noted that her strategy with Mike had worked, after a fashion. Tobias had reacted in a possessive, macho way, but not as she had hoped.

Instead of expressing an interest in having a real relationship, where they dated and got to know one another, *like he had done with Francesca*, he had behaved in the exact opposite way. He had gotten rid of the "threat" Mike had posed by buying him off and shipping him to the other side of the country. And there was only one way Mike would have suddenly gotten a part in the production; Tobias had also paid for that.

As if he had never heard of fighting for the woman he wanted by courting her.

Instead, he had been one step ahead of her, clearing the way so he could have unimpeded access to her for the next month.

His actions were ruthless and definitively alpha, and they informed her that Tobias really did want the sex, enough that he had been prepared to pay for it.

If she hadn't had the state of their "relationship" pointed out to her by the way he was with Francesca, maybe she would have been thrilled by the fact that he had been prepared to go to such lengths to get her to himself.

But, the plain fact was, he had inexcusably changed the rules. Just over two years ago, she had fended off two wealthy men who thought she could be bought with money, gifts and influence.

She hadn't been selling herself then, and she wasn't doing it now.

Jaw set, Allegra dropped her phone into her bag, made an executive decision and walked. On the way, she saw a cleaner mopping up something that had been spilled on the floor, so she stopped and handed her the bouquet of roses.

Holding a bunch of flowers, that looked like they had been bought for her by a lover, now only seemed to symbolize what was *not* in her future. They represented the romantic aspects of a relationship, which Tobias had once very publicly extended to Francesca, but which he had *never* extended to her.

As if all he truly wanted from her *was* the sex.

Tobias saw the moment Allegra turned on her heel and headed for the elevators.

Suddenly over Francesca and her friend, and the incessant girl-talk, he said a clipped goodbye and strode toward the elevators.

At a guess, Allegra had just gotten a call from Callaghan. From the way she had reacted, she knew he'd gotten rid of him.

That meant that either Callaghan had crumbled and blurted out that Tobias had arranged to move him to the West Coast, or she had extracted the information.

He was betting on the second option.

Allegra stepped into the elevator. Her gaze, which was definitely frosty, clashed with his as he stopped the doors from closing with a hand and stepped in with her. "We were in the middle of a conversation."

"Were we? I hardly noticed."

"We were talking about a relationship."

"There's a big difference between the kind of interaction you call a relationship, and what I want." Her dark eyes shot fire. "You paid Mike off!"

A little grimly, he wondered how those two statements fitted together. "I got rid of Mike so we could *have* a relationship."

The elevator stopped at a floor; the doors slid open.

Allegra jabbed a finger at his chest. "You're *paying* for sex!"

There was a small, vibrating silence as an elderly couple, who were waiting for the elevator, stared at them as if they'd each grown an extra head.

Tobias nodded in their direction, took Allegra's arm and hurried her out of the elevator. "How in hell am I paying for sex?"

She jerked free of his hold. "How much did it cost to get rid of Mike?"

He quoted the six figures it had cost him so the producer could be convinced that Callaghan could handle a small part.

She gave him a horrified look. "They make movies about this stuff."

"I just did what worked. Now, tell me how that equates to me paying to have sex with you?"

She met his gaze squarely. "Simple accounting. You've bankrolled Mike's acting career to get me into bed, so now it's almost as if you've paid to have sex with me. You've *commoditized* our relationship."

"I don't see it that way," he said bluntly. "We slept together last night. As far as I was concerned, you *already* belonged to me, so why would I pay for what's already mine? I got rid of Callaghan because he's a guy. If he had tried to touch you, I would have had to deck him."

She stared at him for long seconds, her eyes oddly dark. "You really do want me."

"It's a little more than that." Tobias steered her in the direction of the parking lot. "Like I said before, I wanted to talk about a relationship."

Allegra drove with care through the rain, which was steady now. The clouds above were dark and heavy-bellied, but the temperature was still warm enough that steam wisped off roads and sidewalks. The traffic was thick, but she was still intensely aware that Tobias was once again tailing her, although, this time, she felt entirely different about it. Instead of feeling ruffled and on edge, excited waves of pleasure kept zinging through her.

Tobias wanted a relationship with her. Finally, he was seeing her as "the prize."

She turned into the long driveway to the mansion, hit the garage remote and parked jerkily in her space. Weirdly, she was actually nervous, and felt all thumbs as she grabbed her key. Tobias's black truck glided to a halt beside her convertible.

Her tension ratcheted up another notch as she climbed out from behind the wheel and reached over to grab the tote, but, as she did so, Tobias pulled her into his arms and kissed her, his mouth warm against hers.

Dimly, she registered that she'd let the tote drop onto the driver's seat and, because the door was still open, it had then overbalanced and tumbled onto the garage floor. But, in that moment, nothing mattered but the relief that, finally, Tobias was kissing her.

But, before they made love again, she needed the answer to the questions that had gnawed at her. Planting her palms on his chest, she pushed free. "Francesca Messena?"

He frowned. "What about her?"

"You dated her before you slept with me two years ago, then you dated her afterward. In fact, you *pursued* her—"

"I didn't pursue her," he growled. "Why would I? She's not my type."

It wasn't the answer she expected. It was blunt, male and irritable, but it made her happier than any other answer could. She stared at him for a long, silent moment, because this was *important*. "Am I your type?"

His brows jerked together. "Is this some kind of trick question?"

"No tricks."

A rueful smile quirked the corner of his mouth. "After six years? Babe, you know you are."

She tried not to dance on the spot. "Okay, last question. What kind of relationship, exactly, do you want to talk about?"

"A real one," he said flatly. "I want you with me, so no other guy can get near you. We'll argue, because we're both strong-headed, but, the way I see it, even though things aren't perfect, we stay together and figure it out."

She blinked. Those words could have come out of her own mouth. "Okay. Where did the aliens take the *real* Tobias?"

He grinned, and Allegra stared at him, suddenly transfixed and almost too happy. But, at the same time, there was a peculiar tension at the back of her mind, because it all seemed too quick and easy. Twice, things had gone wrong, so she couldn't quite believe it was going to be smooth sailing this time around.

She drew a deep breath."Okay. Let's try. That sounds good to me."

Lifting up on her toes, she angled her jaw and kissed him. It had been a long, horrible day. She had been anxious, miserable and on edge, and she had thought she had lost Tobias.

Tobias responded by lifting her up, cupping her bottom as he held her against him. Dimly, she registered that they were walking. He set her down as he opened the door that led to the house, linked his fingers with hers, then led her into the hallway that ran past the kitchen.

They didn't make it to the upstairs bedroom. Instead, Tobias swung her into his arms, carried her several steps, then shouldered into a downstairs guest room. White shutters cut out the gloom of the rainy afternoon, throwing shadows over the large white bed.

Setting her down on her feet, he shrugged out of his jacket, dragged off his tie, then pulled her close again. When she surfaced from the kiss, she fumbled at his buttons, pulled at the crisp, gauzy linen until it slid from his shoulders, then slid her palms over hard muscle and heated skin.

Another languorous kiss, and she registered the loosening of her skirt as the zipper glided down. Cool air circulated against her skin as turquoise silk puddled on the floor. She pulled free to undo the shirt, which was tied, then lifted it over her head, along with the soft camisole. Moments later, her bra was gone, and her breath came in as Tobias cupped her breasts, bent down and took one nipple into his mouth.

Sensation shimmered and seared, tension rocketed through her, then they were moving again, backward this time. She felt the brush of cool cotton on the back of her thighs. Then, she pulled at the fastening of his pants, dragged the zipper down and cupped him.

Tobias muttered something short and flat, stilled her hand and pulled her close for another deep, drugging kiss. Seconds later, he peeled out of his pants, then paused to extract a foil packet from the pocket. Breath locked in her throat, she stepped out of her own panties and climbed onto the bed, watching as he tore open the packet and sheathed himself. Moments later, he joined her on the bed, but, as he settled himself between her legs, she pushed at his shoulders.

"Not this way."

He grinned and allowed her to push him on his back, then straddle him and slowly sheath herself.

His hands settled at her hips and, she began to move, a little awkwardly at first, then with growing confidence. His gaze locked with hers as he reached up and cupped her breasts. She gasped as tension coiled and gathered. A split second later, Tobias moved, reversing their positions and holding her beneath him as he slowly thrust inside her. Long minutes passed, during which she clung to his shoulders. Despite the rain, the afternoon was warm, the air thick and humid, making it difficult to breathe.

Reaching up, she pulled his head down and fastened her mouth to his, and the afternoon splintered and shimmered into sultry heat.

Half an hour later, Allegra woke from a light doze and immediately knew something was wrong.

Tobias, dressed only in just his narrow, dark suit pants, his chest bare, was standing in the doorway, one hand filled with expensive, luxurious diamonds. His remote gaze, when it had been so soft and warm before, struck a chill through her. "Where did you get these?"

Allegra sat up straight, dragging the sheet around her breasts. She had been relaxed and warm, but now her stomach was tight and churning, her mind whirling a million miles an hour. Tobias must have gone out to the garage and seen her tote on the floor. At a guess, the case of diamonds had tumbled out and opened. "I think that's my business, but if you must know, the diamonds came from Esmae. They're Mallory family jewelry."

He was silent for a beat. "Try again, Allegra. Everyone knows Esmae was broke before she married my grandfather. Apparently, she had a few Edwardian trinkets, but nothing of any value."

The shock of the words, the way they were said, was like a slap in the face.

Out of nowhere, her heart began to race. Allegra drew a quick breath. "Okay then," she said quietly, "you tell me where I got them from."

"I know about the scandal in San Francisco."

And he was putting two and two together: supposed lovers, gifts of expensive jewelry. "Of course. That's why you ditched me two years ago, so I suppose it's just as good an excuse to ditch me now."

His brows jerked together. "This is not about ditching."

She noticed he didn't refute that he had dumped her because he had bought into Halliday's and Fischer's lies. "So you still want to sleep with me, despite everything?"

She cut him off before he could answer. "If you want to know where the necklace came from, you could always get your little detective, Tulley, to do some more legwork." Her stomach sank when she logged the expression on his face. "Too late. You've already gotten him to pry into my past."

"Only because it didn't add up."

"Of course, it didn't. It's hard to trace where pretty women get their jewelry from, especially when it's given to them by their families or as pageant prizes, or from an elderly aunt. But if you need verification, call a jeweler called Clark who works at Ambrosi. He's doing some checking for me on provenance and value. By now, he should have the record of sale for the pieces that came from Esmae. As for the rest of the diamonds I own, where I got them from is private and absolutely none of your business."

Tobias frowned. "I had to ask—"

"I know. But if you don't mind," she said coolly, winding the sheet around herself like a toga, and stepping out of the bed. "I need to get dressed and get back to work. It's the middle of the afternoon and, now that Mike's gone, we're short-staffed."

Tobias stared at her. For a moment, she almost thought he was going to soften, take her in his arms and say he was sorry for doubting her. That he didn't care where the diamonds came from, and that the only thing that mattered was what they felt for one another.

But then his phone rang, breaking the moment. Placing the jewels onto the dressing table, he slid his phone out of his back pocket and left the room, closing the door behind him.

Allegra stared at the door. She had managed to hide it, but the fact that Tobias had had her investigated, and that he still refused to take her word, had shaken her.

She guessed that, in her heart of hearts, she had hoped he would finally let his stubborn distrust of her go, that if she poured enough love into the relationship, he would understand *who* she was, and allow himself to fall for her.

She had been wrong.

Allegra collected the diamonds, her jaw tightening at the way Tobias had so easily reverted to seeing her as the kind of shallow, cliché woman who would exchange sex for jewelry.

She had zero tolerance for that kind of stereotyping. In Tobias's case: less than zero.

Added to that, she was over the idea that Esmae had married for money and that Mallory women bartered relationships for a cushy lifestyle.

She knew something of Tobias's background, that the narrative was reinforced by his own experience as a child, when his father had lavished jewelry on his mistresses, but it didn't make it any easier to hear. It threw up the barrier that had been standing between them all along: that Tobias didn't seem to trust in love.

And he especially didn't trust in *her love*.

Her problem was, she was in love with Tobias, and had been for six years. However, she was now certain that love was not something Tobias would probably ever feel for her. How could he, when he clearly didn't trust her?

The grim line in Elena Lyons-Messena's book seemed to flash like a neon light in her mind.

If your alpha shows no signs of falling in love, leave. Save yourself.

She had to leave. Today.

She couldn't stay. Not in Tobias's bed, or even this

house. She would lose her shares, but she didn't care, she preferred to keep her self-respect. It just meant that she would do what she should always have done, and buy Tobias out.

As for the clause in the will that said her oldest brother Quin could make some kind of claim should Tobias not manage the resort for the full month, she would tell Quin to stay out of it, and she would tell him why. Once he understood what was at stake, he would take her side. Family was family.

It would be a wrench leaving. It was going to hurt way more than it had two years ago, because now she knew she was in love with Tobias, and had been all along. But she could not stay with a man who did not trust her.

She had kept herself on hold for Tobias for six years, and the plain fact was she couldn't afford to do that anymore.

Opening the door, she headed for the stairs. The low timbre of Tobias's voice registered somewhere in the distance, which only made her feel more miserable, because she had gotten used to the sound of his voice, and used to having him near.

Worried about her heart rate, Allegra phoned her doctor and made an urgent appointment. Afterward, she quickly showered and dressed, choosing a pair of natural-colored linen pants, a white camisole and, because it was definitely cooling down, a white sweater. Moving like an automaton she fixed a pair of silver filigree earrings that were go-to favorites to her lobes and applied basic makeup.

As she coiled her hair into a loose knot and pinned it, she noted that her heart was still pounding too fast. Worryingly, it hadn't stopped, and it was starting to make her feel light-headed.

She strapped on her sports watch, tapped the app on her phone and waited for the reading to come up. The rate was one hundred and thirty beats per minute. She would routinely achieve that when she was doing a workout, but all she was doing was strolling around her bedroom.

Not good.

It was possible the rate would drop, and this was nothing but a false alarm. However, just in case she did need to go to the hospital, she packed a change of underwear, some jeans and a casual sweatshirt in her tote. On the two occasions she had been admitted, the first had been an overnight stay, and the second had amounted to just a couple of hours. She had no idea what would happen this time, but she needed to be prepared to stay overnight. Both times chemical intervention had worked its magic and switched her heart rate back to a normal rhythm.

The decision to leave Tobias, now, before she went to the doctor, settled in. She was twenty-seven; thirty was just around the corner, and the speed with which the years were passing was getting scary.

Marriage and babies had not been at the forefront of her thinking. How could they be, when she had never been able to settle into a viable relationship because she had been hopelessly in love with a man who had no conception of who she truly was?

The plain fact was, she *did* want love and marriage. And she wanted them with a man who could truly love and cherish her.

And that man was not Tobias.

Fourteen

Feeling slightly shaky with adrenaline, Allegra retrieved her suitcase from the closet and began tossing clothes into it. She snatched a Messena jungle-print dress off the hanger, gathered up lingerie, marched out to the bedroom and shoved it all in the suitcase.

Feeling increasingly agitated, *because she had spent so much money on buying Francesca-look-alike things*, she gathered up shoes and packed them into a separate bag. By the time she had packed all of her clothes, the case was stuffed full of Messena pieces. She needed to weed them out, give them away and concentrate on getting herself back.

Not that she had lost herself, she thought grimly. All she had lost was her confidence.

Walking through to the bathroom, she packed her toiletries. Returning to the bedroom, she shoveled her makeup into a carry case, cleared out the dresser and zipped her suitcase closed.

Feeling distinctly breathless, because the rushing around had made her heart race even faster, she snapped the jewelry cases closed and dropped them into her tote. On impulse, she also stored Alexandra's diary in her tote. If she was going to have some downtime in the hospital, or even at home, she might as well read it.

The sound of a door closing brought her head up. It could only be Tobias, because it was late enough that Marta would have left for the day. For a moment, she thought he might stop at her door and knock, but he continued past. She heard his tread on the stairs, then the closing of the kitchen door.

The sound of his truck starting was only just audible through the rain, which had gotten heavier. Bleakly, Allegra slipped into comfortable flats. The weather was supposed to deteriorate more, with strong winds and heavy rain, so there was no point wearing delicate high heels.

Ten minutes later, she had all of her luggage jammed into her cramped convertible. She started the car and activated the soft top. When it was snugly in place, she backed out. It was still too early for her appointment with her doctor, so she decided to drive to her apartment and unload the luggage first.

As she accelerated down the drive, which was already littered with leaves stripped off by the blustery winds, she speed-dialed Janice and told her that she was very possibly on her way to hospital for the afternoon, and asked her to go through their list of part-time therapists and see who was available to come in and take over Mike's classes for the rest of the week.

An hour later, after dropping off her things at her apartment, and the consult with her doctor, she phoned Janice who knew some basics about her condition, and told her she was being admitted to Mercy Hospital, probably just for the afternoon. Luckily, her doctor, Alicia Ortez, had worked at Mercy for a number of years and had been able to get her a referral direct to the cardiac unit rather than sending her to sit in the ER. That wasn't exactly usual practice but, because Esmae had left Mercy a sizable donation in her will, *and* there was a bed available for a few hours, Allegra had gotten seen. And, happily, she could afford Mercy. One of the things her parents had done for her was make sure she had excellent medical insurance.

As familiar as she was with the process after two previous admissions, the procedure was still slightly scary— after all, this was her *heart*. After she'd had her pulse and blood pressure checked by a nurse, she was transferred to a room and hooked up to an electrocardiogram. Half an hour later, a doctor strolled in, checked her stats and asked her a list of questions about what might have kicked off this episode.

The phrase *a broken heart* popped into her mind. But, when her pulse jumped and she saw his frown, she took a slow, deep breath, attempted to exude calm serenity, and mentioned Esmae's death and the stress of work. He ticked a couple of boxes, hooked the clipboard on the end of her bed, then administered a drug she'd had before, Adenosine, which she knew acted to chemically reset the electrical activity of her heart.

If that didn't work, the next option was electrical cardioversion, which she would only agree to as an absolute last resort. It was bad enough knowing that the drug he was injecting would slow, even pause, her heart in order to reset the rate. Allegra did not want to have the job done with who knew however many volts of electricity.

While she waited for the drug to work, she picked

up her phone, which she'd set on her bedside table, and turned it off. Janice knew where she was, and why, so there was no need to be in touch. And the last thing she needed right now was to unconsciously wait for Tobias to call her, then start *hoping* that he would. That was the kind of thinking that had worked against her for the past six years.

Instead, she reached for Alexandra's diary and began to read.

An hour later, she set it down.

The story Alexandra had written in her own hand had been intensely personal and unexpected. She had had an affair with Jebediah, but it hadn't just been an affair; they *had* planned to marry. At a guess, the engagement ring Allegra had had resized that morning had been Alexandra's engagement ring from Jebediah.

Unfortunately, Alexandra's husband, a wealthy and powerful English aristocrat who had a reputation for violence, and who they all thought had died before Alexandra had left England, hadn't died at all. Intent on reclaiming his runaway wife, he had travelled to America, and had found out where she lived. Warned by her lawyer, Alexandra had taken the children and run.

She had settled in New York, hoping to lose herself in the city, but he had eventually found her there, too, and had claimed her house and all her assets. True to form, he had put Alexandra in hospital, then had gone back to England, leaving her broke.

But he hadn't gotten everything. Knowing the risk, Alexandra had systematically converted the oil money into diamonds, an investment she had buried in the garden of the townhouse that had just been sold from under her. Just before she died of her injuries, she had directed Esmae to dig up the jewelry, sell half of it and give the cash to her son, Allegra's grandfather. Esmae was to sell whatever diamonds she needed to live, but to keep as many as possible as insurance against hard times.

But Esmae had clearly been luckier in love than Alexandra had ever been, which explained why she had managed to keep a great deal of Alexandra's jewelry, and why she hadn't ever worn it. In honor of Alexandra, she had kept it hidden away, an "insurance policy" she had then passed on to Allegra.

Tobias strode into his downtown office and dropped his briefcase on his desk. He closed his door, signaling to his PA that he wanted privacy. The last thing he needed was for Jean to be privy to the calls he was about to make.

He had spent the last hour surfing the social media accounts of both Halliday and Fischer, so, when he got hold of Tulley, it was no surprise to hear what he had to report.

Both men had unsavory reputations and a bent for going after younger women. The evidence pointed to Burns-Stein Halliday failing to act on Allegra's behalf because Halliday was the nephew of one of the partners and Fischer was married to the senior partner's daughter. The kicker was, that this wasn't the first time they had covered up for Fischer and Halliday.

Tobias thanked Tulley and hung up. He walked over to his large picture window, which looked out across city buildings to the sea. The wind velocity had gone up, even in the short time he had been in the office, and the rain had come in, turning the city gray, but that wasn't what concerned him.

Allegra had endured a major injustice in her life yet, with all the online hype Fischer and Halliday had generated, he had never heard so much as a whisper of the actual facts. And Allegra had never chosen to confide in him.

And why would she, he thought bleakly, when she must have known that he'd been only too happy to buy into the wrong story.

Collecting his briefcase, he took the elevator down to the street, then a cab to the Atraeus Mall. Minutes later, he walked into Ambrosi. The jeweler Allegra had mentioned, Clark, confirmed that Allegra had phoned to request that he give Tobias the same information regarding provenance that he had given her.

Tobias studied the two sheets Clark handed him. They each had only one record of sale, to Alexandra Mallory. The name Faberge leaped off the first page. The current estimate for the necklace alone was seven figures.

Faberge. It was not the kind of jewelry that men like Halliday and Fischer handed out as gifts. It was investment jewelry. The kind families bought to hedge their wealth. He should know—his grandfather had bought enough of it.

Thanking Clark, he walked back through the mall.

As he walked, the consequences of his actions settled in. The second he had seen the diamonds and felt their weight, he had been flung back in time to the arguments that had used to rage between his parents, mostly about the jewelry his father had lavished on mistresses. Then he had remembered the online scandal around Allegra accepting jewelry for sex and the ground had seemed to shift beneath his feet.

He didn't want to accept that Allegra had been untruthful; he had thought he knew her through and through but, in those moments, he had wondered if he had let lust, and emotion, cloud his judgment. He had wondered if he had been fooled.

He now knew that he had jumped to a completely wrong conclusion. He had let his own trust issues, and the knee-jerk jealousy that had gripped him because it seemed that she *had* slept with Fischer and Halliday, cloud his judgment.

If he could kick himself, he would. As a mistake, it was unforgiveable.

He headed back out to the street, which was now teeming with rain, caught a cab and phoned Allegra while he was en route to his office building. When there was no reply, twice, he tried the spa's number.

Janice picked up. Allegra wasn't at the spa because she'd had to go to the hospital.

Tobias went cold inside. His first thought was that Allegra must have had some kind of accident. "What for?"

"Oh, it's that heart condition she has. It's got some weird name. She just calls it SVT. I don't think it's a major problem, though, since she drove herself to Mercy."

Tobias hung up. His heart was pounding. His mother had died from a heart condition that had come out of nowhere. He had been eighteen at the time, but he still remembered how that had felt.

The cab pulled into his office building. He paid the cab driver. Mercy Hospital was in Coconut Grove. That was about a fifteen-minute drive. He stepped into the elevator and punched in the parking garage. Before the doors opened, he had rung Mercy and was talking to Admissions, who confirmed Allegra was a patient in the cardiac unit.

By the time he had reached his truck, he had checked online, found a description for SVT and read the symptoms. There were ranges of severity and a variety of treatments, including shock treatment to reset the heart. Apparently, stress was often a factor in episodes.

Stomach tight, he swung behind the wheel, started the truck and accelerated toward the exit.

He had made a mistake in not believing Allegra's explanation about the jewelry. He had seen the shock on her face, the way she had lifted her hand to her heart. Now, because of him, she was in the hospital.

It spun him back two years, to a call he had gotten from Lindsay's father to let him know that she had miscarried their baby. A baby he hadn't even known existed. Brice Howell had made no bones about the fact that Tobias's actions in leaving Lindsay for another woman was the reason that baby had died.

He reached the hospital, bypassed Admissions and strode into the cardiology ward, only to find that he had missed Allegra by ten minutes.

Relief filled him. If she had walked out of the hospital, then she must be okay.

Minutes later, he finally got the conversation he needed to have with the doctor who had treated Allegra, and was stonewalled because he wasn't a relative. Although the doctor did inform him that her problem had been "resolved."

Tobias's jaw tightened as he stepped out of the shelter of the hospital foyer into the now-pouring rain. The doctor refusing to talk to him about Allegra's condition, *because he was neither her husband nor her partner*, had struck him forcibly.

That was going to change.

He had messed up, big time. But that wouldn't happen again. *If* she let him back into her life, he would ensure she had the best medical attention. From now on, if Allegra had so much as a paper cut, then he needed to know about it. If she had a medical emergency, he would be there. He would carry her around on a silk cushion, if that was what worked.

By the time he reached his truck and swung behind the wheel, he was soaked.

Dragging off his wet jacket and tie, he tossed them onto the back seat. His shirt was plastered to his skin in places, but that barely registered. As he merged into traffic, he rang Allegra's phone and, again, got no reply.

He didn't think she would go to work, since it was so late in the afternoon, but, at that point, he wasn't about to let any detail slip, so he dialed Janice again.

When Janice confirmed that she hadn't heard from Allegra since she had phoned to let her know she was going to Mercy, Tobias terminated the call. He tried Allegra's number one more time, then concentrated on driving.

He switched on the local radio station, which was broadcasting a storm warning. Apparently, the hurricane that was supposed to veer into the Gulf was now going to hit Miami full on. Even though it was only five o'clock, the light was already murky, so he switched on his lights.

Heavy gusts of wind buffeted the truck as he headed for Esmae's house. If Allegra wasn't there, he would drive to her apartment.

Whatever it took, he would find her.

Fifteen

Allegra arrived at Esmae's house. She hadn't wanted to come back, but, while she was in the hospital, she had remembered the painting she had left in the beach house. After reading the diary, and everything that had gone wrong for Alexandra, there was no way she was going to leave that behind.

As she parked out on the drive, she noticed that Jose, Marta's husband, had already been there and had closed the storm shutters over the windows of the house. There were no lights on inside, so it didn't look like Tobias was home.

Stepping out of her car, she jogged down to the beach house. Even though she was wearing a rain jacket, her jeans were instantly soaked. When she reached the cottage, the wind was even stronger, whipping the sea into a frenzy and filling the air with a misty, salty brine that stung her eyes.

She noted that Jose had missed one of the shutters on the beach house, so she attempted to close it, then gave up when she realized the bolt was broken. Muttering beneath her breath, she had to leave it.

Dragging wet strands of hair from her face, she made her way around the deck, holding onto the rails to anchor herself. It was then that she saw the dinghy, which was attached by a rope looped around a bollard at the end of the short pier.

In his rush to get the house and the beach cottage secured, Jose had obviously forgotten about putting the dinghy out of harm's way in the boathouse. Normally, it was safe enough to be left bobbing lazily at the end of the pier, but, with the combination of a high tide and the storm surge that was supposed to be coming, it was in danger of being smashed against the pier or swept away altogether.

Leaning into the wind, Allegra walked quickly down the steps to the beach and onto the wet pier. Grasping the side rail, she made her way, step by careful step, to the end. Clinging to the rail with one hand, she went down on her hands and knees to lessen resistance to the wind, and began working at the knot that secured the dinghy.

A wave broke, drenching her with spray. Dashing water from her eyes, she resumed working at the soaked rope, but it kept getting pulled tight by the wind and waves, which were dragging at the dinghy.

To ease the tension, she leaned forward and grabbed the rope in order to haul the dinghy in closer and create some slack. She almost had the knot undone when the sound of her name being called jerked her head around. A small shock went through her when she saw Tobias, his face like thunder, as he roared at her to leave the dinghy.

* * *

In that moment, another wave broke, this one bigger than the last, surging over the jetty itself. Her feet went from under her. With a yelp, she tried to maintain her grasp on the rail. The plan was to drag herself upright and hook one arm around so she could haul herself back up, but the wood was slippery, and the power of the water tore her hands loose.

Something, probably the dinghy, caught her a glancing blow on the side of the head as she was swept over the side of the jetty, then she hit the water.

Even though she was wet through, the coldness of the water was a shock.

Her first thought was that she had to get away from the pier itself, because she didn't want to be dashed against the enormous oyster-encrusted poles that supported it. The other danger was the dinghy, which was being flung back and forth by the wind and waves.

Surfacing dangerously close to the dinghy, she gulped a lungful of air and began to swim away from both the pier and the dinghy, which meant out to sea. Even though she was a strong swimmer, it was hard to make headway in the lumpy, turbulent water but, once she was a few yards clear, she could turn toward the shore.

Breathless, she treaded water for a moment and twisted around to get her bearings. A wave surged over her, driving her back in the direction of the shore, which would be a wonderful thing if only she wasn't still too close to the dinghy.

She swam another couple of strokes then braced for the next wave. This time when she came up gasping for air and coughing, because somehow she had managed to swallow some water, movement on the pier caught her eye.

Tobias. Soaked to the skin in a shirt and dark pants,

he was gripping the railing, scanning the water. His gaze locked on hers.

Another wave surged but, this time, she was prepared. Duck-diving, she kicked smoothly through. When she bobbed up on the other side, the pier was empty. Fear spasmed in her chest. Tobias must have been caught by the wave. A split second later, he surfaced beside her. Then, there was no time to think as the next wave broke.

When she came up for air, Tobias's gaze locked with hers. "Are you okay to swim? We need to get to shore before this gets any worse."

The relief that had flooded her when Tobias had popped up beside her turned to an intoxicating flood of warmth, *because he had jumped in to rescue her.* "I can swim."

A few strokes, hampered by the lumpy waves, and she felt the bottom. As she straightened, a wave hit her in the back. Tobias's arm snaked around her middle, anchoring her against his side, and they waded the last few yards to shore. When they reached the hard-packed sand, already littered with driftwood and seaweed, he pulled her close, bent down and kissed her, his mouth hard against hers and tasting of salt.

When he lifted his head, his gaze blazed into hers. "I thought I'd lost you. What in hell were you doing in the water? Haven't you heard, there's a hurricane—"

"I was getting the dinghy—"

"If Jose asked you to get the dinghy, he's fired."

The roar of wind and waves seemed to drop away as she stared at the heated silver of his eyes, fringed by inky black lashes, the intriguing scar across his nose. "He didn't. He'd left before I got here."

"Which means it was all your idea. Why did I already know that?" He pulled her close again, his arms wrapping around her in a hug, which was somehow so much more intimate than the kiss had been.

Allegra wound her arms around his waist, soaking in the heat that radiated from him.

He lifted his head. "You almost gave me a heart attack."

"There wouldn't have been a problem if someone hadn't tied some kind of a weird knot, a million times too tight."

His expression turned wry. "You mean a standard boating knot, a round turn with two half hitches—"

"Whatever. It wouldn't budge."

"You shouldn't have been down here, period," he said flatly. "It's too damned dangerous. And you definitely shouldn't be out in a storm when you've just been discharged from the hospital."

Allegra went still inside. "How did you know about that?"

Tobias pulled her up the shore toward the beach house. "I've been trying to call you all afternoon. In the end, I rang Janice and she told me where you were—"

"You were *looking* for me?"

"No," he said grimly. "I was going *crazy* looking for you."

For a split second, she didn't know what to think or feel, then anger kicked in. She had thought they were finished. She had *grieved* over the loss. Now, suddenly, he was concerned about her—

"We need to get inside. The storm's supposed to peak in the next hour, and they're predicting a storm surge."

The pressurized whine of the wind seemed to lift a notch, as if the hurricane had just found another gear. Allegra glanced out to sea. It was becoming more turbulent by the minute, and visibility was fading as the mist thickened. "What about the dinghy—"

"Forget the dinghy. The way this storm's shaping up, we'll be lucky if the pier isn't washed away."

Tobias kept an arm locked around her waist, as if he couldn't bear to let her go, which was conflicting. Part of her wanted to bask in the happy glow that had started when he had jumped into the water to save her, the other part of her still wanted to fling all of her hurts in his face.

The wind buffeted them as they climbed the steps. Tobias leaned down to pick up a rain jacket he must have thrown down on his way to the pier. Allegra glanced back. The pier was now almost totally submerged. A shudder went through her at the shocking swiftness with which the water had risen, and how easily she had been swept over the side.

She gave Tobias a fierce look. "You shouldn't have jumped in."

"Worried about me?"

She caught his gaze and, for once, didn't bother trying to hide what she felt. Tobias was tough and strong, but the sea was savage. Regardless of how angry she was with him, how crazy he made her, the thought that something might happen to him made her go cold inside. "Yes."

He pulled her up the steps and into the protected lee of the beach house. Seconds later, he had the door open and held it against the wind as she stumbled inside.

Tobias slammed the door closed. The reduction in noise was a relief, even though the sound of the wind buffeting the cottage and the roar of the waves as they pounded the beach, was still frighteningly loud.

The hall was dim, courtesy of the shutters, which closed out almost all of the light. Tobias flicked on lights as they walked from the short hallway into the kitchen.

"You're bleeding. What have you done to your head?"

Allegra touched the side of her head and winced. The skin was broken, and she could already feel a small lump forming. "When I was washed off the pier, I think I caught the side of the dinghy."

Tobias brushed her hair aside, his fingers gentle as he examined the injury. "It's only a graze, but it needs antiseptic. And ice."

While she sat down at the kitchen table, he opened the fridge and found a tray of ice cubes, which he emptied into a clean kitchen towel. He handed her the makeshift ice pack, which she pressed to her head. He then disappeared in the direction of the bathroom. When he reappeared, he had a pile of fluffy white towels and a first aid kit.

The lights flickered as he dropped a towel around her shoulders, at which point she realized she was beginning to feel chilled. It wasn't cold, exactly, but the usual hot temperature had plunged, and her wet clothes were clinging to her.

Tobias pulled a chair close and sat down, his thighs bracketing hers as he opened the first aid kit and extracted a tube of antiseptic. "At least you can swim."

Allegra tried not to notice how mesmerizingly good Tobias looked with his light shirt plastered to the bronze glow of his skin. "Was that in your investigative report?"

His gaze caught hers. "I guess I deserved that. I used to watch you swimming off the beach. But, I admit, I also asked Esmae about you, and she told me you used to swim competitively."

He parted her hair and smeared on the antiseptic. "Although she failed to tell me that you had a heart condition, which makes what you did *even* worse—"

She jerked a little beneath his touch. "I didn't mean to end up in the water, and it's not really a heart condition. It's just a weird kind of electrical thing that happens, usually when I get overstressed."

Tobias stared at her for a long moment, an odd expression on his face, then he pushed to his feet, replaced the antiseptic in the first aid kit and started opening cupboard doors. The anger that had flowed through her, and the desire to be difficult, suddenly burned out, and she was left wishing for the warmth and intimacy they'd shared on the beach.

Picking up the ice pack, she settled it against her head again, and watched as he found coffee grounds and started making coffee. She noticed he had also placed a box of candles and a lighter on the kitchen counter, just in case the power went out. When the rich scent of dark roast filled the air as the machine began to drip coffee into the carafe, Tobias peeled off his wet shirt and dropped it over the back of a chair. Reaching for a towel, he dried himself off. When he was finished, he leaned on the counter and crossed his arms over his chest. "Why didn't you tell me about the SVT?"

Allegra dragged her gaze from his chest. "If you'll remember, we didn't exactly spend a lot of time talking." Suddenly over being passive and looked after, she set the ice pack down on the table, pushed to her feet and began searching out mugs. "If you must know, I didn't tell you because I didn't think it would have mattered—"

"It mattered." Tobias's hand stayed hers as she set out sugar and teaspoons, and, suddenly, tension and a crazy nervousness were zinging through her.

Fingers threading with hers, he pulled her close. "I came looking for you because I knew I needed to fix what had happened this afternoon. Then, Janice told me you were in Mercy Hospital with a heart condition. I missed you at the hospital by a few minutes—"

He loosened his hold slightly. "When you walked out on me, I realized I'd made the same mistake in not trusting you that I'd been making all along." He hesitated. "Before I met you, you know I was involved with Lindsay."

"You were living together."

"For a couple of years. Lindsay wanted to get married. She wanted children, the whole deal. I agreed to marriage. She was already starting to plan the wedding, but, at that point, I knew it wouldn't work, so we broke up."

In terse words, he explained the difficulty he'd had with trust ever since his parents had broken up when he was ten. His father had had affairs then had left his mother to move in with an A-list party girl, the first in a long line, and his mother had become embittered.

"That's why I chose Lindsay," he said curtly. "I was looking for someone dependable and steady, mostly because I didn't want to be like my father. Then, I saw you on the beach and I fell like a ton of bricks. Combine that with the guilt I felt when I finally left Lindsay because I wanted you…"

He released her and walked over to the one window that wasn't protected by a shutter, and stared bleakly out at the storm. "But that wasn't the worst of it. I didn't know it, but apparently, when I left, she was pregnant. Not long after, she miscarried." He shrugged. "I went into damage control, and that meant denying that I wanted you."

A heavy gust of wind hit the beach house, making it creak, but she barely noticed the sound; she was still dealing with the shock of the revelation. "I'm so sorry you lost the baby," she said quietly. "When, exactly, did Lindsay miscarry?"

Tobias turned his head, his gaze oddly dark. "The day after you and I first slept together."

And, suddenly, it all made sense. She had always wondered why Tobias had dumped her cold, when the attraction between them had been so strong and it had felt so good to be together. Now, she knew: it had been the shock of loss, and guilt. "You blamed yourself for the miscarriage."

His expression was remote. "How could I not?"

Then, the online stories had reinforced his decision, ruining any chance of a relationship between them.

Even though it still made her feel angry and hurt, it was time to address the scene in the guest bedroom that morning. "What about your reaction to the jewelry? I'm guessing you read some of the online lies Halliday and Fischer wrote about me."

His expression was bleak. "It hit some buttons, mostly because my father spent a small fortune on jewelry for his various 'friends' and I couldn't stand the thought that you might have slept with Fischer and Halliday. When I walked out to the garage and saw the new jewelry case and the jewels spilled across the seat of your car, I...reacted."

She took a deep breath. "Do you realize how much that *hurt*?"

Tobias crossed the space between them, cupped her shoulders and pulled her close. "Babe, I'm sorry I hurt you, and sorry it took me so long to acknowledge the truth. When you walked out on me, I nearly went crazy—"

They were suddenly plunged into darkness as the power flicked out.

Tobias muttered something beneath his breath. Seconds later, he had the first candle lit and positioned in a glass. Three more candles later, positioned at strategic points, and the kitchen was filled with the warm flickering glow.

The coffee machine had finished filtering, so he poured the coffee, spooned in sugar and handed her a hot mug. "You need to drink that," he said abruptly. "You look too damn pale."

She inhaled the rich aroma. There was no milk, but she didn't care. Hot, sweet coffee when she was wet and chilled was ambrosia.

"There's something else we need to talk about," he said. "I got Tulley to investigate the two men who attempted to destroy your reputation."

Allegra's head jerked up at the way Tobias had framed his words, as if she was *innocent*. She winced a little, because the sudden movement made her head throb. "Why?"

"Because the online stories have nothing to do with who you are. And, as it turns out, those two particular men have unsavory reputations."

"And a lot of money and influence." She met his gaze squarely. "Fischer actually tried to seduce me in my office—"

Cold fury registered in Tobias's eyes, and a small shiver went down her spine. Suddenly, the fact that he had been a Special Forces soldier operating in some of the most violent and dangerous places on the planet was starkly evident.

"I'll kill him," he said softly.

"No need. I hit him with a stapler."

"You did *what*?"

"It was a big stapler." She didn't bother to hide the satisfaction in her voice. "He went down."

Amusement surfaced in Tobias's eyes. It was an odd moment to realize that, just when she had thought everything had fallen apart, he did something masculine and irresistibly *alpha* and, even though she knew he was dictatorial, terminally edgy and *difficult*, she wanted him back all over again.

"I know what they did to you," he growled. "That's why I sent Tulley to investigate them. He did some digging and came up with conclusive evidence that both Halliday and Fischer had been trolling online dating sites and misrepresenting themselves to women for years. There were also a couple of assault convictions that had been quashed, probably because the women had gotten threatened or paid off. To put it politely, their behavior was predatory."

He crossed his arms over his chest. "But, as it happens, Hunt Security and the various businesses the Messena and Atraeus families own, do some business with Burns-Stein Halliday. I emailed Burns the investigative report and suggested that if they continued to employ Halliday and Fischer, there would be repercussions. Also, that they needed to make reparations to you, ASAP, or I would be over there."

Her throat closed up, and, for a long moment, her breathing felt impeded. She had thought she had put it all behind her, that she had healed, but the pressure in her chest told her otherwise.

What had happened had *hurt*. She had thrown herself into study and work and then, practically overnight, it had all been taken from her in the most humiliating of ways.

When she could finally speak, her voice was husky. "What do you mean by *reparations*?"

"For a start, an apology. There's legislation about harassment in the workplace, and they ignored it. Then, there's the matter of compensation for your lost career—"

"I left voluntarily."

"You left because of what happened."

"I can't, exactly, afford to sue them—"

"Which is why *I'm* suing the ass off of them."

That shouldn't be romantic but it absolutely was, because Tobias had finally ridden to the rescue and was now *fighting* for her.

He was on her side, which meant Burns-Stein Halliday was toast. She would not want to be in their shoes if Tobias actually had to go over there. But she would definitely want to be in the room. "When you go, I'm coming with you."

His brows jerked together. "You're not going back to work for those clowns. You've got a great business right here and, as far as I'm concerned, for as long as you want them, the premises at the resort are yours."

A delicious glow of warmth started in her chest. Tobias was being commanding in a totally male, sexy way. Normally, as she had said before, she didn't take orders, but she would take this one because she was in complete agreement with it, and she totally loved that he was intent on protecting her. "Why would I go back to BSH? It would be like redoing the beauty pageant thing. I liked the pageants, and I liked winning, but then I got over them, and they just weren't my thing—"

"Babe, you're losing me."

She gave him a patient look. "The point is, I liked getting the degree, I liked the study and the achievement, but I didn't get the degree so I could work for Satan."

Tobias lifted a hand to his mouth to conceal the fact that he was laughing, although that was a pointless exercise, since his shoulders were shaking. "I assume you mean Burns—"

"That's right. Satan. I don't even know why you asked the question. And, back to that other thing you said about the lease… Since I'm perfectly happy in Miami, plus

I'm beginning to think I've finally gotten a boyfriend, of course I'll be staying."

An emotion flashed in his gaze that made her heart stumble.

He muttered something short and flat and did what she was aching for him to do… Reaching her in one stride, he took her mug out of her hands, set it on the table, then hauled her into his arms.

They were both still damp and salty, they needed showers and fresh clothing, but Allegra was loath to give up these moments. She wanted to hold onto Tobias because, despite everything that had been said, a kernel of fear still existed that this newfound intimacy could vanish. "I wish I could have known all of those things about your relationship with Lindsay two years ago."

"Ditto to knowing about Halliday and Fischer," Tobias said somberly. Then, he rested his forehead on hers, which was totally cute. "We didn't know…but I'm pretty sure someone else did."

"Esmae."

"She knew I'd fallen for you."

And, in that moment, Allegra's heart soared and happiness expanded inside her, warm and bright and intoxicating enough to make her feel just the tiniest bit giddy. And not in a *get-to-the-hospital-for-drugs* kind of way.

She tipped her head back so she could study the lean contours of his face, the tough set of his jaw. "Fallen?" she probed, just to be doubly, positively sure.

Tobias's mouth quirked. "As in totally, head over heels, in love."

A slow smile spread across her face. "Just the way I am with you." She felt like dancing, like doing a victory lap, but she settled for hugging him hard and close.

He bent to kiss her. By the time he lifted his mouth,

Allegra was clinging to his shoulders, soaking in his warmth and the steady thud of his heart. "I can hardly believe this is happening. It feels like a dream."

Tobias reached over to the back of a chair, where he'd tossed his jacket, and pulled a small jewelry box from the side pocket. "We can make it even more real. That is, if you'll say yes."

He opened the case, which bore the Ambrosi crest, and took out a solitaire diamond engagement ring that was breathtakingly beautiful in its simplicity. White fire glittered in the flickering light.

"It's beautiful."

"And it's brand new," he said flatly. "No history attached."

She drew a swift breath. *Now* it was real. "You bought it for me."

Tobias went down on one knee. "Allegra Mallory, will you marry me and be my love?"

There was only one answer she could give.

"Yes, yes and *yes*."

She held out her hand so he could slide the ring onto her finger and, as he did so, tears burned at the back of her eyes, but this time they were tears of joy.

Finally, she and Tobias had their happy ending.

* * * * *

COMING SOON!

We really hope you enjoyed reading this book.
If you're looking for more romance, be sure to
head to the shops when new books are
available on

Thursday 4th
March

To see which titles are coming soon, please visit
millsandboon.co.uk/nextmonth

LET'S TALK
Romance

For exclusive extracts, competitions
and special offers, find us online:

 facebook.com/millsandboon

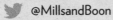 @MillsandBoon

@MillsandBoonUK

Get in touch on 01413 063232

For all the latest titles coming soon, visit
millsandboon.co.uk/nextmonth

MILLS & BOON

THE HEART OF ROMANCE

A ROMANCE FOR EVERY KIND OF READER

MODERN

Prepare to be swept off your feet by sophisticated, sexy and seductive heroes, in some of the world's most glamourous and romantic locations, where power and passion collide.
8 stories per month.

HISTORICAL

Escape with historical heroes from time gone by. Whether your passion is for wicked Regency Rakes, muscled Vikings or rugged Highlanders, awaken the romance of the past.
6 stories per month.

MEDICAL

Set your pulse racing with dedicated, delectable doctors in the high-pressure world of medicine, where emotions run high and passion, comfort and love are the best medicine.
6 stories per month.

True Love

Celebrate true love with tender stories of heartfelt romance, from the rush of falling in love to the joy a new baby can bring, and a focus on the emotional heart of a relationship.
8 stories per month.

Desire

Indulge in secrets and scandal, intense drama and plenty of sizzling hot action with powerful and passionate heroes who have it all: wealth, status, good looks…everything but the right woman.
6 stories per month.

HEROES

Experience all the excitement of a gripping thriller, with an intense romance at its heart. Resourceful, true-to-life women and strong, fearless men face danger and desire - a killer combination!
8 stories per month.

DARE

Sensual love stories featuring smart, sassy heroines you'd want as a best friend, and compelling intense heroes who are worthy of them.
4 stories per month.

To see which titles are coming soon, please visit

millsandboon.co.uk/nextmonth

JOIN US ON SOCIAL MEDIA!

Stay up to date with our latest releases, author
news and gossip, special offers and discounts, and
all the behind-the-scenes action
from Mills & Boon...

 millsandboon

 millsandboonuk

 millsandboon

It might just be true love...

MILLS & BOON
True Love

Romance from the Heart

Celebrate true love with tender stories of heartfelt romance, from the rush of falling in love to the joy a new baby can bring, and a focus on the emotional heart of a relationship.